MARIGOLD

Reviewers Love Melissa Brayden

"Melissa Brayden has become one of the most popular novelists of the genre, writing hit after hit of funny, relatable, and very sexy stories for women who love women."—*Afterellen.com*

The Forever Factor

"Melissa Brayden never fails to impress. I read this in one day and had a smile on my face throughout. An easy read filled with the snappy banter and heartfelt longing that Melissa writes so effortlessly."
—*Sapphic Book Review*

The Last Lavender Sister

"It's also a slow burn, with some gorgeous writing. I've had to take some breaks while reading to delight in a turn of phrase here and there, and that's the best feeling."—*Jude in the Stars*

"I have loved many of Melissa Brayden's characters over the years, but I think Aster Lavender may be my favorite of all of them."—*Sapphic Book Review*

"*The Last Lavender Sister* is not only a romance but also a family saga and a journey of transformation for both characters."—LezReview Books

Exclusive

"Melissa Brayden's books have always been a source of comfort, like seeing a friend you've lost touch with but can pick right up where you left off. They have always made my heart happy, and this one does the same."—*Sapphic Book Review*

Marry Me

"A bride-to-be falls for her wedding planner in this smoking hot, emotionally mature romance from Brayden...Brayden is remarkably generous to her characters, allowing them space for self-exploration and growth."—*Publishers Weekly*

"When I open a book by Melissa Brayden, I usually know what to expect. This time, she really surprised me. In a good way."—*Rainbow Literary Society*

To the Moon and Back

"*To the Moon and Back* is all about Brayden's love of theatre, onstage and backstage, and she does a delightful job of sharing that love... Brayden set the scene so well I knew what was coming, not because it's unimaginative but because she made it obvious it was the only way things could go. She leads the reader exactly where she wants to take them, with brilliant writing as usual. Also, not everyone can make office supplies sound sexy."—*Jude in the Stars*

"Melissa Brayden does what she does best, she delivers amazing characters, witty banter, all while being fun and relatable."—*Romantic Reader Blog*

Back to September

"You can't go wrong with a Melissa Brayden romance. Seriously, you can't. Buy all of her books. Brayden sure has a way of creating an emotional type of compatibility between her leads, making you root for them against all odds. Great settings, cute interactions, and realistic dialogue."—*Bookvark*

What a Tangled Web

"[T]he happiest ending to the most amazing trilogy. Melissa Brayden pulled all of the elements together, wrapped them up in a bow, and presented the reader with Happily Ever After to the max!"—*Kitty Kat's Book Review Blog*

Beautiful Dreamer

"I love this book. I want to kiss it on its face...I'm going to stick *Beautiful Dreamer* on my to-reread-when-everything-sucks pile, because it's sure to make me happy again and again."—*Smart Bitches Trashy Books*

"*Beautiful Dreamer* is a sweet and sexy romance, with the bonus of interesting secondary characters and a cute small-town setting." —*Amanda Chapman, Librarian (Davisville Free Library, RI)*

Two to Tangle

"Melissa Brayden does it again with a sweet and sexy romance that leaves you feeling content and full of happiness. As always, the book is full of smiles, fabulous dialogue, and characters you wish were your best friends."—*The Romantic Reader*

"I loved it. I wasn't sure Brayden could beat Joey and Becca and their story, but when I started to see reviews mentioning that this was even better, I had high hopes and Brayden definitely lived up to them." —*LGBTQreader.com*

Entangled

"Ms. Brayden has a definite winner with this first book of the new series, and I can't wait to read the next one. If you love a great enemies-to-lovers, feel-good romance, then this is the book for you."—*Rainbow Reflections*

"*Entangled* is a simmering slow burn romance, but I also fully believe it would be appealing for lovers of women's fiction. The friendships between Joey, Maddie, and Gabriella are well developed and engaging as well as incredibly entertaining...All that topped off with a deeply fulfilling happily ever after that gives all the happy sighs long after you flip the final page."—*Lily Michaels: Sassy Characters, Sizzling Romance, Sweet Endings*

Love Like This

"Brayden upped her game. The characters are remarkably distinct from one another. The secondary characters are rich and wonderfully integrated into the story. The dialogue is crisp and witty."—*Frivolous Reviews*

Sparks Like Ours

"Brayden sets up a flirtatious tit-for-tat that's honest, relatable, and passionate. The women's fears are real, but the loving support from the supporting cast helps them find their way to a happy future. This enjoyable romance is sure to interest readers in the other stories from Seven Shores."—*Publishers Weekly*

Hearts Like Hers

"Once again Melissa Brayden stands at the top. She unequivocally is the queen of romance."—*Front Porch Romance*

Eyes Like Those

"Brayden's story of blossoming love behind the Hollywood scenes provides the right amount of warmth, camaraderie, and drama." —*RT Book Reviews*

Strawberry Summer

"This small-town second-chance romance is full of tenderness and heart. The 10 Best Romance Books of 2017."—*Vulture*

"*Strawberry Summer* is a tribute to first love and soulmates and growing into the person you're meant to be. I feel like I say this each time I read a new Melissa Brayden offering, but I loved this book so much that I cannot wait to see what she delivers next."—*Smart Bitches, Trashy Books*

First Position

"Brayden aptly develops the growing relationship between Ana and Natalie, making the emotional payoff that much sweeter. This ably plotted, moving offering will earn its place deep in readers' hearts."
—*Publishers Weekly*

Soho Loft Series

"The trilogy was enjoyable and definitely worth a read if you're looking for solid romance or interconnected stories about a group of friends."
—*The Lesbrary*

How Sweet It Is

"'Sweet' is definitely the keyword for this well-written, character-driven lesbian romance novel. It is ultimately a love letter to small town America, and the lesson to remain open to whatever opportunities and happiness comes into your life."—*Bob Lind, Echo Magazine*

Heart Block

"The story is enchanting with conflicts and issues to be overcome that will keep the reader turning the pages. The relationship between Sarah and Emory is achingly beautiful and skillfully portrayed. This second offering by Melissa Brayden is a perfect package of love—and life to be lived to the fullest. So grab a beverage and snuggle up with a comfy throw to read this classic story of overcoming obstacles and finding enduring love."—*Lambda Literary Review*

By the Author

Romances

Waiting in the Wings

To the Moon and Back

Heart Block

Marry Me

How Sweet It Is

Exclusive

First Position

The Last Lavender Sister

Strawberry Summer

The Forever Factor

Beautiful Dreamer

Lucky in Lace

Back to September

Marigold

Soho Loft Romances:

Kiss the Girl

Ready or Not

Just Three Words

Seven Shores Romances:

Eyes Like Those

Sparks Like Ours

Hearts Like Hers

Love Like This

Tangle Valley Romances:

Entangled

What a Tangled Web

Two to Tangle

MARIGOLD

by

Melissa Brayden

2023

ISBN 13: 978-1-63679-436-5

This Trade Paperback Original Is Published By
Bold Strokes Books, Inc.
P.O. Box 249
Valley Falls, NY 12185

First Edition: July 2023

Credits
Editor: Ruth Sternglantz
Production Design: Stacia Seaman
Cover Design by Inkspiral Design

Acknowledgments

Dreaming about what you want and going after it are two different things. The latter is definitely more daunting than the former. But crafting the love story between Alexis and Marigold served as a strong reminder that reward doesn't come without (sometimes terrifying) risk. Marigold is a character who consistently puts her own life on pause, and for far too long. If you're reading this, and that's you, today's the day to hit the unpause button because your story is just waiting to be written. Don't lose another precious moment.

I want to wholeheartedly thank my publisher, Bold Strokes Books, for letting me tell the stories I long to tell in the way that I want to tell them. Creative freedom is a wonderful thing, and you've always granted me that.

Ruth Sternglantz, thank you for always telling me like it is but doing so delicately so I can absorb, regroup, and craft the best story possible without rocking in a corner clutching a Pop-Tart. I trust you and value our little team.

Inkspiral Designs, much gratitude for the cover that offered such inspiration as I worked through the ins and outs of Marigold and all she was and is.

To the production team at Bold Strokes (Cindy, Stacia, Toni, and the wonderful proofreaders), I'd buy you all donuts if I could—and perhaps one day will! Thank you for making all the magic happen that, voilà, produces a book!

To all those close to me (you know who you are), and anyone who's reached out to share a laugh, thank you! The pep talks are especially helpful. The friendship is invaluable. The wine definitely helps. You make my heart full.

To Alan and the blond curlies, you're the best for letting me drift off to fictional lands on a Saturday when I should probably be making lunch. I hope I make you proud!

Readers, we've been through so much together both on and off the page. I hope you have it in you to join me for more romance, more angst, more fun banter, and definitely more kissing in the future. Ooh la la. Onward and upward!

For bridge sitters everywhere. Your time will come.

PROLOGUE

Marigold Jane Lavender escaped into her fictional world at every possible chance. Regularly unleashing her imagination, she explored made-up cities, embarked upon perilous missions, and more commonly lived out the most romantic moments between herself and her dream woman du jour. There was no doubt about it. She was a dreamer and proud of it, counting the moments until she could sneak away from the rest of civilization with a killer coffee or gourmet sandwich and lose herself in a scenario of her own making. She preferred make-believe, where everyone was funny, romantic, playful, and dramatic. Who wouldn't want to watch their favorite self-constructed moments play out over and over again with little tweaks to make each time even better than the last? They offered her a break from day-to-day reality, calming her soul and exciting her spirit. Her daydreams would blossom, wander, and linger deliciously. They got her through the more mundane have-tos in life and offered her hope that her future would usher in a lot more excitement than her present.

Marigold was proud of all she could accomplish with just a little scenery and her unencumbered thoughts. Did that give real life an awful lot to live up to? In more ways than she could count. It was likely the reason she was still single. No real person could possibly make her feel what imaginary Marigold experienced when she was in fake love, all starry eyed and goose bump laden. How could she *not* be, when she'd been wined, dined, and taken up against the wooden dresser, before waking to a trail of rose petals leading to a perfectly cooked breakfast on a terrace somewhere in Europe with a monument looming out her window and a violin underscoring all of it. Ooh la la. In her daydreams, she was always smiling, perpetually gaga for her significant other, and often kissing the face of that special woman, whoever she turned out to be that particular day. And there had been many she'd cast in the role.

She had the perfect fantasizing spot, too. Her go-to sit-and-dream location was the old wooden footbridge just outside of her hometown of Homer's Bluff. It didn't have a name these days, but a little research had taught her that it had once been known as the Chapman Bridge, named after the family who had once owned the land. She'd been visiting the Chapman Bridge, dangling her feet over its edge, watching the river float peacefully by below ever since high school when she'd saved enough to buy a clunker of an Oldsmobile and explored every inch of town, even the outskirts, her way of getting away from the demands of high pressure teenage life. Grabbing space for herself was still a common coping skill.

When she thought about it, each of the Lavender siblings had their own way of unwinding. Her brother, Sage, threw himself into work as his escape, riding his tractor through the lavender fields for several more hours than necessary. Her younger sister, Aster, found a quiet bench and a good sci-fi novel to drift into. Violet, the oldest of the Lavender kids, busied herself worrying about the people she loved and inserting herself into their conflicts to escape her own. She grew more and more like their mother as time went on, self-sacrificing and helpful. Marigold? She dreamed her troubles away on a gorgeous, empty footbridge and wondered about a life a little bit bigger than this one. She wanted to catch flights, brunch with friends, join the board of some important charity, and land that hard to get reservation at the fanciest restaurant in the most exciting city.

She wasn't complaining about her current existence. Not really. Her life came with plenty to smile about. In fact, she considered herself lucky in the grand scheme. Blessed, even. She liked Homer's Bluff, Kansas, and its petite size. The simplicity of small town life allowed her to focus on enhancing the details. There were no surprises, missed opportunities, or strangers. The dependability delivered a peaceful night's sleep because there was safety in repetition. At least, that's what she told herself today as she dipped a toe in the cold water skating by.

The highlight for Marigold? Her family. The Lavenders were known throughout the neighboring towns for owning and operating one of the largest independently owned lavender farms in the country.

In fact, her great-grandfather had changed their last name to make it memorable. It had worked. They had the farm of forty acres, the family's home where her dad still lived, and the store—and their products were in a rather large distribution channel. For her part, she and Violet managed The Lavender House, the on-site store that sold just about any lavender product one could dream up, most made with lavender straight from the farm just a few feet away. People seemed to really like that component and were willing to pay premium prices for local and fresh. The log house structure that housed the store smelled heavenly upon entry, and Marigold basked and danced every time she walked through its heavy door. Home. The scent of lavender would always mean home for her. Speaking of which, she checked her watch. Dammit. She'd lost track of time. Her extended lunch was coming to a close, and she would have to say good-bye to her friend the Chapman Bridge and the sound of water heading downstream, music to her ears.

"You're back. How was Bridgerton?" Violet asked, wrapping bars of soap in purple tissue paper so she could tie them neatly with twine. They were nothing at The Lavender House if not cute and rustic at the same time. *Yes, we will wrap your pretty soap with on-the-nose paper, and we will tie it up with tree parts like the forest nymphs we are.*

"Ah-ah." Marigold shook a finger. "You know that's not its name. Its name has been long forgotten by people around here. That's part of its beauty and mystery. Only I know." She booped her sister's nose because it semi-annoyed Violet, and Marigold lived for their sisterly back-and-forth, rooted in love but thriving on shenanigans.

"Any specific revelations today?"

"Yes, as a matter of fact." She logged into the point of sale station so she'd be ready to assist the next customer. Business tended to pick up after lunch, and getting the little things accomplished early set them up nicely. "I've decided I should be named town princess and gifted a tiara. I've dropped it into the suggestion box at city hall. Now it's just a waiting game."

"You beat me to it. I was hoping for princess status." Violet slid a strand of her dark hair over one ear. She'd cut it noticeably shorter a month ago. It hung several inches shy of her shoulders now, sophisticated as well as gorgeous. Her sister was a force and carried her eldest sibling status with grace. It hadn't always been that way, but when they'd recently lost their mother, she'd naturally assumed a more ever-present role in the lives of her siblings. Marigold loved her for that.

"You were too busy with soap, and now you're in the princess cold."

"Damn. Cursing myself for it."

"Next time, you'll be faster. Did Aster come by while I was gone?" Their younger sister, an impressive chef with her own restaurant just outside of town, was the only Lavender not involved in the family business. It just hadn't been for her, but it made for excellent guilt trips.

"Negative." She glanced over her shoulder. "And I have the moisturizer Brynn likes set aside behind the counter for when she does, so don't sell it." Aster was wildly in love with her fiancée, Brynn Garrett, one of the town's two veterinarians. They were expecting a child in just a couple of weeks, and Marigold couldn't wait to get her hands on the wedding plans once the two were ready to set a date.

"We should toss in some of the essential oil, too. Aster said it helped Brynn sleep now that she's so uncomfortable."

Violet reached behind her and grabbed a bottle, launching it to Marigold, who caught like a WNBA superstar. "Why haven't they recruited me yet? I keep waiting."

"On Bridgerton. Staring off into the wonderment of the horizon. Probably reciting sonnets."

"Stop it. My poetry never rhymes."

"Are you two fighting again?" Aster Lavender appeared next to them like a ninja, never one for grand entrances. She was quiet, thoughtful, and brilliant. With her dark hair pulled into a low ponytail, she was the more youthful version of Violet.

Aster looked from Violet to Marigold and blinked with her customary slight head tilt. It wasn't always easy to tell when Aster was joking, but this had to be one of those times. Marigold and Violet *rarely* fought. She'd even let go of that time when she was thirteen and Violet read her diary entry about how she didn't know how to kiss and told Sage, who mercilessly teased her.

She did now. Thank God. Even if she was short on recent practice. Something to work on.

"Fighting? Yes," Violet said blandly. "I'm sending Marigold to work the fields with Dad and Sage."

Marigold laughed. "That's literally the worst thing she could think of. That tells you how opposed she is to manual labor."

Violet studied her manicure. "Imagine the abuse one's nails would take."

"Poor runner-up princess. Don't do that to yourself," Marigold said with an empathetic pout. She swiveled to sister number two. "We have wares for you. It's a good day." She bent under the counter and popped up with the bag. "Here."

"Oh." Aster brightened. "Thanks to you both. Brynn is going to be so relieved to see more of the oil. It really did help her relax."

"Anything for my future niece and her gorg mother," Marigold said with confidence.

"Or nephew," Violet tossed in. "We don't know yet. You can't just proclaim."

"Speak for yourself." Marigold placed a hand on her heart and smiled. She'd always trusted her intuition when it came in as strongly as this inkling. She was having a niece. No one could convince her otherwise. "I still don't understand how you've gone so long not knowing."

"We like the idea of finding out when we meet them," Aster said.

Violet raised her shoulders and dropped them. "You have willpower of steel."

Aster shrugged. "We just want a happy baby and a safe delivery for Brynn. That's all that matters." She blew out a slow breath, a signal she was uneasy. "I've been reading up on the process. There's really a lot involved and a number of different variables for both patient and doctor to consider." Aster was nothing if not thorough. She did her research on, well, everything. A gift and a curse as far as Marigold could see. But Aster's impressive brain had to be fed, and for her that meant gathering information.

"You're diving deep on childbirth?" Marigold asked and gave Aster's hand a squeeze. "Are you sure you want to overrun your brain with all that? Let the doctors worry."

Violet was immediately at her side. "Plenty of time to create a list of things to worry about." In actuality, however, the baby could arrive anytime now. They were not far from Brynn's due date.

Aster leaned against the counter. "I'm keeping it all in perspective.

The odds are in our favor for a smooth delivery. I've checked on those, too. Ran all the statistics."

Marigold squeezed her hand again. "Of course you have. If you're worried, let us know. Big sister rescue squad over here ready to shake you up a martini of joy."

Aster laughed. "I've had your joyful martinis, and they aren't for the weak. Knocked on my ass after two last time. I went home and told Brynn that if she loved me deeply, she would play with my hair and sing me Taylor Swift songs in a whisper voice until I fell asleep. She still hasn't let me forget."

"Now, nor will we," Violet said sweetly.

"People go to amazing lengths when they're in love." Marigold sighed dreamily. "How do I get in on that?"

Aster grabbed that one. "Well, if you're me, you pine after the same woman for years until you royally screw it up before she sweeps you off your feet forever. Now I rub her feet while she reads, and we debate baby names. It's rad."

"Timing is everything," Violet said with a nod.

"Speaking of which, I have news besides the impending arrival of a child." Aster's eyes flashed, which said this was big. She didn't dole out eye flashes over mundane tidbits.

"Perched and ready," Marigold said, offering her full attention.

"I'm going to imagine you're familiar with Alexis Wakefield."

Marigold frowned. "Is she on a soap opera? I'm obsessed with those with no time to watch."

"If we were on a soap opera," Violet noted, "I could smack you in the middle of the workday." She pretended to do so, and Marigold fell right over, not one to miss a chance for a little dramatic action.

"Perfectly timed!" she said, popping back up. They needed an Oscar.

"Okay. Are we done being weird?" Aster asked. Her mouth pulled, but she held back the grin, probably because she knew better than to encourage them.

Violet checked her watch. "Yes. Sorry. Tell us what you have cued up."

"Alexis Wakefield is a very popular food critic, the one everyone talks about for both good and terrifying reasons. Pretty famous, actually."

"Vaguely sounding familiar," Marigold said. She offered the gimme-more gesture. "Keep going."

"She has a column with the *San Francisco Journal*, but it's her social media that really puts her on everyone's radar. I mean, I follow her. I'm surprised you don't, but I guess you're not in food."

"Wait, wait, wait." Violet frowned. "Is she the one with the short snarky clips on Instagram where she side-eyes the camera at the end and sometimes takes a bite of something? She has really great lips."

"Yes! That's her."

The mouth comment tipped her off. Marigold squinted. "The make or break you woman, who cuts right to the chase?"

Aster's eyes went wide. "Okay, yes. She's the one. She's coming to Marilyn's on Tuesday."

"What?" Marigold looked to Violet, who looked right back with the same *holy shit* expression.

Aster held up a finger. "Or at least that's what a friend of mine who knows her editor told me. We won't know for sure until then." She paused. "It's a big deal for Marilyn's. For me. I don't want to screw it up."

"She's coming here?" Marigold asked, excitement arriving like fast moving floodwaters. "To Homer's Bluff? This woman is famous."

"Very. She's on top when it comes to viral reviews," Aster said.

Violet crossed her arms. "But she's been known to rip people apart."

"Our menu is first rate, and I stand by my food. It's all I can do."

"How did this happen?" Marigold asked. The smile on her face felt large and permanent. This was the best news! She loved it when good things happened to the people she loved, and no one deserved more acclaim than Aster and her fantastic restaurant. "The last exciting thing that happened in this place was Mrs. Brumfeld letting the air out of Mrs. Hastings's tires for not returning the new Parker Bristow novel to the library in a timely manner."

"In fairness, she'd been waiting on that copy for weeks," Violet said.

Aster shrugged. "I guess we're next. Apparently, Marilyn's pulled in some chatter online, and Alexis Wakefield wants to check the place out for herself. See if it lives up to its reputation. Restaurants in lesser known places are surfacing as trendy. The big cities are played out."

"Well, it will live up," Marigold said emphatically, pulling Aster in with one arm and squeezing her tight before placing eighteen kisses on her baby Aster head. "What do you need from us? Anything."

"Anything," Violet echoed.

Aster shrugged and reddened, her voice just a whisper when she said, "I just wish Mom could be there."

Marigold's smile dimmed. They'd lost their mother to cancer, and the family was still very much healing and figuring out who they were without her. She had been their core, the center of everything good about the Lavenders.

"So I was hoping, you know, if you're not too busy, that you two might come on Tuesday. Moral support. Just knowing you're in the room, eating my food, would make me feel so much more at ease. A little bit of Mom."

"You got it," Violet said quite seriously.

Marigold nodded, her chest tight and an aching lump forming in her throat. "I'd be honored, Aster. In fact, I'm already mentally scanning my closet for the perfect outfit that says *My sister is the best chef ever.*"

Aster seemed to process this in that all-too-thoughtful manner in which she did everything. "Okay. Seems like a lofty fashion goal." Nuance was not her strength.

"She can do it," Violet said easily, leaning her forearms onto the counter. "This is really cool news," she told Aster, placing a grip on her forearm. "And you're going to kill it come Tuesday."

"I'll be offering a chef's tasting menu that night, just in case, a selection of our best features, so come hungry."

"I already know my order," Marigold said.

It turned out to be a really good day. Aster's news had elevated Marigold's mood and kept her smiling even through the mundane moments. Her siblings' victories were hers, a lesson learned from her parents.

As she stood alone in front of the mirror that night in her turquoise boxers and white sleeveless tee, she smiled at the slight resemblance to her mom. While she and Sage had their father's lighter complexion and strawberry-blond hair, her smile was all Marilyn Lavender's. Nothing could make her happier than carrying that special piece of the woman who'd made her life warm, fun, and safe. She missed her mother with her whole heart, nearly breathless with grief at points. She wondered if the effect would ever leave her. In many ways, she hoped it didn't.

"I love you, Mama," she said quietly, believing wholly that their mother was still with them in everything they did. "You would be so proud of Aster. Can you even believe it?"

Marigold was a go-getter in her own right, but she didn't come with Aster's talent or Sage's drive. She'd love to have an ounce of Violet's ability to project-manage. But Marigold hoped that her tenacity and desire to always learn and improve herself contributed to the world, too. She wanted to see more of it. Experience new places. Travel. Get an apartment and look down at a bustling city and know she was a part of something much larger than her.

She climbed into her California king and stared over at the pillow next to hers. Empty. Cold. She was uncomfortably alone. Helena, the woman from her daydream earlier, the one who'd made a big pot of soup and had it waiting because Marigold had had to work late, well, she hadn't materialized. Nor had her sexy white dress shirt that Marigold had taken off her with skilled precision. Damn, she was good at the sensual stuff in her daydreams. If only she got to practice more in real life.

She pressed her cheek to her own pillow and smiled at the memory, whether real or not. Longings were longings, and she fell asleep that night remembering her hands on those buttons and all that was revealed to her beneath.

"One day, Helena. You and me," she said wistfully moments before sleep claimed her. Whatever her name was, her person was out there. What was she doing right now? Pouring a late-night glass of wine? Tuning in to her favorite show? Or was she looking up at the stars and wondering about her, too?

CHAPTER ONE

Alexis Wakefield scanned her inbox and mentally arched a sculpted eyebrow. A hundred and seventy-three new private messages to her Instagram account since the night before. The number was not out of the ordinary. Her followers were nothing if not zealous and opinionated, praising her for her latest review or rebuking her, point by point, in defense of their favorite restaurant. Cute of them. It was part of the package deal that came with being a public personality. People wanted to interact with her, feel like they were a part of her world, just as she was a part of theirs.

"Yeah, can't do it," she said, closing the window. She tried to answer a few each day. Keep them hungry with an occasional reply. But tonight was not the time. She lacked the fortitude to answer a single message and instead skimmed her inbox for anything or anyone she actually knew. Oh, there was one critiquing her outfit in the actual subject line. She still wasn't sure when her fashion and appearance had become part of the mix, but they certainly had. She'd been dubbed glamorous, trying too hard, beautiful, fake, filtered, and everything in between. She didn't let it get to her and shrugged off the comments, understanding that the internet was a viper pit, and if she wanted to survive, she had to become a viper herself.

And, oh, she *had*.

Alexis, when reviewing, leaned in to the snark and did not hold back her criticism. She never was dishonest about her opinions or exaggerated for attention, though. The integrity of the review mattered. The food had to be the spotlight, and she was a straight shooter. Alexis swept a wayward strand of long dark hair from her eye and went to work putting the final touches on her latest write-up before officially filing it with her editor. She'd post it to her own social sites after the column went to print and let the likes flow in.

"Sorry about this, Punctuation Kitchen and Bar," she murmured as she uploaded a photo from the hip little eatery in North Beach, San Francisco. Crowds were flocking, reservations were hard to get, and her little review was about to poke a hole in that happy state of success. The restaurant wasn't at all far from her perfect Eastlake Victorian home that about broke her with its price tag. "Fuck it," she'd said as she'd signed the paperwork a year ago. You only lived once. San Francisco had a dynamic food scene, and she couldn't imagine living anywhere else. But Alexis definitely tried to manage the quantity of reviews of establishments in her home city to not exclude her national audience. Plus, the trends were all about finding obscure eateries in lesser known cities and putting them on the map. Her readers ate that formula up. It had her on the road periodically, but other than the less than luxurious accommodations half the time, she didn't mind. She was a hustler who cared about pulling in views. This local write-up, though, she'd budgeted for. And the restaurant, Punctuation, hadn't disappointed, until it had. She'd had high hopes after all the early buzz, but as she wrote in her column, Punctuation unfortunately came with no exclamation point.

Her impression of the place was simple. The restaurant came with a fantastic selection of bourbons and an executive chef who appreciated the details that made each dish pop. His first downfall was his inability to self-edit. His dishes were crowded and trying to do too many things. Secondly, he was so caught up in the wow factor that he forgot the basics, like good seasoning. Her review was no-holds-barred and chronicled her journey at the restaurant from her first steps through the door to the farewell bite. It wasn't her fault the food did not impress her. It was her job to report her opinion to her followers, who were growing by the second, in as entertaining a manner as possible. Was she sharp tongued on purpose because it garnered her more shares on social? Of course. She wasn't a fool. Her harsher words were what her readers hung on for. She also had no problem delivering a glowing review when a restaurant deserved it.

She blearily checked the clock. Close to one a.m. A night owl, always. She typed up the last of her review, which would appear in the *San Francisco Journal* later that week. Papers didn't get much bigger than that one, and she was proud that she'd landed there. She'd started her original column on the back page of a small food magazine nearly fifteen years earlier. Since then, she'd slowly clawed her way to the top.

> *In the end, I wish I could recommend Punctuation, the little restaurant that didn't. But unless you were born to hate any kind of true flavor whatsoever, keep driving. What could have been for Chef Michael Kowalski, if only he'd paid more attention in culinary school? Tsk, tsk. Someone send him back to basics, and I'd welcome a return visit with a side of that fifteen-year bourbon. In fact, I feel like I've earned a stiff drink after that food.*

She nodded, proud of her work. The regrettable part would be the damage it would do to the restaurant's foodie business and Chef Kowalski's bruised ego. But she imagined they'd rebound and maybe even learn to bolster and edit the bland food they'd served her. All part of the gig. Nothing personal.

She rolled her shoulders and turned around to her best friend on the planet, Carrot the blond and amazing dachshund. He'd been patiently waiting for her to finish with work while curled into a circle on top of a throw pillow. Her bed was his bed during the day, and he laid constant claim. When Alexis showed Carrot the tiniest bit of attention, he stood and wagged his whole body in sleepy celebration. He even smiled, his signature move. Not a lot of dogs had that ability. Carrot nailed it.

"Handsomesauce over there, I think you've more than earned about eight thousand kisses."

Carrot's response was to leap on top of her and smother her with kisses of his own in a frenzy.

"Ah! Someone is incredibly cute right now, and it's not me," she told him, holding his sweet little face. She would literally hurl herself off a building for this dog—she loved him that much. "What do you think about this compliment? Shall we celebrate it with a puppy treat or two?" His response was to turn in an excited little circle while standing on her stomach. "Oh, wow. Look at the poise. Look at the balance. Nine-point-five out of ten." A pause. A lick. "Fine. You won me over. The whole ten points. Follow me to the goods."

She snagged Carrot a bacon-flavored treat, his favorite, and scrolled her calendar for a reminder of the week ahead. She was traveling somewhere obscure. That much she remembered. She tended to ignore the details until they were upon her. Aha. Apparently, in just a couple of days, she was headed to Nowhere, Kansas. Why? She paused a minute and then remembered that Tatum had called with a request that she check out this restaurant she'd heard about from a friend, who'd fallen all over herself after eating there. It fit her lesser known goal, and Tatum, who was a fantastic editor, was also a good scout, so she'd agreed. A quick scan of the local blogs told her that the pecan dusted pork medallions seemed to be their fan favorite. But Kansas? Seriously. "Carrot, are you up for a little middle of the country adventure? I'm talking tumbleweeds and dirt. At least, I think I am."

Carrot didn't care. He was all in and signaled as much with four circle turns and a rear back, his customary answer to anything that ended with an inflection in Alexis's voice.

"Well, at least we can try to snap a few photos of you in some bandanas. Add to your puppy book. Rugged dachshunds are where it's at, and I wouldn't lie to you about that. You know me."

Because life was too short for cheap wine, Alexis indulged in a glass of the good stuff and let the day slide off her. Ready to sleep at last, she took off everything but her Dolce & Gabbana panties, pulled back her fluffy comforter, folded it neatly at the edge of her bed, slipped beneath the cool sheets, and waited for Carrot to snuggle into his own bed nearby. Just as she was about to flip out the lights, her phone danced eagerly to life.

She studied the readout. A text from Sadie. It took her a moment to place the name until…oh yes. The brunette who squealed when she was touched in just the right way. An interesting choice. Not that she minded. Their night together had certainly been a unique experience and, honestly, memorable.

Tell me you're up and thinking about me, the text read.

She paused. Because she was up but that was about all she could say. *About to go to bed. Sweet dreams to you.* That should do it, right?

I hope yours involve me. Because you're the star in mine.

She frowned at the reply. That was the problem with hookups. They didn't always stay that way. She was a busy girl. She didn't do sweet nothings or lazy snuggling, or even enjoy small talk that much. Once everyone was satisfied, there were things to accomplish, empires to claim, and lots of food to taste. You couldn't fault her for having goals beyond pillow talk and chasing them. Women were lovely, amazing even. But Alexis didn't pine for the warm fuzzies of a relationship. In fact, she was glad to be out of her last one, short lived as it had been. Not everyone was built the same. She had her dog, her column, and her travels, and occasionally a buddy comedy on the plane ride home to make her laugh. An orgasm on the go with a woman from a bar and she was set. All the good things in life.

"Good night, Carrot-Man," she said, reaching down to give her dog's ears a hearty scratch. "'Night, Sadie. Hope you find yourself a hookup tonight."

With a click of the light, she began her journey to slumber, knowing it wouldn't take long. Alexis Wakefield lived a fabulous life without anything complicated hanging over her head. Didn't get much better than that. She'd sleep like a damn baby that night—if babies were at the top of the food chain and sitting on lots of money. A smile. A sigh. She was off.

❖

Country music from a decade or two before her time settled all around Marigold like a salve. The people she'd known for most of her life filled the busy space all around her because this town didn't have too many options when it came to nightlife. But the beer was cold and the company was good, so she wasn't complaining.

"Marigold Lavender, what I don't understand is why you won't marry me."

Marigold took a sip of her citrusy hefeweizen atop her customary stool at Larry's Last Stop, Homer's Bluff's only true bar if you didn't count the miniature ones inside restaurants. "Tillman, if I've told you once, I've told you eight times, maybe nine. I'm gay and thrilled about it. Do we need to go over again how I know? It's time you faced the fact that you and I will not be riding off into any kind of sunset together. You don't even own a horse."

"I'd buy one for the esteemed honor of your company."

"You're missing the point. You're not a woman."

"I guess I was sorta hoping that you'd tell me you're what they called fluid. Bisexual. Pansexual. Falling in love with the person"—he touched his chest—"and their overflowing heart."

"Except I'm not. I've dated men, present company included, in fact. Your adorable ass wasn't for me, but it's cute in a pair of jeans. I'll admit I do admire it from time to time. No desire to go a single step farther, though, and don't you think that's telling?"

"You're ripping my soul in two." He dipped his head and looked up at her with those big brown puppy dog eyes. He was harmless and a good friend, probably her best outside of Violet, who he just so happened to live next door to. She kind of enjoyed that her two favorite people were lined up in a row. Small towns were like that, and it gave her peace of mind knowing he kept an eye on her sister and nephew. Tillman was good people. She knew he was serious about wishing for more between them, but his playful side was certainly on display tonight after they'd killed two beers together.

"Tillman, what we need for you is a new woman, someone not from around here to wow your socks right off your big feet."

"But I have eyes for you."

"We'd live a sexless life. I'm a boob woman."

He gave her the steely eyes. "What can I do to be better? Seriously. I'll take notes."

"Slow down. Step one." She took a long sip from her glass, grinned, and winked, hoping it softened the blow.

His face fell. He leaned in and whispered, "Are you talking about my bedroom performance?"

"Aww. Is that not what you were asking about, sweet cheeks?" She laughed as he sank straight to the floor and stayed there on his back like roadkill. She joined him down there as those around them barely blinked. Just Marigold and Tillman on a regular old night out. "The love game is hard. I'm finding that out myself."

He sat up and turned to her, sobering. He knew when to be a cutup and when to turn it off and be her friend. "You're not finding what you're looking for out there? I thought you were checking out all the dating apps." He looked sad for her, and that helped her confess the truth.

She nodded. "I was. But for some of these people, it's all just a game. I don't think I'm cut out for ghosting, hookups, and all the fake photos and manipulation that happens on them."

He squeezed her hand and removed his blue Jayhawks ball cap, which she knew to be his favorite, showing the dark blond locks beneath. "You have a tender heart, MG, and anyone who wastes your time is not worth it. You hold out for the best, or you'll have me to talk to."

"That's the nicest threat I've ever received."

"You two gonna sit on the floor all night?" Larry hollered. He was in his late sixties and didn't hear real well anymore, walked with a limp, and read a lot of gardening magazines.

Tillman stood and offered her his hand. "Nah, we were just making sure you were getting your dollar's worth with that cleaning service, Lar. Tell 'em not to skimp on the corners."

"Couple of weirdos," Larry said, shaking his head and moving down the bar, magazine tucked under his arm like a security blanket. Marigold had a soft spot for him, too. Call her sentimental. Larry was a fixture in Homer's Bluff and a surly surrogate granddad to many, herself included.

"Do you really think I'm…fast?" Tillman asked quietly, glancing around to make sure no one overheard their conversation.

"Oh, Tillman." She shook her head and left it there.

"Damn." He put his cap back on his head and focused in distress on the wall ahead of him. "Just double damn."

"Plenty of life ahead of you, Till. Another round on me to ease your sorrow. Then I have to go home, and you'll need to walk me like a proper gentleman best friend."

"I agree to this," he said, still pouting but looking a little happier now that a free beer was coming his way.

She touched her mostly empty glass to his longneck. "Peas."

"In a damn pod," he said back, finishing their two-decade-old motto. They'd enjoyed a tight-knit relationship ever since he'd fallen over backward from rocking in his chair in their sixth grade homeroom. On purpose. While the other kids laughed and cheered him on, the kind of attention he still ate up, Marigold had been the one to pick him up and give him a stern talking to about safety and not acting like a dumbass all the time. She'd actually used the word. From that moment on, he'd been taken with her in a sweet way. They'd run in different crowds as they got older but always picked up easily with each other. Tillman had been popular in school, but never arrogant. He was gentle and fun and tried to always do the right thing even though his boneheaded tendencies had sabotaged his efforts on more than a few occasions. Marigold was always there, however, to place him back on course. His moral compass. The two of them grabbed a beer at least once a week these days and did a good job of centering each other. To this day, his grandma baked her fresh bread for every single holiday. Bless Hilda and her amazing abilities with a proofing box.

"What do you think, Tillman? Are we going to make it?"

"Damn right we are, MG. You hang tight a sec. I need to play my favorite song on the juke." She smiled as he headed to the retro jukebox that had seen better days. Moments later, because there wasn't a lot of competition, "You Never Even Called Me By My Name" strummed over the speakers.

"Hey."

She turned, confused because Tillman's stool had been stolen by her kid brother, who looked like he'd asked for a lollipop and had been gifted eight.

"Well, someone's out of the house."

Sage held up a hand. "Not that I was dying to be, but life with a teething baby makes nights at Larry's fewer and farther between. I miss talking to other adults who aren't Tyler, as great as she is. When I pointed a burp cloth at the TV and tried to change the channel with it from across the room, she told me to grab a beer. I gotta say"—he placed his hands flat on the bar—"I practically sprinted out of there."

"And in an hour, you're going to miss those two adorable girls so much that you'll pay the tab and race home."

"Don't bust my ass. I can't help it that my family is awesome. But for now, I'm gonna grab a brew with you folks and bask in fully verbal company." He grinned and flashed the dimples that made women across town weep the day he married Tyler, his very own high school best friend. The two of them had danced around each other for years, denying that anything romantic floated between them. The whole rest of the world knew plain as day. Once Sage finally admitted to himself that Tyler was the woman for him, they'd lived happily ever after in marital bliss. Well, bliss and sleepless nights with a teething Wrigley. Good thing her niece was possibly the cutest little baby ever made with Sage's blond hair and Tyler's spunky confidence. Marigold could just eat those cheeks for breakfast.

"How's Dad today?" Marigold asked. Sage and their father oversaw the lavender farm and worked closely side by side each day, much the way she and Violet did at the store.

"He was super quiet again." It had been over two years since they'd lost their mom, and she'd watched as their dad made every attempt to press on without her, stay active in his kids' lives, and find his own happiness. But lately, he'd been fading into himself more and more, losing the battle. It slashed at Marigold and kept her up at night. None of this was fair. Sage stroked his chin, boasting two days' worth of stubble. "My opinion? I think we need to do a better job of popping in over there. Especially in the evenings. When the sun goes down, I think his loneliness sets in. He's more aware of the empty spot on the couch next to his."

"I hate hearing that." Marigold knew lonely. She didn't broadcast how much she struggled watching her siblings raise their kids and enjoy life with their partners while she dreamed of her own, curled up in an empty bed. In fact, she did everything in her power to hide her feelings on the topic. Even her fictional worlds had her feeling pathetic these days. She was thirty-five years old and watching her life slip away. Violet was raising her son, Ethan. Sage had Tyler and Wrigley, and Aster was about to welcome a new little one of her own with Brynn. So if there was someone who had the time to check in more on their father, she was the perfect candidate for the job. Maybe she and her dad could help each other feel a little less isolated. "I'm all over that," she told Sage. "We can brief Aster and Violet and all do a little more checking in on him, but I don't mind being project leader."

"I appreciate that, Mare. The guy's lost, and I'm not sure what to do anymore. Even at work, I watched him drift. Forgets to put in orders. Mixes up the calendars." Sage shook his head. "And it's not that he's getting older and forgetful. He's just lost his motivation. He doesn't care."

"He misses *her*," Marigold finished. She knew for certain that there was never a love story more perfect than the one that belonged to her parents. They were high school sweethearts who'd never spent a day apart once they found each other, supremely happy living in adoration and love for the other. They were two halves of a whole, separated way too early by an unfortunate cancer card. Unfair.

"Exactly." Sage's blue eyes, a family staple present in one-half of the Lavender clan, met hers. "Theirs was a kind of love that doesn't come around too often."

"I've never seen anything like it." She smiled on the verge of tears as she thought back to the quiet looks her parents used to exchange over dinner when all four young kids were creating chaos at the table, fighting, singing, and reaching for seconds. When they'd all been tucked in for the night, their parents would sit on the wooden swing hung on the back porch. There, in the dark, they'd hold hands and catch up on each other's day. She knew because she used to sneak out of bed and watch them through the window. Her sweet parents, moonlight kissed and happy. "When Mom passed, she took a big piece of him with her." She sighed and studied her beer, foamy and cold. She no longer felt as celebratory.

Sage placed a strong arm around her shoulders and gave her a squeeze. "If anyone can help Dad out of this, it's you. You're unstoppable, and that's why we love you. Our kindhearted guard dog."

It was true. She was a persistent devil, hell-bent on protecting the people that she loved. And she'd stop at nothing to achieve her goals, even when they were pinned to other people.

"I'll swing by. Make him dinner." In fact, she wondered if it might turn into a weekly date. She wouldn't mind that at all, quality time with just her and her dad in their family home. She tapped the bar and pushed her beer away. It was no longer the vibe, nor was this loud music. She could use a quieter venue about now, her conversation with Sage having dissolved her mood. Yet she didn't budge and knew exactly why. Leaving Larry's and heading home meant she'd be on her own once again. The concept crippled her.

So there she sat.

After singing a handful of songs across the bar with his buddies, Tillman re-emerged and hopped onto the stool next to Marigold's. "Are you impressed with my solo? Been working on the big notes in the mirror." He was grinning with pride, his hair spiky with sweat.

She tried not to wince. "Tillman Lee, wow. You nailed it."

Sage offered him a fist bump across Marigold, which he heartily smashed back. "Thank you, Lavender folk. You're too kind."

Marigold stifled a yawn and offered Tillman a kiss on the cheek.

"You really think I go too fast?" he whispered, unable to let the topic die. "I kind of think of it as effective service. I'm working to get the job done. Don't want to make her wait."

"Bless your heart. Your nickname was jackrabbit," she told him plainly, trying to inject sympathy into at least her stare. Best it come from her. They'd had sex exactly one time when they were twenty-one and tipsy, and it was not an experience she ever needed to repeat. Thank God she'd finally admitted to herself that women might be for her. It had been like a glorious veil lifting. Conversely, her first sexual experience with a woman had solidified exactly why she'd never enjoyed sex before, because hot damn, she was as gay as the day was long. Now she understood where all the acclaim came from. Sex was just about the most amazing thing there was. It was better than hot buttered popcorn, which was her absolute favorite, but she'd hand you her tub for a little naked action. She was sadly not getting enough of it around here. Yet another reason she longed to pack up her bags and flee this town. One day…maybe.

Tillman craned his neck to better see her brother. "Sage, let me ask you a question, my brother. Any woman ever tell you to slow down, you know, between the sheets?"

Marigold winced at the reference. They were really going there?

"Um. No, man," Sage said with an easy smile and went back to his beer. She'd heard rumors about his satisfied partners, but Marigold chose not to think much about her brother engaging in such acts, because gross.

Before she could cover her ears, she was saved when a voice behind them called, "MG, you up for some darts?" It was Tammy from Spaghetti Straps, the cute boutique in the center of town.

She actually wasn't a darts fan but, again, not exactly ready for her noticeably quiet home. "Sure. On my way." She heard the weariness in her own voice as she trudged over. Surely, the universe had more in store for her than a series of nights like this over and over, right? She felt like she existed in a perpetual waiting room, watching everyone else live, twiddling her thumbs patiently as she longed for her turn. Just not your time yet, she'd say to herself. Only these days, she wasn't so sure she believed it.

"Am I first?" she asked.

"You get it, girl," Tammy said and watched.

Marigold threw and watched as her underthrown dart arced low and landed off the board in the empty black abyss. She dropped her shoulders. "Damn it, Mare," she muttered. Well, wasn't that just the perfect metaphor for her sagging personal life?

CHAPTER TWO

Marilyn's was bustling when Marigold arrived for her seven p.m. reservation for a fancy dinner with her date, Violet. The restaurant was simple, elegant, and rustic with a menu designed around elevated American comfort food. Thick wooden beams lined the ceiling and a gorgeous oak bar stood to the right of the dining room, which was dotted with round tables designed for groups to be able to cluster close, rather than be separated down a long rectangular table. The lighting was soft and made the room glow. A unique, nearly romantic, ambiance draped gently over the room. The kitchen was open, and eight chef seats lined its perimeter.

For dinner, Marigold had selected a peach-colored sundress and let her blond hair fall loose on one side, pulled back on the other, a style that had always earned her compliments in the past. Her hair with its gentle curls had always garnered her quite a bit of attention, and she leaned in to it. Apparently, it was her most coveted feature, and she was someone who valued her brief moments to shine.

"Is that your natural color? That golden and strawberry combo? Gorgeous."

"Marigold, how do you get your hair so shiny?"

"These locks are so thick. I'm jealous and not afraid to bitch."

She silently thanked her father after each compliment that came her way and learned to toss her hair just so to pull attention from across a room. She had no shame and owned it. If only her well-practiced tosses weren't wasted on so many small town straight people she had no interest in sleeping with. Ah, life and its annoying roadblocks to getting good and naked.

Violet arrived in the dim entryway of Marilyn's moments later and scoffed. "Flag on the play. You outdressed me again." She narrowed her gaze like a fashion cop on a mission. "This is the third time in a month. I should come to expect it, you traitorous hussy. I thought we were going *casual* chic." Violet folded her arms in betrayal, but in reality, it was an overblown bit rooted in half truth.

"And that's what I've done. Sundresses are very laid-back, Vi. The chillest of all dresses. Everyone knows that."

"But I'm wearing jeans, so a dress is instantly dressier. Even the chillest of all dresses outdresses jeans."

"Yes, but you're in *dressy* jeans, so it's hard to compare. Dressy jeans and dresses are both dressy enough."

"But jeans, dressy or not, are objectively less cute than a dress of any variety."

"Fine. Next time I'll text a full-length photo before I get in the car."

"Holding you to it." Violet exhaled slowly and smoothed her maroon top with the lace sleeves that made her look like a supermodel. Marigold had no idea why she'd ever worry about her appearance next to anyone. Violet radiated. "I will live with my fate because tonight is about Aster."

Marigold felt her grin tug. "Who's gonna kill it tonight. I have butterflies." She touched her stomach. "Do you realize I couldn't sleep last night I was so excited for her?" She kept her tone hushed because you never knew who was listening and there were still several other diners waiting to be seated ahead of them. "Vi, this reviewer could put our little baby Aster and Marilyn's as a whole on the map. We're talking national attention." She leaned back for emphasis and let her words shimmy in the air. "And that could mean everything for her career. An explosion of fame and focus. People will take road trips to taste Aster's food. Her pork medallions could be in magazines."

"They should be," Violet said.

"She might wind up on TV on one of those food shows that highlight eateries. Maybe I'll get to sit at one of the background tables. We'll both wear dresses that time."

"Hi there, beautiful darlings," Monique said. She'd served as assistant manager since Aster had opened the restaurant and did a great job of making the customers feel special and cared for. Young, friendly, straight dark hair that swung a little when she walked like there was a runway beneath her high-heeled feet. "I was waiting for you. We have your favorite table reserved. The one with the great view of the action." She meant *kitchen*, because Marigold loved to watch Aster command tickets. Monique held two tall menus to her chest and gestured for them both to follow her into the dining room. "As always, Jack Daniel's pork medallions are my recommendation, but the short rib risotto is also worth a visit."

"This will take some serious thought," Marigold said as they followed Monique to the four-top with the scripted *Reserved* notice in the middle. Very elegant. Monique scooped up the small black sign, then left them with their menus and a wine list. "Enjoy your meal."

They definitely would. Aster's open-concept design was Marigold's favorite part of the dining experience at Marilyn's. A show before their meal. It allowed diners to glimpse Aster's small team of chefs as they prepared the food, moving meticulously around each other in what seemed to be a choreographed dance, firing off tickets, flipping things in pans, and plating with impressive finesse. Marigold never got tired of watching her little sister, the one who used to sort the flowers in their front yard by color, run a full kitchen. Yet she did it with precision five nights a week as executive chef.

"I'm going pork medallions," Violet said. "I'll dream about that Jack Daniel's sauce all night if I don't."

"Then I'll go risotto and we can swap bites, but don't skimp."

"I'd never."

They folded their menus in tandem just as Byron, their favorite server, sauntered up to the table. "Wow me. What are we having?"

"Medallions for me. Risotto for the blonde," Violet said. "Oh, and can we split the wedge salad to start with maybe some extra candied bacon on the side?" She looked to Marigold, who nodded.

Byron snapped his leather pad closed. "Done. You've nailed it yet again."

Violet glanced back at the door. "Is she here yet? Do we know?"

"Not yet," Byron said. "But we're eagerly awaiting her esteemed presence." His black shirt had been pressed within an inch of its life, and his dark hair had an impressive height to its coif. There was an anticipatory energy that blanketed everything tonight, almost like you could reach out and touch it.

Marigold had also been scanning the room like a mother whose toddler had a fondness for matches. Not only that but she'd googled *Alexis Wakefield* and would recognize her in a heartbeat. Brunette. Pretty. She seemed to carry herself with a sophisticated air. And from what Marigold had read on her review site, she could be brutal when she wanted to be. That wouldn't be a problem for Marilyn's, however, because it was probably the best restaurant in the world. That was simply the end of it. She was convinced. With her mother's name and her kid sister's immeasurable talent and flavor innovations, the place was a hero just waiting for someone like Alexis Wakefield to introduce it to the world via her keyboard. And tonight could be the very night it happened.

"I think you have to play it a little more cool," Violet said, placing a hand on Marigold's.

"I don't know what you're talking about." But she heard the edge in her voice.

"Your energy is vibrating. Let go of the tablecloth." Marigold did. "You're in poodle mode, and it shows." She seemed to catch Byron's eye across the room and nodded. "Lemon drops are in order."

Marigold swiveled her attention back to her sister. "You know damn well I can't say no to lemon drops." Lemon drop martinis were her kryptonite. She sipped them slowly because she was no fool. But maybe it wasn't such a bad idea. "If we have lemon drops, we do guarantee ourselves a less stressful event."

Violet took a sip of ice water. "You can breathe."

"I can *luxuriate*. I think we're owed."

Her sister nodded seriously. "We had a hard day. At least twenty customers."

"And we want to remember the night Aster rose to glory and supported us financially into our old age."

"I get the rocker in the good light."

"Like hell you do."

"Let me guess. Lemon drops?" Byron asked with an arch of his brow. Damn him. He had their number, almost as if they had a reputation or something. Which, honestly, at Marilyn's they did. They ate there more than any other place in town. Sometimes Marigold came alone and ate at the bar. It was a nice way to get out of the house without looking pathetic. She was simply visiting her sister. An easy explanation for her perpetual party of one.

"I think we could be persuaded to enjoy a lemon drop," Marigold said as if it was the best new idea ever. "This is why we love you."

He grinned and placed two cocktail napkins on the table. "Coming right up."

Marigold opened her mouth to thank him but went still. "Don't move a muscle," she said, channeling her inner ventriloquist. "But she's here. This is not a drill."

Violet turned all the way around and stared, breaking every possible rule. "That's her? She's gorgeous."

"You can't just stare," Marigold hissed as Monique led the new arrival to a small table across the room.

"But I am," her sister said, undeterred.

And now Marigold was, too. *Oh, my.* Violet wasn't wrong. Sweet molasses on Sunday. Alexis Wakefield was stunning in every sense. It was like real-life Hollywood had just invaded Homer's Bluff. She was even prettier than the online photos had indicated. She wore a purple dress, businessy in its nature, with black pumps and what had to be a Prada bag. Marigold coveted Prada bags, but who had the money for such a splurge? Apparently, Alexis Wakefield. Her dark hair was down, semi long, parted in the middle, and impressively shiny. What kind of conditioner offered those results? Another glance said Ms. Wakefield wore subtle makeup applied to perfection. She certainly knew how to put herself together. The effect of all the components combined sent Marigold to her new existence: liquid. A warm, mesmerized puddle.

"MG, you in there?"

She was, but she wasn't actually either. Her mouth went dry, and her cheeks were doing this weird hot thing as if the universe had just touched her forehead with a magic wand, declaring her incapable of continuing on as she was.

"Mare?"

If she had been a cartoon character, her eyeballs would have shot out of her head and back, with little hearts in place of her pupils.

"Hey. I'm serious. You okay?" Violet asked, touching Marigold's wrist and studying her with drawn brows. "You haven't moved or spoken in about forty seconds. I'm afraid of still, quiet Marigold."

Marigold held up a finger. "That woman. She's…more than I

expected." She reached for her water glass and downed a gulp, making sure not to turn around again so Violet would have a chance to take a turn for reference.

"Me, too. The whole room shifted when she walked in. All eyes moved to her."

Marigold held out her arm. "She gave me the goose bumps. Very few people can do that."

A smirk appeared on Violet's lips. "Well, well. Someone has a crush, and we like to see it. Aster's gonna love this."

"What will I love?"

Marigold blinked up at her little sister, who was standing next to their table, staring down at them with what their mother used to refer to as her Bambi eyes. Big, brown, and earnest.

"MG has noticed your critic in a big way." Violet bounced her eyebrows, and understanding washed over Aster's expression.

"*Oh*, you're into her." She nodded with wide eyes. "That's only a little surprising. She's pretty."

Marigold, unsure how to describe the reaction she'd just had, tried to move them back on track. "But aren't you supposed to be cooking? Don't let us distract you. You feel free to focus and pretend we're not here."

"I could never do that," Aster said seriously. "But I have to leave. That's what I came over here to tell you."

That's when she realized that Aster wasn't wearing her monogrammed Marilyn's chef's coat. "Why would you do that? What are you talking about?" Marigold asked, cartwheeling out of her love-drunk state into big sister concern. "You can't leave."

Violet covered her mouth. "Is the baby coming?"

Aster nodded and flashed a wobbly smile. "Brynn's having contractions, and they're getting closer together. She's already heading to the hospital in Wichita. Tyler's driving her, and I'm going to meet them there."

"What do we do?" Marigold practically shouted, slamming her palms flat on the table. She had this urge to boil water or run laps around the dining room. Then she remembered the importance of tonight for the restaurant. The drop-dead gorgeous food critic waiting to make Aster's career was just over there. She half considered racing into the kitchen and jumping on the line to help, to flip something in a pan, but her skills placed her on the underqualified list. What now? There was no plan.

"Do you think one of you could speak to Ms. Wakefield, explain the situation, and the other could calm Henry the hell down? Monique has tried, but he has a crush on her, and she only makes him more on edge." She raised her eyebrows. "He's freaking out that he's about to handle such a big night without me."

Marigold squinted because which one was Henry? "The second chef guy?"

"Sous-chef. Yes." Aster hooked a thumb, and Marigold followed it to the person in question. "He's fantastic. Fully capable, but his nerves get the better of him."

"In that case, maybe this isn't the best night," Violet said. "Should you just call the review off?"

"That's not how reviews work. She's free to dine here and write about us whenever she wants. It's not an agreed-upon event." Aster pressed on, stealing a glance across the room to make sure she wasn't overheard. "She's here to review the restaurant, not just me, and we still have service tonight. And it's okay. My menu, my recipes, my staff will tell her everything she needs to know about my work."

Which essentially meant this was happening. Marigold nodded, vowing to help. "How are you so calm? There's a baby on the way. And you have to leave your restaurant on such an important night. That's a lot of things to mentally juggle," Marigold pointed out. She tried to imagine herself demonstrating similar control, and nope, that would never happen.

"Have you met Aster?" Violet asked, giving their sister's hand a squeeze. "She's got this, right?"

"I do." Aster smiled and exhaled slowly. "But the truth is that my heart feels like a jackhammer operated by a cat on speed, so I better go."

"Yes. Dammit. Get out of here!" Marigold dropped her napkin onto the table. "Message us with the first hint of news. I want centimeters, the pushing schedule, and fifteen photos from the baby's first moment of life."

"You got it," Aster said, radiating. She held out her hands and flexed her fingers. "I can't believe this is actually happening. I'm going to be a parent. Like Mom." Her smile was tentative but incredibly sweet. To her credit, she hadn't mentioned the stress of leaving the restaurant or the big reviewer. She was focused on what mattered, Brynn and their baby. God, Aster had her life together. Her priorities were in line, and it showed. Marigold was not only proud, but she admired her for that.

"You're going to be the best mom," Violet said. She stood up and cradled Aster's face, always the nurturer.

"It's feeling very real about now. Are you sure you don't mind smoothing things over?"

"We were made for this," Violet said.

"Marilyn's has a team of fantastic chefs and two very passionate family ambassadors to stand in for you. Don't give it another thought," Marigold added, projecting manufactured confidence.

Aster nodded a few times. "Okay, then. I'll be in touch." She hugged each of them, raised a hand in farewell, and quietly left the restaurant through the kitchen.

As soon as she was out of earshot, Marigold spun around to Violet. "What the hell? A baby and a career changing review in the same night? The universe is busy."

Violet didn't seem as concerned. "Everything will be fine. Let's divide and conquer. Do you want to chat with Ms. Wakefield, the love of your life, or would you rather address Henry?"

Marigold eased a strand of hair behind her ear and gave her shoulders a shimmy. "I don't mind taking one for the team. How's my hair?" She gave it her signature toss.

"A halo of honey blond. Va-va-voom," she stated in a businesslike tone. "Now get over there."

Marigold took a deep breath, tabled her own simmering feelings surrounding Alexis Wakefield, and remembered the cause. Her baby sister meant everything and needed Marigold's finesse in this moment. She would deliver.

She concentrated on a hospitable walk and a warm smile as she approached the table and took a final centering breath when Alexis's striking features came into better view. Wow. She clasped her hands in front of her. "Hello. I don't mean to bother you, but I wanted to introduce myself."

Alexis raised her gaze, adjusted her hair a half inch, and slid into an easy smile. "Hi, there."

"Yes, hi. It's so nice to meet you. I'm Marigold Lavender. You're Alexis?" Of course she was. Just look at her.

"I am. Nice to meet you." A pause struck. She hated those. "Are you a follower of my work or...?" Right. She should probably explain herself.

"Oh. No." That sounded bad—she rushed to recover. "I'm sure it's great. But I'm the sister of the owner and executive chef."

"Okay." A pause. "That's fabulous," she said in a voice that didn't communicate the sentiment at all. That was weird.

"We're just so excited that you're here. I know Aster wanted to prepare each dish personally."

"Right. That's...lovely." She inclined her head as if waiting for the point.

"Except she had to leave."

"Oh. Okay." She folded her arms casually. Was she bored? Yep, she was a really good-looking bored person. What in the world was happening? Marigold was generally a well-liked person who was used to others reciprocating her friendly overtures, matching her friendly energy, or at least attempting to. Alexis Wakefield was apparently immune to any kind of rapport-building. This left Marigold floundering and wanting to work twice as hard.

"You see, it's a big day for our family. Aster's partner, Brynn, is in labor as we speak." She beamed and waited because who doesn't love a good baby on the way update? Nothing. "So Aster had to dash off to the hospital just now. Totally unexpected. As most labor and deliveries are, I suppose." This didn't seem to be going well. Or rather, it wasn't going at all. She found zero genuine investment from this woman. Certainly, Marigold had to be missing something.

"Congratulations to all of you," Alexis said evenly. She sipped from her water glass, leaving a faint maroon imprint that matched her lipstick. Apparently those were all the words she planned to devote to the topic, which sent Marigold into a very weird compensation mode. Now *she* had to use more words to make up the deficit.

And, yes, here they came. "This is their first child, so you know how huge this must feel. Not that I know." She placed a hand on her chest. "I don't have any children, and forgive me for presuming you would know. Maybe you don't either. I imagine it's pretty universal, though." She shrugged. "I'm just emphasizing the importance of today for our family. For Aster specifically." Heavens to Kevin Jonas, she was talking way the hell too much. It's what she did when she was uncomfortable. What she needed was an *in summary* statement, an exclamation point to end her spiel because Alexis was watching her like a grasshopper encroaching on her picnic. "In summary, the point of all this is that Aster is so sorry that she couldn't be here. But Violet— her other sister—and I want to welcome you in her place." A pause. "I don't know why I said *in summary*." She laughed. "High school speech class for you."

Alexis didn't smile. "I appreciate you letting me know about your family news, and I wish you all nothing but the best. But honestly and, I suppose, *in summary*, I'm here for a meal. That's all." Clearly, that was meant to be the end of the conversation. It felt very much like Alexis Wakefield didn't want to be bothered, which made sense. Aster had explained that most of the reviewers didn't announce their presence or inform anyone when they might be dining. Anonymity might have been her preference, and here they'd gone and made a big deal out of her presence. These things were very much outside of her experience.

"Right. Well, I'll leave you to your dinner." She offered a nod and a lingering look at those really perfect pouty lips. "And it was really nice meeting you."

"Likewise," Alexis said like she was concluding a business meeting. Marigold walked away, picking the stray icicles off her dress, the ones that had been thrown in the midst of that chilly conversation. Was it that hard to try for pleasant? Act excited for a new baby? The gorgeous Ms. Wakefield clearly had a heart of stone. Now more than ever, Marigold worried about the forthcoming review. The woman couldn't be easy to please. She exhaled and took comfort in the knowledge that Aster's food was the best she'd ever tasted. If this reviewer knew anything, she'd agree before the night was over.

"All I'm saying is that you're more amazing than you give yourself credit for."

Marigold frowned as she approached the open kitchen and saw her sister with a hand on Henry's shoulder. Luckily, the chatter of the dining room made it impossible to hear much of their back-and-forth.

"I don't think I can do this," he said, whisking a bowl of eggs, staring at them like they held the key to his future. "I've never been good under pressure. It's why I got Cs on all my finals in culinary school."

"You're so far beyond that now," Violet said, always the voice of reason. "You're a professional, and this is your kitchen. You create these same dishes daily. You just have to do what you always do. Just another night of…"

"Service," he provided.

"Yes. That. Amazing service, too."

Around them, line cooks stole concerned glances as they worked tickets. There was no leader. Everyone was fending for themselves. She didn't know a ton about restaurants, but they needed someone to captain the ship. This was desperate. Marigold decided Henry needed a more personal approach. "Hank. Do people call you that?"

"My Grandma Ginny does. She lives in Minnesota." He stared at her hard, his eyes moving back and forth between hers, as if searching for an anchor.

Marigold took his big hands in hers and gave them a squeeze. "Hank, Grandma Ginny very much wants you to remember how amazing you are. Aster has all the faith in you, too. Do you have pets?"

He nodded enthusiastically. A smile blossomed on his face. "Elmo. He's a turtle."

"Elmo can't wait for you to come home a rock star. He's prepping his shell for a major party."

"Yeah?" Henry asked. His wide-eyed gaze communicated such hope.

Violet turned to Marigold with a look that said *Is this really happening?*

Marigold stayed focused. "Totally. Elmo is sending you a steady hand and a clear head to make the perfectly crafted dishes you always do. The chefs in this kitchen need your leadership tonight. This is your moment to shine, Henry. Are you up for it?"

He exhaled. "I'll do it for Elmo."

"Yeah, you will!" Marigold said, smacking the side of his arm. "Now, Violet and I are going to go sit down and enjoy the evening. You got this."

As they left the kitchen, Violet stared straight ahead. "He doesn't have this, does he?"

"Nope. Not even a little bit."

"We're gonna pray a silent prayer to Grandma Ginny."

Marigold winced. "She might be alive."

"Stop killing my hope. These are stressful times, dammit."

"You know what?" Marigold took her seat. "We're either gonna sit here and practice our deep breathing exercises…"

"No."

"Or we're going to nurse lemon drops like they're our security blankets until Ms. Wakefield sees herself out."

"Lemon drops for the honeys at table five." Violet patted the white tablecloth. "That's my vote."

Marigold caught Byron's eye and shot him the number two. This was going to be a stressful night. At the end of it, if they had a healthy new baby and a glowing review, Marigold would spend her days repaying the universe out of her very own pocket of luck. "Don't let me down," she murmured to the team of writers she imagined were penning her story.

"Are you talking to the writers in the sky again?"

"They need to hear from me, Vi. Accountability is key." She made an I-see-you gesture to the heavens. Her team needed a nudge now and then.

"Could they talk to my people, please? Tell them my ex is late with his child support and that I need my boyfriend to consider proposing sometime within the next decade."

"Will do. My writers won't fail your writers. Cruz will likely pop the question by Christmas because we're that effective."

"Ooh la la. Life is about to get good."

"Is he back in town soon?" Violet's very sweet boyfriend had moved four hours east for work at an engineering firm specializing in luxury private planes. The two kept their relationship afloat through sexy Zooms and stolen weekends. It was all very romantic in Marigold's opinion. The pining. The angst. The separation. If all went well, Cruz DeHoyos just might become her new brother-in-law.

Marigold happily accepted her newly shaken lemon drop martini in the exact moment she saw Alexis Wakefield served her crab starter across the restaurant. "Here we go. It's on."

Violet exhaled slowly. "Cheers to Aster Lavender, soon to be mom and culinary rock star."

"I'll drink to that."

They clinked glasses, all the while Marigold's heart thudded like a jackhammer. She gave Violet's hand a squeeze and hoped for the best on all counts. The night felt bigger than all of them, and she had a distinct feeling her life was about to change forever.

CHAPTER THREE

Alexis never got used to Middle America, no matter how many different cities she dropped in on. So different from any metropolitan city on either coast. However, the town of Homer's Bluff was truly an anomaly. While it had all the technological comforts she was used to in life—ATMs, Wi-Fi, streaming services, and even a charging station for electric cars just outside of the city—it also made her feel like she'd drifted back in time. The people moved at their own pace, rarely in a hurry for much. No one was lost on their phone as they moved down the sidewalks. No one spoke animatedly into their AirPods as they moved from one location to the next. New, yet old. Alexis couldn't get over its uniquely dual existence. The small town was warm and fuzzy with a touch of quaint. It wasn't quite a Hallmark movie, but it was certainly a second cousin to one.

As she grabbed a cappuccino from a walk-up coffee window in the center of town, she watched in astonishment as people greeted each other by name and mentioned things like *the pancake breakfast on Saturday*. It was the most interesting place she'd ever visited. Granted, most of her work took her to flashy establishments in large to medium cities. She generally shied away from the tumbleweed towns for a reason, but something about this particular venture felt ordained. It's why she'd stuck around an extra day. Why not soak up the local culture? It was certainly memorable.

"You're gonna love this. There's even a dog park, Carrot." They hung a left on their walk as she sipped her piping hot cappuccino. Not half bad. "They've thought of nearly everything in this tiny place." The directions that the woman at the bed-and-breakfast had supplied were surprisingly easy, but then it would be difficult to get lost in a place that simply revolved around a sizable town center. As they rounded what had to be Main Street, she squinted, scanning the scene for the fucking *Back to the Future* clock tower, to no avail.

The dog park was like most she'd visited, with the exception of the ice cream sculpture that was actually a doggy water fountain. She liked that touch. She let herself inside, closed the gate behind her like a responsible dog owner, and let little Carrot off his leash to run free as the wind. "There you go, buddy!" she yelled, raising a fist as the zoomies celebrating his freedom commenced. She folded her arms, closed her eyes, and let the warm breeze brush against her cheeks. Pretty day. In fact, it was a really pretty place. It called to her more than she would have expected.

Shame about the review she'd have to write about their beloved hot spot. She sighed. It would have been nice if little Marilyn's had pulled out a win, but the pork medallions that everybody apparently raved about were overcooked, the sauce was too thick, and the risotto was slightly runny. The only wins had been the crab starter and the butter cake for dessert. It didn't give her much to work with. The meal had been a legitimate miss. Whether the executive chef's absence factored in was not for her to say. She was there to review her meal, and she would.

Her phone buzzed. Her ex. She closed her eyes and felt Carrot, back from his frolic, nudge her ankle. He was such an intuitive little guy, already offering moral support. "Judith. Hi. What can I do for you?" They'd been broken up for well over six months, and it hadn't even been that long a relationship to start with. Why was she still dealing with fallout?

"Don't be casual with me. You turned off the electricity."

"No. That didn't happen. I'm incapable. I'm not the electric company."

"Well, the lights are off."

"I told you that I paid through the summer and you would take over the payments from there. Did you not? It's the end of August, and it's your rental now. You took over the lease a long time ago."

"A reminder would have been nice."

"We broke up. That's not my job anymore." She kept her voice even but wasn't surprised by this. Judith relied on the world to do things for her, getting by on her good looks and the way they affected others. That's how she'd managed to have virtually every door opened for her without lifting a finger. You had to give her credit for her track record. Their year and a half together had comprised some really hot nights in the bedroom and a frustrating existence outside it.

"You're a piece of work, Alexis." Judith's voice turned biting, and Alexis imagined her moving the phone to directly in front of her mouth. But then again, maybe she couldn't see it very well if she was in the dark. "I can't believe I gave away a year of my life."

"It was actually longer than that." She sighed. "I'm sure they'll turn the power back on just as soon as you pay them."

"How do I do that again?"

"I left you the login and password and had it all transferred to your name, remember? It's all in the white binder."

"Now I'm going to have to go find the damn thing."

"Yes, I think you're going to have to."

"Don't call me again."

Alexis paused. "Judith, you called me."

"Bye, Lex. I hope your day sucks." That sentence was followed by the harsh beep of the call ending.

Why did everything have to be so contentious with Judith? There was simply no reason for the abject hostility. Now that they were broken up, Alexis could look back and see the very same manipulation tactics her older sister had used on her. Growing up, Aspen had always been Alexis's friend and hero until the very second she didn't get what she wanted. Her sister had framed Alexis on more than one occasion for her own crimes, too, the worst being the time she'd blamed Alexis for the dent in their father's car that Aspen had put there herself after sneaking out—not that Alexis had caused when she'd borrowed the car *with permission* to go to the grocery store for ingredients. She'd been grounded for a month while Aspen ran free with her friends like the perfect angel she certainly wasn't. It bothered her that she'd been drawn to someone just as self-serving in her romantic life. She had to do better. She would. Either that, or live life on her own, which she had to admit was certainly less stressful.

Getting out of the city to somewhere a little slower paced like Homer's whatever-this-place-was was actually helpful for perspective.

She had a second night here, to avoid flying two days in a row. But in that moment, it didn't feel like a hardship. She was looking forward to the cleaner air and the chance to quietly write up her review without the pressures of her actual life. Tatum, her editor, didn't need it filed until the next day, and her notes were specific and lengthy. She'd have some choices to make. For now, she could exhale. Who would have ever guessed that Alexis Wakefield could find such comfort in the objectively mundane? It sounded harsh. It wasn't. This was a sleepy place with less than exciting people. It wasn't their fault they lacked sophistication, much like the pork dish from the night before. Poor little rubbery things. Even the citrus seasoning had been missing. The orange slice, pictured in photos on Yelp, was noticeably absent from her plate. A big oversight.

"Oh, Dill, you found a friend."

She glanced up at the words and saw Carrot running around with an adorable little black and white dog. She watched as the new dog bowed his body and shook his entire backside at Carrot, inviting him to play. The two took off for a race around the park's perimeter.

"It doesn't get much happier than that," Alexis said to the blond woman with the lazy curls. She had bright blue eyes. The kind that were lighter than most other blue eyes. Like the sky when it only had the most wispy of clouds.

"Dill, over there, adores other dogs, but most of the ones we've seen lately have been bigger. I think he's overjoyed to find someone his own size. Enjoying your stay?"

Alexis tilted her head. There was something familiar about this woman. They'd spoken. But where?

Apparently, picking up on her confusion, the woman helped her out. "Marigold Lavender. We met last night at Marilyn's."

"Oh, right. Nice to see you again." The overly chatty sister of the owner. How could she forget? "Your pup is adorable."

"He's my dog-nephew, actually. I'm dog-sitting for my sister because—"

"She's having a baby. I remember."

"My other sister, Violet, was supposed to meet me with Aster and Brynn's second dog, Pickles, but they're running late. It's a whole thing with an unruly garbage disposal. You know how they can be. Her boyfriend is an engineer who lives out of town. He's coaching her through the steps." She made a face as if the world had an understanding that garbage disposals were not to be trusted. Unique take.

"That sounds really rough."

"I don't think anything is going to get us down today. My brand-new niece was born just after three a.m. She has tufts of blond hair and the sweetest eyes. They're Brynn's. Gorgeous. They don't have a name for her yet."

"She sounds incredibly sweet. Congrats to you and yours."

"So, how was your night last night?"

Alexis was fairly confident that the question was the sister's attempt to take her temperature about the meal. But with her review not yet public, she had no intention of divulging that kind of detail. "I appreciate you asking, Lily, but I can't really discuss my thoughts until I've had a chance to file my review."

"Marigold. My name is Marigold." Her smile had dimmed to fifty percent.

"My apologies." Lily, Marigold. It was hard to keep the flowers straight.

"I'm sorry, too. I didn't intend to pry for information about your review. I was just trying to be friendly. No ulterior motives." She gestured to Alexis. "But I sense you're uncomfortable, so I'll give you your space."

Well, now she felt a little bad. "Hey, you don't have to do that. Sorry if I was less than welcoming."

"Little bit. But that's okay. We all have our own stuff going on."

"I'm used to people who are maybe a little less well intentioned." She held up her phone. "I also just received a phone call from my ex right before you came over." Why in the hell had she just said that? Weird.

"Oh. I'm sorry."

"I'm not picking up next time." She folded her arms across her chest. "Some tethers are best left cut."

"I'm sure he's full of regret." Then she held up a hand as if rethinking the comment. "Not that I would know. Maybe he's simply a total asshole. Ignore my projections." She tossed in an apologetic smile. "I tend to try to see the good in people to a fault."

She decided not to correct the pronoun. "Life must disappoint you a lot."

She watched as the light in Marigold's eyes faded. She'd done that. Damn. She didn't enjoy knowing that. She had to remember that people around here didn't have the thick skin she was used to. Maybe that wasn't a bad thing.

"I've had my fair share. Anyway, I'll let Dill and your guy run around. Enjoy your day." She raised a hand in farewell.

Alexis watched as the flower woman crossed the lawn to the dogs and followed after them, laughing at their antics and tossing in words of encouragement. "That's right. You can catch him." At one point, Carrot went up on his hind legs seeking a kiss, which she leaned down and granted. Such a sucker for the ladies, that dog. Off to the side, she watched quietly. Alone. Not at all wondering what it was like to be that happy. Carefree. Nope. Not at all.

CHAPTER FOUR

Marigold's heart ached with love. There was nothing quite like a new little life, only days old, blinking up at a person. The innocence, the trust, the uncomplicated affection was almost too much. Little Cara Jane was a dream that Marigold hadn't anticipated. She'd held a variety of babies before, gushed over them, and memorized their faces the way any decent baby addict would. She adored her nephew and niece and had gushed over each of them when they were born. But this child was different, heaven-kissed and seemingly wise in the way she stared straight up at Marigold as if she knew all the world's secrets. And who knew? Maybe she did.

Marigold shook her head and marveled from where she sat on Aster's couch and sighed. "I know the review is scheduled to hit any minute, but I can't stop staring at this little girl."

Brynn smiled with a combination of joy and exhaustion unique to new parents. "I do the same with her. I just can't stop staring. The way she grips my finger when she nurses. My heart can't take it." She shifted her focus to Aster, who sat in front of her laptop. "Anything yet?

"Not yet," Aster said with a smile that was slightly tighter than usual.

"Nervous?" Marigold asked.

"No. What will be, will be. I have everything I need right here." She gestured to her new family of three. "That's all that really matters."

Marigold loved her little sister with her entire heart, which made the happiness that sprang off Aster the past few days addictive. Aster smiled, but she rarely beamed. Yet when it came to welcoming Cara to the family, it was like she couldn't stop. The tapping of her foot beneath the table indicated that the review did carry some weight, however.

Marigold leaned forward. "You're going to be opening a rave any second now."

Aster watched her screen. "Is it pathetic that I've hit refresh five times in the last sixty seconds? Everyone says she usually posts at— Oh, wait. Here it is."

The room went quiet as Aster scanned the article on the screen. Marigold and Brynn exchanged a wide-eyed look as anticipation licked through the room. It seemed to take a lifetime as they awaited Aster's report.

"Well. All right." She turned from the table to face them.

What did that mean? Marigold couldn't take it another second. She'd aged eight years since Aster had opened the review.

"Is it good?" she asked. But Brynn seemed to already know and sat back in resignation. Marigold refused to give in. There was still a chance. "You're killing me over here."

"It's not. But that's okay, right?" Aster's face didn't match her words. Her eyes were earnest and her mouth pulled in. She blinked way too many times. "Maybe Henry was off his game. He's a great chef."

"Let me read what this woman has to say," Brynn said, stalking to the laptop screen with purpose. "Baby, I'm so sorry." She went quiet to scan the review and stood straight up. "Well, she can go to hell."

"What?" Marigold had never heard Brynn speak like that in all the time she'd known her. Her heart sank. Was it really that bad? She headed to the kitchen table, cradling Cara. Standing next to Brynn, she scanned the title of the article: "The Little Eatery That Simply Could Not." Oh no. She took her time and read every word on the screen. Brynn, seemingly shocked, gently took the baby from Marigold and joined Aster on the couch.

"You know none of that is an accurate representation of Marilyn's, right?" Brynn took Aster's hand. "It was a strange night for the restaurant. How could it not be? The stress of a big-time reviewer, coupled with you having to dash away last minute. That's not a typical day."

"And it all worked out the way it was supposed to. Look at her," Aster said. "I wouldn't change a thing about that night." Marigold listened from her spot across the room. Her sister was trying to not let on, but she could hear the effect of the review in her voice. "I'm gonna take a minute and regroup. Be right back."

"Take your time," Brynn said. "We're good here."

Meanwhile, Marigold went back to reading. She grew more angry with each word. Then something occurred to her. It wasn't necessarily the fact that the reviewer didn't enjoy the food that infuriated Marigold, it was her *tone*. It was one thing to write an unfavorable review—it was something else entirely to have fun ripping someone's life's work apart. And that's what this Alexis woman did in the article. She employed dripping sarcasm, biting wit, and unnecessarily cruel wording to express her thoughts—for no reason other than to be mean.

I tried not to laugh at the unfortunate attempt at a risotto. I mean, they seemed to be trying. Gold star, little kitchen, you get a participation trophy. But, fellow foodie, I have to warn you that Marilyn's short rib risotto should have been served with a straw. After three bites—excuse me, slurps—I politely moved on. If only that had been the worst thing on the plate. Can we talk about the famous pork medallions?

Marigold forced herself to breathe. She was mocking them. After all the work and worrying, the attempts to please this woman, she was laughing in her sister's face, dragging the restaurant with her mother's name, making them her own personal joke to entertain her fans, who had to be awful humans.

She sat with the words for a moment, knowing in her heart that she wouldn't be able to let this stand. Alexis Wakefield might be a bigwig in the culinary review world, but that didn't mean she was excused from common decency. There had to be justice in the world in order for Marigold to live comfortably in it. And this was one injustice that called for her attention.

But first, she had to focus on her sister and what she needed. In fact, Marigold canceled her plans with Tillman that night and spent the next few hours attempting to distract Aster in any way possible. Questions about Cara's birth brought the light back into her eyes for a little while, but inevitably, the rain cloud seemed to follow her, making various appearances throughout the evening, which Marigold understood.

"I guess it's more of an embarrassment than I'd anticipated," Aster finally confessed. "I don't think I prepared myself enough for bad news, and now…" She sighed, grappling for the vocabulary to explain herself. She ran a hand through her dark hair. "I feel uncomfortable and I'm questioning my own abilities. I'm supposed to go back to work in ten days and feel stripped of my confidence. Just because one woman wasn't a fan. Isn't that weird?"

Brynn, always soothing in her approach, took Aster's hand. "It's not. You're shaken up. That's okay."

Marigold nodded. "If it helps, I think people like her just enjoy being mean. They thrive on the attention it brings them."

Aster nodded. "It did seem extra aggressive, didn't it?"

"You think?" Marigold asked, her anger flaring. "Here's my advice, not that you asked. You concentrate on your sweet nugget of a new baby and your amazing career, and let the miserable people be miserable in the corner of life's room. Lonely and awful."

"Wow," Brynn said. "MG, you have some feelings. But you know what? I do, too. You're right, and Alexis Westworld can kick rocks by herself."

"Lonely and miserable," she reiterated. They fist-bumped.

"Wakefield," Aster supplied quietly. "Her sister is Aspen Wakefield. Little trivia for you."

"Get out," Marigold said. "The actress? That's not fair. Hateful people shouldn't get to have the novelty of celebrity siblings. Especially not attractive ones."

Brynn scrunched one eye. "I've read Aspen Wakefield is awful to work with."

"Well, that certainly tracks," Marigold said. "The whole rotten apple section. I wonder how many others there are in that family." She heard the intensity in her voice and slowed her roll. She didn't want to stoop to Wakefield's level. "Sorry. I'm fired up."

"Mean people suck." Brynn was right there with her. "Marilyn's doesn't. End of story."

"Thank you," Aster said. "I'm glad I'm with the two of you right now." She looked down at Cara. "The three of you. My apologies." She smiled down at her daughter. "We just keep going. That's what we do."

It was a great plan for Aster, but it wasn't close to what Marigold aimed to do. She wasn't exactly sure what action to take, but she knew she had to do something. Should she reach out to Wakefield? Send her an email with a piece of her mind attached? No. It was likely something like that would fall flat or never even reach her at all.

As she sat at home that night full of indignation for her sister and the restaurant, she acted on impulse. Her feelings bubbled and simmered, and if there was a time to capture them, harness them as fuel, it was now. She couldn't hold off until she'd had a good night's sleep and distance from the review. Watered-down feelings weren't the motivation she needed. She clenched her fists, refusing to give herself any chance to chicken out. Had to be now.

She turned her phone on herself, sat back in her desk chair, and let it all out. She told the camera in the most succinct terms possible that meanness wasn't the way to go and it was up to them, collectively as a society, to push back. That Alexis Wakefield could dislike all the food she wanted but shouldn't be rewarded by followers for making it personal. She looked into the camera on her phone, found her conclusion, and spoke from the heart. Her words were improvised, but sincere.

"So what I'm asking of the person sitting at home watching this video is that, together, we stand up to cruelty for the sake of entertainment. We say no to that brand of behavior once and for all and boycott the *San Francisco Journal* for printing it. If we don't push back, then who the hell are we becoming? Oh"—she tented a hand over her eyes—"my name is Marigold Lavender. I should have led with that." She felt heat blossom on her cheeks. "My mother, who passed two years ago, named me as well as my three siblings after flowers. She thought flowers were beautiful. In fact, she thought the whole world had the potential to be. Alexis Wakefield wouldn't know beauty if it sat in her lap and fed her dinner. She hurts people and smirks about it. It's time to tell her that's not okay."

With a few clicks and a couple of hashtags, the video was off into the world. Marigold killed the lights in her home and went promptly to sleep. Who knew that anger and indignation took so much out of a person? She was past the point of exhaustion, and with an outstretched hand in its usual spot, the empty pillow next to her, Marigold was asleep before her brain had a chance to get going.

For the best.

CHAPTER FIVE

Call me.

C   What? No. It was too early for the average person. Alexis liked to get in a run and shower before dealing with the world. But that's all the text message from Tatum said. Mysterious and unlike her. Alexis, who was in the midst of brewing her first espresso of the morning and already dressed in her running gear, frowned down at her phone. So she wasn't engaging. She shrugged off the message and moved through her morning. She'd get to it eventually. She and Tatum had worked together for years. Tatum understood Alexis, which was why they worked so well together. They had a shorthand, which was exactly what you longed for in a critic–editor relationship.

An hour later, as she toweled off from her run, she had two missed calls. Finally, a second message came. *I'm serious. Pick up your phone.* It promptly rang and she begrudgingly slid on. "Hi, Tatum. How are things?"

"Really? That casual after I've been beating down your door?"

"I was trying to bask in the glow of my meditation session." She grinned because she'd never meditated a day in her life, and Tatum damn well knew it.

"I'm afraid I'm about to ruin your fictional zen."

"Dammit all to hell." She was still smiling. Whatever it was, they'd handle it. They always did. She could still imagine Tatum adjusting her brown cat-eye glasses. She was likely wearing argyle and pacing the small hallway near her cubicle. Very corporate Scooby-Doo on purpose. The ultimate written word cliché. Tatum was way more suited for New York than California, but that actually made her unique. She was a novelty, fun at parties, and always wound a little too tight, which Alexis added points for. Someone in her camp needed to be.

"Why? What new deadline are you about to shoot my way?" She turned the pages of *Food & Wine* as she stood at her kitchen counter and paused, prepared to tell the paper to fuck off if it was about to demand more. She'd earned that kind of power and already felt spread thin. Hell, she'd put their lifestyle section on the map.

"The Marilyn's review from the town in Kansas?"

"Yeah." Another page flip. How was Chardonnay on the rise?

"It's blowing up."

She raised a shoulder and closed the magazine. "Awesome. I haven't been online today yet. Are you calling to give me a raise?" She shifted her gaze to Carrot sleeping on her couch in a swirl on top of his favorite chenille blanket.

"Pause right there and reverse course. It's bad. Apparently, the sister of the chef has gone viral and the public is demanding an apology for your cruel delivery. Our phone lines are also overloaded."

"What? You're kidding." Alexis stood and side-eyed the wall, attempting to process the ridiculous news. "I'm really sorry she's upset, but that delivery style is exactly what my readers want from me. I'm *successful* because I tell it like it is. It's entertainment, for God's sake. So, wait, the sister?" She scanned her brain. "Jasmine or something."

"Marigold."

"God, yes. She's a nonfactor. You don't have to worry about her. Tell her to churn butter and we can circle back to her another time. Not that we will." She was being petty but only because she was annoyed.

"Well, you do have to worry. Major gossip sites are reposting her already skyrocketing video. The views are climbing by the second."

She exhaled. "Really? They're trying to cancel me over having some fun with some unfortunate food?"

"Trying is an understatement. Brad is going to have a decision on how we respond by five. He wants to wait and see how the rest of today goes."

She closed her eyes and leaned back against her counter. "Please tell me he's not going to issue an apology. That's the worst thing to do in a situation like this. It's the equivalent of admitting guilt."

Tatum paused. "He's getting pressure from the paper's owners to make it go away. I wouldn't be surprised if your hands are tied in the future."

"You can't censor me over this. *Tatum.*"

"I think it's fair to say I'm not going to be the only person signing off on your column, at least in the short term."

"Temporary handcuffs. Perfect." She walked the length of her kitchen. "My column in tepid form makes me want to throw a glass at the wall and watch the shards rain down."

"I don't think that will help your cause. Stay tuned. Gotta run. Pick up your phone when I call."

"Got it." Alexis dropped the phone onto the couch and stalked to her laptop in search of the video causing all the trouble. It took her all of two seconds to see what Tatum was in a tailspin about. Alexis's notifications were through the roof. Her private inbox was overflowing with newly minted Lavender supporters who were angry. Most were demanding she rewrite the review and apologize. Like hell she would. She clicked through to the fifty-two second video and sat back in awe. If she had a tiny violin, she would have played it to underscore this woman's sad tale. The big bad food critic had stomped on poor, pure-hearted Aster Lavender. They even had a hashtag: #cancelalexis. What complete shit. She shoved her laptop away, disgusted with the whole thing.

Carrot wagged his tale and whined softly, beckoning her over to the couch. She needed a distraction, and work wasn't going to be it today. So it was settled. She'd take the damn day off, stay off social media, and snuggle with her dog while she watched something violent and satisfying. This whole thing would blow over. Everything in life was temporary.

When Tatum called that evening, Alexis had to replay her words multiple times to make sense of them. "What do you mean the *Journal* is dropping my column. For how long?"

"They're replacing you with Scott Marks."

She stared at the gray wall of her living room in utter awe. "He's a hack. He likes avocado toast."

"The decision came from above. There was a whole meeting about it behind closed doors. Brad's hands are tied. I'm honestly shocked myself, but we live in a cancel culture, and it seems you're the next victim."

She was scrambling now. Words weren't coming easily. Her palms itched. "Tatum, they can't be serious. We can't let a woman from the middle of nowhere with a cell phone upend a major newspaper."

"Hey. You're going to be okay. You have your website, your social media following, and the means to post your reviews all on your own. You don't need the paper."

"Yes, I do. I'm a legitimate reviewer, not some influencer wannabe. I attend James Beard dinners. Does that not count for anything?"

"You're gonna land on your feet, Alexis. You always do."

"Damn right I will. That isn't the point." But it wasn't Tatum she was angry at. Tatum had shown herself to be loyal, kind, and a friend in a lot of ways. She didn't have a ton of people in her inner circle. She kept most people a sizable distance from her real life, and it would be smart to hold on to the ones she had. They truly mattered. Tatum had come up with her. They'd ascended the ranks side by side. "I'm sorry for my tone, and I value your advice. I'm just trying to find the pieces of my career scattered on the floor."

"I know," Tatum said quietly. "I'll check on you soon. Go visit your mom. See if she got the coffee I sent her from my South American vacay. Go drink some of it in sunny LA and decompress."

Alexis exhaled slowly. "Yeah. Maybe." This was just so out of the blue. One minute, she was fine, and now she was supposed to flee town and figure out what to do next? How was this possible? God, her head was now pounding. Carrot licked the back of her hand tentatively as if trying to make things okay for her again. She stroked the soft blond fur on the back of his neck, appreciating his presence more than he would ever know.

Things were worse when she woke up the next day. The internet had collectively decided she was the mean girl of the food scene and wanted her punished in a highly public manner. Everything started to come apart. The hard-to-get reservation Alexis had snagged for dinner at The Blue Boat for the following week was unceremoniously canceled via email. No explanation was given. The baristas at her favorite coffee haunt, the same two who used to laugh with her and dish on all the best pizza dives, now avoided eye contact. Two of her sponsorship deals dropped with a brusque apology. Doors were closing left and right. Her calls weren't being returned. She had the plague, and it was all the fault of one overly sensitive woman in Kansas.

"What are you doing here?" her mom asked, holding her pink bathrobe with the boa collar across her body with one hand and the storm door open with the other. The sun was halfway up, but the sleepy street in the Hollywood Hills was quiet, dormant. Rich people slept in.

"I couldn't sleep." Carrot, done with the morning air, ran straight into the house. He was no fool. Summer was on the way out, and the early September temperatures were making that clear.

Her mother blinked. Her pretty brown eyes didn't yet have the false eyelashes and perfect liner, but her beauty was hard to dispute. She made her early sixties look like a cakewalk. Lorna Wakefield had been a runway turned print model in her day, and more recently ran a consulting business for those aspiring in the industry. "Are you telling me you and my grand-dog drove through the night? Who does that? Find a Four Seasons somewhere. Hop a quick flight. What is going on with you? Is this about the bad press?"

"It's cold and I don't have a quick answer. Can I come in and tell you at your kitchen table over a cup of coffee I would wrestle God for?"

"Of course. Of course, come in. God's down the hall." She opened the door and Alexis shuffled inside.

"Funny as always, Lorna."

"Where do you think you get your way with words? Not your father. Did you know he had his neck done? It was a whole thing, but the bastard is starting to look like a rubber chicken, and I love that more than bread."

"Mom. Can we not?"

"My apologies for insulting the man who ignored you most of your life and placed his focus solely on waffles and beer pong."

"Valid point. Proceed."

As she entered the kitchen, the sound of the morning news played from the television on the counter. Her mother was a media hound and had a TV in nearly every room. She gestured to the screen. "Aspen's going to be on celebrity *Price Is Right* this morning. She's hoping to beat Carly Daniel, the returning champ. I hated her last film. Not enough action. All character work. She's also doing something new with her hair I don't like."

"A game show, huh? Is this promotion for the Netflix movie? Aspen's."

"Yes. It's her first holiday foray. I told her she needed to get on her agent about finding a way to wholesome up her image. For once, she listened to me."

"A Christmas special to distract from bad press. Could work."

"Exactly that. Lots of boob and Santa hats."

Alexis frowned. "I thought you said *wholesome*."

"Lots of things fall under that definition, babe. Cream and sugar?"

"Black. It's that kind of week."

"I saw some of it. Brutal. Unfair."

"You did?" Alexis stared at her mother. "Why didn't you reach out? Say maternal things that were supposed to make it all better but don't. Isn't that a thing moms do?"

She thought on it, stirring her own coffee. "You're an adult now. You don't need me. Plus, I figured I'd hear from you sooner or later. Baby, your eyes are a sight." She laughed and Alexis felt two inches tall. "You haven't slept well, and it shows on your face. I have some cream upstairs."

Alexis's hands flew to under her eyes automatically. "If I'd been sleeping, I wouldn't be driving to LA from San Francisco in the middle of the night."

"You need cantaloupe, too."

"Hmm. I'm not thinking that will fix all that's wrong in my sphere."

"Yeah, but it'll help with those eyes."

In response, Alexis closed them. Of course that would be her mother's top concern. Not her bruised ego, sunk reputation, or her dead-in-the-water career, but the unattractive circles under her eyes. She hated Hollywood. There was a reason she'd left. "Well, thank God I came to the right place for fruit on a Tuesday morning. The hours in the car were worth it. Good-bye, circles."

Her mother set a half a cantaloupe down in front of her with a spoon. Next, she cradled Alexis's left cheek. "My baby. They really came for you this time, huh? I'm sorry."

That made her soften. She needed someone to care. Her mother wasn't a bad mom. She just emphasized the superficial. "An internet witch hunt of the standard variety." Alexis shook her head. "I hope it blows over. For now—"

"You need to hide."

"I need to hide."

A smile hit. Her mom threw two hands in the air, celebrating. "We can watch Bravo and do facials."

Alexis tried not to wince outwardly, though it was difficult. She scratched her top lip. "We could. I know you love those Housewives."

"Yeah, but Beverly Hills is getting out of control. I'll catch you up later." Her mother clapped her hands. "Aspen is gonna love this."

Alexis held up a finger. "She isn't. She tolerates me until I stop doing things for her, or she feels her position of top dog is threatened, and then it's claws out. I mean that literally. Have you seen her nails?"

Her mother, as always, brushed off the negative mention of her older daughter because she was, after all, living the exact life her mother had wanted for herself. Aspen was the little darling of the family, even if she wasn't darling at all.

Two days later, her nightmare came true. The front door opened in the middle of what had been a peaceful day of Bravo, three cups of coffee, and a good book. Alexis had lost herself in a murder mystery novel she'd found tucked away on the bookshelf while her mother held a client session with a young woman working to secure an agent.

"Alexis! Get over here and hug me." Aspen stood in the entryway in all her made-up glory, hand on her hip, boobs on display, and sass in her voice.

Alexis mustered a smile, discarded her book, and hugged her sister. "Hey, Aspen. Good to see you." In a way, it was. She didn't hate her sister, but she was always wary.

"You've been canceled and the paper dropped you. Awful." She shook her head as if reliving the worst kind of tragedy. "I read all about it."

"All facts. Strange that I didn't hear from you."

"Nonexistent cell service in the hills," Aspen said dismissively. "Is there food? Like a burger. I like the kind with the spicy cheese." She waited.

"Strangely, no fresh burgers sitting around," Alexis said, frowning at the dark kitchen in the next room. Her sister really did live on another planet.

"Any chance you could grab my bag from the trunk of the Jag?" She touched her lower back. "Been sore lately."

"You want me to get your *bag* for you? As in suitcase? Does that mean you're staying?"

"Hell, yeah. I'm not going to let you have all the Mom fun." Did that mean Aspen was seriously every bit as possessive and jealous as she had been growing up? Because she literally lived twelve minutes away.

"You're here because you don't want Mom paying attention to me? How is that a thing?"

Aspen shrugged and sighed, uninterested. "Just help me with my bag, okay? Back, remember." She took a seat.

Alexis stole a moment to assemble her strategy, pinching the bridge of her nose. "You know, maybe later."

"Fine. Be a bitch." Aspen stood, stalked past her, and headed up the stairs to the shrine of her high school bedroom. Their mother had touched none of it, including Aspen's beauty queen crowns, her homecoming queen scepter, and the ten to twelve headshots that still hung in a collage above her bed. Alexis found it all very pathetic. But then, she'd never bought a ticket for the Aspen train. Carrot swiveled his focus back to Alexis with a whine. "This isn't good," she told him. "You stick with me." He tucked his face back into the crook of her knee. She tried to settle back into her book, but from that moment on, peace was nonexistent.

Her briefly quiet world in LA blew the hell up.

Instead of getting away from her troubles, Aspen made sure they followed her. "Alexis, did you see this meme of you with evil red eyes?" She flipped the phone around, and Alexis's spirit hit the floor. "They are coming for you so hard. Wow."

"Still, huh?" she'd asked around her morning coffee. Her hand shook as she attempted to raise the mug to her lips. She set it back down again. This was a form of anxiety she wasn't used to. Carrot inched closer on top of her bare foot beneath the table.

"I don't think your sister wants to hear all that," her mother said, letting her hand drape on Alexis's shoulder as she passed. "She needs to clear her head. Let her get away from the world instead of you dragging it in."

"I'll stop," Aspen said with the demure smile she'd perfected. Perceived innocence was always her goal.

But she didn't stop. That night she turned her phone around with a shake of her head. "Now the actual celebrities of the food world are weighing in. June Genevieve says she's never been a fan of your caustic tone in reviews and applauds the call for change."

Alexis blinked, because June Genevieve was her childhood hero. She'd grown up obsessed with her cooking shows. While her family followed Aspen around to her pageants and TV gigs, Alexis sat in front of the television taking detailed notes. June was the person who'd first taught her how to set a soufflé. Her heart sank. "Oh."

The truth was she'd been thinking a lot on the backlash, how she got to this place. It was slowly dawning on her that a lot of the blame was truly hers. When she traced it back, she'd never set out to be mean and had gone with the over-the-top critical tone to get her foot in the door. Once she noticed it was getting her attention, she'd amped it up even more, a tactic to garner extra attention for her little column. Then it became the style she was known for. All this time, she'd considered her reviews one part informative, one part entertainment, like the judges she saw on reality TV shows. Looking back, seeing how people she respected were now responding, she had regrets. In fact, they were beginning to swamp her. It had taken her days to get here, but she had.

"That one's gotta kill you. She's your hero, right? Ugh. I'm super sorry, kiddo." Aspen pulled the phone back slowly and pocketed it.

Alexis offered a shrug, holding back the tears that threatened to brim. She knew without a doubt that she had to get out of this house or else wither under Aspen's manipulation and sabotage. She wasn't strong enough in her present state to endure Aspen's expert assaults. It seemed no matter how old they got, no matter how much she hoped, Aspen would never change.

"Wait a minute. Where are you going?" her mother asked from the doorway to the guest room as she tossed her clothes one at a time into her suitcase like the shot clock was about to expire.

"I'm not sure, but I can't stay. Bad idea. Aspen is Aspen, and I'm not equipped."

Her mother nodded and sighed. "I get it. I'm so sorry. I've tried to rein her in, but she's on a tear. Please tell me you're not running to your father's."

"Nope." She handed Carrot a bacon treat and stashed the bag in her suitcase. "I need low stress, not a babysitting gig."

"I'd walk you out, but I promised Aspen I'd do her toes. That girl certainly has a lot of daily demands. Starting to wear on me, if I'm being honest."

Alexis sighed. "It's okay. I know the way. Take care of yourself, Mom." She kissed her cheek and took a moment to enjoy the squeeze her mother offered back. It helped. She longed for more.

"Let me know what you're bringing to Thanksgiving. Your dishes are always my favorite. Oh, maybe make an extra batch of that stuffing. Aspen will be in the midst of a shoot, so she can't really contribute."

"That last part should be stamped on her forehead. I love you."

"I love you back. Wish you could stay longer."

"Another time." Alexis gave Carrot a toss of her head, and he followed her with his jaunty step right out of that unfortunate situation.

A larger question loomed. Now what? She sat behind the wheel of her car, contemplating her next move. She didn't want to go home. She had no friends reaching out and offering up their homes, even though she would have thought one or two would have. Fair-weather folks. Carrot stared out the window from his dog seat, patiently waiting. Where's the one place no one would expect to find her? Where she remembered feeling the most relaxed she'd felt in ages. She shook her head. It seemed ludicrous, and it might just invite more trouble. Or maybe returning to the scene of the crime was the only way to put things right. "Should we do it?" Alexis tapped her lips, kissed Carrot's head, and started the engine. If she knew one thing for sure, it was that she was headed to the one place Aspen Wakefield would never set foot. That sealed the deal. Done. Decided.

CHAPTER SIX

Marigold lay flat on her couch with her head facing the TV, watching the movie *Nine to Five*. Tillman lay flat on the floor in the opposite direction.

"They're gonna kidnap this man?" he asked, twisting around in horror.

"How have you not seen this? Women's empowerment before it was a real thing."

"No, I haven't." He sat up and pointed at the screen. "Because my sweet mama protected me from violence. Good fucking fireballs. They *are*. They're gonna keep him in that room."

"It's a classic. A favorite of my mom's."

"Are you scratchy again?" He turned around and frowned.

She paused midscratch because her neck was itching like crazy. "Ever since I posted that video, my skin's been blotchy and irritated."

He squinted. "No hives. No bites."

"It's guilt. I'm allergic to guilt. I did an aggressive thing, and even though I stand by the video I made, I can't help but notice that Alexis Wakefield has been dragged through the streets of the internet by trolls in the thousands, maybe millions."

He nodded, a light bulb went on, and he pointed with an outstretched hand at the TV about eight times. "Remind me never to cross you."

"That's right. I'll sic the internet on you or put you in a room on a leash." She sat up. "It's Saturday and we're in my living room watching an old movie. Why aren't we more exciting? We're supposed to be out and living our best lives."

"Larry's?" he asked. "That insurance firm is sponsoring a dart tournament. Five hundred dollars and free beer for a week."

Marigold scrambled to her feet. "I'm game. Let me get my hoochie outfit on."

He supplied a hip bump. "I'll run my fingers through my luscious locks and meet you in the truck in fifteen."

"Done." Marigold shimmied into her good jeans and navy spaghetti-strap top and draped a white button-down over her arm in case it got chilly. Hoochie status was important, but the cold trumped everything.

"Get it, girl," Tillman said as she hopped in the truck.

"I'm even wearing a low heel."

"Every lesbian in town is going to—"

"Do nothing because there aren't any?"

"Don't forget about your sister and that one other couple."

"Who are all completely useless to me."

"Yeah, sorry about that. Must suck to be gay away from gay people." He cranked up the country station and drove them straight to Larry's Last Stop, where the crowd was already gathered around the dartboard, cheering on the competitors.

"We have a ringer over here," Heather shouted to Marigold as they approached the bar. Heather had been her lab partner in biology and now owned Bella Beautiful, the cutest little boutique in a row of three similar stores in town center. "No one can touch her."

"Her?" Tillman asked. "Is it Mrs. Finkelman with the blue hair? I've always believed she was a spy wearing disguises. That's no one's real look."

"Lots of spies in small-town Kansas," Marigold deadpanned.

"That's what they want you to think, MG. So naive," Tillman said with an added *tsk*.

"Not Finkelman," Heather said. "Some lady I've never seen before. Two beers in and her hand is as steady as a rock."

Marigold frowned and wandered over to the board, stepping between patrons to get a look at the ringer. Holy hell. Holy moly at Satan's dinner table. Hell's gate had swung right open. *Alexis Wakefield.* No. There was no way that woman would show her face in Homer's Bluff again. Marigold blinked to clear her vision, but the most beautiful woman she'd ever seen, who also happened to be cruel beyond measure, landed a double twenty to the sound of the crowd's roar. Alexis's dark blue eyes flashed victory, and she geared up for another throw. This time a bull's-eye. Marigold wanted to turn away, deny this woman another second of her attention, but the cut of the black sweater she wore offered a glimpse of cleavage, and Marigold didn't know how to reconcile what her own head *knew* and what her body proclaimed. She'd never been a cleavage hound before, so why was this different? Why was it enough to temporarily combat the anger she carried in her heart for Alexis Wakefield, whose lipstick had faded and eyeliner dissolved, making her appear less sophisticated and more girl-next-door? How was it even possible for her to look innocent in any way? Marigold refused to be fooled.

"I think we're staring at your nemesis," Tillman said. "Yup. That's her. What's she doing here?"

"Excellent question," Marigold said, narrowing her gaze to glare status. Alexis had some audacity, showing her face in town after all she'd done. She was civil enough to wait for the tournament to conclude before telling her so personally. The story of Marigold's video had certainly made its way through town, but apparently no one at this bar had put two and two together about who the mysterious dart thrower actually was. She decided maybe that was a good thing. She wasn't in the mood for high drama.

When the tournament concluded, however, there was a second round of bad news. Alexis had taken the win and was celebrated immediately with her prize. The rumor rippling through the bar was that she'd pledged the prize money to Larry's itself toward that new state-of-the-art jukebox everyone had been hoping for.

"Mare, did you hear that woman didn't keep the check?" Heather asked in a whisper.

"Yeah, about eight people mentioned it."

She tried to make small talk with Tillman and ignore the flutter of activity. She also wasn't sure what to do with her hands. She decided another drink would help. She needed to drown these anxious, angry feelings. This was her turf, and she wasn't planning on surrendering.

"Marigold Lavender, I was wondering if I'd run into you." Alexis sipped from her free beer and leaned her back against the bar next to Marigold's stool. Guess her luck had run out.

"Why are you here?" she asked. "Haven't you had enough fun at our expense?"

Alexis opened her mouth and then closed it, seemingly choosing a calmer approach than her initial instinct. "When it comes to throwing punches, you don't have a lot of ground to stand on here. You canceled me, remember?" She turned to face forward again, clearly waiting for service.

"Rightfully so."

She turned back. "Possibly. But if there was anyone going for blood, it was *you*. I was simply doing my job." She had such deep blue eyes, almost royal. So different from her family's signature shade. Marigold blinked, attempting to clear her field of vision. Nothing about Alexis was to be admired.

"Oh no, no. I was simply making the world aware of the fact that kindness matters. Decency matters."

"It does," Tillman said loudly, leaning over.

Alexis ignored him and returned her casual focus to Marigold. "I don't know. You're pretty vicious yourself."

"Excuse me?" Now that riled her up. She found herself squeezing her pint glass, wondering if it might burst in her hand like she was The Incredible Hulk.

Alexis signaled for a beer. "Could I have dropped the snarky, cold-hearted-bitch persona at some point once my career picked up steam? Sure. And maybe I should have. But I never set out to hurt anybody. Can you say the same?" She picked up the full glass and took a sip.

Marigold opened her mouth to speak, but her head was spinning. Alexis had the ability to get under her skin in such a way that she couldn't gather the appropriate words.

Tillman leaned over. "Ma'am, Marigold Lavender is a stand-up person only looking out for what's right."

"And you are?"

"Me? Oh, I'm just Tillman." He nodded. "We dated once. She seems to have regrets about that."

"Tillman!" Marigold hissed and sliced through the air near her neck.

"Peachy." Alexis folded her arms and regarded him.

"But she's gay, so it's not gonna happen for me."

Marigold briefly closed her eyes in defeat. Bless Tillman's heart but he wasn't cut out for run-ins in a bar.

Alexis raised an eyebrow, her gaze flicking with interest back to Marigold. "Who would have guessed? Mary Sunshine likes ladies."

"Now you're going to make fun of my sexuality? Do you know what year this is? Have you heard of hate crimes?" Marigold straightened, ready to go to battle with this overly attractive human surely carved from Satan's personal soap. Alexis was sent to Earth to torment her.

"Settle down. I'm as lesbian as the day is long. Apparently, you didn't google my personal life. I applaud your sexuality. I question your use of a cell phone camera and Instagram account."

Tillman gave her a little shove in her lower back, as if to say *You found one!*

She elbowed him back to an intrigued stare from Alexis. "Why are you two wrestling?"

"It's just a thing we do," Marigold said with indignation.

"I'm not even a little surprised. Anyway, I'm not in town for you. In fact, I was hoping I might miss running into you altogether because I might have some personal growth to work on, but so do you. You're aggressive." She reached for her drink. "I'm here for darts and beer. Enjoy your evening." With that, she raised her glass and floated back to the dartboard, leaving Marigold mystified and indignant.

"She just called me aggressive. I'm not. I'm a gentle soul. She's aggressive. And awful. Right, Larry?"

Larry blinked slowly from behind the bar, trying to catch up. "She's hit quite a few bull's-eyes tonight. Pretty good if you ask me."

She brushed off his biased answer. "Tillman. Weigh in here."

He got serious for a minute. "You're the most wonderful person I've ever met, MG. You just did an aggressive thing, and that's okay. Sometimes it's called for."

"I stood up for what's right. I let the world know about a bully behind a keyboard."

"Right. But she did get fired over it, so she might be a little hurt." He held his palm up. "Even though she's awful, I mean."

Hurt. The word didn't compute in relation to Alexis Wakefield. Even her name sounded like a villain's. But she also hated that she'd hurt someone. Anyone. "It was a necessary side effect," she said with a shrug. "The world is better without her beating up on small restaurants who just had a bad night."

He clinked his glass to hers, but the whole run-in had her ordering a third beer, which was more than her usual limit. Then Tessa from Yay Clothes! asked her to do a shot, so they did. She knew she'd been overserved, but the escape was actually kind of nice. "What's he drinking?" she asked Larry, pointing at one of the insurance guys down the bar. His drink looked fancy, sophisticated. She wanted to be like the insurance man.

"Scotch on the rocks."

"I'll take that."

"MG? You don't drink Scotch," Tillman said like it was the funniest thing he'd ever heard. He was a little gone himself. Luckily, they could walk home.

Minutes later, she sipped from the beveled cocktail glass Larry had deposited in front of her with a dubious grin and a sigh. The bad news was it tasted like gasoline, but she was already this far in. "Lovely," she said through tight lips that now buzzed. Wait, now they'd gone numb.

Tillman lost it. "Oh, my life is made. Please keep drinking that."

Well, she had to now. "I don't know what you're talking about. I'm just as sophisticated as that guy. And Alexis Wakefield."

"Oh, someone has Ms. Wakefield on the brain."

"Pshh." Another three sips. That was strong stuff, and the top of Larry's head was kinda fuzzy like her lips. Did he always have fuzzy hair like a Muppet? She decided probably. Just had never noticed before. She swiveled around. Another two swallows. "I'm not bad at darts. I could beat the really pretty mean lady."

"This is probably not the night for that," Tillman said, but then he got pulled into a conversation with Sage's baseball buddy, Mick Normandy, and Marigold was off and heading toward the board on a mission. The few steps she took, however, let her know that throwing sharp objects was not the best plan. She could watch, though.

When she arrived, Alexis and Ray Dobbs from the auto body shop were in the midst of a match. Ray seemed to be ahead, but Alexis laughed and smiled like she didn't really care. That was unexpected because Marigold would have guessed she hated everyone all the time. Didn't she? Weird.

"Nice one, Roy," Alexis replied to his double sixteens and flashed a smile that seemed genuine.

"It's Ray. But thank you, ma'am."

"My bad. Ray it is." Alexis lined up her shot and threw, landing a twelve. "Too many beers for me. I better surrender now." She offered up a conciliatory high five, and Ray smacked her hand. "You're a good player."

"You, too," he said, clearly smitten. Dear Lord. "Come back tomorrow."

She offered a one-shouldered shrug. "I'm in town for a while, so I just might."

Confused by Alexis behaving like an actual person, Marigold blinked her way to the restroom, mildly aware of the fact that she was mumbling to herself. The hallway was blurry, and she placed a palm on the wall to steady herself. The empty two-stall accommodation was kept remarkably clean for a bar. Larry had his priorities, and though he left the jukebox old and dusty, the restrooms sparkled.

"Marigold, you doing okay? You don't look so upright." Heather. She recognized her voice easily. "I saw you downing scotch, and honey, you don't strike me as a scotch gal."

Marigold squinted and slid back into her jeans. "I'm not *not* a scotch girl." Why was she trying so hard to stretch into a cooler persona? It wasn't her. She knew why and refused to examine the reasoning too carefully. Embarrassing. She'd never considered herself someone who could be affected so easily. Yet being called aggressive by a woman she hated but still had the capacity to objectify had kicked her into defensive mode. "But I'm fine. Really. I'm just not cool." She pushed open the door to the stall. "Heather?"

Why was Heather a whole new person?

She stopped short next to Alexis, who was now in Heather's spot.

"No Heather," Alexis said. "She glanced down at her phone and hightailed it out of here as I came in."

"Oh." Her skin went prickly. Alexis smelled like the raspberries that used to grow in the back field of the lavender farm. Marigold used to sit by the patch for hours making up stories and plays. She still had some of them. The sweet smell pulled her in and made her feel more comfortable than she had any business being. Yet the dangerous cobalt eyes that looked her up and down pushed her away. What a dance. She was dizzy from confusion, or maybe the damn scotch.

"Whoa. You okay?" Alexis's hands were at her waist. She felt those hands, the fingertips. If she wasn't already drunk, that would have done it. "You're swaying."

"I don't need your help. Ever."

"And yet without it, you would have fallen over." Alexis sighed. "Listen. I don't love the stunt you pulled. You don't love the way I express myself. That's just part of life. You don't have to like everyone."

"Well, I really dislike you."

Alexis lifted a hand, palm up. "And I'm the mean one."

She had a point. Maybe Marigold was kind of aggressive. This was such new territory, and the way the room decided to start spinning was not helping matters. She blinked and attempted to focus. Yet the only thing her eyes would focus on was Alexis's full mouth.

"What are you doing? Are you looking at my—"

Like a lifeline, Marigold leaned in and claimed those lips without hesitating because that was all she wanted, a brief moment with them. But once her lips were pressed to Alexis's, instinct took over because the payout was too damn good. Her breasts tingled. Her midsection went tight. Her logic was clearly offline—blame the scotch—and that was for the best because her body took over and allowed her to have much more fun. "Why are you so hot?" Marigold murmured, deepening the kiss, nodding ever so slightly when Alexis allowed herself to be walked to the wall and pressed to it. This was the best moment ever. Why didn't she make good decisions like this one more often? Alexis parted her lips, and that was all the permission Marigold needed to slip her tongue inside. *Perfection.* She melted, wondering how she was even standing. She was taller than Alexis Somebody and loved that. Alexis still had her by the waist, and Marigold's palms were now flat against the wall on either side of Alexis's face. Their bodies pressed together as the distant sound of the country music on the jukebox underscored. Some kind of angry female getting revenge, which honestly felt apropos. The exterior door to the restroom shook, signaling someone on the other side trying to get in. *Go away*, her brain supplied. Wait. That meant the door was locked. Who the hell had locked it? Alexis. She remembered losing Alexis's arm for a moment. A knock came. Marigold stepped back, blinked, and began to float back to herself.

Alexis stared at her, eyes wide. She touched her lips and gave her head a shake. Then an amused smile blossomed. "Where in the world did that come from?"

Marigold's face was hot and brain still fuzzy. *Damn you, sophisticated scotch man.* She touched her still pleasantly buzzing lips. "That wasn't supposed to happen."

"No. I would think not."

"Excuse me. Who's in there? You can't just lock the door! I'm going to get Larry in a minute."

Marigold, feeling startlingly sober for a glimmer of a moment, turned the lock just in time for that busybody McKenna Walters to bust through with an accusatory hand on her hip. They'd been in school together their whole lives. Marigold had never been a fan.

"What's going on in here?" Her gaze shifted from Alexis to Marigold.

"That would be none of your concern, McKenna. Not everything is. We were having a conversation about…pockets." She blinked, attempting to clear her field of vision as the alcohol effects tightened their grip. "I love 'em. She doesn't. Don't you have business to attend to?"

"Pockets. Really? That's all you got?" With a pointed glare, McKenna breezed past them into a stall. Marigold, floored with what had happened in the last five minutes of her life and grappling with a body that clearly didn't have her best interests at heart, was unsure what to do next. Thereby, she promptly opened the door and fled the scene.

"Come on," she said to Tillman. "We gotta get out of here fast. Walk me home. Pick up those feet. Those clompers can't hold us back."

He flashed a wounded puppy look as she passed. "But Larry just ordered pizzas. With banana peppers."

"You've had pizza before," she tossed over her shoulder. "Hurry. I'll owe you a slice or eight."

She heard his barstool screech as he followed her out. "You are so not yourself tonight. You gotta watch the booze, MG. This isn't like you."

She dropped her head back dramatically as they walked down the darkened street, leaving his truck for the next day. "I know. I do things that are downright shocking these days. Is it my thirties? What's going to happen in my forties? Am I going to start robbing grocery stores?" Her voice was unusually loud, but she couldn't seem to rein it in. "I've surprised myself, Tillman. I'm Satan's ride or die."

"Wait up."

Marigold turned around, horrified to see Alexis exiting Larry's and gaining on them. What in the world could she possibly want? Wasn't Marigold's embarrassment enough? She paused because turning this into a footrace would be weird. "There's really nothing to talk about, okay?" she called. "We had a moment. It's over. Sorry about that!"

"What moment?" Tillman asked.

Alexis paused in front of them and frowned. "If you're referencing the kiss, no worries. You left your bag in the bathroom."

Horror of horrors. She glanced down at her small mint canvas cross-body and wanted to climb under the concrete. "Oh. Thanks."

"Just thought you might need it to get into your house. Even evil food critics are capable of an occasional good deed."

"Probably just hit your quota."

"Ouch. Claws are still out, I see."

Marigold winced internally. Comments like those weren't like her. She *was* being aggressive. Alexis was right. She just had a way of bringing it out in Marigold. "I shouldn't have said that. Thank you for my bag. Tillman?" She inclined her head in a *let's go*.

"You guys kissed? You hate each other." He looked from Alexis to Marigold with his mouth open. "How does that happen?"

"I had a similar response," Alexis said. "Anyway, enjoy your night."

Alexis headed back to the bar, leaving Marigold staring blankly after her, wrestling with questions she had no answers for. Why was Alexis in town? Why had Marigold kissed her? Why couldn't she concentrate on anything other than Alexis when they were in the same room?

"I think I get it." Tillman held out a hand as if trying to work a puzzle. "You want to take that woman to bed and use all that anger and tension to really tear up the sheets." He flipped his ball cap around and offered his best smolder. "Like those movies. You should go for it."

"Stop that, Tillman Lee, or your face is gonna stick. Let's go eat frozen pizza in my kitchen." She shook her bleary head. "Forget tonight forever."

"Seems like a pretty sad backup plan to what I suggested, but okay."

He'd nailed it. That was Marigold. Sad and full of backup plans to what should be the prime of her life. Now she'd gone and acted a fool on top of it all. What a mess she was. She needed chocolate and an intervention.

Tillman slung an arm around her shoulder, likely because she was walking wavy. "I got you. Peas."

"In a pod. Thanks, Till." She sighed, lost and shook, wondering who the hell she was these days. She stared up at the night sky, looking for answers and receiving none.

CHAPTER SEVEN

R ight this way, Ms. Wakefield."
The quaint little office building that housed Homer's Bluff Veterinary Clinic reminded her of something you'd see on a postcard. The cute red door was welcoming, as was the quiet, friendly receptionist at the front. "You can take a seat. I recommend the green couch. Would you like a mint?"

"I'm fine. Thank you, though." Carrot, piecing together that this was in fact a vet's office, his enemy in life, jammed his head behind her back, refusing to face his fate.

She hadn't anticipated needing a vet during her stay, but the limp that had descended upon Carrot twenty-four hours ago showed no sign of letting up. She refused to let him suffer if he happened to be in pain.

Five minutes later, Alexis followed a second woman, this one much louder with volumes of red hair on top of her head. She was led down a short hallway with Carrot trotting begrudgingly next to her. "I don't seem to recognize you. Just moved to town? We love new neighbors."

"No. I'm just visiting. I needed a quiet place to relax and get away from it all."

"We have a lot to offer. You'd be surprised. Have you swung by Spaghetti Straps just yet? They're having a sale on anything pink. Even hot pink. That's my favorite of the pinks. It has a lot more to say than the others. You just have to listen."

Alexis pondered the statement. She wasn't exactly wrong. "I've never heard anyone say anything close to that before."

"Well, now you know."

"In here?"

"Yes, ma'am. Dr. Brynn will be with you in just two shakes. Make yourself comfortable, and feel free to grab a lollipop over there on the counter." She indicated a fully stocked lollipop tree and beamed. "Those aren't part of the office budget. I brought them myself."

"Incredibly generous of you."

"Eve. That's my name." The woman tapped her plastic name tag and closed the door.

Alone, Alexis inspected Carrot's paw just in time for him to pull it away. Yep, still tender. He'd gone hard at the dog park the day before and had been limping on his right front paw ever since.

"Good morning," the cheerful vet said upon entering. Pretty. Blond with a calming presence. "I'm Dr. Garrett."

"Alexis Wakefield."

"Yes, I saw your name on the chart. Nice to meet you. This must be Carrot."

"It is." Alexis scooped him up onto the exam table and explained the series of events that brought them in. "He's a pretty active dog who doesn't realize he's middle-aged now."

"Isn't that always the case?" Dr. Garrett asked with a smile. "Let me take a look at this most handsome fella."

Alexis watched as Dr. Garrett gave Carrot a full exam. She was exceptionally gentle with him and even made sure to talk sweetly to him the entire time, narrating her actions. Impressive. It was clear this woman was a good veterinarian, and Alexis was grateful she'd found her.

"Here's what I think. We can take X-rays to be sure, but I'm fairly confident we're dealing with a slight sprain to his hock, here, which is the doggy equivalent of an ankle."

"Oh. You sprained your ankle?" Alexis said to Carrot and gave his ear a scratch. "That tracks. What do we do?"

"I'm going to send you home with an anti-inflammatory to make him feel better, a cold pack, and the instruction to give his foot a rest for the next week. No wild afternoons at the dog park for a bit."

"He's going to be devastated, but I'll try to give him extra snuggles on the couch."

"That's the way to do it." She smiled and met Alexis's gaze straight on. "Are you reviewing another restaurant in town?"

Aha. Dr. Garrett knew her work, which made her puff up a little because she liked this woman a lot. She had a great energy about her. "Not quite. Just some time away."

"Well, we'd like to invite you back to Marilyn's. Maybe you'll enjoy it more this time."

"We?"

"My partner, Aster, is the executive chef and owner."

"Oh, damn," Alexis said without thinking, and then promptly deflated, which was unlike her. That meant Brynn also knew Marigold Lavender, kissing bandit with skills she tried to no avail to banish from her knowledge base. "You probably hate me, yet you've been so nice. Very professional of you. I appreciate the care you showed my dog today, in spite of our…differences." She swallowed.

"I don't hate anyone." Dr. Garrett raised a shoulder and closed the chart. "I didn't like the review, though. How could I? I love Aster very much, and I'm a big fan of her work. I think you just got this one wrong is all. It happens to the best of us." She offered a wink and headed for the door. "Eve will get you set up with the good drugs for my new friend, Carrot. You give that foot a rest, young man. Stay handsome."

And the really nice doctor was gone.

Alexis, not sure what else to do, took a seat with a hard thud. That damn review had come back to bite her again. Never had she rethought any of her harshly worded reviews as much as this one. Yet she stood by her assessment. But she was starting to agree that her words weren't exactly the most tactful. Seeing their effect helped with that and certainly killed the buzz. That, and the whole tanked career. Maybe she could get a job at that Larry's place. Sling beer until she withered a slow, shameful death.

Eve reappeared with a bag of drugs for Carrot. "I think you should take her up on the offer. Try the restaurant again."

"You knew who I was?"

"Honey, I've been reading your stuff on the Insta for years. I didn't mind your sass until it was aimed at the sweet folks I love. Then I gotta cut a bitch." She said it with the sweetest smile. "But I'm glad you've come back to make it all right. We're forgiving people."

"That's not exactly why I'm—"

"Marigold Lavender can certainly get a job done. She's our resident activist. Sunshiny disposition and all."

Alexis chewed her lip in frustration but also saw this moment as an opportunity. She leaned in. "What's her deal anyway?"

"Marigold? She manages The Lavender House with her sister Violet. Great store."

"Another flower."

"They're all flowers. Their mama and dad made sure. Marigold sits out on the bridge at the edge of town staring at the water and writing in her notebook. A dreamer of the truest sort."

"Really? Like someone in a wistful romance novel? Real people do that stuff? Who in hell has the time?"

"She does. Everyone loves Marigold. She's sassy and fun and sometimes slips me free lotion for dry elbows." Eve turned thoughtful. "But a sensitive soul underneath the confidence. At least, that's always been my suspicion."

"Interesting." She wanted to brush away the information as inconsequential, but Marigold had worked her way under Alexis's skin and then against her lips and now she was this *entity*. Alexis couldn't shake her even though she'd been trying.

Eve arched an interested eyebrow. "I hear you're related to Aspen Wakefield, and I'm a big fan. Any chance I could get an autograph or maybe a phone call? I'm on Zoom, too."

Alexis sent her an apologetic look. "She's pretty hard to pin down."

"Oh, I bet. I heard she's not only beautiful but smart, too. Turned down an opportunity with NASA to be an actress instead."

Alexis laughed out loud because the thought of Aspen tackling even a basic math problem was out of the realm of reality. "That last part didn't happen, but I'll certainly tell her I met a fan."

Eve's entire face glowed with joy. "This is the best day. I'm ever appreciative even if you are the mean girl that made the Lavenders sad."

And there it was again. "No problem," she said, scooping up Carrot, the one soul who still loved her. She stole a lollipop, checked out, and walked the fairly quiet sidewalk down what she now called Main Street, USA. She tried to enjoy the mildly cool weather and sunshine. So Aspen was a NASA superstar. Marigold was a justice-fighting dreamer. And she was a nationwide pariah. The trifecta.

She ruminated, walking at a slower pace for Carrot, giving him intermittent breaks. What she came to realize was that she was in a unique position. The pause button that had been placed on her life certainly gave her space to reflect. That was new. She was beginning to absorb how others saw her. Insensitive. Self-serving. A bully. The truth was that she didn't want to be any of those things.

Maybe, just maybe, this was her chance to reinvent herself a little. She had space and time.

"Who do I want to be?" she asked the reflection looking back at her in the candy store window. That's the part she had to figure out. Next would be the execution.

But first and foremost, she wanted to be the girl with a big bag of chocolate malt balls and planned to make that happen right now.

❖

"Welcome in to Edna's Sweet Treats," Marigold called in response to the bell above the door. She was trying to do things just as Edna would and sell as much damn candy for the woman as any other day of business. She craned her neck around the Good Ship Lollipop display to see who she might be helping.

"Hi. Just looking around. Do you by chance have malted milk balls?" the floating voice asked.

"Do we have malted milk balls? Only several drawers of them. You've come to the right place."

"Marigold?"

As they came face-to-face on the other side of the display, she found Alexis carrying the adorable blond dachshund she'd met a couple of weeks back in the park. She swallowed because their most recent interaction that she'd tried to forget about came rushing back to her now. She touched her cheek absently to see if it felt hot. She was still incredibly embarrassed by the kissing session she'd initiated at Larry's and the fact that she'd replayed each moment about eleventy times. That part she was learning to live with, but what did it say about her that she was lusting after someone who'd bullied her kid sister in front of the entire world? Who did that? She had some soul-searching to do for sure. She mentally added some bridge-sitting penance to her calendar.

"What are you doing here?" she asked Alexis.

"Is that how you greet all of your candy store customers?"

She looked around, remembering herself. "You're not my customer. You're Edna's customer." A pause as she reflected. "But I am Edna today. She would have greeted you nicely. So, welcome in," she said quickly and with half-hearted enthusiasm. "Can I interest you in a free sample of fudge before you leave?"

"Yes," Alexis said slowly, eying her with suspicion. "Why are you Edna? I'm so lost."

"Edna is having a much needed root canal, and rather than close up shop and lose a day's income, I offered to cover for her today, and Violet is covering my shift at The Lavender House. It's what people who are nice do for each other. You wouldn't know."

"Edna would never insult me in this manner." Alexis folded her arms and raised an eyebrow in challenge. "In fact, I think I'll come back when she's in. Maybe I'll even bring a get-well-soon card. Bye, Marigold."

Dammit. She'd gone and been aggressive again. "Wait." She pinched the bridge of her nose and gathered her grace. It wasn't Alexis's fault that Marigold hated herself for that kiss. She was a pawn in the scheme of memorable kisses. "I admit that I shouldn't have said that last part."

"No. But it's clear my mere presence upsets you, so I'll get out of your way."

"Give me another chance. Just let me show you some delicious malted milk balls!" Marigold blurted to Alexis's retreating form. "Please?" She exhaled slowly. "I'll be a delight. I swear."

Alexis eyed her in hesitation. "All right. If you're sure you're up for it."

"I am. Right this way, valuable customer."

"You don't have to overdo it."

"That's fair."

Marigold had studied the aisles of the candy shop before her big shift, refreshing her memory on all Edna had to offer. She put that knowledge to use now. "My personal favorites are the original malt balls, but I hear the mint is her best seller. The peanut butter looks delightful, and I wish I could tell you more about the butterscotch, but the idea confuses me. I'm sure they're quite good, too. Edna knows candy."

"Hence the root canal?"

She winced. "Perhaps."

She felt Alexis's gaze on the side of her cheek, and that made it go warm again. She needed to work on temperature control around this woman.

"Well, now I'm intrigued by the butterscotch." Alexis's voice was noticeably quiet in the already silent store. It sent a tingle across Marigold's skin. She covered the spot on her arm.

And now she was secretly imagining them kissing right there in the malted milk ball section just moments after she'd been so angry to see Alexis. How did both moments exist? The world was surely trying to teach her some sort of lesson. Hell if she knew what it was.

She blinked herself out of the daydream and shrugged. "You could always, um, live a little. Try them all. Butterscotch first." With the tiniest plastic tongs she'd ever used, she retrieved a sample and placed it in Alexis's waiting hand. The world went still for Marigold as Alexis raised the chocolate to her lips and took a bite. Marigold was well aware that she was watching Alexis's lips as she tasted the sweet candy, but it was too good to look away. In the back of her mind, she knew this was new material for later when she sat alone in her house imagining a nonexistent romance with a fictional woman. She refused to entertain thoughts of actual Alexis. That would be…too much.

Alexis's dark blue eyes went wide. "You know, I gotta say, Edna knows her stuff. The butterscotch is excellent."

"Hmmm?"

"The butterscotch. Are you okay?"

"Yes, and so excited you like it!" She clapped once. "Yay! Now the original." They went through the flavors, and Marigold wished she could say that she remembered herself and got it together, but the reality was that Alexis only got more expressive as she taste-tested the other flavors, and Marigold fell into captivation. She remembered she was dealing with a food critic, who came with knowledge and opinions and took this whole thing very seriously.

"Okay, I've made my decision. Let's go with a quarter pound of the butterscotch, a half pound of the peanut butter, and another half pound of original."

"Cha-ching," Marigold said, pleased to have made the sale on Edna's behalf. "I regret saying that, but it is a fun word. Follow me to the counter, unless you and Carrot would like to peruse the store."

Alexis went soft. Had Marigold seen that right?

"You remembered his name."

Well, well. Marigold had just found a source of weakness, and it was the adorable little dog making eyes at her. To try to make up for her earlier behavior, she followed the thread, hoping to make their final exchange a little more pleasant. "Where did you two meet?"

"A few years back, I went with my sister's girlfriend at the time to pick out her new puppy. Taylor had second pick of the litter and chose her dog, Raisin, who is just the sweetest thing. I had no intention of getting a dog. I mean, at all."

"Let me guess. He had other ideas."

Alexis lit the hell up. Wow.

"Exactly. Pushed his nose into my hand."

"Aww."

"And crawled right into my lap as if he belonged there, while his siblings played."

"One can't say no to that kind of divine intervention. I believe in fate."

"Thank you for saying that. I think so, too." This topic had Alexis energized. She simply radiated joy. "So given he was Raisin's brother, Carrot seemed like a fitting name."

"Do the dogs ever see each other?"

"On occasion." Alexis hesitated. After all, this was the first time they'd attempted authentic get-to-know-you conversation. But Alexis seemed to make a decision and went for it. "Taylor and my sister split up, but she's great, and we make occasional playdates for them whenever I'm in LA. They go nuts together. The zoomies are intense." She pulled out her card and looked up at Marigold, who made that register her bitch. She didn't know candy, but she knew retail. "What do I owe you, pseudo-Edna?"

"That will be twenty-two fifty."

"For milk balls." Her expressive eyes widened as she handed over her card. "All right, Edna. I see you."

"Small town hazard. Everything costs a tad bit more. No big box stores."

"No argument. I don't mind paying for quality. Thank you for your help today, Gladiola."

"Very funny. And look, we made it out without a further disagreement."

"What are you talking about? We didn't make out at all. See you soon." Alexis waved over her shoulder without looking back.

The parting words left Marigold grappling for a response. "Right. Bye," was all she came up with. She hadn't expected either of them to ever mention that wayward kissing session ever again. As in take it to the grave and call it drunk weird happenstance. Yet Alexis had gone and done it right there in Edna's Sweet Treats. Did that mean she kissed people in bars regularly, making their encounter just another Tuesday? She also didn't like that idea. In fact, she hated the thought of Alexis repeating their moment with someone else, which was too bold of her. She didn't care. Why was she all of a sudden jealous of Alexis and prospective other women? Did they kiss like magic together, too? No. And what was she even copping to right now?

"Are you having a wild conversation with yourself in your head right now?"

She blinked, startled back into reality. Aster. When had she shown up? "No."

"Are, too. I just spotted Alexis Wakefield. Remember her? The food critic you went all vigilante on?"

"I do." She squinted. "How would you figure I forgot that?"

"Good point." Aster rocked on her heels. "You do tend to hold on to things with an impressive viselike grip."

"Yeah, well, it was *your* restaurant. Similarly, I don't know how you let go of something like that so easily."

"Because I gave myself three days to wallow and pout, and then when the time was up, I had to move forward. I have customers. They're hungry. I must feed them. Plus, this felt like a challenge to do even better."

"Why is everything so cut-and-dried for you? Damn you for being so refreshing and mature. Where do you get off?"

Aster laughed. "Thank you. I had a nice family raise me right. A good mom."

The pesky lump in her throat was back. Grief was tricky. Just when you thought you had it under control, a casual mention made you want to well up.

"Oh." A pause. "I'm sorry. I just think about her a lot. It helps to keep her a part of my everyday."

"Never apologize for mentioning Mom. In fact, we should mention her more. All the time."

"Yeah." Aster paused. "I feel her so much in Cara. I think she watches over her."

"Yeah? I love hearing that." Her eyes had filled. Not a surprise. "I know she does."

"Where's Edna, by the way?"

"It's root canal day, but I'm tearing up the sugary sales. Make a big purchase, so I can be the candy queen of Homer's Bluff."

"How does six pounds of milk chocolate sound?"

Marigold's eyebrows reached for the stars. "I like the sound of that. I'm just not sure where to—"

"She has a back room. I'll show you."

Clearly, Edna and her sister had some sort of chocolate arrangement happening, but she was happy to help pack the thick sheets into the pretty blue boxes Edna set aside for chocolate purchases. "What are you going to do with all this?"

"The perfect chocolate drizzle for a caramel torte I'm working on."

Marigold closed the last box and headed for the door. "I'm coming with you. Edna will figure it out."

Aster laughed. "I'll bring two by The Lavender House later this week."

"Violet is going to sob with joy. I will hang your photo up as favorite sibling of the week."

"That's fair." Aster stacked the boxes and Marigold bagged them. "So did Wakefield say why she's back in town? That's odd, right?"

"She's probably wildly obsessed with me after I ended her."

"I was actually a little worried the opposite was true."

"That she has a vendetta and is here for sweet, sweet revenge? I hope not. We kissed the other night." Her hand flew to her mouth. It was her proximity to chocolate. Had to be. She was chocolate drunk and saying things she should never confess to anyone.

"I certainly misheard you."

"Aster, I wish you had."

Her kid sister's eyes were luminous and questioning, and she set her huge bag of chocolate right the hell down. "Why were you kissing the woman you can't stand?"

"In addition to her status as internet bully, she also happens to be really attractive, and scotch made me forget the former. Never drink it. Who knew?"

Aster marveled. "You had scotch and Ms. Wakefield, in that order."

"A stretch. There was no *having*. Don't tell Violet. Any of it. Lock your lips right now and let me watch."

"She deserves to know. Violet adores gossip, and you just delivered a doozie dose." Aster said this with the earnest quality of a trusting child. "It would be wrong to withhold. Wouldn't you say?"

"No. I don't say." A pause. "But I suppose I'd be indignant if the tables were turned."

"Very intuitive of you. I have to run. Chocolate sauce, dinner with Brynn, and then I'm on baby duty."

Marigold sighed. "You live a really nice existence."

"Couldn't agree more. See you soon." She paused, searching for words. "Don't kiss anyone else, ya know? Unless you really mean to. Then go ahead."

"Wise. I like the way you think, kiddo. Bye again."

Traffic at Edna's was slow, so Marigold spent the time moving through the aisles, staring at all the wonderful confections that surrounded her. She was literally that kid in a candy store and enjoying every moment of her day. In between candy awe, she let her mind do what it always did and drift off to somewhere wonderful.

She'd cast a new girlfriend recently, Iliana. They were barefoot on a warm beach together, waiting for the sun to dip low enough in the sky for the perfect golden hour photo. Marigold wore a yellow sundress, off the shoulders, of course, and Iliana had her dark hair down. Every so often, the wind lifted it, and Marigold would forget to breathe.

"I can't wait to get you back home," Iliana would say. She'd mean the fancy hotel suite, but Marigold translated.

Her flash fantasies. That's what she called the quick ones. Interestingly enough, each one always seemed to end on that last line. Something about it inspired a shiver each time. Probably because even in the beautiful moment, and they were always beautiful, there was the anticipation of something even better waiting for them.

"Oh, Iliana. Say it again," she murmured to the white-chocolate dipped pretzels, knowing damn well she was a silly fool. What adult lived in their daydreams? Clamping down on every moment alone to lose herself in pure fiction. She did. And it was becoming a little sad. A palate cleanser. She would think about a mundane event. Taking her dry cleaning to Sly Sleeves on Fourth Avenue. She closed her eyes and was immediately back on that beach with Iliana. Pause. Only it wasn't Iliana. Her stomach clenched as she looked back with trepidation at the blue eyes she knew all too well as belonging to Alexis. The deep blue was cold, but the quality behind them was warm and wonderful. She felt her real life lips relax into a grin as her fingers threaded Alexis's. *Bubble burst.* Wait. What? Where was Iliana, and why was Alexis now crashing her very private fantasies that no one *real* had ever appeared in?

"No, no, no, no," she said out loud, accusing the pretzels and informing the universe that she wasn't down for this woman. "We're not doing that, okay?" She raised her voice and sent her focus to the sky. "We like nice people. It's a hard stop for me. I'm going to have a peanut butter cup and drown your visions the hell out."

While she was sad to shelve her fantasy world, she would do what she had to in order to take back the keys to her thoughts. Romance be damned. Alexis Wakefield was not worth her time. Not even her shiny dark hair or the soft sway of her hips when she crossed a room. *Well, maybe those.* "No! Dammit."

CHAPTER EIGHT

When alone in a small town without much to occupy one's time, what's a foodie to do? Alexis didn't have to ask herself that question more than once before deciding she would do what she did best. Explore the food scene. She would visit every local eatery she came across, starting with the incredibly funky doughnut shop that snagged her attention on the drive into town.

Hole in One had a drive-through line wrapped around the building when she pulled into a parking spot that Tuesday morning. She'd been in town six whole days and now understood that the town layout was organized with two loops and a grid system. Easy enough to find most anything. The doughnut shop occupied the outer loop, away from town center. An interesting choice.

On the way up the walk, she admired the mural painting on the exterior brick. The painting covered the entire wall and showcased three different doughnuts and a glass of milk with a fancy straw. It seemed to work, because now she wanted all four items, along with some coffee. Effective.

She pushed open the door to the interior. *Whoa.* Alexis was caught off guard by the heavenly aromas already overwhelming her senses. The sweet rich flavors that swirled in the air about brought her to her knees. An excellent sign. It meant fresh oil, fresh ingredients, and honest-to-goodness know-how. The trifecta was the only way to achieve that kind of aromatic perfection. Hole in One was already impressive, and she hadn't laid eyes on a single doughnut yet.

Of course there was a line inside as well, forcing Alexis to remain in the doorway until there was room for her to properly join it. She used the time to study the handwritten sign that served as the menu. They had only four doughnut flavors available to choose from, a call she applauded. Do one thing and do it well. She'd seen too many businesses take on more than they could handle and thereby half-ass every dish they presented.

Let's see. Today, they offered Nutter Butter Rama Roo, Cinnamon Savage, Chocolate Murder, and Hazelnut Fig Face. Her choice was easy. One of each. She was also awarding them imaginary bonus points for creativity. If the flavors rotated daily, and she enjoyed what she ate, she'd most certainly be back.

"Hey, there. Welcome to Hole in One!" a cheerful redhead enthused. "We hope you're having an amazing morning. How could you not be with doughnuts in your future?" She met Alexis's gaze, tilted her head, and paused. "Wait. Pause the show. Aren't you the famous food critic?"

"I think so. I am a critic with a column. Well, former column."

"Uh-uh. You're not nice. I don't know about doughnuts for you."

Alexis closed her eyes. Seriously? They were going to do this at the doughnut shop, too? She felt the now judgmental stares of the people in line behind her. This was embarrassing. Plus, she had limited choices because she needed those doughnuts. "I get it. I posted a less than kind review of a local restaurant."

"Worse. Try our founder. The woman behind our concepts, our doughnuts, and our early success." The redhead whose name tag said *Tori* placed a reverent hand over her heart.

Well, that was news. "Aster Lavender opened this place?"

"Hand-painted the mural out front and curated each and every recipe. She even comes in and whips up new ones just because she cares. We're lucky to have her."

Alexis had to give credit where credit was due. Also, she was willing to say what she had to. "Well, so far, I'm really impressed. I'd like to see if the doughnuts are as awesome as they seem. Can I find out?" A veiled challenge. That seemed to pique Tori's interest. She wanted to prove an Aster Lavender point, and Alexis was prepared to let her if it earned her four of those bad boys on the cooling rack behind the counter. Her mouth had been watering since she'd arrived.

"Okay, but you better prepare to apologize for every negative thing you said about Aster."

"Technically, nothing. I reviewed her restaurant." She knew better than to push the issue.

"I'll make you a deal. If you like what you try, you have to promise to tell Aster, personally."

"What? No. We're not making deals." The woman in line behind her shifted in impatience.

Tori took a step back. "Then step aside. I have a line getting longer by the second."

Alexis sighed, studied her Prada boots, and made a decision. "Can I have one of each flavor? And a coffee of the day."

"Adventurous spirit," Tori said, trying to mask her approval. She signaled one of her employees, who dutifully went about boxing her order. "A plate, too," she instructed him. "Fork?"

"I'm not a heathen."

"A point for you," Tori said.

Alexis was able to snag one of the very few tables in the small space and got to tasting. She cycled from one doughnut to the next, sampling, savoring, sorting through her thoughts. She divided the notes section of her phone into a grid to keep track. She wouldn't be posting an official review because she was currently not welcome online, but old habits died hard. The fruit doughnuts popped, the cinnamon dazzled, and the rich chocolate anchored the final doughnut like an Olympic sprinter hell-bent on gold. The verdict was easy. These were the best four doughnuts she'd ever tasted. Aster Lavender might not be an overhyped hack after all. How did she admit that gracefully to Tori, who eyed her every second she took up space in the shop? Finally, Alexis dabbed the corners of her mouth and returned the plate to the counter. She was keeping the leftover portions in the box for later.

"I treasured each bite. Truly a victory. Congratulations on an amazing shop."

Tori's features blossomed in triumph. "We're just so very thrilled to have another satisfied customer."

"This place is the best ever," a middle-aged man in a pharmacist's coat called out.

"Mr. Landry is a regular."

"I would be, too," she said with a slight head bow. "And if I ever meet Aster in person, you can bet I'll deliver the compliment."

Tori held up a red fingernail perfectly matched to her Hole in One shirt. "No. No. You go find her and say the nice words in person. You have a lot of making up to do after what you wrote."

"I'll do my best." It's wasn't like she had that busy an agenda, and the woman was certainly shaping up to be a mysterious figure that she'd begun to wonder about. She could take a few minutes and swing by Marilyn's. Why not?

"If you want another doughnut from this establishment ever again, you best hold up your end of the deal. You hear me? In person." The male employee behind Tori nodded his encouragement. Maybe that meant Tori didn't go to the mat often. She seemed like Hole in One's resident do-gooder, who also didn't mind stepping out of her comfort zone for battle. This town had several of those, Marigold Lavender included. Of course that thought prompted the movie to play in her mind of the night Marigold caught her in a lip lock for the ages. Alexis felt that memory all over. She wasn't sure why it had such a hold on her.

But because she always tried to keep her word, one thing they *couldn't* call her on, Alexis-of-the-unemployed waltzed into Marilyn's that afternoon, metaphorical hat in hand, in search of Aster Lavender. "Excuse me, ma'am. Is Aster available?" she asked the wide-eyed woman behind the host stand.

The woman, who she vaguely remembered, didn't say anything at first, probably not expecting public enemy number one to just waltz into the scene of the crime.

"It's okay if she's busy." She slid a strand of hair behind her ear and smiled expectantly, hoping to put the young woman at ease.

She held up one finger, never taking her eyes off Alexis. "I'll be right back."

"No problem." Alexis took the moment alone to look over the mostly empty dining room just ahead. The restaurant would be in that lull that occurred between lunch and dinner service. Servers moved through the space, preparing it for the evening and speaking to each other informally. Having worked in a series of restaurants herself, Alexis enjoyed that particular time in the day. The calm before you got bulldozed along with your teammates.

"Hi."

Alexis turned to see Aster in a chef's coat, peering at her curiously. She recognized her from photos online. Striking. Brunette with luminous eyes and shoulder-length hair pulled back in a ponytail.

"Aster. We haven't met formally."

"No, but you've kissed my sister."

The woman at the host stand swiveled toward them. Alexis felt her eyes go wide. Aster had said the words with such ease, almost as simply as remarking about the weather. It certainly erased from her brain every word Alexis had planned. She tried to regroup and realized she was flailing.

"I'm not upset about it. Just making conversation." Aster was certainly a to-the-point human. "Would you like to sit?" She gestured to the bar seats that overlooked the open kitchen. Alexis nodded and they grabbed two chairs. "Cory, maybe some bread and the garlic hummus?" He nodded and dashed away. "How about a glass of white wine? I have an Albariño that pairs perfectly."

All of this caught her completely off guard. "Sure. That's hospitable of you."

"I was sorry you didn't enjoy your meal the last time you were here. I always want my diners happy and satisfied with their food. What brings you back to town?"

Alexis pulled her shoulders toward her ears. "I'm still trying to figure that one out, but I needed somewhere to escape the larger world, and this town seemed kind of full circle. I wish I could explain it more specifically."

"I think I understand what you're saying. Marigold got you canceled, and now you're hitting a pause button. It's a good spot to do it. Kissing was probably an unexpected event if I had to guess."

"Definitely unexpected. She's something. Marigold."

Aster beamed with pride. "She's amazing. Give it time, and you'll believe it, too. Even though she did take you down."

Alexis held up a hand. "Let's not get carried away."

Aster stared at her blank-faced. "I'm not."

"Okay, then. Well, I'm back at your restaurant because I made a deal that if I loved the doughnuts at Hole in One, I had to personally seek you out and tell you." She made a half-hearted bow-down gesture. "So here I am. You rock at doughnuts."

"Tori."

Alexis grinned. "Wouldn't serve me unless I agreed to the deal."

Aster really seemed to like that. "I'm sorry everyone is giving you such a hard time. I didn't like getting reviewed so harshly, but I respect you and your opinion. I get the game more than the people who love me. If anything, I want to be better."

Okay, even she was starting to really like Aster Lavender. And this garlic hummus. "This is incredibly bright."

"Made in-house. Top-secret ingredients."

She sipped the Albariño and basked in the complementary relationship. "You know your wine, too."

"Flavor profiles are my favorite. I get obsessed and devote way too much time. I love to take things apart with my mind and palate. See what makes them what they are."

"You and I would get along nicely had we met on other terms."

Aster sat up and unbuttoned the top two buttons on her jacket. "I think we still can. Is it true your sister is a movie star?"

For once, she was grateful for Aspen. "It is true. Aspen Wakefield is my older sister. You might have seen her on *Thicker Than Water*. You probably won't believe me, but I'm the nice one."

Aster laughed. "I can't wait to tell Brynn. She used to have a little crush on Aspen."

"I met her! Dr. Garrett. She's wonderful. Took the best care of my dachshund. Probably too nice for Aspen, if we're being honest."

"Thank God. I would like to hold on to her." Aster looked thoughtful. "Come over for dinner next week. I have Sunday nights away from the restaurant. I'd be happy to cook." She leaned in. "Let's skip the review, though. Just enjoy really sinful food together."

"Really?" Alexis almost couldn't believe this was happening. None of the other chefs she'd lambasted had ever reached out and offered any form of friendship. But the gesture might have been exactly what Alexis needed for her soul to right itself. She hadn't liked the person looking back at her in the mirror lately, and making amends with Aster Lavender felt wildly refreshing and the right thing to do. "I'd love to have dinner with you and Brynn."

"And Cara. She's our baby girl. Can't forget her. Don't worry. She won't let you. Cara's the life of the party and generally closes the place down."

"Cara. That's right. She was born the night I was here."

"The most important day of my life. Hence, the disarray you walked into."

"Maybe I should have accounted for that and come a second time before writing a word. I wish I'd done that. Two visits certainly would have made for a more well-researched review." It wasn't until this moment and looking into Aster's kind eyes that she felt really awful about stamping that day with anything negative. God. She had to start thinking about the bigger picture in life. She'd try. She would.

Aster glanced skyward. "Thank you for saying that. I think both our lives took a turn that night."

"Yours was definitely a more positive shift than mine." She tossed back the wine for comedy, reaching in to keep the rapport with Aster going. Alexis needed this like a salve to a wound she hadn't even realized was so deep. She felt something in her loosen the slightest bit, and relief rained down on her as she sat there. God, it was nice. And foreign. Had she really been wrapped so tight? Her time in Homer's Bluff seemed to be freeing her, one step at a time.

Aster laughed. "I can't fix your career, but I do make a killer scallop and ham risotto. Nothing soupy about it."

"Sold. Risotto is my weakness in life. Are you spying on me?"

"I promise I'm not," Aster said earnestly. This time it was Alexis's turn to laugh. They exchanged numbers, and Aster vowed to text her all the details for Sunday. "I'm glad you stopped by. It was nice to have a one-on-one conversation." Aster shrugged. "Since we were linked so publicly."

"It was honestly all my pleasure. You're a class act, Aster. Gonna go imagine that risotto until we meet again."

"Don't kiss any more of my sisters, okay?"

She paused midstep, grappling. "You have my word." If her face was hot as she headed to her Range Rover, she pretended not to notice. The day was feeling like a good one, and she refused to let Marigold Lavender and their complicated history overrun her thoughts. At least… she'd try.

❖

Marigold's childhood home, with its exterior of dark wood and big crisscross beams that lined the porch, was located just behind and down the road from The Lavender House. Marigold had a soft place in her heart for the house. Everywhere she looked inspired a memory of boisterous kids running all over each other. It all still echoed in her ears like it was yesterday. Sage with his signature ball cap. Aster trying desperately to keep up with her three older siblings. Violet lording her older sibling knowledge over all of them, and Marigold concentrating on painting her nails perfectly so everyone in the fourth grade would vote for her for class vice-president. It felt like watching a movie of a big, noisy family. She loved it.

Tonight, the house glowed cozy in the waning evening light. It was a little more empty these days, belonging only to her father, but it was every bit as welcoming. Violet would close up the store that night, and that freed Marigold to pop in on their father, part of their new initiative to be more present on a daily basis.

Sage had been right.

He wasn't himself. He was still friendly and loving in that quiet way he'd always had, but the twinkle was gone from his eyes. He moved around that big house like he was carrying bricks on his shoulders. He was alone now and very much aware of it.

"You in here, Mr. Dad?" The nickname she'd had for him most of her life was born from his attendance at her very proper childhood tea parties. She smothered a smile at the image of him crammed into one of those tiny chairs, attempting to sip imaginary tea with his pinkie in the air, as instructed by Marigold, of course.

"What's that?"

"It's me. Marigold. Your absolute favorite. Here for a weekly gossip sesh. Show yourself."

And there he was, her burly dad, emerging from the bedroom just off the living area. "Mare. Hi. Just finished my shower." He ran a hand through his strawberry-blond hair, same as hers. "Dirty today. Dust all up in the fields."

"Well, thank God you're presentable." Her father and Sage oversaw the lavender fields along with their staff, long days outside doing the kind of manual labor that made Marigold want to crawl in the corner and hide. She wasn't cut out for long stretches of dusty work. Her mom, however, had been different, pitching in wherever the business needed her. She was the brains behind the lavender farm-to-product operation but never shied from jumping in anywhere. Whether it was behind the register at The Lavender House, working the books or marketing at home, or on top of a tractor. Marigold smiled at the image as she threw open the fridge and grabbed two beers and tossed one to her dad, who caught the can easily. He seemed pleased with the gift. "What should we eat?"

"Oh, you're staying for supper?" He sounded both surprised and hopeful as he cracked the beer.

She took a swallow of hers, cold and crisp, as she perused his freezer. "I'm crashing your party. What about these pork chops? Aster taught me how to season the hell out of them."

He brightened even more. "Yeah. Definitely. That could be real nice."

"Done." She tossed the chops onto the counter and went to work. She was no pro, but she liked the challenge. Garlic and black pepper were key to her chops. Once they were sizzling in the pan, she turned to her dad, who watched from the kitchen table nearby, the hub of so many family dinners. Holy ground, yet also just a regular kitchen table. The best.

"What's new with you?" he asked. The brewski had loosened him up. He was serving up smiles now. "You posting any more internet videos? Sage says you have far-reaching power. World better watch out for my girl."

She kicked a hip against the counter. "I'm like Wonder Woman with a webcam." She shrugged. "I think I might be hanging up my online crusader cape, though." She let the pork chops rest and took a seat next to him.

"If you do that, who will you be? I kinda like Marigold."

She hesitated but then decided to give him the dish. "Okay. So there's this woman, and she makes my heart race, but she's the one I went all Justice League on, and now whenever I see her I behave horribly. I think she inspires big feelings in me."

He blinked. "We've never girl talked before. I'm trying to figure out my role."

She dropped her head onto the table with a quiet thud. "This is me being dramatic, Dad. You pull me back. That's what Mom did."

"Okay. Let me see." A long pause. Finally, she lifted her head and stole a peek through one eye. "Sorry. Got it now. Mare, I think first we have to understand the nature of your reaction to this woman. The reviewer, right? Who's back in town?"

"You know a lot." She sat up, intrigued. Turned out he wasn't bad at this. "Yes. That's her. Go on."

"Well," he said, running a palm across the bottom of his half white, half blond beard, "do you really carry hatred for this, uh, individual, or is there maybe some other emotion that's inspiring these microbursts?"

"Good word! I'd like to check the *other kind of emotion* box."

"Interesting. Don't you think?" He sported a proud grin. Her father was enjoying the role, which was nice to see.

"It's possible I have a minor crush on her." She felt the warmth invade her cheeks. "She's over-the-top attractive. I'm sure I'm not the only one who feels that way."

"Been there." A fist bump. "When I met Marilyn, my concentration on anything important went out the window. I rode the bench for weeks playing high school ball because I kept missing the damn tackles. I turned into a bumbling cartoon."

She ruminated, forging a comparison. "Okay, okay. So here it goes. *A*, I do find myself preoccupied ever since she showed up in town. *B*, but how can I legit have a crush on my sworn enemy? It's wrong. It goes against so many principles I thought I valued. This isn't *Days of Our Lives*."

He nodded, cool as a cucumber, and kicked back in his chair. "That one is easy. The opposite of love isn't hate. It's apathy."

She stared at the man who had always been a guy of few words, content to smile, hug his kids, and be silly when called for. Though she loved him to pieces, Marigold had never considered her father to be the foundation of family wisdom. She'd been wrong.

"Okay. I can actually work with that. Wow, Mr. Dad."

"Don't sell your old man short. I pay attention to things."

She decided to go for it. Broach the subject they'd all been tiptoeing around. "What about you? It's been more than two years now," she pointed out delicately. At the same time, she strove for nonchalance, worried she'd frighten him away. "Have you thought about dipping a toe into the dating pond? Seeing what's out there?" The idea of her dad with a woman other than their mom was jarring. However, she couldn't stomach the idea of him spending the rest of his life, likely decades ahead of him, all alone. She imagined him fading further from vibrancy into a quiet, lonely existence.

"See, that's not gonna happen for me because I'm just not

interested." He offered a shrug. "My person is gone. And that's the end of it."

"Dad. I know it's hard for you to imagine, but we're nowhere near the end of it. Mom is with us still and is going to love you always. But she would also want to see you happy. She'd demand it, actually."

"I'm as happy as I'm gonna get. I got my kids. I got my grandkids. Got my tractor. Tonight, I have pork chops, a beer, and excellent company. Feeling good about that."

She sighed, knowing when to take her fingers off a bruise. Maybe he just needed more time, which was entirely his right. "Just keep an open mind to whatever signs the universe sends your way, okay?"

He stared at her. Her blue eyes were his. "I notice you're not attached. Is that what you're doing? Keeping your mind wide open?"

"No." That one landed. It did feel like the powers that be were trying to hit her over the head with something these days. She just couldn't imagine that the cosmos thought Alexis should play any kind of role. Shiny hair and perfect lips be damned. They butted heads. Every day would be a battle.

"You know what?" her dad said. "I'll give you the same advice you gave me. Keep an open mind. Don't always think you know how everything is going to turn out."

She blinked, turning that last phrase over. "Is that our deal?"

He hesitated, consulted the ceiling, and came back to her. "Deal, second child." And then quickly moved out of it. "Those, uh, pork chops rest long enough?"

"Yep." She pushed away from the table. "Coming right up. Green beans, too."

He watched her plate the food. "Your sister came by yesterday. You kids on a schedule? Someone draws the short straw and has to check in on old dad?"

She laughed. "We all just love you. But there were no short straws involved. I don't know." She lifted a shoulder. "I kinda like having a dinner companion. Maybe we can make it a more regular thing."

"Fine by me." He messed up her hair with his humongous hands as he passed. The same hands that always made her feel light as a feather when he'd scoop her up for a squeeze or so she could snag a better view from on top of his shoulders.

They enjoyed a delicious dinner together, if she did say so herself, just the two of them. The more they chatted, the more he opened up and ultimately relaxed. The rain cloud that he seemed to tug on a string behind him was gone for a time. She was feeling lighter, too, with a bit more direction, all thanks to Tom Lavender's unexpected insight.

Marigold would count that as a much needed win.

For both of them.

Chapter Nine

A lexis was late and she hated it. Her straightener had overloaded the outlet at her Airbnb. Carrot had taken his time downing his dinner before promptly curling into a ball for his early evening snooze. And her hair hadn't done what she'd wanted it to. At all. Which meant the autumn sky had already gone dark when she pulled up to the address Aster had provided her. Surely dinner engagements in small towns didn't run on time. Nowhere in the Western Hemisphere did, right? Fashionably delayed was the way to go.

She snatched the bottle of bordeaux she'd secured as a host gift from the passenger's side and slid out of her Range Rover just in time to see a cute white hatchback pull up at the curb. When a headful of pretty honey-blond curls sprang from the driver's side, she knew instantly who she was about to encounter...and it could go a lot of ways.

"Alexis." A statement, not a greeting. Marigold frowned, trying to assemble the puzzle pieces, perhaps. She carried a cute little brown sack with red and white handles. "Are you looking for...Aster?"

"We're having dinner," Alexis supplied. "She doesn't hate me as much as you do. Are you joining us?"

Marigold seemed to pause and reset herself. "No. Nope. Just dropping off a couple of outfits for Cara. I can't seem to help myself when I see the tiny baby clothes at Spaghetti Straps."

"That's sweet of you." Alexis had caught a glimpse of that boutique near town center. Lots of bright colors that typically fell outside of her wardrobe's color scheme. But then again, she'd been trying on lots of new habits lately. Maybe she should swing by. Check out a lime-green sweater or a fuchsia pencil skirt. What could it hurt? She'd literally hit rock bottom. She couldn't quite explain why it didn't exactly feel as awful as it should. Something about this little place acted as a salve.

Now they were both making their way up the walk, practically side by side, just in time for the door to swing open. Aster's eyes went wide as she surveyed Alexis and then Marigold. "Did you two come together? Is this an extension of the kissing thing? That's okay if it is."

"What?" Marigold said with a laugh that seemed way too loud. "What in the world? God, no. I was just swinging by to spoil my niece a little." She handed off the bag and turned to move off the porch. "As you were."

"MG, get back here. Now."

"Marigold's here?" Brynn appeared over Aster's shoulder. "Marigold. Hey! Please eat with us. I need backup when two foodies get together. I get lost in the flavor profile shuffle."

Alexis turned to Marigold. "I promise to be on my very best behavior. Nary a snarky comment or judgmental retort."

"How will you survive?" Marigold asked, but to her credit she tossed in a highly winsome smile that Alexis admired for probably a beat too long.

"Okay," Aster said loudly, seeming to have noticed. She also shattered the enjoyable tension. "It's settled. Marigold is staying. I'm cooking. Brynn, can you pour the wine?"

Her eyes lit up. "My favorite task ever."

Aster gestured between her and Marigold. "You two can mingle… or whatever it is you do."

As they entered the home, they simultaneously opened their mouths to balk at the implied characterization but closed them when they noticed the commonality. Aster was right. They were a complicated duo with a strange history between them. It was likely she wasn't the only one feeling off kilter. Alexis wasn't sure whether to follow her curiosity and run toward Marigold or remember exactly why she'd lost her job and stay the hell away. Tricky. She needed that wine to decide.

Brynn placed a glass in her hand in under a minute. "How is my friend Carrot doing?"

It had been more than a few days since their appointment, and Carrot had rebounded nicely. "Back to his old tricks. Thank you for the great care." Right on cue, a black and white terrier mix tore through the living room followed by a second one that looked quite similar.

Brynn gestured toward them with her chin. "Pickles likes to make Dill chase her around. She's the mom and prefers to keep him in check."

Alexis leaned into the huge grin she couldn't hold back. "I love that you have both of them."

"Aster was a hero and is responsible for their reunification."

From the open kitchen, Aster nodded and called out, "My one good deed in life."

"Not everyone would rescue an entire litter of puppies miles from civilization."

"You rescued puppies?" Dammit all. Aster Lavender was an honest-to-goodness saint, and Alexis was starting to understand why so many people went to bat for her.

Marigold stared at Alexis from behind her wineglass. "You light up anytime you're around dogs." Then, realizing she'd said the musing out loud, she held up one palm. "Just an observation."

Alexis met her gaze and ignored the delicious shiver, the kind she got when she was wildly attracted to someone. "Always had a soft spot for animals. They're so earnest. So trusting." She stared into the depths of her glass. "Most of the people in my life have ulterior motives for the things they do."

"That's incredibly sad," Marigold said with a frown.

"You may need new people," Brynn added. "You've come to the right place." A cry erupted. "In fact, we have one more trusting soul for you to meet." Moments later the smallest little person with big green eyes was placed gently in her arms. The world slowed down.

"Hi, there," she whispered.

Brynn beamed with pride. "Meet Cara. She likes middle of the night snuggles, warm milk, and interesting things to look at."

Alexis's heart swelled. Looking down at the little girl caused her to launch automatically into baby-speak. "Well, look at you. Yes, you. Hello, sweet girl. That's your foot. It's a nice foot, too. I see it."

Marigold stared in shock. "I stand corrected. Dogs and babies."

Alexis laughed. "What can I say? I'm a softie at heart." She raised a finger. "I realize you likely won't believe that."

"I might," Marigold said. Right then Alexis caught Brynn and

Aster having some sort of private, wide-eyed exchange. She let them have their fun. This wasn't anywhere close to a double date, yet part of her also realized that she could do a lot worse than someone like Marigold, who relished goodness and seemed to be well intended. She omitted the fact that she found herself hugely drawn to Marigold physically, pulled in by the way she carried herself, formed words, and tossed her hair with such casualness that it was clear she didn't know how gorgeous she was. *Fuck.* This was a thing, wasn't it? And seemed to be becoming more of a thing with each tick-tock of the second hand. She lifted her shoulders and inhaled as the room gushed with warm conversation between her three dinner companions.

She needed to decide on a strategy. Alexis was not a figure-it-out as she went kind of woman, and her approach to Marigold was in need of a plan of action. *Make a move, get it out of your system, and turn it all the hell off.* Not bad.

The trio now looked at her expectantly. Someone had apparently addressed her, and she'd missed it in her haze. "Sorry." She frowned. "Can you say that one more time?"

Brynn had been the source. "Is it too personal to inquire what you thought of your sister's statement to the press yesterday? I imagine it must be difficult."

That didn't bode well. She squinted. It wasn't unusual for people to ask her about Aspen. She was definitely the more exciting sister to the general population. But Alexis, not being an avid fan herself, didn't follow her sister's many appearances or snippets in the news. "You might have to be more specific. I've purposefully unplugged since I've been here."

"Because of me," Marigold said with what sounded like a crumb of remorse. Maybe more. Interesting development.

Alexis, reaching for rapport, raised a shoulder. "Well, me, too."

She refocused on Brynn, who was searching for something on her phone. She began to read. "*When asked for comment on her sister's cancellation and dropped column, Wakefield smiled ruefully. 'You know, it's one of those things. It's a shame but also a testament to the fact that what we put out into the world comes back on us twofold. Alexis is a big girl. She'll figure it out.'*"

The room fell silent. It shouldn't have hurt. Aspen had hung Alexis out to dry more times than she could count. Yet it still did. "Well."

Brynn and Marigold shared a look while Aster stirred the risotto and followed along quietly. The mood had shifted, and it was all her fault.

"You hadn't seen that yet," Brynn said. "I'm so sorry to have brought it up."

"No. Not your fault at all. But, as always, Aspen has to Aspen. She tends to step on the hands of people who've fallen as she elbows her way to the top."

"That's quite an unpleasant visual." Brynn took a very snuggly Cara and set her in her nearby bassinet to gaze at the mobile of stuffed elephants twirling.

"We're not exceptionally close," she explained. "Nothing like your family. It's just the way it is."

"I'm sorry to hear that," Aster said solemnly.

"No need. Just another day at the Wakefield office." She tried to smile, doing her best to convince the room that she was totally unaffected by the quote. She stood. "That smells amazing over there. What can I do to help?"

Aster smiled and didn't miss a beat. "How are you at firing scallops?"

"Not bad. My scallops have pulled me a compliment or two, but I'm no pro."

"Tell you what, you sauté those bad boys, I'll finish the risotto, and we can plate together. Bring your wine. It's the best part of cooking."

Alexis smiled back, grateful to Aster for pulling her out of the emotional spiral she'd been close to falling into. She grabbed her glass and went to work, all the while very aware of Marigold's gaze on her as she worked. From her barstool pulled up to the counter, she watched Alexis's hands, her face, and if Alexis wasn't mistaken, she might have caught Marigold checking out her ass. So this was mutual. No denying it. They locked eyes in that moment, and Alexis raised an eyebrow. Marigold looked quickly away, grabbed her wineglass, and wandered over to Cara's bassinet. *Chicken.*

"What's funny?" Aster asked, spooning the risotto into shallow bowls. "I hate when I miss the amusing moments."

Brynn closed in. "I think your sister and Alexis over here might have had a moment," Brynn whispered in an overly loud voice, leaning between them. She didn't miss a lot.

"Are you three talking about me?" Marigold asked, widening those big blue eyes. Alexis's midsection rippled as she imagined Marigold lying on top, bare breasts pushed up against her own. She leaned in to it.

"Yes," Brynn and Aster answered in unison. Alexis had to laugh. This was turning into a fun evening. No one was trying to show anyone else up. No jockeying for position, or attempts to outshine or outwit. Just…friends hanging out. Refreshing and foreign. How did Alexis get this in her everyday life? Had she seriously been surrounding herself with assholes and social climbers? With a little distance, her world now seemed so acrimonious and fake that it made her nauseous.

They gathered around the table and shared a fantastic meal that night. The risotto was stunning in the bowl and tasted even better. She shook her head, savoring her last bite. "The ham is such an enriching flavor. It assists but lets the scallop be the star."

Marigold nodded and swallowed. "I enjoy it when food knows its role."

"That's what I love about it, too," Aster said, ignoring her sister's quip. She seemed reasonably happy with the meal. No bravado needed. Aster was what you see is what you get. "I'm glad you like it."

She didn't hesitate. "I more than liked it. This rivals your doughnut recipe."

"Well, let's not get crazy," Brynn said, holding up a hand. "Have you tried Peanutbutter McCrunchalot?"

She laughed. "Gonna add that to the list."

"Someone is extra complimentary all of a sudden," Marigold said around a sip of wine.

Alexis sighed and sat back. Marigold was simply never going to let her fully off the hook, and it was tiring at best, frustrating at worst, and now that she'd had two glasses of wine, a fabulous dinner, and was feeling relatively comfortable, she went for it. "Let me explain something that I think requires clarification. I love food. I root for food. I always want to walk away with a glowing review. But I also realize that I work, correction, *worked* in the entertainment industry. My readers pick up my column or open my Instagram not just to learn about a new restaurant, but to see how I'm going to dismantle the meal."

"That's fair," Aster said quietly. "They do show up for that."

"It reminds me of the Greeks," Brynn said thoughtfully. "Or public executions. Human nature is such an interesting dichotomy."

Marigold scoffed. "Well, I hate it." She gestured with her glass. "As I let the world know."

"I get it, Marigold. You're not a fan of mine. You remind me every chance you get."

"Just making sure we're all on the same page."

"Oh, we are," Alexis leveled back. "Would you like my sister's number? The two of you can get lunch and discuss all the ways I disappoint."

Marigold opened her mouth and closed it. Alexis got the feeling she didn't like the comparison. Marigold's posture shifted to defeat, and she suddenly found the contents of her glass intriguing before setting it aside entirely.

"I have dessert," Aster said loudly. But the mood had shifted, and recovery felt unattainable.

Alexis set her napkin on the table. "As nice as that sounds, I don't think I could eat another bite. Let me help you with—"

"Yes. Me, too," Marigold said, lifting her plate and Brynn's. "I'm the crasher. Let me get this."

The group cleared the table together, as Marigold scrubbed a stubborn pan. Once everything felt under control, Alexis stole the moment to exit.

"Thank you for your gracious invitation. It was a wonderful evening."

Brynn checked on the sleeping baby and linked her arm through Aster's, and they walked Alexis to the door. Marigold tossed her a wave, but her forehead showed creases indicative of stress or deep thought. It was hard to tell which. Alexis waved back, refusing to let her gaze linger. If she did that, the surge of electricity would move through her and it would take another hour to move past it. She refused to devote that kind of time to Marigold, who was never going to cut her an inch of slack. Decision reversal. *Avoid this woman at all costs. Wipe her from your brain. Move forward with your life and out of Homer's Bluff as soon as possible.* She would let her Airbnb host know of her impending departure.

It had been a strange and much needed respite from the harsh real world, but Alexis had a life waiting for her, and it was time she got back to it.

❖

"What in the world is wrong with you?" Aster asked once Alexis was gone. She regarded Marigold from the barstool across from the sink. Her tone was sincere, however, and her eyes earnest. "You were not yourself tonight, and you've been washing that same *clean* pan for at least ten minutes."

"I don't know," she said quietly.

Brynn joined them with a shake of her head. "The tension was so thick between the two of you. Are we not going to acknowledge the chemistry?"

"We can acknowledge it," Marigold said. "I don't think I could deny its existence if I wanted to, but the simple truth is that when I'm around Alexis, I'm likely to commit a felony. It's an urge I've never experienced, and I don't think there are too many romances built off the beginnings of violent crime."

"Please," Aster said. "You're the least violent person I know. Maybe you're misinterpreting your impulses, if you know what I mean."

"I agree," Brynn said. "Sometimes when the feelings are coming at us at such a high volume, our brains don't know how to handle them. A mislabeling. What we do know is that she affects you. It's honestly intriguing as hell to watch play out."

Marigold shook her head. "Whether or not I find her attractive, she's a ruiner of things. She has no soul. She's like Siri but with judgment."

"A tad harsh," Brynn said. "She works in a cutthroat industry, and I think she's figuring out that there are ramifications for playing the game too hard. Offer her some grace. We have."

Marigold glared. "You're too nice." She scrubbed away on that pan because it honestly felt good. All the while, she turned over the evening in her mind. She deflated. "Except that I want to be nice, too. It just always goes so wrong when I'm with her."

Aster turned to Brynn. "I think fireworks are fireworks, right?"

"Oh, definitely. I saw about eight different varieties tonight." She made an explosion gesture with her hand. "Bang. Pow. Fireworks are fireworks."

Marigold pinched the bridge of her nose. "You're talking in couple code. I'm annoyed and envious. A decoder ring, please." She looked around the kitchen.

Brynn took the lead. "I think what we're saying here is if you can transfer that off-the-chart anger into passion for your subject, you're going to have quite the bonfire on your hands."

"So many metaphors. My brain hurts." But at the same time, this all sounded familiar, and she combed her memory for the words. Finally, she snapped her fingers. "The opposite of love isn't hate. It's apathy. A quote from Dad."

The room went silent as the words shimmered in the air. "I need to write that down," Brynn said.

Aster nodded, marveling. "Go, Dad. He's entirely right. He just said it better than we did."

"I don't know. The fireworks thing was pretty good, too," Marigold said. She pursed her lips as she considered how to put all of this together to help her cause. Step one was to figure out her next move. What would she do if this was anyone but Alexis? "I should probably apologize. She seemed to deflate when she heard about what her sister said in the press. And then I went and made her feel even worse about herself."

"Eve told me she's staying on Wesco Loop. The little green house with the geraniums growing from the barrels?"

"Take her some doughnuts," Aster said, grinning. Her eyes danced and her shoulders scrunched in an uncharacteristic show of excitement. "I have to say, I don't know if it's because it was my restaurant that sparked all of this, but I'm fully invested. So is Cara. It was her birthday that brought you two together."

"This is the best soap opera," Brynn mused.

Aster nodded and dropped her voice to the dramatic. "Will they find forever love or wind up in criminal court? Tune in tomorrow."

Marigold eyed her kid sister. "You're enjoying this way more than I ever would have predicted. Have you been hanging out with Violet?"

"I really should be. She will eat this up." Aster put a note in her phone, probably to loop Violet in. Perfect. Arm the one person she spent most of her days with.

Marigold circled around the one piece of this thing that really tugged at her. As much as she didn't care for Alexis, she truly disliked that Aspen had been so awful to her. She'd seen the air fall straight out of Alexis's sails, and it had rattled something primal in Marigold. Why did she hate it when other people were assholes to Alexis, but she was perfectly happy to be on the attack herself?

Marigold raised her gaze, deciding the pan was, at last, clean. "I'll take her the doughnuts."

Brynn wrapped an arm around Aster from behind. "Did you hear that?" Excitement rained down. "Tomorrow's show is an apology episode."

"And do you know what apologies lead to?" Aster asked.

"Tell me."

She stole a look at their sleeping child and switched to a whisper. "Firework sex."

Brynn gasped playfully. Seriously, these two. "There's nothing better. Why do you think I pick fights with you every so often?"

"Like I didn't know that," Aster deadpanned.

Marigold dried her hands hurriedly. "Okay, that's my cue to go before it happens here and now. You two are gems for letting me eat your food and fight with your houseguest. Let's do it again real, real soon." She quickly kissed Aster's cheek, then Brynn's, and blew a kiss to her snoozing niece.

Well, that was certainly a night she wouldn't soon forget. She chewed the inside of her cheek as she drove home, only her car didn't quite make it there. Nope. It drove, to her own surprise, straight to Wesco Loop and a little green house with geraniums out front.

Chapter Ten

Alexis's Airbnb host called himself by his first and last name in most every document he'd left for her. Barney Hershel, while hospitable and informative, had also left Alexis a strict to-do list to keep the property picture-perfect. "Barney Hershel would like you to take out the trash," Alexis said quietly to herself as she tilted the can onto its back wheels. "Barney Hershel would prefer you not leave the can on the curb too long after pickup." Acting as a responsible renter, Alexis dragged the big green can onto the curb just in time for a pair of headlights to hit, making her squint and step back. Had the trash collectors detected the can and shot over? That would be too much. Maybe it was Barney Hershel himself checking up on her. She waited for the reveal.

The white car with the Pink Panther hanging from the rearview paused in front of her. Marigold leaned out the open window. *Well, wonder of small town wonders.* The streetlamp caught the blue of her eyes. She was a fantasy. Her curls were unruly and wild, likely from driving with the windows down. She had a desperate look on her face, and Alexis was struck by the perfectly unexpected image in front of her.

"Do you have a minute?" Marigold asked. She was nervous but also seemed to need Alexis to say yes.

Alexis glanced at the trash can and back again. "Just freed up, actually."

Marigold pursed her lips, mirroring the swirling uneasiness Alexis wrestled with. She pulled into the driveway and stepped out of the car. For an extended moment that left Alexis in suspense, she didn't speak. Instead, she seemed to be explaining something silently to the grass, gestures and all. Finally, her eyes found Alexis and held on. They were absurd in their beauty, those eyes. "I wanted to make sure you were okay. That's the thesis statement."

Alexis didn't hesitate. "I am." She always was. That was just her. There were big blows and little blows. She took 'em on the chin and kept going.

"You know you don't have to be. Strong." She held out an arm and let it drop as if she was desperate to get through but didn't know how. If only Marigold knew that no one got through. By design. She evicted any vulnerable tendency the second one showed up. Weakness was for the uninspired and often left you burned. "At least not with me." Marigold blinked rapidly and scurried to correct her meaning. "I just mean we barely know each other. Nothing to lose. That's all." She touched her chest just above the soft swell of her breasts. "I promise I'm not here to be mean again. I'm hanging up my boxing gloves."

"That would be nice." Alexis nodded. "Except I'm really fine. In fact—"

"What if we got to know each other? Novel thought." A beat. Another. "But what if?"

"What?" Alexis never would have predicted the question and had no idea how to answer it. "Why would we ever do that?" She hadn't intended the words to come laced with doubt. She held up a reconciliatory hand. "Let me back up. Can I ask what brought this on?"

Several seconds of silence crept by. Marigold was policing every word that came out of her mouth. "I guess I'm doing this. Okay." A slow exhale as if gearing up for battle. She refocused on Alexis. "I'm really attracted to you." She nodded once, as if the mission was complete. Battle won.

Alexis tilted her head. She'd guessed as much but never thought she'd hear the words flow from Marigold's especially kissable lips. Too tempting for their own good. She softened. "I think you're beautiful. There's my half of the confession. But the reality of the situation is—"

"We drive each other up the wall."

"There's that. It's a factor."

Marigold tilted her head and held direct eye contact. Their chemistry distracted. Alexis felt it close to bubbling over, a pot they couldn't seem to keep the lid on. "No one brings out my emotions to the extent you do," Marigold confessed. "I have all of these big feelings that I can't seem to grab hold of"—she shifted her weight from one foot to the other—"but what if they were good big feelings? I can't help but think—"

"That we might be something underneath all the ire." The concept was intimidating and alluring at the same time. They'd be dynamite without their clothes on. But what about out of the bedroom? She couldn't quite think past the physical because it found a way to overwhelm everything else. She felt it all the way to her fingertips.

Marigold shook her head slowly as if working a puzzle. "It sounds ludicrous given our history."

"The little matter of you seeking to destroy my life and career."

"After you took down my little sister."

"Right, so…"

Marigold raised a finger. "What if we treated it as an experiment?"

"Hmm." Alexis tapped her lips, her face warm even while battling the chilly weather. Where was this going and why was she so tingly? She was too purposeful a person to tingle. Yet here she was, tingling like a fourteen-year-old at a school dance. "Tell me more."

Marigold took a step forward, and Alexis felt every inch of their new proximity. "We spend a little time together and find out if we have any common ground beyond…"

"Impressive kissing compatibility."

Whether absently or on purpose, Marigold's fingertips brushed her lips as if in memory. The action brought on a surprising ache low in Alexis's body that she found unfamiliar and insistent. The thought of those lips pressed to hers, moving against them or other parts of her body made her take a literal step back to regroup. She needed her bearings for this conversation, but her knees were shaking. Unhelpful. Marigold was right about the strong reactions they brought out in each other. She could admit that part as she stood smack in the middle of an exhibit A moment.

"Are you okay?" Marigold asked, reaching as if to steady Alexis from feet away.

"Of course. I told you. I'm fine."

"I get it. I was just trying to—"

"I know." A break in the action. The streetlight along the sidewalk flickered twice like a wink. "I think…yes. Let's do it."

"It?" Marigold blinked, lost to a daydream, perhaps.

"Spend time together."

"Right. God, I didn't mean…" She held up both palms, a signal fired to stop herself. "That would be nice. This is good. I think it's good. Surprising. Yeah. Okay."

"Take it easy."

"I'm on easy street over here. I don't know where you are."

"It feels a little like an alternate reality."

That earned a laugh, which neutralized the tension. "But we could probably use a few parameters."

"Should I have my attorneys draw up a contract?" She added a smile, but Marigold wasn't grinning with her.

"I don't think we have to go that far." She eased a strand of curly blond hair behind her right ear. "Let's keep it PG. I don't want all of this"—she gestured to the empty space between them—"to cloud my judgment."

"So no more surprise kissing." Alexis enjoyed the way Marigold's lips parted slightly at the mention. *Same, Marigold. Same.*

"Right. No kissing."

"No sex, obviously." She'd only said it to greedily see Marigold's reaction. She was gifted a visible swallow. The side effect was that it also did things to Alexis and her already uncomfortable lower half. Now she was imagining walking Marigold backward into the bedroom inside Barney Hershel's little green house, anticipation prickling her skin.

"No. No sex. We agree on that."

"If you say so. Personally, I think it might be a nice way to—"

"No. Uh-uh. You cannot tempt me. That's a rule, too."

"So many rules. Are you like that in the bedroom, too? Do you like to—"

"Stop that."

Alexis sighed, produced her phone, and handed it to Marigold. "In the name of science, can I get your number?"

Marigold softened, though the pulse at the base of her neck continued to thrum. "Anything for a noble cause." She typed quickly into the phone and returned it. "Message me when you're free." She returned to the driver's side door before hesitating and spinning back. "I'm really sorry your sister wasn't kind. Your family should be there for you, thick and thin."

"Oh. Thank you." She wasn't sure anyone had ever expressed anything similar on her behalf. The words landed and melted over her. Marigold only made it halfway down the street before Alexis placed the call.

"Hello?" the familiar voice said in greeting.

"Lunch tomorrow?"

"You're serious?" A short laugh. "You don't waste any time."

"Who am I to stand in the way of scientific discovery?"

"You're on."

❖

Wow. When Alexis Wakefield walked in a room, people noticed her. Marigold wasn't sure she'd ever witnessed anything similar. And not quick glances to see who'd arrived on the scene, but full-on stares that followed her progress and the gentle sway of her hips as she walked by. The woman came with a brand of glamour that couldn't be taught. She had presence, beauty, and poise. Marigold was reminded again of all those things when Alexis arrived at Kip's Diner, and fifteen to twenty guests swiveled to gape. Marigold happened to be one of them, and that made her a little uneasy. Was she out of her depth with this mission? What kind of make-believe was she playing? She needed to find a way to silence the overt captivation if she had any hope of figuring her and Alexis out.

Alexis, wearing a black sweater and a rose gold pendant necklace, scanned the room and glided her way. A flicker of concern crossed her features as she slid into the red booth across from Marigold. "You're already here. I thought I'd be first."

"We said we'd meet at noon and it's twelve fifteen."

"Right. Who arrives at the agreed upon time? Twenty minutes is standard."

"Twenty minutes is rude. I was here at eleven fifty-five. Maybe even eleven fifty-four."

Alexis seemed perplexed and then surrendered with a deflating of her shoulders. "This place is so different. I keep forgetting we're not in Kansas anymore." She opened her menu.

"No. Actually we are," Marigold pointed out. "We're literally in Kansas."

That pulled a wide smile. Alexis had a great one. Didn't matter. That's not why they were here. *Focus*. "You got me. How often can you employ that phrase and be literally corrected?"

"Most every day of my life."

"Got me again." Alexis looked skyward. "I'm going to quit while I'm behind. What's good here? Don't hold back." She eased a strand of dark hair behind her ear. "I came to play."

Marigold tapped her closed menu. "It's Monday, so that means the meatloaf special, but I'm a sucker for the turkey club with homemade chips. The BLT is pretty popular. One can always count on the double cheeseburger."

"What'll it be?" Ronnie asked, rolling up with a lot of extra energy. He might as well have been on roller skates. His morning energy lasted all day, like a caffeinated Woody from *Toy Story*. "Usual club-hold-the-tomato for you, MG?"

"You got it. And can I get a side of extra ranch for the chips?"

"Done-zo. And for you, Companion of Marigold?"

Alexis raised an eyebrow but pressed on. "Give me the greasy double cheeseburger and fries. Oh, and your spicy ketchup."

"Comin' up in about four songs on the radio."

Marigold was honestly taken aback. Alexis didn't seem the type to get messy at lunch. "I was predicting a chicken Caesar before you got here."

Alexis frowned. "Who comes to a diner and orders a salad? Show me to this person so I can try to get through to them. We can call people together for an intervention." She sat back against the padded booth. "I think we just stumbled upon your first mischaracterization of me. I love food. I will dive right in every time."

Marigold turned this over in her brain. "I guess that actually makes sense." She sipped her cherry soda. "How did you wind up a famous snarky food critic?"

"Right. That." Alexis mulled over the question. "I honestly thought I'd take Aster's route. Open up my own restaurant in Los Angeles, and all the powerful Hollywood types would fight for a reservation."

"But?"

"I wasn't as good a chef as I wanted to be in the end. But beyond that, my own restaurant meant that I'd be stuck in one spot, married to a menu and a style." She shrugged. "My palate is adventurous, and I wanted to get out there and experience all types of foods and preparations. I didn't like the idea of being tied to one building."

"Does that mean you travel a lot?"

"Short trips here and there. But I enjoy traveling." She took a sip from the iced water in front of her just as the sun slanted in over her deep blue eyes. Marigold glanced away. It nearly hurt to look at Alexis. Likely a side effect of her own guilt for objectifying a woman she barely knew. "But my home base is San Fran. Have you always lived in, uh, Homer's Bluff?" She smothered a smile.

"You say the words as if they're comical." Her defenses peeked out, but she reminded herself of the facts. She didn't entirely disagree with the implied jab, so why was she holding Alexis to a standard that didn't exist? She issued herself a loosen-up directive and did.

"You have to admit that the name's a little, I don't know, silly sounding."

Marigold nodded. "Here's the problem. It's not silly enough to sound quaint. Aster always says that if you're going to name a small town, make it count. Do you know there's a Dreamer's Bay out east? A Tanner Peak out west? Why couldn't we have gotten one of those names? Homer's Bluff is fine, but not nearly as charming as it could be and, thereby, forgettable." She held up a finger. "But only we can make fun of it. You can't. That's a total rule."

"Noted. I think you've hit the nail on the head. But I will say this. Those TV movies seem to be based on at least a kernel of truth. I wouldn't have guessed that until visiting here. There's a town square, for fuck's sake. In this day and age, that's surreal. Pardon my language."

Marigold waved her off. "Speaking of here, that brings us to the big question. How long are you staying?" She folded her hands on the table. "That particular detail impacts the experiment, wouldn't you say?"

She shrugged one shoulder. "I'm not on a timeline. I don't have a job. I'm on the run from the public eye."

"I forget that I'm looking at a public scandal of my own making."

Alexis held up a challenging finger. "Hey, we both played a part. Don't go stealing all the credit." They shared a smile, because how did they even get here? To this very moment. On a date. Drawn together by a series of events stemming back to one evening.

Ronnie arrived with their food and grinned. "You're in for a treat.

Thomasina's on the grill, and she rocks a good burger." He slid the plates in front of them. "Gonna have to order me one after the lunch rush dies down. Your fault," he whispered to Alexis with a wink. Then he was gone, and Marigold had the distinct honor of watching pristine, designer-clad Alexis Westlake pick up her juicy double cheeseburger and get to work. There was savoring. Studying. And finally, melting in sweet surrender. There were several points in their meal where she outright paused, placed a palm flat on the table, and closed her eyes.

"Thomasina should adopt me. This kind of food makes me happy. Back to basics on Monday morning. Nothing pretentious or heavy-handed. Just a good old-fashioned cheeseburger with the works." She smiled—correction, *glowed*—and sat back to bask. "Thank you for suggesting this place, Begonia."

"Well, we only have about four full service restaurants. But I'm glad you liked it." Before today, she wouldn't have imagined that Alexis was someone who could enjoy a quick and messy meal at a diner. In her version, Alexis would have balked and turned her nose up at their baskets of fried food. How surprising that the opposite had occurred, giving her something to learn from. Maybe she'd made other false assumptions about Alexis. It wasn't fair, and she would work to undo them until she knew better.

When the bill came, Alexis slid her credit card to Ronnie with purpose and held up a hand when Marigold attempted the same. "On me. Please." She acquiesced and tried not to show how important it made her feel. It did, though. Truly.

"Thank you."

They shared a quiet exchange of eye contact that made Marigold's limbs go numb. She'd never seen a more attractive woman, and in that moment, Alexis's beauty reached a whole new level. *Just look at her over there.* She was relaxed, happy, and in no hurry to get out of there. The combination more than worked for her. "Do you ever wear, I don't know, joggers and a T-shirt to go and grab a jug of milk?"

Alexis nodded. "I do. I'm also a runner. I go two to three times a week." She gestured with a tilt of her head. "The park on the outskirts of town has a few impressive trails. It's gorgeous. Want to come with me sometime?"

The idea of Alexis in athletic wear that clung, and a thin sheen of sweat beaded across her skin, almost caused Marigold to short-circuit. She dug her nails into her palm to regroup. "Hard no. I don't run. The athletic genes went to Violet and Sage. I'm woefully uncoordinated."

"The great thing about running is there is no defense." She leaned in with a challenging gleam in her eye. "Could be fun. Just you against the world."

"Us," Marigold said, then nearly choked on the words once she heard them out loud. "I meant that there would be two of us running, so theoretically, we'd fight off the nonexistent defense as a team. A duo. Like in comic books."

"You're at your best when you get red and flustered." Alexis tapped the table as Marigold attempted to recover. The compliment had danced and shimmied its way down her spine. "Not that I want to, but I better let you get back to work."

"Right," Marigold said, joining Alexis so they could walk out together. "Violet would probably like her own lunch break."

"I haven't met her yet. I give it another forty-eight hours. The town is only two feet wide." They paused in the parking lot, the impending parting ways hanging sadly across Marigold's shoulders. That was another surprise to note. Alexis leaned in and kissed her cheek in a move that seemed so natural that it left Marigold staggered. "Take care, MG. Isn't that what all the cool kids call you?" Alexis asked, walking backward down the sidewalk looking like a candy bar Marigold wanted to unwrap…slowly. She was so out of Marigold's league that it was absurd.

"A nickname, yeah. What's yours?"

Alexis paused, looked skyward, and shook her head. "I don't think I have any of those."

"That sounds like a challenge. Bye, Lexi." Alexis wrinkled her nose. It didn't fit. "I'll keep trying!" she called.

"Do!" Alexis yelled back.

Walking to her car alone, Marigold realized that her cheeks ached from all the smiling she'd done. She touched them, reliving the highlights of the conversation. It had been a fun lunch, and shockingly, they hadn't infuriated each other once. No one slung an insult. Neither had walked out. Marigold couldn't help but wonder: What would have happened if the two of them had met under different circumstances?

Would she have offered to buy Alexis a drink? Would Alexis have noticed her in a crowded bar? Her romantic fantasies had never come with much conflict, which was maybe why their fiery dynamic felt so foreign. Love on a straightforward path sounded awesome, but maybe there were other routes to romance that she shouldn't count out.

"Where are you right now?" Violet asked later that afternoon as Marigold paused mid-shelf restock. She held a purple kitten piggy bank in each hand as she stared off into the distance. "One of your fictional daydreams?"

She smiled, reanimated, and floated back. "No. This one was actually quite real, thank you very much. I think I'm ready to tell you all about it."

Violet's dark eyes flared with interest, and she leaned her chin in both hands from behind the checkout counter. "Well, raindrop my roses. Storytime is my most favorite thing."

Marigold started at the beginning of her and Alexis, including the portions Violet already knew. This time she put it all out there, peppering the details with the *feelings* she hadn't been as forthcoming about.

"Wow. There's so much to unpack. Where does a girl start?" She straightened and regrouped. "So, you've been reliving that kiss over and over?"

"Against my will. That's what she does to me. A complete mind and body takeover, until I'm fully...consumed."

"Hot damn. I want to be fully consumed." Violet fanned herself. "It sounds like the new goal is to channel the fireworks for good rather than the acrimonious."

"Exactly that. It's lofty, but at lunch today? After the first few minutes, it was like we settled into a comfortable-slash-*awesome* rhythm. We're different enough to make things interesting, but I found out that Alexis values the simple things in life just like me. You should have seen the joy she found in this greasy cheeseburger at Kip's. And you should have seen her eating it." Marigold slunk to the ground.

Violet laughed. "Ooh la la. How badly did you wish you were that burger?"

She covered her eyes. "Okay, yeah. I can't lie to you. I wanted to take her home then and there. You're like my human truth serum, which is why I've avoided telling you all this. When it's just you and me, I can't be anything but honest."

Violet softened. "You do the same for me. Grateful for you, ya know?"

Since losing their mother, Marigold made sure to treasure each one of her family members and never take for granted the love and happiness they brought into her life. Violet, though? She was a standout. Marigold's ride or die, the closest person to her on planet Earth. "I'm grateful right back and would raise the money to buy you the planet Mars if you asked." A pause. She'd been going on about her own issues for the better part of forty-five minutes, but her sister had been notably quiet about her own life's happenings. "How have you been these days?"

Violet offered an anchored smile. "Ethan's been a handful, but it's his age. I read about it. His brain is growing rapidly right now, and he's in that I-can-do-everything-for-myself mode which results in standoffs between the two of us, most often before preschool." Her nephew was the sweetest boy, but he was definitely testing the fences to see if they would hold. Five going on sixteen. "It's wearing on me, I think. I don't have the same energy I used to. Frustrating."

Marigold laughed. "I think that means we're officially getting old. Though I do have two years before I'm you."

"Way to flaunt it."

"I would be happy to take him off your hands a bit more. We could go to the park. See some movies."

"That'd be great, actually. I'd welcome the help."

"Done. Me and Ethan are going to paint the town." She dropped her tone. "I'll make sure it's washable." A happy thought struck. "That would also give you and your cute boyfriend more time to make out on the couch like randy teenagers."

Violet brightened. "Yes, that would be amazing."

"Consider it done."

Violet was a single parent, and with Ethan's asshole father pretty close to absent, she didn't get a ton of help. Marigold could be that, fill in the gaps their mother would have normally handled, and offer Violet more of a break. She could choose a specific night of the week, though she'd need to work around check-ins with her dad and helping

Brynn with Cara while Aster was at the restaurant during the week. Her calendar was overflowing, but it was important work, keeping this family afloat. Someone had to do it, and there was no one else with an entirely flexible schedule. Sign her up. She'd always been the helper type, and now she had an even more important call to action.

CHAPTER ELEVEN

It was downright frigid, considering that it was only October. Kansas was serious about its weather, something Alexis never would have expected. As tough as her morning run made her feel, it didn't excuse her from a few overt shivers as she walked the rest of the route back to her little green home away from home. She'd just started her poststretch routine, using the front step for tension, when her phone rang. She glanced down. Tatum. A spark of excitement sprang.

"Hey, Tatum."

"Alexis. You picked up. I wasn't sure you would."

"Well, I'm not dead." She rolled her shoulders forward and then back.

"Of course not. But…where are you? Your socials have gone dead, and no one's heard a thing."

She nodded. "Right. Well, I think I had some soul-searching to do. I needed some space to clear my head and regroup."

"Fair. You want to grab a cappuccino? Maybe we could brainstorm some next steps. Obviously, I'd love to bring you back to the paper someday, but the temperature needs to be right."

Tatum knew the drill just as clearly as Alexis did. When someone with a platform was canceled, it was essentially a long-form time-out. There was always the potential to rise from the ashes, but rule number one was that enough time had to go by. Everything was apparently forgivable with the flipping of the calendar pages. People loved a good redemption story.

"I'm in Nowhere, Kansas."

Tatum took her time with that one. "Right. Okay. Why?"

"I ask myself that question daily. Scene of the crime. No chance my sister would show up. It was also the first place I've visited in a long time that felt completely, I don't know, peaceful. And I needed peace."

"Let's be honest, are you there to tell off that woman on the video?"

"No. In fact, we're kind of dating."

Another long pause. "I can't tell if you're joking because I have no way of seeing your face. Alexis, what the fuck is going on?"

The endorphins from her run still fired, acting as chemical courage to just put it all out there. "I'm not joking. We really hated each other. Then we were kissing. Now we're doing a lot of eating and talking and it's a whole scientific thing. Stay tuned, sweetheart. My life is more than weird right now, but I'm not sure I mind."

"Who even are you?" Tatum said with a laugh of disbelief. "But you sound happy, which I did not predict. You're well?" There was a skepticism in her voice and a sidecar of concern.

"It's hard to believe even for me, but I am. Uncharted territory. I'm riding the spontaneous wave."

"Well." She could almost hear Tatum searching for words. "That's *really good* to hear. Hit me up when you're back, and maybe we can grab that cap."

"You're on, pal."

Though Carrot had shown himself to not be a running companion and thereby stayed home, he did enjoy joining her for her cooldowns. She opened the front door and let him scamper around, masquerading as a dog who'd just completed a long run and now basked in the afterglow when he'd likely just scored a forty-five-minute snooze.

Her muscles tugged with that pain of accomplishment. She touched the back of her neck, feeling strong and proud. Afterglow. The word now took her places and helped keep her warm. Her lazy thoughts ambled right to where they always seemed to these days. She imagined Marigold turning to her just as the sunlight slanted across her eyes, highlighting their hue and the vibrancy behind them. In fact, she had an impulsive thought for how she might spend the late morning.

An hour later, she found herself walking into what could only be described as a lavender explosion. Marigold hadn't been lying. The Lavender House sold every product one could shove lavender into or onto or around. The one-room store located in what appeared from the outside to be a two-story log cabin smelled amazingly of soft lavender. It boasted lots of natural light from the front-facing windows. While the outside made her want a stack of buttery pancakes, the inside made her long for a luxurious massage. A pretty brunette brightened when she saw Alexis approach. A little bit Marigold in the mouth and nose, but a little bit not everywhere else. The older sister.

"You must be Violet."

The woman paused, giving nothing away. It was possible she hated Alexis. If she'd learned anything, it was that the Lavenders were a tight bunch and fiercely loyal. "And you're Alexis Wakefield. Oh, I've heard all about you."

Alexis arched a tentative brow. "That could go a lot of ways."

"Oh, it does. But I'm most interested in your take on my sister." She held up a clarifying finger. "Marigold."

"Winsome smile. Feisty when she believes in her cause."

"Convenient in bathrooms?"

Oh damn. The older sister didn't mess around. That one had her grappling. "To be clear, *she* kissed *me*," were the juvenile words she went with, forcing a wince. "Not that I wasn't a willing participant." Why did it feel like she was sitting across from the principal in her office? She'd been in the store under two minutes and had already been called out. Violet was a force. *Oh no.* A force who was reaching for a nearby shelf to steady herself before sinking to her knees. Alexis reached for her. "Whoa. Are you—" But Violet's eyes were rolling back and then she was out. Unconscious. *Oh God.* Luckily, Alexis had been able to cradle the back of her head the rest of the way down, crushing her own knuckles between Violet and the wooden shelf in the process. She gently eased Violet to rest on the carpet as her mind scurried to remember her CPR training from when she used to babysit as a teenager. "Violet, can you hear me?" No response. She made sure she was breathing. Thank God, she was. She also had a pulse. More relief. She smoothed the hair across Violet's forehead. "You're going to be okay," she said as she fished for her phone, which of course had to have fallen to the bottom of her bag.

"I need medical assistance at The Lavender House. I don't know the address." She looked around the space quickly as if there would be a neon sign broadcasting that information. It was not to be. Meanwhile,

Violet's eyelids fluttered. "Oh God. There you are." That was a good sign. "Hey. Hey. Violet. Come back to me." She touched her cheek, and Violet's eyes opened fully. "You're just fine. You went over."

"Oh no," she said, looking around. She grabbed a fistful of the fabric of Alexis's pants, clearly panicked.

"No. It's okay. I promise. I have you."

The calm voice on the other end of the 911 call continued to ask her questions as Violet floated back to them more and more. Alexis did her best to answer, now holding tightly to Violet's hand. "She's awake now. Yes."

"You don't have to call anyone," Violet said. "I'm never out for more than a minute or two."

"We do," Alexis mouthed to her. "Wait. So this has happened before?" she asked, realizing the implication. "No, she didn't strike anything before losing consciousness."

Violet pushed herself into a seated position. "A couple times. Not a big deal. I probably need more sleep."

"Yes, breathing normally."

"Cancel. Cancel." Violet took the phone. "Hi, is this Helen or Mary? Mary, hi. It's Violet Lavender. I fainted, but I'm fine." Her voice was weak, but she was at least making sense. "Tell Kevin and the gang that they don't need to race over here. I probably need some sugar."

Everyone sure did know everyone around here. It was remarkable how things worked.

"Right. No, I appreciate that. Say hi to your mom for me. Tell her we got that three-wick candle in last week. Lavender orange." A pause. "I promise that I'm fine. Talk to you soon. Mm-hmm. Bye."

When she clicked off the call, the room went quiet, and they regrouped, catching their breath.

"I'm so sorry that happened," Violet said finally with a nervous laugh. "Thank you for helping me."

"Do you think you can stand?" She offered Violet a hand, which was when she noticed that her own was trembling. Not only that, but her heart rate danced in the stratosphere. "That was really frightening. I don't think I've ever seen someone pass out while I was in the middle of talking to them."

"Can we not mention this to Marigold? As in absolutely don't. I implore you."

"Why would we not?" she asked delicately. She didn't know this woman, but it seemed like an odd request.

"Because then it will become a *thing*. And she's such a worrier, you know? She'd take it upon herself to follow me around all day just in case it happens again. Why do that to her?"

"Well. Maybe it's good to have people worry about you in this case. You said it's happened before." Part of Alexis felt like she was crossing a boundary into territory that wasn't hers, but at the same time, the here and now *was*. They'd just experienced this dramatic moment together. Alone. There was no one else who could say these words, especially if Violet wasn't sharing the details with her family.

Violet exhaled slowly. "A couple of times. Yes." She looked around as if trying to remember where she left something valuable. "I'm going to make an appointment. I probably need an iron supplement or something. My diet could really be better." But the look on her face contradicted her nonchalance.

Alexis swallowed. "Please let me know if there's anything I can do to help. That sounds like something people just say, but I mean it." She did, too, and surprised even herself. Something about her time in town had her open to connecting with others in a manner she wasn't accustomed to. It felt…nice.

"You could start by buying something lavender." A mischievous smile appeared. Violet was moving them purposefully away from the topic. "My sister would love it, too. She's especially fond of the honey-lavender soaps over there."

Alexis glanced over her shoulder, reluctant to move on to soap when she'd been on a 911 call just minutes before. "I'll take a look." A pause. "Is Marigold here?"

"She had an appointment."

"You're never going to believe this." Alexis knew the voice drifting from behind them. "You're not going to freaking buy it." Right on cue. Marigold. Alexis smiled and relaxed. She watched as Marigold arrived on the scene and completely took over with her energy, passion, and downright insistence that what she had to say was important.

"We're waiting," Violet said, folding her arms.

Marigold halted like she'd run into an imaginary door. Her eyes went wide. "Alexis is here."

"I noticed that, too," Violet said, moving around the counter as if she'd simply been there, normal as could be, the whole damn time. A sham.

Alexis offered a wave. "Don't let me get in the way of the big news."

Marigold held out her hands as if a big declaration was forthcoming. "I had my allergy test today for the itching, and we have a verdict. I'm allergic to lavender."

"You are not," Violet said. She covered her mouth with both hands. "Are you sure? What happens now?"

"It's a rare allergy, and I likely developed it over time. Contact dermatitis. The oils on my hands are what's causing the itching. I have some as-needed medication and a directive to wash my hands more often when handling anything with oil."

"You work at The Lavender House. Your last name is Lavender. And you're allergic to…lavender?" Alexis asked, smothering a smile.

"You have to just laugh," Marigold said, "because it sounds ludicrous. Yet it's my path in life."

"Only you, MG," Violet said.

Alexis shot a look to Violet, waiting on her to make the right move and bring her sister up to speed on all that had happened. Yet Violet was content to straighten the areas around the point-of-sale station.

Marigold seemed to note the interaction. "I take it you've met Violet."

"You would be correct. She doesn't take prisoners."

Marigold looped her arm through her sister's and smiled at her like she'd hung the moon. "Were you giving Alexis a hard time? That's okay. She deserves it. Don't hold back."

Alexis gasped and looked on coolly. "The nerve of these Lavenders." Then she eased things with a smile. "I had the afternoon free, so I thought I'd swing by and see where you work." She shrugged, feeling instantly like a shy seventh grader. "I hope that's okay."

"The tour commences now," Marigold said with a sweeping one-armed presentation. Behind her, Violet stared blankly at the surface of the counter. Alexis made a promise to herself to check in on her later, concerned about all she'd learned. For the time being, she followed an admittedly adorable Marigold and her honey-blond curls around The Lavender House.

"Comfort products over here. Socks, scarves, earmuffs, bedtime teas, teddy bears. On the far wall, you'll find the beauty hall of fame. Moisturizers, shampoos, collagen creams, lotions. Books are yonder."

"Yonder?" Their gazes connected. The smile that passed between them flickered with a hint of heat. For the first time, neither she nor Marigold looked away, allowing their attraction out to play for the first time. No one was hiding anything.

"Yonder," Marigold said, a hint quieter, and led the way.

Alexis sucked in a breath and dutifully followed. "What do you recommend? Do you have a favorite product?"

"Oh yes." Marigold paused in front of a shelf in a corner nook. "There has never been a softer blanket than this lavender infused godsend." She handed the blanket tied with purple twine to Alexis, who had to agree. It was in the top tier of soft blankets. "For you. On the house."

"Really?" She glanced down at her new treasure. "You sure? I don't mind paying."

"What's the point of running a store if you can't manage a freebie or two for the people of your choosing?"

That meant she'd been chosen. Impossible that something so innocuous seemed to matter so much to her. A sign of the new times. "Thank you."

Marigold tilted her head. They were secluded, sandwiched between the meeting of those shelves. "Look at Alexis Wakefield, suddenly all sincere and earnest. It looks really good on you."

"It happens once in a blue moon. Don't blink."

"I wouldn't dare." Marigold's eyes dipped down. They found Alexis's lips and lingered before moving back up. It was a delicious moment, and she wanted to live in it for so much longer than what she was afforded. "Should we get together soon?" Marigold didn't move a muscle.

"I have nothing but time on my hands. How about a run tomorrow?"

"A run? I'm pretty sure I'm supposed to have breakfast with Tillman." The corner of Marigold's mouth pulled in a partial smile.

"Do you always half smile when you lie?"

"Yes!" Violet yelled from the counter.

Alexis arched a brow. "I'm learning more every day. We can skip the run, but I want a rain check. I'm serious."

"Let's make it a lovely scenic walk with snacks, and you're on." Marigold's eyes danced when she negotiated. They flared when she was fired up in anger. But nothing compared to the way they darkened after she was kissed.

"I agree to the terms." Alexis wasn't a nervous person, but a fresh batch of butterflies swarmed her. She attempted to shrug it off and reclaim her calm, collected, in-control default. "Where should we meet?" she asked. Why did her voice sound weird? Syrupy and with less volume behind it. The way people spoke when they ended a sentence with the word *sweetie*. She was going soft!

Marigold relaxed, thoughtful. "There's a wooden footbridge just outside of town off Spyglass Road. Seven thirty a.m.? It's early, but I have to work at nine."

Alexis didn't hesitate. "Early works. I'll bring coffee."

"Then I'll bring bagels."

"The bridge, huh?" Violet said, attempting to make a point. "Wow."

"You refrain from wowing," Marigold called through the shelves of lavender riches.

Her answer came immediately. "I'm not sure you have jurisdiction over uttered phrases."

"I do, though. I checked the handbook."

"I wish *my* sister came with a handbook," Alexis said, perpetually amazed at the differences between the Lavender siblings' dynamic and the Wakefields'.

Marigold wilted with compassion. "Aspen seems complicated."

"No. She's pretty simple. Hell-bent on the world adoring her and willing to cut throats to make it happen. A typical narcissist with a lot of power."

Marigold gave her hand a squeeze. "That sounds terrifying."

The current of electricity that flowed between their hands seemed to shock both of them. Marigold pulled hers back quickly. "Probably not supposed to touch. Personality experiment and all."

"Let me guess. Handbook?" Alexis asked.

"Yeah," Marigold whispered. "Section nineteen. Don't ruin your chance to discover something that might actually…" But her words died.

"Might actually what?" Alexis asked, never needing the end of a sentence as much. "You have to finish. Section twenty-one."

Marigold swallowed. "Turn out to be pretty amazing."

A long silence enveloped them. The weight of the words coated everything. "Then I guess we better not fuck up the experiment."

"Oh, for God's sake, fuck it up!" Violet called. And then quieter. "Oh, hi, Mrs. Tuffs. I didn't see you sneak in. Nice weather today."

Alexis smothered a laugh, but Marigold didn't hold hers back. "Perfection," she mouthed.

Alexis gave her new blanket a squeeze "Thank you for this. I'll see you for the scenic bagel walk tomorrow."

"Don't be California late."

"News flash. It's not just California. Bye, MG."

"Bye, Lex Luthor."

Alexis turned back and arched a brow.

Marigold sighed. "I'm not feeling that one either. I'm not giving up."

"Whatever you say."

On her way out, Alexis passed Violet purposely and sent her an inquisitive look with a thumbs-up. A question. Violet confidentially passed her back a thumbs-up sign of her own, which was fine for the moment. But today had Alexis shouldering more questions than answers about what might be going on with Violet Lavender.

❖

"Do you remember the woman I kind of hated, and you made me make that pact about keeping an open mind?" Marigold asked.

Her dad studied her, taking in the question. Of course he remembered, but Marigold needed to set up the conversation properly. Their weekly dinners were proving helpful, and she figured she'd leverage his free advice while she had his full attention.

"Ah. Yup. The food woman who didn't like Aster's second-in-command."

"Yes, that's her."

He frowned. "Did she do something awful?"

"No. And I keep waiting for her to."

"Huh. After talking to Violet, I was hoping you two might bury the hatchet. Life's pretty short, you know."

"That's just it. I'm starting to wonder if she's not as awful as I thought." Marigold held up a hand in pause and finished her bite of spaghetti. Her mom's recipe, savory and amazing. "Jury is still out, but it's a theory I'm working with."

"Interesting. So, what's the plan?" He kept eating, waiting for her explanation. He was turning out to be the best listener.

"We're supposed to take a walk tomorrow, and that feels, I don't know, extra personal."

"It's just walkin'. No vows or commitment required, if I remember the act correctly." He took a pull from his beer. "I talked to a woman at the grocery store."

She froze, mid noodle twirl. Her head probably looked like a prairie dog as she popped to attention. "You did? Say more words."

"I don't know. You got in my head the other day, so I just said to her that the green beans looked better than usual."

"Okay. A little green bean small talk. I like it."

"She said, *Thank God*. And so I high-fived her."

Marigold nearly choked on her own tongue. "You did not high-five her. Dad."

He set down his beer with satisfaction. "Did so. And finished my shopping."

She swallowed any and all tips on flirting with strangers and instead celebrated his victory. "You are a rock star of the grocery aisle. But next time maybe just get her number." A pause. She eased up. "I suppose a high five is a great start, though."

He laughed. Actually out loud. Rare and wonderful to hear. She smiled right along with him, basking in this small victory. "I was just feeling brave and silly. Pretended I was Sage." He laughed again and shook his head sheepishly. "I don't have his dimples."

"You don't need 'em. You're a catch."

He gestured to the spaghetti with his fork. "This is good. It's been a while."

Grief circled and spun around her heart, giving it a generous squeeze.

She didn't think about things like her dad no longer getting to have his favorite spaghetti. "I like it, too. Takes me back to when I was a kid." She looked around the room. "It used to be so busy in here. Remember?" Echoes of the past surrounded them.

"Still is when the four of you get together. Look out."

"That part's true. And the littles. Three grand-Lavenders. Can you believe it?" She was the only one who'd yet to have a child, which was surreal. She'd always imagined she'd settle down young, raise her kids, and look forward to soccer Saturdays and putting cookies out for St. Nick. Yet it was still just her. "I think being the only one without a family has—"

"Made you think you're even cooler than the rest of us? Hardly." Sage. He'd popped in the back door and jumped right in. He sniffed and moved closer. "What is that? Tell me you made Mom's recipe, and I will fall to my knees and admit that you're cooler."

She grinned and folded her arms. "Get ready to bow down because I did."

"Grab a plate," her dad said. "Two Lavender kids."

Marigold tried not to bristle that her one-on-one had been disrupted by her little brother because that's just what Sage did.

"Am I joining some kind of party already in progress?" Violet stood in the doorway along with Aster, who held baby Cara.

Marigold turned to her father with wide eyes. "I think you summoned them."

He beamed. "Your mom did. The spaghetti is a Bat-Signal."

Aster crept in. "Sorry to just show up, but I'm off tonight and giving Brynn a baby break."

"And I was finishing up at the store and saw each of the cars go by." Violet shrugged. "Can't be left out. Why are we gathering?"

Marigold laughed. "I'm here to see Dad. Sage is here for food. Sounds like Aster's looking for a place to chill with the baby, and you have total FOMO, per usual. Caught up?"

"Yes. Thank you," Violet said, sliding into the chair across from their father.

"I can't believe you hooked us up with this spaghetti," Sage said from the stove, shoveling a meatball into his mouth like the good-looking barbarian that he was.

"I love not having to cook," Aster said, grabbing a bowl. "Total bonus to this unexpected venture." Sage bumped her with his fist as he passed.

"Speaking of hookups, you all should have seen Marigold Lavender batting her eyes at the store today."

"Offense and objection," Marigold said, holding up a finger. "I was being hospitable to a customer. There's a difference."

Violet scoffed. "You gave away the merchandise and fluffed your hair like a pretty peacock."

"Do I need to cover my ears?" Sage asked. "Feels like I should do that."

Their dad shook his head. "No. They only kissed the one time in the bathroom at Larry's."

All eyes flew to him. He jutted his chin in Marigold's direction. "Just so happens that we talk, okay?"

Sage held up his hands. "Pop's coming in hot with the info. That's new and notable."

Violet leaped in. "Speaking of new, I saw Dr. Stanley on my break this afternoon, and he wants to run some tests." She reached for the Parmesan.

More whirling. The room was getting whiplash. "What kind of tests?" Marigold asked, trying not to leap to any dramatic conclusion. The problem was that their family had been through a lot already, and her sensitivity showed it.

Violet nodded. "See? That look on your face was the exact reason I didn't want to mention anything."

"Of course you mention it," their dad said, finger to the table, his go-to gesture for when he meant business. "Always. What did Dr. Stanley say, and why did you go see him?"

"I've had a couple of fainting spells. Nothing too serious. But I thought we should get to the root cause."

"Define *a couple*," Sage said, setting his bowl on the counter and moving closer. His brows drew in. Aster stood frozen a few feet away, Cara blinking drowsily in her arms.

"Four times over the past two weeks."

The room went silent. Not again. "Vi," Aster said quietly.

"I'm sure it's just a vitamin deficiency. But my lymph nodes seem swollen, so we're gonna continue to explore what might be wrong." She turned to Marigold. "Please apologize to Alexis for me when you see her tomorrow."

"Alexis? Why would I do that?"

Violet looked apologetic. "It's possible she had to call 911 when I fainted in the store. I maybe made her promise not to mention it to you."

The room went silent before erupting.

"That's not okay," Sage said, raising his voice.

"We don't do that in this family," her father said on Sage's heels.

Meanwhile, the baby began to cry, and Aster raised a hand. "How would you feel if one of us pulled a stunt like that?"

Marigold was the only one sitting silent, frustrated with Violet and just as upset with Alexis. How could she have held back such important information?

"I get it," Violet said, "which is why when I saw all of you were together, I seized the opportunity to bring you up to speed. Now, I need to pick Ethan up from his grandparents' house." She turned to Marigold, "I'm sorry to bail early on your spaghetti."

"It's okay."

Violet kissed their father's cheek, turned, and addressed the room. "It's really no big deal. I promise."

Once she'd gone, the rest of them shared a moment.

"She has looked really tired lately," Sage said.

"True." Marigold shrugged. "I thought it was just that Ethan was running her ragged."

Her father, however, had gone pale.

"You okay, Dad?" Aster asked, bouncing Cara. But they all knew what he was thinking because the same thoughts trickled into the backs of their brains, too. This had a similar feel to what took their mom, and genetics could certainly be a factor in Violet's case.

"Whatever happens, we'll get through it together," Sage said, placing a hand on their dad's shoulder. Their father nodded and took his bowl to the sink.

"She's fine, Dad," Marigold said.

Because this was Violet, their fearless leader, their courageous big sister, and the closest thing to a mom that they had. She had to be okay, because the alternative was simply unthinkable.

He braced with either arm alongside the sink. "Yeah. You're probably right. But what if she's not?" he asked.

No one had the answer.

CHAPTER TWELVE

Alexis had woken up three times the night before. Her brain was too active for any kind of effective sleep. She was worried about her path, her trajectory in life, and her career. She had a little money put aside, but it would only last so long. She had a dream that night that she'd applied for a job at a library and was told by the librarian that nobody liked her and she should stop applying for jobs in general. Of course, her sister had money, but in no plausible scenario could she imagine asking her for financial help. Aspen would delight in either turning her down or waving the favor over her head until the end of time. In the meantime, she was aware of the ticking clock. She'd need a plan soon.

With Carrot snoring nearby, Alexis spent the second part of her night thinking of Marigold. Her smile. The annoying tenacity that never quit. The gentle heart underneath. A part of Alexis searched her brain for where all of it was going, and how she could have so many overwhelming feelings for one person. Thoughts of Marigold carried her to Violet and the scary episode at The Lavender House. No matter which way she came at it, she knew what she had to do. And that was loop Marigold in, which meant breaking her promise to Violet. There was no other possibility.

After banking maybe three hours of sleep, Alexis made the decision to tell Marigold on their walk. With two creamy coffees in a cardboard tray, she approached the footbridge where they'd agreed to meet. *Oh damn.* She paused when it came into view to simply take it in. The bridge was absolutely beautiful. Rustic and serene just like you'd see on the pages of a magazine or calendar. Sitting three-quarters of the way down was Marigold, holding a bakery box and dangling her feet above the river below.

"I'm on time," Alexis called out.

Marigold looked up and smiled in greeting but there was something else there, too. Wariness? Tolerance? She couldn't decide. Marigold patted the spot next to her for Alexis to sit.

"Bagel with three types of cream cheese because you're a food person and I didn't want to get it wrong."

A thoughtful touch. "I'll steal the plain."

"A purist."

She hadn't known Marigold for very long, but in that time she'd learned to recognize her most common facial expressions and their meanings. This one didn't bode well. "You seem like there's something on your mind."

Marigold nodded, her gaze trained on the water and the horizon. Alexis followed it to where the two met, ready to listen. "Violet told me about losing consciousness in the store. I'm struggling with why you didn't tell me. Kind of important. Huge, actually."

Alexis sighed. Beaten to the punch. It was her own damn fault. "Because she asked me not to say anything. I realize, having had time to push it around, that it wasn't my best call." Her voice sounded flippant. A habit. She had to work on that.

Marigold turned to her. "You can't do that. You flat can't. It's out of bounds. My family is everything to me."

The urgent look in her eyes coupled with the gentleness of her tone affected Alexis to her core. "I'm really sorry. It won't happen again. You have my promise."

Marigold took Alexis's hand in hers and turned it over, palm up. Alexis watched in captivation, barely able to breathe. "Here's the thing." With a delicate forefinger, Marigold traced the lines on her hand. It was a moment Alexis knew she'd never forget. "I want us to be open and honest about everything right down to how we're feeling." Her voice floated in the air as softly as the tracing of Alexis's hand. She was flooded with emotion, staggered, and overwhelmed. An uncomfortable lump ached in her throat like an arrow sign over all she felt. The moment was outside her comfort zone. Not many people treated her with such tenderness. In fact, she couldn't come up with a single name.

"Yeah. Me, too. I want the same." Her voice sounded hoarse and unrecognizable. She didn't care.

Marigold threaded their fingers, gave her hand a squeeze, and let go. Alexis instantly experienced loss. "I think our little experiment said no touching."

"Did it?" She passed Marigold a soft smile. She wasn't even aware she was capable of soft smiles. "Hard to remember." A pause. "Is there an update on Violet? Is she feeling better?"

"Thank you for asking." The sound of water lapping underscored. "She seems okay, but her doctor wants to run tests."

She stared off at the fluffy white clouds in the distance. "I'm glad she went in. She seems strong-willed. Like someone else I know."

A sideways smile from Marigold. "Can't imagine who that is. Eat your bagel. I want to see you get all thoughtful and contemplate each ingredient."

"I don't do that."

Marigold covered her mouth. "Oh, Alexis."

She liked the sound of her name on Marigold's lips.

"You don't have the vantage point that I do. You do, too. It's your reviewer face."

Alexis took a bite and chewed, very aware of Marigold watching her. "Decent bagel. Not gonna remember it in a month, but it serves its purpose in the moment. Enjoyable. B plus."

"We agree."

"What? Apparently, it's possible, after all. Jot that into your data log."

"Later. Right now, I want to sit here with you and enjoy my favorite spot a little longer." Alexis handed over a coffee. "Thank you."

"That means you come here a lot. If it's your favorite spot."

She nodded. "I've always been a dreamer. I sit here and get lost in all sorts of fantasies and—"

Alexis arched a brow.

"Not like that."

"Just checking."

"Well. *Mostly* not like that." Rose flamed her cheeks. "I think a lot of people grow out of their imagination. I'm an exception. I never did."

"What are these fantasies about?"

Marigold pulled her shoulders in. "Mostly about finding my

person. Spending evenings together. The things we say. The things she does. How much we love each other and pine away until we're reunited."

She'd never wanted to star in a fantasy more in her life. "You're a romantic."

"Self-admitted."

For a brief moment, Alexis allowed herself to acknowledge that she very much would like to be that person for Marigold in real life, realistic or not. Bring her coffee in the morning. Sit on bridges with her and eat warm breakfast in the sunshine. Watch her brighten every room she walked into and fight tirelessly to right every wrong. It didn't at all line up with the life she'd been leading in the slightest, and that part puzzled. Her day-to-day was fast-paced and seemingly shallow in this moment, so far removed from the authenticity of Homer's Bluff that it astounded. She attended parties where people air-kissed and discussed who wore the wrong designer to the event. Pretentious and even a little cutthroat. She hadn't realized it until recently, but she didn't have friends, she had colleagues. At the same time, she missed her old life. She wondered how this version of her would fit. When she did go home, could she bring a little of the peace she'd found here with her? She truly hoped so.

She turned to Marigold in a confession mode of her own. "I don't think I would characterize myself as a romantic. Maybe that's why my relationships haven't worked out."

"Have you had a lot of those?"

"Really? We're going there?"

Marigold clapped her hands once. "Full steam ahead. Seems like important information. For science and all."

"That's fair. Four actual girlfriends. Various hookups in between. One situationship." She wrinkled her nose. "I have regrets about several of those entries."

Marigold nodded, absorbing. "And a lot more experience than me. It makes sense. You're so beautiful that sometimes it hurts to look at you."

Alexis swiveled, processing this new information. Marigold really found her that attractive? She swam in the words an extra moment. By view of her family, the media, and the public, she was the also-ran to Aspen's God- and surgeon-given beauty. "Thank you."

"When you walked up in this"—with her finger, Marigold gestured at Alexis from head to toe, indicating her black running pants and white zip-up jacket—"I almost forgot that I was upset with you."

"And now I'm learning how to get out from under Marigold's fist. Valuable intel." They shared a smile. "Tell me about *your* dating history."

"Less exciting. A couple boyfriends when I was young and naive, then a really long dry spell until I realized why I wasn't into any of them."

"I bet that was an enlightening moment."

"You have no idea. It's been less than two years now since I came out."

"Really? That wasn't long ago."

"That's me. Still in the intro to lesbian class. I've been on maybe ten dates. Nothing serious ever manifested." She shook her head, staring out at the horizon. "But that's being gay in a small town."

"Did you ever think you'd get married and settle down with that Tillman guy?"

That pulled a laugh. "No. Our blip of a sex life was so awful, Alexis." She placed a hand on Alexis's leg for emphasis. The warmth took root and spread, causing Alexis's stomach to go weak and her limbs to tingle pleasantly. She tried not to let on, but she didn't want that hand to ever move. "He just didn't know it."

"He has a thing for you. It's sweet."

"Yes. But he knows better than to hold out hope. Smart guy. Big heart." She took her hand away and Alexis wanted to cry.

She sucked in a breath. "That's okay. And the relationship thing? You have plenty of life left to lead."

"I really just think I'm looking for *her*, though. My person. And I think she's out there."

Alexis nodded. "Hey, maybe you're having coffee and bagels with her right now." She tossed Marigold a sly smile from around her cup.

"See, I can't tell if you're being serious or not."

"Guess you'll have to put in the time." She looked around, taking in the protective way the trees framed the water. The blue morning sky enveloped it all like a blanket. "And it's beautiful up here. Perfect for sorting your thoughts. Or fantasizing, as you say."

"Dreaming. I don't know why, but it was important to me that you see it. If you're getting to know *me*, my heart, you almost have to start at this bridge." There was love in her eyes, and Alexis went soft.

"I want to know your heart," Alexis said without thinking.

"Good. Here we are." She kicked her head to the side. "Shall we walk?"

They did. They spent the next forty-five minutes walking the perimeter of town, swapping stories and stealing glances at each other like sixteen-year-olds. She loved the way Marigold paused her stories to search for the perfect word and was never in a rush to get there quickly. Her silence hung in the air until she was good and ready, a grin accompanying the correct adjective, verb, or noun once it was located.

"When was your first kiss?" Alexis asked, jealous of whoever had the honor.

"Thirteen, behind the cafeteria with Randall McDougall. He brought me a carnation the next day that I'm pretty sure he swiped from the funeral home his mother worked at."

"At least he showed ingenuity."

"Wasn't a great kisser, though."

"Then let's move on. Best kiss of your life?"

"I refuse to answer that one. What about you?"

"Same. I plead the Fifth." But now Alexis was thinking about kissing Marigold, and everything around them went fuzzy and unimportant. Her body hummed, and her skin prickled with sensitivity. She struggled to keep the conversation moving forward because she wanted to use her mouth for other things. Marigold was watching her with intensity. Did she know? Could she tell how much Alexis wanted her and that her need grew exponentially with each minute that passed?

"So, what's your assessment of our little experiment?" Marigold asked quietly.

"I'm tired of the rules." Alexis pressed Marigold up against a nearby oak and gave her the space of time to say no. The tension in the air hung thick, and heat flared. Instead, Marigold's tongue wet her bottom lip in anticipation, all the while her gaze trained on Alexis's mouth. She could hear the quiet sounds of their accelerated breathing. Could feel the slick fabric of Marigold's workout shirt beneath her fingertips. That tiny movement from Marigold, the touching of her tongue, flooded her system, making her forget to think. For the best. She tilted her head and leaned in, catching Marigold's mouth with hers. The rules were banished. And in that instant, everything else recessed—the sky, the ground beneath their feet, the sound of the birds going about their morning routine. It was only them. She was reminded just how perfectly they fit. She hadn't wanted to admit it that last time at Larry's and had written off their utter chemistry. Nothing but alcohol creating a fuzzy memory. But this kiss only confirmed it twofold. As Marigold's mouth moved over hers, exploring and seeking, Alexis was consumed. She spun uncontrollably out of herself, hovering somewhere near heaven. This had been worth waiting for. The kiss was different than their last, insistent yet soft. Marigold ran a hand up Alexis's arm to her jaw and cradled it, leaving a trail burning behind. Craving more, Alexis pressed herself closer, wishing she hadn't worn the outer zip-up. Too many layers between them. One long kiss and then another. A short one, then a long. She slowed their pace, trying to hang on to control. She pulled her mouth away to check in, only to have Marigold place a hand on the back of Alexis's head and pull her in for more. She swallowed a whimper when their mouths came together and ignored the fevered ache Marigold sent straight down her body. Marigold in command was a whole separate level of hot.

"That wasn't supposed to happen," Marigold said, but her hand was still on the back of Alexis's neck, her fingers threaded through Alexis's hair. Neither seemed to have any intention of moving back into her own space. "But it was too good to stop."

"Maybe we just wing it from here."

Marigold didn't say anything. Her gaze moved across Alexis's features. "Your eyes don't give much away. Today they did."

She swallowed. "You seem to have an outlying effect on me."

"But your mouth is my favorite. The most expressive part of your whole face. Sometimes you bite the inside of your cheek when you're working through a thought. You pucker your lips ever so slightly when you don't like the words that are said to you. But when a smile happens? It's important, because you don't hand those out to just anyone. Well, at least the real ones."

Alexis blinked, shocked that Marigold had noticed those subtle details about her, honored even.

She kissed her softly. "What's my mouth saying right now?"

"So many things it probably shouldn't."

"You're thinking too much," she said after another kiss.

"I have to agree. Because when I stopped, things got so much better."

"Can we think less in the future?"

Marigold smiled and nodded. Just as Alexis leaned in for more, a quiet alarm sounded. Apparently, Marigold had her hearing bells.

"That's me." Marigold straightened and reached into her back pocket. "I have to go. That's my half-hour warning for work. I have an alarm on my phone programmed, so even if I get distracted, I'm never late." She pointed at Alexis. "You are the biggest distraction I've ever met in my damn life."

Alexis's widened her eyes, aiming for pitiful. "We have to stop?"

"We do and we should. It's the *woods*."

"Mysterious and sexy."

"You cannot use my far-flung sense of romantic adventure to convince me to open the shop late and make out with you up against that tree." She paused, defeated. "You actually probably could, but I ask you not to try." A pause. "Dammit." She stepped back into Alexis's space, grabbed two fists of her jacket, and went in for a hungry kiss, walking her backward until she was pushed against that very tree. "I'm a responsible manager. Violet won't be in until midmorning. It's just me. I gotta be strong." She stepped back purposefully and sighed with deep regret.

"And people desperately need lavender products in the early morning hours?" Alexis loved the swollen quality of Marigold's lips. She'd done that. God, she'd happily kiss this woman into next week.

"Yeah. They really do. Vitally."

"Not convincing."

Marigold seemed to be drinking her in. "Your hair is so sexy after fingers have been run through it. I want to stand here and stare at you." She held up her hands. The dazed quality that had come over her since their kiss slowly began to evaporate. A travesty. The stolen moment dissolved back into life as scheduled. "I know a shortcut." Marigold pointed with her head. "I can show you."

Alexis studied her options, distracted by her body demanding something that she couldn't give it in this moment. Follow Marigold, or continue along the trail a few miles. "I think I need to work off a little energy after that, um, stolen moment," she said with a laugh. "A run might be best."

"Maybe I'll see you later," Marigold said, a veil of politeness descending. She hated it. She wanted the unencumbered Marigold, who'd led with her instinct, not her head.

"That would be great," Alexis said, seizing the same unexciting crutch. She held up a hand in farewell and left it there like a dad waving his daughter off to school. Cringe.

Five minutes into her run, panic arrived. She wasn't used to this level of vulnerability, or the feelings that still swirled without her damn permission. It felt like she was on board a runaway train and needed to figure out her strategy for leaping before it crashed.

"No, you don't," she said, dropping with her hands on her knees, out of breath, chest screaming. In the center of that well-worn path, she attempted to wrestle back control. "You're fine. It's just new." The sound of her own voice acted as a calming agent. "Just new," she said again, straightening. She pressed on. As she continued her run, she replayed every moment of that make-out session because there was no better thing to think about. The scorching memory loosened her muscles. Her heart. Her brain. Thoughts started to roll without obstacle. She systematically sorted through all the ways she could take back her career, reinvent herself, adopt a more respectable tone without losing readers, and highlight food in a whole new way. Alexis didn't want to call the morning's events an awakening, because how clichéd. But she went back to her Airbnb with renewed energy and excitement...about so many things. That kiss had lasted maybe a few minutes tops. But it had flipped her perspective on its head. Had she ever experienced a moment with such power before? Absolutely not. But she had a harness on things she'd only been able to grapple with just a day ago.

Excited, hopeful, motivated. She was all those things.

Alexis had a life to lead, and now, more than ever, she was excited to get to it.

❖

While country music wasn't Marigold's go-to genre, she had to appreciate its storytelling abilities. In the past three minutes, she'd listened to a man lose his mom, his girl, his dog, and his job and somehow manage to live life for what he called *the good stuff*. She sipped her beer, contemplating his perspective, and how he'd rhymed *try hard* with *die hard*. Just as perplexing as it was catchy.

"Okay, so what is going on with that food critic woman? What have you done to her?" Marigold's brother slid onto the barstool next to hers at Larry's. Happy hour was in full swing, and the crowds showed it. She and Sage often ran into each other there each Thursday evening after work when beer dropped to two dollars and Larry busted out the gourmet snack mix that Mabel Montgomery made in her kitchen and hand sold by the pound.

Marigold ignored the way her cheeks flamed at Sage's question because she knew *exactly* what she'd done to Alexis two days ago up against an unsuspecting, wholly innocent tree. She smiled against the rim of her pint glass, victorious vixen that she was. "I don't know what you're talking about."

"I saw her an hour ago at the mini-mart. She was buying a case of spring water, smiling at everyone she came in contact with. She even gave me a damn side hug. What the hell happened to her?"

Marigold was surprised to hear it. She wondered what had sparked the change, while secretly hoping that she knew. "Maybe she's just having a good week."

"Understatement. But hey, whatever works. It looks really good on her."

"Stop that right now." She whirled in her seat. "You're not allowed to find Alexis attractive."

"What? Because you do?" A pause as he signaled for a beer. And then, "And yes, I can, too."

"Sage, I swear to God."

"You gonna run tell Dad?"

She glared at him, feeling that same ire she did when they were kids and he'd take her iPod shuffle and mess up her perfect dreamy playlist. "I will pummel you. Tackle you in the parking lot."

"I believe you, too. But here's the trouble. I'm bigger than you now, so you'd go down like the pretty little flower you are." He was enjoying this way too much, messing with her on purpose. No woman held a candle to Tyler in Sage's mind—he was just trotting out his annoying little brother act.

"You kids need to be separated?" Larry asked. He was in the midst of cutting out photos of tomato plants. Did Larry have a dream board they didn't know about?

"No," they said in unison, as Marigold remembered her age and sucked it up. "So, she really did seem happy?"

"For sure. The energy was entirely different. Welcoming. Charming. *Good to see you, Sage!*" he said in his best impression of an overly friendly woman. "*The fruit here is so fresh.*"

Alexis shook her head. "She did not say that last part."

"No. I added it for effect. You get the point."

Marigold couldn't hide the proud grin. Part of her was terrified of the big feelings that seemed to smother every rational thought in her brain. The other part desperately wanted to dive in headfirst and see what trouble they could get into together.

"Darts later," Larry said to Marigold specifically, as he ambled by to serve a customer down the bar. That meant Alexis might be by. Larry was tipping her off.

"Does everyone know everything around here?" she called after him. He didn't turn back. Just shrugged the way Larry always did.

"They do. *We* do," Sage affirmed. "You gonna do it?"

"Do what? Play darts? Probably not."

"Go for it with the smokin' reviewer. What are you waiting for? You've been in a dating holding pattern forever. We all think so, and it's dumb."

"You *all*? What? Have you been having meetings?"

"Yeah, once we did."

"Shut up. Lies make a man ugly-age." A pause. "You actually have?" Then she realized that was exactly the kind of thing her close-knit family would do. Aster probably brought snacks. She deflated. "Great. I'm officially the spinster sister everyone thinks is going to die alone. But that's not me! I'm the fun Lavender."

"I mean, if I'm busy, you are."

"I'm the person people call when they need something."

"That part is accurate. You're always doing things for other people. Too many things. It's why you have no time for hookups."

"Do we have to talk about hookups?"

"I don't love it either, but someone needs to get through to you. Didn't you redo the floors in Mrs. Abernathy's house when you didn't have a clue what you were doing? That's an overreach."

"Well, she was so sick, and there was no way she was going to be able to figure out those ridiculous instructions." She waved off his point. "They were just snap into place laminate strips."

"And you're always walking people's dogs and picking up their mail and making sure all of us are in love and happy and shit. You sit on that bridge thinking about your own life but never really seizing it by the throat and making any of it reality."

Okay, those words landed. Hard. "I just figure…there's a plan for me. God, the universe, whoever just hasn't gotten around to me yet." She heard the doubt that had crept into her voice.

"Oh, Mare. You're breaking my heart." He made a show of grabbing his chest. "If anyone deserves love, a fantastic life full of silly romantic gestures, and a partner who adores you, it's you."

"Well, I'm fine." She smacked the bar in punctuation. "Take that information back to your cohorts. No one needs to worry about me." But she worried about *herself*, wondering if life was passing her by because she lived with such high romantic expectations that she refused to leap unless it was a sure thing. But nothing was. Alexis sure as hell wasn't. They'd gotten off to such a rocky start—was it actually possible that Alexis could be her endgame? Wasn't it supposed to be perfect from moment one? It was, in her fantasies.

As if reading her mind, Sage leaned in. "If you're waiting for a neon arrow sign to lead you where you're supposed to be, I'm here to tell you that it ain't like that. Tyler is the best thing that ever happened to me, but it took me years to figure it out. Best advice I have? Don't wait years."

She pushed her fingertips through the stray curls on her forehead only to realize that her hand was shaking. Because Sage had just touched on what was her biggest fear, one that she didn't dare utter— missing out on the important parts of life because she got in her own way. "I hear you," she said, forcing a smile.

And then the door opened and a gust of wind ushered Alexis Wakefield inside as if the divinities had summoned her for this very moment. Sage spun around to the door and then back to Marigold. "Well, if that isn't a damn arrow sign. I don't know if she's for you, MG, but I think it's worth finding out." He tapped the bar. "Gotta get home to my girls. Tyler is having dinner with Brynn. They'll probably talk about me and my hard to resist baby blues. Maybe my dimples."

Marigold rolled her eyes. "You have to get over yourself."

He gestured to his face. "Who could get over this? Honestly. *Who?*"

"Hi, Sage."

He turned. "Alexis. We meet again. And you're still happy. Marigold is, too." He turned back and gave her hair an annoying ruffle. "Gotta go. You can have my seat."

"Thank you. Do I not *usually* seem happy?" she asked Marigold as she slid in next to her.

"Not overly."

"Can I buy you a drink?"

"Are you trying to pick me up?"

"Yes."

"In that case, I'll take a beer."

Alexis signaled Larry and passed him the number two. He seemed excited to see them together and moved faster to pour those beers than Marigold had seen him move in years. He clearly had an opinion. "I've never spent time with a woman whose go-to drink was beer. I think I like it."

"Well, Alexis, you might be *spending time* with the wrong kind of people. Who doesn't love a good brewski and a game?"

"You watch football?"

"Oh, I more than watch. I holler. I sometimes throw things. Harass the neighbors."

"The neighbors?"

"Cowboys fans. I just can't."

Alexis laughed, and it was low and awesome. That sound curled around Marigold's spine and sent heat…everywhere. "We should take in a game sometime."

"Tomorrow. Chiefs take on the Raiders."

"You have yourself a date. We'll need football food."

"My specialty."

Alexis sipped the newly arrived beer. "What is this? Hoppy."

"You know beer, too?"

"Marigold Lavender, I'm a fucking connoisseur of anything one can consume. By the way, that's a category you fall very much into." She passed Marigold a sexy smile and glanced over her shoulder. "They're starting. I better go."

"What? Wait." But Marigold was left alone to blink and find her ability to think once again. After that comment, her words took a cruise to the land of languid and lustful. She spent the next hour turned around on her barstool, watching Alexis throw darts in the most perfect pair of jeans ever cut, designed specifically for her perfect set of curves. It was honestly two shows in one. Watching Alexis school the other competitors was a glorious thing. By the end of it, the entire bar was behind her, cheering loudly when she landed another bull's-eye. Marigold had lost count of how many of those she'd hit tonight. With each one, she turned back and met Marigold's gaze.

"Your sworn enemy just kicked my ass," Bruce Milberger said, landing alongside the bar. Marigold didn't mind in the slightest. She basked in his loss. Bruce had been a popular football player in high school who'd made fun of her for caring about things like student politics and gender equality. She'd never forgotten that and made sure he didn't either.

"Maybe you're not as good as you think you are, Bruce," she said in an overly sweet voice. "Remember that time you fumbled the football three yards from the end zone? I feel like that game was the championship. Correct me if I'm wrong."

"Are you ever gonna let me off the hook for being an asshole in high school?"

"Nuh-uh," she said, but this time the smile was playful. He was a meathead and knew it. That part helped. Still smiling from the conversation, she turned to see a woman unfamiliar to her train her iPhone squarely on Alexis as she prepared to throw. Ten minutes later, the woman was getting a shot of Alexis from the other side of the room. Apparently, the whole world thought she was every bit as attractive as Marigold did. She nursed the beer over the course of the next hour. Was it possible she timed her exit to coincide with a certain dart game coming to a close? Oh yes. And Alexis had smoked the competitive group once again.

"Why is it you never play?"

Marigold turned around, not at all surprised to see Alexis, but ready to play that off. "What? Oh, hey. Probably just that I'm too good. You know, I wouldn't want to steal your thunder." She sobered. "That's a falsehood. I suck at darts and would die a slow death if anyone saw how badly."

"You're blushing."

She gulped air. "Happens lately. A whole thing. It's this out-of-town problem."

Alexis smiled at the insinuation.

"Where are you off to?" Marigold asked.

"Your car. I'm walking you there to make sure you arrive safely."

Her heart squeezed. Their sexual tension bounced around them like a pinball in a machine, but small gestures like that one offered a warm anchor. "Oh. That's nice of you." She took Alexis's hand in hers and felt a shot of energy ripple through her arm to her midsection. She realized how much she wanted the short walk to last. When they landed at her car, one of only a few in the parking lot because most people walked to Larry's, Marigold exhaled. She leaned back against the door and brought Alexis with her. The glowing streetlamp dropped a convenient puddle of light and shadow. Helpful and mysterious.

"Oh, hi. What are you about to do with me?" Alexis asked. Her eyes said she wanted.

Marigold didn't speak. She let the press of her lips do the talking. They sought Alexis's and began to move in a slow dance, pulling a quiet murmur of appreciation from Alexis. It undid Marigold. A whole new level of longing unfurled. She slid an arm around Alexis's waist and pulled her closer, enjoying the press of soft curves, reveling in the satisfaction of taking what she wanted. This was what Sage had been talking about because for the first time in years, Marigold felt like she'd come alive.

"If we keep doing this, I'm going to explode," Alexis breathed, cupping her jaw as Marigold held her close. "It's not that I don't love making out with you up against...all the things."

"But we're two adult women who continue to kiss and kiss."

Alexis nodded. "We're like a spinning tornado when we get going."

The visual layered in, and Marigold couldn't believe the accuracy. They were, in fact, a tornado born of this perfectly placed chemistry. "I once nearly blew up a science lab. Two powerful chemicals coming together in the same space."

"Can have a powerful effect," Alexis said, tracing Marigold's collarbone.

Pure torture. She wanted to take Alexis home. She wanted to lace up that explosive quality they carried and let it run. Tonight seemed like the perfect night for it, too.

"Hang on," Alexis said, straightening. The loss of her weight, her warmth, caused Marigold to sag, lonely against her car. She watched curiously as Alexis took four steps into the parking lot, craning her neck around the blue pickup three spaces down.

Marigold blinked. "What in the world are you doing?"

"There was someone there. I swear it."

"It's the time of night when people head home. Happy hour is over, and folks realize the drinks aren't so cheap anymore."

"It was a woman with short hair, and she had her phone out."

Marigold's hand flew to her mouth. She'd forgotten about the woman in the bar. "Yes. I saw her inside. She took about three dozen photos of you playing darts." Marigold shrugged. "It was weird, but I figured she was one of your many admirers. Your fan base."

"It's possible," she said, sliding her hands into the back pockets of the jeans that were made to taunt Marigold. "But that felt different."

Marigold straightened. "Different how?"

"Like a member of the press. An aggressive blogger, maybe. She looked like a woman on a mission, not someone who wanted to say hi and snag a selfie."

"You think they tracked you down?" It hadn't even occurred to Marigold that Alexis would have people trying to report back on her whereabouts and status. How surreal. "Here?"

Alexis shrugged. "They can show up anywhere and do. I'm sure Aspen's recent comment shook up interest. They probably want me to respond and hope it's inflammatory. Intrusive and fucked up is what it is." She shook her head and peered down the sidewalk. "Seems like I scared her away."

"Good." Marigold placed a hand on the back of her head, off center and scrambling to get back to the extremely charged moment she'd been pulled out of. It was simply too good to abandon now. She rested against the car and hoped Alexis came back to her.

"But that reminds me." Alexis took a few steps in, clearly excited about something. "I'm thinking about writing a new piece. No respectable publication will touch me just yet, but my social media has a big reach." She mirrored Marigold's position and leaned back against the car.

Better. She luxuriated in their recaptured proximity. "What kind of piece are we talking about?"

"I'm thinking an apology letter wrapped in a blueprint for a new approach to food and my reviews. Maybe you'd be willing to read it before it goes up? As my ultimate naysayer."

"Of course." What Alexis didn't realize was she had a woman who would say anything but *no* tonight. "Whatever you need." She turned to Alexis and sent her *eyes*. That was a clear signal, right?

But instead of rejoining their scorching moment from earlier, Alexis promptly straightened and hooked a thumb behind her. "Actually, I think I'll get started on it tonight. I'm feeling inspired."

Marigold wanted to shout expletives from on top of her car and protest this decision to her fullest abilities. Instead, she straightened, too. Resignation was her queen. "That's so awesome. The inspiration."

"You going to make it home okay?"

"Yes, totally. You need a ride?" Maybe she'd be invited in and they'd stare into each other's eyes before realizing that keeping their hands to themselves for a short little nightcap was simply an impossibility. She clenched her stomach muscles, bracing against the rapid flutter of butterfly wings.

"I'm good. My Range Rover is around the corner. I hope I see you soon." Alexis squeezed Marigold's hand, offered a quick kiss and a lingering smile, and was on her way. That left Marigold turned-on, alone, and—honestly—a little flabbergasted by the about-face. Maybe Alexis didn't experience what Marigold did when they kissed. Because now she was questioning everything. One thing she knew for sure—as she stomped to the other side of her car and started the ignition, there was a woman taking her photo.

CHAPTER THIRTEEN

Alexis poured her second black cup of coffee that morning. She was going to have to pull out the mega concealer to cover the circles under her eyes. She'd tried to work the night before, harness the abundance of energy the evening out left her with. It had been a dead end. She'd sat in front of her laptop staring. But her thoughts continually led her right back to that parking lot when Marigold Lavender, justice fighter, had hauled her in for a demanding kiss that scorched Alexis's socks right off.

She knew unequivocally that she wouldn't have behaved herself if she'd stayed a second longer in Marigold's presence. She'd already steamrolled Marigold's rules once the other day on their walk. The ball was in Marigold's court and would stay there. If they were going to take things farther, it had to come from Marigold.

Texting was completely in bounds, however, and she fired off one to Marigold that morning as she begged the caffeine to trickle through her system already.

Do you realize you've hypnotized me? Kept other thoughts from spending too much time in my brain. It's wild.

She smiled, set the phone down, and scooped up her extra-cuddly dog, who in a shocking turn had no trouble falling asleep. He flopped over in her arms as she cradled him like a baby and kissed his neck, his big ears reaching for the door. Her phone buzzed on the counter, inspiring a smile as she wondered what Marigold might have to say to her small invitation to flirt. She freed Carrot, who took off on a playful tear through the room as she checked the text.

"What the hell?" she murmured, perplexed and annoyed. She read the words again. Her mother.

U hooking up with the woman who canceled you? Why did she feel the need to construct texts like a teenager? Second of all, how in the world did she know anything about her interactions with Marigold Lavender?

Are you spying on me? she typed back and waited while Carrot, at full speed, raced onto the couch, froze, and zoomed straight into the bedroom.

Her answer was a link to *The Entertainer*'s website where everything pop culture was reported on, discussed, and scooped. The headline appeared after a click. "Alexis Wakefield Caught in a Lip-lock with Woman Who Got Her Canceled." Whoa. She checked the time stamp. The article had been up for twenty-eight minutes. As if on cue, her phone shook in her hand, screaming that she had an incoming call. Her editor. She impulsively slid on.

"Tatum."

"Alexis. We're all dying to know."

And here we go. "What my favorite dining spot in Kansas is shaping up to be?"

"Are you still canoodling with the Marigold woman who ended you?" Her voice was loud with a stripe of amusement. "There are like four of us hiding in this office eating Ruffles potato chips and desperate for the verdict."

"We're getting to know each other," Alexis said conservatively.

"It's not a stunt? Half of us bet on that option."

"Not a stunt." She loved Tatum, but they didn't actually work together anymore. She'd wondered if their friendship would stand on its own, but after she'd been dropped from the paper, she'd been dropped by Tatum, too. Their lighthearted text thread had gone cold. Apparently, her relationships weren't as authentic as she'd believed them to be. No one from her life had really reached out to check on her once she became untouchable. She remembered what Marigold had had to say about it. *That means you're hanging out with all the wrong people.* She'd offer a cute little shoulder shrug and her face would go all soft and kind. It would fill Alexis with actual hope and make her want to curl up with her lavender blanket. Maybe even sit on a footbridge.

Wow. The potency of her thoughts surprised even Alexis. "Enjoy your morning gossip and chips. Gotta run."

What she needed to do was warn Marigold. She had no idea who in Homer's Bluff might be following an entertainment news site, but it was probably best she got ahead of it and sent up a flare. She placed the call and waited. Marigold's voice greeted her moments later.

"Do you know there's a photo of us kissing on Instagram?"

Alexis winced. "I knew *The Entertainer* had picked us up, but I was hopeful they didn't funnel us to their socials, too."

"They did. We're funneled. Tillman says that Heather texted it to him, which means Heather texted it to the whole town. Now what?"

Alexis sighed, sitting with the guilt because she'd dragged Marigold into this. "We just live our lives." She pinched the bridge of her nose. "But it's likely someone is going to reach out to you for comment or more information."

The line went quiet. "I guess I better make sure my hair is done."

Alexis paused, taken aback, and then fell into laughter. She had not been expecting that particular takeaway, but it tracked and it was wonderful. Marigold's world wasn't falling apart. She didn't seem angry at Alexis for dragging her into high-profile coverage. She wanted to make sure her goddamn hair was on point, which of course, it would be. That honey-blond chaos couldn't lose.

No one but you can crack me up like this. I just love you," Alexis said automatically, and then caught herself. "For the record, I just meant that I love the way—"

"No, no, no." Marigold leaped in with a voice that said she was wagging her finger. "Too late. Your words are in stone. You just declared unending love. I gotta call the news back and let 'em know how you feel about me. Bye, Alexis. Pine for me." The phone literally beeped in her ear, and Marigold was gone.

"Seriously?" That earned another hit of laughter from Alexis alone in the kitchen. That could have been an uncomfortable and touchy exchange. In fact, in any other relationship from Alexis's past, it would have been. Yet with Marigold, it had turned out to be the most endearing one. Carrot raced in from the bedroom, did a lap, froze, stared at her with wild eyes, and raced out again.

"Same, Carrot. Same."

❖

"My God. The way she angled her head," Violet said, leaning in for an imaginary kiss. She stole a glimpse at her propped-up phone. "And holding you here," she continued, cupping the jaw of her imaginary kissing partner. "And then just going for it." She hopped to the other side of the counter. "And you're all"—she dropped her arms to the waist of the invisible woman—"give it to me good."

Marigold held up a finger. "Never said that. Never would."

"Why not? Because then maybe she'd oblige."

She couldn't hold back the laugh. "Really? Is that all it takes?"

"Give it a try sometime."

Marigold cringed. "If you say so, Vi."

Violet gave her hips a sassy shake as she walked to the back of the store, ready to open for business.

"Work it, girl," Marigold said. "That's what I'm talking about. Hey, did you hear that Dad talked to a woman at the grocery store? An actual one. I mean, I think it was an exercise at best, but it tells me that he's trying." She scrolled her email and peered around her phone for Violet's response. "Violet Jo Lavender?" When she still received no answer, she raced to the front of the store to find her sister sitting on the floor against the wall, a palm on the carpet, one arm around her midsection. She looked up at Marigold with concern.

"I'm fine. I just got this overwhelmingly woozy feeling. Came out of nowhere. I thought I should join the ground before it claimed me."

"Oh no. Again?" Marigold sank to her sister's level and met her gaze. "What do you need?"

Violet took a deep breath. "Just sit here with me until it passes?"

"Of course." She nodded and slid in next to her sister, taking her hand and pulling it into Marigold's lap where she held it as the seconds that felt more like months ticked by. "Feeling any better yet?"

"No," Violet said, clearly trying to harness a slow breathing pattern. "They taught me to do this when I had Ethan."

"Using what you know. That's good." Their voices sounded too quiet. They were being extra polite, too. *Because we're scared.* "Should I call someone?" Marigold finally asked.

Violet squeezed her hand. "No. I think I'm good now." She sat forward, but Marigold pulled her back. They looked at each other, trying to figure it all out, will it to go away.

"Violet, I'm scared."

Her sister's beautiful brown eyes shone with fresh tears. "Yeah, I know. Me, too," she said in a strangled voice. The unspoken existed. They'd lost their mom to an aggressive cancer that barely gave them time to understand what was happening before she was gone. History simply couldn't repeat itself. That would be unfair. "There's…" But the emotion stole the remainder of her sentence. For a moment, she couldn't speak. "There's Ethan," she whispered at last, as two tears raced their way down her cheek, followed by a third. Violet's son was everything to her. They were a duo. It was her and Ethan against the world since the moment Violet became a single mother. "I'm not leaving him. I can't."

"We're nowhere close to that."

"Still. Promise me that you'll be there for him. You know, just in case."

"You have my word. But we're going to get answers," Marigold said with a ferocity she very much meant. "Ethan will be just fine, and so will you." But in her heart, a fear took root and tangled itself around every inch of her being. There were hints of what might be ahead, and Marigold couldn't look away from them. She began quietly making plans that would see them through whatever was wrong with Violet. She would be the rock, filling in for their mother, no matter how hard things got. She'd be the one to pick up the slack. And dammit, she would hold her sweet family together if it took every last ounce of energy and persistence she had.

"I hope you're right. You often are," Violet said. "I think I'll just grab some water and take the morning slow."

"No. I can cover the store, Vi. Go home and rest."

"And let you have all the fun? Not a chance," she called over her shoulder. "And when these spells show up, they're short bursts, and then they're gone."

She tried to take comfort in that. Violet was experiencing a few blips. Nothing to cry about. Yet. "Well, at least the nation isn't critiquing your kissing skills from their armchairs." She'd said it to lighten the mood and move them to somewhere sillier. By comparison, Marigold's morning drama didn't quite compare, and they both knew it.

"That saucy clip? They're probably taking notes. You two are just a giant firework when you're together. Now here's the make it or break it."

"Hit me."

"Do you like her?"

It was a valid question. "At first, I wanted to run her out of town by mob."

"Noted. I do remember the warpath."

"When I put down my pitchfork, I started to notice her nicer qualities. My passion for little-sister revenge had eclipsed them all."

"As it should."

"Here's the thing." She came around the point-of-sale counter. "I'm not getting caught up in romantic delusions."

"Isn't that your entire definition? You live for that stuff."

She shook her head adamantly. "But nothing like this has ever presented itself. Do you know how it feels when you see one of those corn mazes from a ladder and it looks super easy?"

"Those things lie."

Marigold held out an emphatic hand. "Yes. All's great until you're inside. Then you can't tell which way is up, and all you want to do is run for the damn exit before an axe murderer whirls around the corner and offs you to the *Friday the 13th* theme song." She was aware of how loud her voice had gotten but couldn't seem to intervene.

Violet placed a hand on her hip. "The specificity of that analogy is startling."

"I've given it some forethought."

"Yeah." She bounced her finger in Marigold's direction. "Maybe stop doing that. You're freaking yourself out."

"My point," she said, eager to explain, "is that the idea of a great romance and the reality of what it feels like are wildly different things."

"An idea lives in your brain. A romance lives here," Violet said, touching her chest. "You feel it."

"Right. That's the jarring part."

Violet chuckled to herself. "The maze." She shook her head. "I never thought I'd see Marigold Lavender proclaim that romance was too scary for her."

"I see what you're doing. This is like when we were kids and you'd say *I bet you can't run upstairs and get my hairbrush and be back in ten seconds.* Then I had no choice but to prove you wrong and you'd win." She squinted hard.

"You were on to me that whole time?"

"No." She stood a little taller. "But I am now." A pause as she rearranged the gathering of purple candles near the counter. "I just am taking a moment to navigate the maze now that I'm dropped in the middle of it."

Violet laughed. "You've got it so bad. You should have seen yourself the day she walked into Marilyn's for the first time. Your brain went to mush, and you literally gaped like a cartoon character. Hearts and stars chased each other over your head."

Marigold remembered that day. Before the review. Before the canceling. Before the feelings. Now it was all a jumble of confusing wants, needs, and sensations tied together in a… She gasped. "This is my knot."

"Oh," Violet said, nodding. "It really is. You have a knot of your own now."

When Aster and Brynn and Sage and Tyler were all working out their romantic problems, she could see it, clear as day. The couples were perfect for each other, but each had their own brand of knot to untangle before finding their happily ever after. They had to put in the work. But once they did, they were quite capable of riding off into the sunset.

"But how do I untie mine? Where's another me offering sideline advice when I need it? I can't see the forest for the maze."

"Only you can unlock the curse," Violet said in an overly ominous voice. "And get yourself some."

"Oh, where has my wisdom gone?" Marigold shouted loudly to the ceiling. She tossed in a shaking of her fist for proper reckoning.

"I was just looking for a pair of fuzzy socks. Do you have those?" Joan Martinhouse asked. The petite woman who worked the front desk of Tyler and Brynn's veterinary practice peered at them in fear.

"We do," Marigold said, attempting to rebound into the land of lavender sock retail. "We have regular purple socks but also our lavender-infused, which I highly recommend for decompressing."

"Are you sure there's not some kind of curse I should know about? I don't want to find myself in some kind of lavender predicament."

Marigold laughed. "No, ma'am. We were just discussing my unique love life with the heavens."

"As one does," Violet added.

"I did see you kissing someone passionately on my phone."

"We all did, Joan. All of us," Violet said dryly.

"I vote yes to kissing all you can. Life without banging is just not life at all."

Marigold exchanged a wide-eyed look with Violet and said, "Damn, Joan. Just putting it out there like that."

The demure and generally soft-spoken woman smiled. "Life's just too fucking short for anything less. I'll take the lavender-infused, please."

Leave it to the universe to send quiet Joan in on its mission. "I see what you're doing," she whispered to the ceiling as she rang her up. "On to you."

Chapter Fourteen

It had been a fairly typical workday at The Lavender House, but Marigold's phone had received three different voice mails from media outlets, which meant Marigold was, ahem, sought after. That's right. An actual famous parking-lot harlot. She tried not to let the acclaim go to her head as she helped Tori pick out the perfect infuser set for her mother, or when she swung by her dad's place to make sure his fridge was full. She did, however, move with more purpose just in case those silly paps needed another shot. All levity aside, once she was home for the night, she made the decision to return one journalist's messages just to see what it was they were after.

"Ms. Lavender, mm-hmm, thank you for getting back to me." The woman on the other end of the call sounded like she was working on seven other tasks and, perhaps, walking on a treadmill as they spoke.

"Of course." The woman, Shelley Something-with-a-D, from *The Entertainer* had no way of seeing Marigold, but she still touched her hair absently to make sure it passed the standard curl test. Can't be talking to the press with tragic hair. Not too wild, not too flat. Thank God. She was in luck, which fluffed her confidence.

"I'll jump right to it," Shelley said with impressive vocal fry. "The photos and video we ran of you and, uh, Alexis Wakefield were a big attention getter. Basically, because you hated her with such passion. Now there's lip-locking in Smalltown, USA." A quiet chuckle. "Can I ask for a comment for our follow-up?"

"I don't know that I have anything I can add, except maybe a request for privacy. Your scout captured a private moment."

"I completely understand. Mm-hmm. Yeah. Just doing our job.

Can you speak more on the topic? How do you feel about Alexis Wakefield? Have you come around to her side, or was it a moment of weakness in a parking lot?"

Marigold wasn't sure what she should say or not say. This felt like a trap. "I think she's smart and beautiful and comes with a lot of opinions."

"Perfect." She was too happy. This couldn't be good. There was a knock on the door behind her.

"Wait. Can I undo that? The quote." Another knock. "I mean, doesn't everyone think those things about her? I'm confident you've seen her. She should be in magazines. Oh, actually, I bet she already is. I haven't bought one in a while."

Another chuckle. "Mm-hmm. Well, I think it's a great quote. All of them."

"Those last ones are quotes, too?" She reran her words—that had admittedly flown freely—from as many different angles as she could. *Knockity. Knock. Knock.* Whoever was there clearly knew she was, too. "Okay. I should probably go before more quotes spill out. Bye now, Shelley D."

"Please keep my number and call if you ever want to talk about all you have going on. I'm a good listener. Pictures are bonus points." Marigold winced. The conversation had been less fun than she'd been anticipating.

She opened the door, phone at her side, and relaxed into a happy haze at Alexis standing there, dog in her arms. The sun was setting and caught the blue of her eyes just right. The breeze lifted her hair and set it back down again. "Hi! I have visitors."

"Carrot wanted to come over." Alexis held up her dog. "He's pushy. I tried to tell him we weren't invited and hadn't even called first. He literally didn't care. Who just shows up?"

"Well, here's the thing. Carrot and I are cosmically linked. He gets me. I get him. He's always welcome at my place. You can come in, too, since you're with Carrot, and tell me all the ways I just screwed up my first call with a reporter."

Alexis's eyebrows leaped toward her hair. "You were talking to a reporter? Let me guess. Shelley DeSinso from *The Entertainer*. She eats the garnish off party trays."

"Bingo. Though we didn't delve into garnishes."

"I told her no comment. If they want to get me to talk, it's gonna have to be at the hands of a bigger fish."

Marigold pulled her face back. "You are a show business elitist." She switched her focus to adorable Carrot. "I'm merely a girl, standing in her living room, making eyes at a sandy dachshund."

"What did you say to Shelley?"

"That you had really nice lips and mad skills for days, especially that move where your fingers go into my hair. I told her I gave you extra credit for that."

Alexis stood there. The expression on her face was completely unreadable.

"C'mon." Marigold laughed. "I'm from a small town, but I'm not naive."

Alexis swallowed and shook her head. "No. I was too busy basking in the fiery glow of that compliment to care about a midlevel reporter." Carrot wiggled in her arms, and Marigold gestured for Alexis to set him free. The little dog took off, eager to sniff every inch of her house and acquaint himself with her most comfortable lounging spots. "I'm not sure I'll ever see him again."

"I'm down for a new roommate. Does he snuggle?"

"When he feels like it." Alexis took a few steps past Marigold and into the house. "It's so bright in here. Beautiful."

"You came at the right time of day for the show. Golds, pinks, and oranges for the next forty-five minutes." Marigold was excited Alexis had noticed. Not everyone did. "Natural light is my favorite. I don't have blinds on any of the windows and had new, bigger windows installed when I was able to afford it. It was a pretty significant purchase for me. I get the impression you're rich." She covered her mouth. "That sounded awful. I speak before thinking more often than I care to admit."

Alexis's lips were parted and tugging as if she was watching the most amusing movie flicker in front of her. "That tracks—she said with love."

"There you go with the love again. In the third person this time. You're a little obsessed with me."

Alexis's beautiful smile eased sideways into cute as she turned around and made her way back to Marigold. She stopped smack in the middle of her space like she owned it. Marigold wondered what it would feel like if she did. If Alexis was all hers, and she was Alexis's. How would their two worlds mesh? How would *they*?

"You're not wrong. I think about you more than I admit."

"Yeah?" Marigold reminded herself to breathe. She was feeling a little off balance by the way Alexis eyed her with this dose of unapologetic determination.

"Is that bad? Tell me the damn truth."

"The damn one?" Marigold asked, not really even sure what words she was speaking as each little part of her came undone. Why was the world so different when Alexis was in her sphere? It made her want to make a casserole, jump out of a plane, garden, get hard-to-score tickets to a concert, or take a trip to Acapulco and sip drinks with tiny umbrellas. "Could you eat buttered popcorn all night without getting tired of it? Tell the truth."

"Without a doubt, yes. Is there someone who couldn't?"

"Unfortunately. But I can't imagine tangling with them," she said, touching her chest. "I need someone who likes popcorn and bridges." She looked behind her. "And cute dogs."

"And justice and people with the last name Lavender."

"Those are big, too." A quick beat. "You make me nervous because you're a maze, but I want to find my way into you."

Alexis's eyes went wide and Marigold slapped her forehead.

"Not like that, though," she rushed to explain. Alexis tilted her head and squinted. "Well, maybe a little."

Alexis looked behind her with regret. "I would rather not move a muscle because this is getting good, but my dog is quiet. That could go a lot of ways."

They turned in tandem to see that Carrot had located Marigold's turquoise sofa with the sculpted back and swirled himself into a circle, snoring softly. Marigold turned back to Alexis only to find that she'd stepped even closer. The scent of her raspberry body wash intoxicated. God. Alexis adjusted a strand of Marigold's hair from in front of her shoulder to behind with such intention that it inspired a shiver. It skated smoothly across Marigold's skin. She blinked, taking in each sensation. Alexis's hand slid to her waist, and she leaned in, hovering just shy of the column of Marigold's neck before closing the distance fully. She placed a warm, open-mouthed kiss on the skin there. Marigold went soft, her muscles Jell-O. She nearly sank to her knees in surrender, never wanting this moment to end. The anticipation, the raw desire, the ever-escalating heat moved through her, one inch at a time. The warmth of Alexis's lips pressed to her neck, her tongue exploring, was the most gratifying-slash-torturous experience ever. But Alexis wasn't done and refocused her efforts. She found Marigold's mouth and moved in, kissing her slowly, thoroughly.

Marigold was wet and aching already. There was no way around it. She'd been indulging in sexy thoughts about Alexis for weeks, and three minutes of the reality was her utter undoing.

"I'm sorry that I'm breaking the rules," Alexis breathed. Her voice wasn't hers, which meant she was just as turned-on. The knowledge added to the urgency.

"Let me be clear," Marigold said. Another kiss because who could wait? "The rules were nice. They are obsolete."

Alexis blinked. "I'm sorry. I'm a sucker for words, and that is a really good one."

A pause as they stared at each other, attempting to secure air. "How about tantalized?" Marigold asked. "I've always liked that one."

Alexis's cobalt eyes went dark. She nodded and backed Marigold up until her backside hit the entryway table.

"Luxurious," Marigold said with a teasing smile. Alexis unbuttoned Marigold's jeans and nodded. "Effervescent." Her zipper was slid down. Her eyes fluttered closed as little sparks of anticipation shot off her. She hadn't yet moved, but at the same time, she was reaching for satisfaction with everything she had. She needed to be touched. "Majestic." Her jeans were tugged to the floor, and she dutifully stepped out of them. She'd better be able to come up with another word. "Pleasure." With both hands, Alexis ran her fingertips from Marigold's midthighs upward. "Unadulterated." Alexis cupped her through her underwear, and their mouths came together in a hungry clash. The words were through. They were bathed in a wash of pink and orange and spinning wildly out of control against a table whose main purpose was to hold her phone and keys. What life was this?

"Is this okay?" Alexis whispered in her ear. The tickle of her voice sent a shiver.

"Yes," Marigold hissed. "Right here."

Alexis slid the small square of fabric to the side and touched

Marigold fully. She made a strangled sound, and Marigold outright swore, gripping Alexis's shoulder with one hand and the table with the other. Alexis's fingers explored delicately at first and then with more determination. This was what heaven felt like. Marigold's hips began to rock, searching out that perfect rhythm and purchase. Her skin was hot, and her head went swirly. Only her body knew what the hell it was doing and took over completely, leading her down a path where she abandoned inhibition, logic, and fear. If she'd been lost in the maze, Alexis had found her and brought her to this very unexpected moment. Wasn't she just on the phone?

"I can't get over you. This." Alexis began to stroke more purposefully. "You're the sexiest woman I've ever met," Alexis said. There was reverence in her voice, but surely the words couldn't be true. Didn't matter. They were hers for now, and she was keeping them. They found their rhythm, and Marigold finally opened her eyes to find a picture she knew she'd never forget. Alexis, lost. Her head was tossed back slightly, her dark hair fell down her back, and she bit her bottom lip as she carried Marigold higher and higher. Alexis was fully dressed, but the combination of lust and determination was perhaps the most erotic thing she'd ever seen. She'd never known the kind of ache she had for Alexis that bloomed in her stomach and moved through every part of her. It culminated now as she angled her hips just perfectly, asking Alexis silently for more. Her wish was granted when Alexis entered her swiftly and with purpose. The air whooshed from her lungs, and a fullness took over that she never wanted to end. At the same time, she very much needed release. Fire crackled and danced across every nerve ending. "Please," she murmured.

Alexis nodded, shifting her attention to the one spot that would push Marigold over the top. Her thumb circled and pressed. The pressure built to staggering heights until it broke and she was falling from the tip-top of a tree, aware of Alexis clinging to her, breathing rapidly, kissing her neck, and along for the ride. "We just did that," Marigold finally said, but there was no air. She was gasping, and everything felt very much underwater. She heard her own voice but *felt* so much more. The aftershocks stole the show, and she allowed herself to revel in each one. "Who are you again?" Alexis had just played her body like a beautiful solo on a violin, and Marigold was still dumbfounded in its wake.

"You're really cute when you're hazy."

She was aware of the buttons on her shirt being worked. "What are you doing? I already—"

"Who says there's a limit?"

"There's no limit?" A fairly new concept. "I don't think I've ever—"

"Then you've been doing this with all the wrong people." Beautiful Alexis winked at her, and she laughed.

"Plus this part's a little bit for me." Marigold's shirt was parted to reveal her light turquoise bra with the tiny lace designs, her favorite from the cutest little lingerie boutique with an LGBT mission and an online store. She was glad she'd worn it and enjoyed the feeling of Alexis sliding the straps down her shoulders one at a time. Her skin tingled, still sensitive. "May I?" Alexis whispered. Marigold nodded, impressed at the one-handed unclasping that followed. Alexis slid the bra down Marigold's arms and allowed her gaze to trail from her face to her breasts. "Another word. Exquisite."

"You're the writer," she said, already noticing the breathy quality her voice took on at the new exposure. The pulse of Alexis's gaze was every bit as potent as her touch. She traced the rounded outside of Marigold's breast and, as if she couldn't resist, wrapped her arms around Marigold's waist, dipped her head, and pulled a nipple into her mouth. She wasn't shy, licking and sucking, bringing Marigold's body roaring to life like a growing kitchen fire.

"I think I love you topless," Alexis said, angling her mouth to Marigold's other breast. "No. I know I do."

"You hard-core can't stop saying you love me," she said, eyes clenched, fingers in Alexis's hair. They were rocking together again. Alexis seemed hell-bent, and Marigold couldn't argue with a woman on a mission. Alexis dropped to her knees and placed an open-mouthed kiss between Marigold's legs, eased them apart, and used her tongue to trace the most agonizingly perfect circles, light and delicate. The pressure gathered. Before she knew it, she was well on her way, curving her hips to meet Alexis, reaching for more until she shattered a second time in a surprise. The orgasm had been closer than she realized. She hadn't been ready, and it toppled her, taking over every muscle. Each thought. She gripped the table behind her, her body a shooting star. "Oh, you're good," she said, riding it out. "And it's not done. Okay. Hang on. Whoa."

Alexis chuckled. "I've never heard someone walking me through their payoff before."

Marigold exhaled, steady and slow before addressing the issue. "I needed you to know my experience."

"I enjoyed every damn second of it."

"I love when you swear. You do it so well."

"I'll fucking do it more."

Marigold parted her lips, straightened, and kissed Alexis, ready to turn the tables, eagerly looking forward to seeing desire darken those deep blue eyes. She wanted to touch Alexis, make her feel all the intense sensations Marigold just had. She wanted her naked and undone beneath her fingertips.

After a few passion-filled kisses, Alexis pulled back. "I'm thinking I should go."

Record scratch. It was almost as loud in Marigold's ears as if it had actually happened. "Now? No, no, no. There's more."

Alexis stole another kiss. "I want that, I do. But what if there is? More?"

Marigold understood. Alexis was overwhelmed by it all. Standing there, mostly naked in her house as daylight faded, she understood. Alexis was every bit as scared of this thing as she was. Silently, Marigold laced their fingers. "Then we figure it out together. You and me."

"You and me," Alexis repeated, gently trying it on. She raised her gaze to Marigold's and nodded. The mood had shifted, yet their connection had just taken a key step forward. Marigold led Alexis quietly through her living room, up the short flight of stairs to her bedroom, and pulled her into her arms, holding her tightly for a long moment. She cradled her face and studied it. Stunning.

"Hi," Alexis said with a new vulnerability written all over her features. The guard was down. This was simply…her. The woman. No bravado. No quips.

Marigold stroked her cheek. "You feel so different from anyone I've ever been with."

Alexis shifted her weight. She was nervous, which was unthinkable. The confidence from just ten minutes ago had dissolved before her eyes and what was left was a tenderness Marigold hadn't been prepared for. Yet she loved it.

"Come here," Marigold said, sitting on the side of her king size bed covered in the big, warm quilt she'd found for a steal. She gave Alexis's arm a light tug and pulled her into her lap. Oh, that was good. Too good. Marigold could live here. She slipped a hand underneath the hem of Alexis's mauve shirt—knitted, with a slight blousing on the sleeves. She wanted to go slow. Taking her time with Alexis, letting her feelings be known through her touch, felt as vital as air. She kissed her softly, reveling in the short kisses that melted into deeper ones. The lazy sweep of Alexis's tongue intoxicated until there was nothing lazy about what they were doing. The touches were more purposeful now, and she removed Alexis's clothing piece by piece until only her bra and panties remained. She took in the sight. How did she get this lucky? Marigold crawled on top, living happily in the anticipation of undressing her fully. She settled her weight to a murmur of appreciation from Alexis, who cupped Marigold's ass, pulling her snug up against her. "Why are these still on?" she asked, indicating Marigold's one piece of remaining clothing.

"You first," Marigold said. "Allow me." She bent her head, capturing the hem of Alexis's panties and tugging them with her teeth as Alexis watched in captivation, slipping out of them the rest of the way. Marigold kissed the gorgeous legs she'd been admiring for weeks right up to the insides of Alexis's thighs, blowing gently on the soft skin there and what she found between. Alexis lifted her hips, a request. "No, ma'am."

That earned a laugh. "Fine. Your turn."

Marigold stood and removed her underwear, a move that had Alexis's eyes hooded, her bottom lip bit. In response, she sat up and unclasped her bra, freeing the breasts that Marigold had imagined more times than she could count. She went entirely still, taking in the view. This whole thing was unreal. Perhaps a dream she'd soon wake up from? Until then, she planned to enjoy every second afforded to her. She moved back to the bed, nodded, and eased Alexis back down, following her there. She nuzzled the neck she'd long admired and then kissed it thoroughly, reminding herself to go slow while luxuriating in the raspberry scent she couldn't get enough of. "I love the way you smell." She slid her body to the side and let her hand run down Alexis's shoulder to her arm, her stomach, around the curve of her breast, and down again, longing to explore every inch. She would, too. She lifted

Alexis's breast and circled a nipple. Alexis tossed her head back as Marigold pulled the nipple into her mouth, driven, drunk. Longing shifted to hunger. The sound of Alexis's shallow breathing encouraged Marigold, liquid fire in her veins.

"Unreal," Alexis managed as her fingertips gripped Marigold's hair, encouraging her.

Marigold watched in awe as Alexis slid on top and straddled her hips. She surrendered control but only because the view was too good to pass up. Long dark hair touched the tops of bare shoulders as Alexis's breasts moved with her in a gentle rocking. Marigold couldn't resist. She cradled both breasts, candy to her hands, and studied Alexis's face. Each shift in her expression was worth memorizing. Her hips began to press and rock against Marigold's stomach. A quiet murmuring that didn't equate to words accompanied the motion. She closed her eyes, which made Marigold sit up, having lost that precious window in. "No. Look at me. Please." Alexis did, unleashing those blue eyes. The bedroom evaporated, and their lips came together. Marigold lost herself in the rapid beating of their hearts, having never craved anything this much before. Alexis's mouth, slow and hungry, moved down her neck, and Marigold allowed the momentary distraction before taking over. They were in sync to a staggering degree, each touch, each kiss, every look. That was it. This was Marigold's show now. As such, Alexis was deposited on her back, and Marigold slid downward, parted her legs, and tasted. Once. Twice. And again. Alexis grabbed a handful of the comforter beneath her. Motivated and reveling in the feel of Alexis beneath her mouth, Marigold found her stride and lost every inhibition. Liberating as hell. She carried Alexis higher and higher until she raised her hips and went still, crying out and twisting beneath Marigold's touch, wild and unencumbered. Marigold held her tightly but didn't forget to watch the pleasure as it rippled over and through Alexis, who'd never been as beautiful. Her eyes were closed and her hair fell back, brushing the quilt like a waterfall. Marigold was overwhelmed with emotion, and grappling to name it. But there were no words.

The room went quiet, yet she felt anything but alone. She lay alongside Alexis and quietly took her hand while examining the whole experience.

"I'm shaking," Alexis said finally, offering an embarrassment-laced smile. "I'm not sure why. I'm sorry."

It was a relief. It meant Marigold wasn't alone in the things she was thinking, feeling, and experiencing. Her own world felt entirely different with Alexis in it. But if Alexis was afraid, too, somehow that made it manageable. They were in this thing together. "I think we're both a little...surprised."

"I knew we'd be good together." She almost left it there but didn't. "The experience was more than I'd planned, and I'm working through that."

Marigold turned onto her side to face Alexis, earnestly needing to explain something before she lost her courage. "There are quiet moments that I want with you. Is that strange?"

Alexis turned as well, mirroring her. They were close, as if telling important secrets. That offered a veil of safely. "Tell me about them."

She heard the tentative quality of Alexis's voice, the slight tremor. "We've been getting to know each other. Going to restaurants, on walks. Running into each other in the world. But what about the small stuff? Just...life?"

"The humdrum."

"Passing the newspaper at breakfast." She touched Alexis's cheek softly. "I find myself wondering what it would be like to be the person you call when you're annoyed with your day, or want to just watch TV on the couch."

"We would argue over shows," Alexis said with a smile. "And the remote."

"Until I tackled you for it, and we compromised on what to watch."

"I'd watch your show, if you'd watch mine."

Nothing had ever sounded better, leaving Marigold terrified to hope. But how would any of that happen? They hadn't gotten into how their lives would mesh if they did decide to take this thing somewhere formal, which at this moment felt like *the* looming question circling the room.

She sobered for a moment. "We're very different people."

"Maybe that's the part that has me so fixated. I've been with a lot of people just like me. From my very same world. Too many, if I'm being honest."

"The ex on the phone that day in the dog park."

"Yes." Alexis looked skyward and nodded. "Shallow as hell. But I was, too. Still am." A beat. "I don't want to be, though. I see that much so clearly lately. This whole side trip away from real life has been... eye opening. I don't want my existence to be about follower counts, sponsorships, and invites to all the important parties."

Marigold grinned. "Okay, but I do love a good party."

"I think I'd like them more with you there, too."

"Stop. Are you inviting me to a fancy party?"

Alexis nodded. "I think I am."

"This feels like a step."

Alexis held up her thumb and forefinger. "But before I ruin it, I should go."

That sucked the fun right out of the room. "Oh. You don't have to."

"I don't think you want me to move in, and we're not great at middle ground."

"What? You mean we hate each other until we're—"

"Naked and giving your house a workout."

Oh, the way she said those words was as good as a frosty mug of beer. She tapped her cheek. "Here's an observation for you. You flee the scene a lot."

"Do not. I preserve it." Alexis kissed Marigold, slow and thorough. "Thank you for today."

"You're welcome? That's weird."

Alexis winced. "I know. I'm not good at navigating Marigold just yet, but trust me when I say I'm a quick study and will put in the effort." Her eyes drifted down Marigold's naked form before returning to her eyes. "And I'm highly motivated."

That sent a rather impressive shiver through her limbs. "Ooh la la."

Alexis danced into her clothes as Marigold watched with a smile. The best part? After what they'd just done, she didn't feel the need to look away and offer Alexis her privacy. She basked in their newfound intimacy.

"What are you grinning at?"

"The very unexpected direction my life has taken. I'm staring at you naked in my bedroom because now I'm suddenly allowed to in a way I wasn't just hours ago. Also, you're really hot. Stay naked forever."

Alexis barked a laugh. "A compliment from you goes a long way.

But you're the show-stealer here." She sat on the edge of the bed. "Do you realize that when you walk into a room, everyone automatically smiles like they know they're in for the best time."

"I guess I'll have to pay more attention."

"You should." Alexis touched her cheek softly and sighed, her gaze roaming yet again. "I can't get over this body."

Marigold felt the heat flame her cheeks. "I'm happy to hear it."

"I hope I see you soon, Marigold Lavender."

"You will. Leave the dog."

"Not a chance."

Once the sound of six feet leaving her home faded, she lay back on the bed, tossed an arm over her face, and basked in the most unexpected and memorable afternoon of her entire adult life. "What is happening to me?" she asked her friend the ceiling and laughed. "And how can I get more of it?"

❖

Alexis didn't want to leave Marigold. At all. In fact, she ached for her now that they were apart. That was the headline. She'd never been a sentimental person, and cuddling, chatting, and basking with her partner after sex had never been her favorite. But in yet another first time, she found herself longing to do just that.

As she drove the sleepy streets of Homer's Bluff, she allowed herself to drift back over to Marigold's place, where in an alternate reality, they'd stayed right there naked and wrapped in Marigold's quilt, talking, touching, and getting to know each other until they couldn't keep their damn eyes open. But that very same need was also the reason she'd decided to leave and offer both of them their space instead. Did she even know how to cuddle? What were the rules when you had these big feelings swirling? It was dark out, which seemed an appropriate time to leave someone's place on a weeknight, especially if you knew staying over was not the best move. She squeezed the steering wheel. "Damn it, you are so awkward with this stuff, it hurts." Marigold Lavender had just knocked Alexis's world into a much more satisfying place, which also came with an intimidating list of side effects.

She wanted to pick up her phone and call a friend, but quite honestly, they'd all hit the deck the minute she became untouchable.

Looking back, her connections had all been superficial. She thought about Marigold and the way she was with Tillman, or her sisters for that matter. She craved those kinds of relationships now, mourned for what she didn't have. She was a lonely, isolated woman who'd done this to herself. She'd invested in all the wrong things in life. What was she supposed to do about that now as she sat in her thirties in a moment of personal crisis, grappling for a foothold? She shook her head as tears of regret sprang and ran. "That's okay," she whispered, attempting to harness this new, more emotional version of herself. "You're here now. You're figuring it out." She smiled through the embarrassing waterworks. "And you have a really nice person who will help you do just that."

Alexis Wakefield was changing with each day that passed.

She could feel it as plainly as she saw the stars overhead sanctioning her strides.

The world was calling, and she planned to listen, which admittedly had never been her strong suit. After a lifetime of believing she knew it all, it was her moment to shut up and pay attention.

She arrived home, tossed her keys on the counter. Dating rule number one said you gave it time before calling a woman you'd just slept with. She tossed it the hell out the window and did the exact opposite.

"Hi," Marigold said upon answering. She sounded sincere and bright. "You called me already. Did you forget something?"

"I needed to hear your voice again. That simple." Everything in Alexis offered up a dreamy sigh at the sound of the gentle, feminine vocal quality that was all Marigold. It tickled her ear and settled her down. "What are you doing now that I've given you free time?" She began to walk circles around the white marble topped kitchen island because she was now a schoolgirl.

"I don't want to tell you because it's not nearly as sexy or cool as I want it to be."

"You want me to think you're sexy and cool?" She laughed. "Honey, you don't have to worry about that."

"I like that." A pause. "You calling me *honey*."

Her smile drooped. She did, too. "I miss you, and I only left ten minutes ago." This was a big moment for her. She didn't confess these kinds of things to people. Ever. She was standing on what felt like a very flimsy limb above a steep drop-off, but she was doing it. She slammed her eyes closed and waited, heart thudding.

"I was actually feeling very much the same," Marigold said. "You should have stayed."

Alexis nodded. "Okay. What if I did next time?"

Silence. Was that a presumptuous comment? She would now hand over her favorite Chanel bag to take the question right back.

"I would love that. When can we arrange that very set of circumstances?"

Alexis laughed, relief and excitement raining down. "You'll be shocked to hear that my schedule is wide open."

Silence hit. "About that...I could really get used to having you around."

"Me, too."

"But I can't help thinking about the fact that you're going to go back to San Francisco at some point." A pause. She was feeling Alexis out. "I mean, is that still the plan?"

Alexis heard the hope in Marigold's voice. She kind of liked the idea of existing in this perfect little imaginary life she'd crafted together for herself here. But her reality was back home. Eventually, she had to face her career and figure out what was next. She missed the narrow hallways of her cozy home. The wooden floors. Her own bed. But the idea of leaving Marigold made her ache.

"Yes. I do imagine I'll be going back to California at some point." Her mind raced as she tried to make it all fit. "I don't know where you're at. I wouldn't presume. But maybe we don't have to just cut this off." She didn't recognize herself. She *always* cut things off at the easiest opportunity. Tonight, her heart overruled her head. "I mean, if that's the route we choose to go at the time." She rushed to explain. Her vulnerability was showing. "Just playing around with options. Thoughts? You can ignore me." With warm cheeks, she worked to tame her wayward nerves that squirmed and vibrated. "Sorry."

"This is a moment."

"I know." She rolled her lips in and waited.

"I don't think I've experienced you as anything but the picture of cool and in control. Well, earlier this evening excluded." Alexis smiled at the reference, remembering Marigold taking her body easily to the brink.

"Who says I'm not those things right now?" She heard the forced bravado behind her voice.

"You're so not."

Softer. "I'm not."

"Alexis, you're the most confusing person I've ever met. One minute, I want to *ruin* you and the next I'm searching for ways to *keep* you."

"I feel like both can exist." A laugh. "Certainly adds to our fire."

"God, the fire will be the end of me."

Alexis closed her eyes because the statement did things to her, and she was half tempted to hop in the car and drive straight back to Marigold's house. "The fire is noteworthy."

"Do you know that your voice drops a tad when you acknowledge anything that falls into the sexy column?"

"I do now."

"It's one of my favorite things."

She smiled lazily against the phone. " 'Night, Marigold. I'm glad I called."

"Me, too. But I want to answer your question first because I do have thoughts. I'm not scared of San Francisco. The prospect of it. Visiting. Spending time there."

"Moving."

She heard Marigold pull in a breath. "If the adventure suits."

They were actually having this conversation. Did the phone somehow make it easier? "The adventure. I like the categorization."

" 'Night, Alexis."

"Good night to you."

She took a moment to blink and marvel, tapping her still swollen lips that had just confessed to a whole hell of a lot. She scooped up her dog, peppered him with kisses, and instead of doom-scrolling the internet, she selected a promising-looking book from the story-lined shelf in the living room. A romance, in fact. *Well, well, Barney Hershel. I owe you one.*

CHAPTER FIFTEEN

Alexis sat alone at one of the small tables in the dining area of Hole in One, still wearing her running clothes, admiring the Chocolate Murder doughnut on the small plate in front of her. She'd come to the shop because it really was the most wonderful-smelling place she'd ever experienced, and she planned to spend as many mornings basking in its glory as possible. Her trip in was earlier than she'd planned. Still wasn't quite seven a.m. Lately she'd traded in her night owl routine for the early bird equivalent. Four miles of hard-core running and a hearty round of overthinking had earned her this bad boy of chocolate wonder. Her mouth watered and her body sagged at the wonderful chocolatey aroma. She was going to savor the warm doughnut and cup of coffee for as long as possible.

"You thinking about Marigold Lavender or about how you plan to get your good standing back in the foodie community?"

Alexis's eyebrows shot up and she regarded Tori, who stood alongside her table with her flaming red hair pulled back in a French braid. "A little of both." She squinted, feeling seen and called out. "How do you know so much?"

"We're the doughnut shop," she said with nonchalance. Alexis waited for more, but none came. Apparently, that was all there was to it.

"Right. Okay." Small towns certainly took getting used to. Apparently, the doughnut shop was at the heart of it all. Who knew?

"Can I offer you some advice and top off that coffee?"

"I won't say no to either."

"Marigold Lavender isn't your average woman. She is a force." Tori wasn't wrong and had her attention. "But underneath it all, there's a delicate quality there that a lot of people don't see. The very same ingredient that fuels her heart of gold. She puts other people before herself and pays the price later. Don't let her settle for less than she deserves or Satan will get you for it."

"Wait. What?" That took a turn.

"You heard me," Tori said, sauntering back to the counter, leaving Alexis to wonder if that last part was just sassy fun or sincere warning. But the core message had landed. It made sense. Alexis thought on all Marigold seemed to do for her family. *She* was the one they called on when they needed something. Marigold was the rock for Violet, cooked dinners for their father, and showed up with new clothes for baby Cara. But what about what Marigold might need? In that instant, Alexis wanted more than anything to be the person to do those kinds of things for Marigold, put her first, and make her feel like the most important person in the world. About as awesome as this kissed-by-the-gods doughnut was making Alexis feel.

"I can be the doughnut," she murmured.

"I don't know what that means, sweetheart, but you run with it," Tori called, demonstrating her impressive eavesdropping skills. "You can be anything you set your mind to, baby girl!"

"Thanks, Tori. I really feel like you get me," she called back.

"Well!" She shrugged. "We're the doughnut shop!"

"You might need that on a T-shirt."

Tori reached beneath the counter and emerged with a red T-shirt with those exact words on the back in swirly white script.

"Sold!" Alexis stood and stalked to the counter. "I'll take a medium." A pause. "And a second one for Marigold."

"See? Now that's how you do it. You're learning already," Tori said, her green eyes sparkling, giving the color of her hair an extra added pop. "Come back in tomorrow. I got some special flavors lined up. I'm not talking about them, though." She made a point of turning an invisible key in front of her mouth. "But banana frosting is involved." She cringed. "I've already said too much." She leaned forward. "There might also be a caramel coconut mash-up. Dammit. Shut up, Tori. Why do you always have to spoil it?" She shrugged helplessly in answer to her own question.

Alexis blinked. "That was quite a journey."

"You sound like my mama."

"I've not heard that before."

"How's the murder?"

"Lock it up, it's so good. I can't resist the sparkle of a well-made doughnut."

"Another satisfied customer! Hit it, Drew!" Tori called to the back of the small shop. Her employee promptly rang a bell to celebrate the moment. It seemed like a great idea, and Alexis wondered why she didn't ring more bells when things went her way. A quick glance at her watch told her that Marigold would be waking up soon. Maybe she'd shoot her a *Good morning, sexy* text. Her lips tugged, and she went all smiley. It was official—she was a walking cliché. She decided to embrace the madness and own her puppy dog status. There were worse things to be.

❖

Marigold heard her alarm sing its rousing tune, but she chose to ignore it for just an extra moment or two. She was too busy reveling in the most wonderful dream in which she and Alexis had finally thrown caution to the wind and ripped each other's clothes off in her entryway. She grinned with triumph when her slightly sore and satiated body reminded her that that was no dream. After another few blinks, her brain floated back to her. Oh damn. The alarm was actually her phone ringing, and it had been doing so for quite some time.

She fumbled for it and slid on to the call. "Tillman Lee, it's barely seven a.m. To what do I owe the distinct honor?"

"Well, Ms. Marigold, I'm here with my next-door neighbor, Violet, and we're thinking she needs to go to the ER."

Marigold sat straight up, no longer groggy in the slightest. "I'm getting dressed. Maybe I should skip getting dressed. What happened? Is she conscious?"

"She is. Had a weak spell and went over. Unfortunately, it looks like she twisted her ankle real good and can't put any weight on it. I could take her, but she doesn't want me to wake up Ethan."

"You stay with Ethan." She slid into a pair of jeans. "Can you? I'm coming for Violet."

"Dream team. Peas in a pod. Let's do it."

"Hey, Tillman?" She danced her way into a shoe.

"Yeah?"

"You're the best."

"Shucks, MG. Don't make me all red and embarrassed." She heard a muffled conversation. "And Violet says don't speed, and keep your eyes on the road, not your phone. Oh. And that she's fine."

"I'm fine!" Violet yelled in the background.

The hell she was, and Marigold was tired of waiting on the tests to clear the insurance hurdle. Gripped by fear, she slid into the driver's seat and smacked her steering wheel because she knew in her heart what they were about to confront, and it was familiar and awful. "Nope," she said out loud. She had no plans to let it win this time.

When she pulled into Violet's driveway, Tillman stood on the sidewalk with Violet's arm slung around his shoulder. "A bad sprain at best. It's already swelling up nice and pretty."

"Ouch," Marigold said, because the telltale colors were already starting to emerge.

"He's dramatic," Violet said. She turned to Tillman. "Are you sure you and Ethan will be fine?"

"Hell, yeah. He loves *PAW Patrol*, and so do I. We're gonna have a cereal party and see where the morning takes us. Maybe hit up the park or Hole in One. Larry's opens after not too long. Does he like stouts or lagers?"

"No. None of that. He has preschool at nine."

Tillman sobered. "Right. You mentioned that. Just seeing if you were still lucid." Violet smacked his side. He winced. "Yep. She's one hundred percent herself."

Unfortunately, his attempted levity was lost on Marigold, who was swamped by fear. She squeezed her hands to stop them from shaking. Adrenaline shot through her veins in excess. "Help me get her into the car?" She moved opposite Tillman and slung Violet's free arm around her shoulder. They offered her a full-on glide to the passenger's side.

"Thank you for coming by." Violet said, as if they were old acquaintances. That formality meant she didn't quite know how to handle herself. She was just as scared. "I guess we can just open a little late today?"

"The people of Homer's Bluff will find a way to get by without the ability to purchase lavender dish towels for one damn day."

Homer's Bluff's small clinic was good for viruses and stitches, but their problem felt bigger. Marigold made the executive decision and drove them the thirty minutes to Wichita, where they joined the masses in the ER at Ascension. The whole thing felt like a tidal wave. They waited two hours in the waiting room to find out that Violet's foot was, in fact, sprained, but Marigold wasn't about to leave it there. There was a larger storm looming, and it was time they met it head-on. Ninety minutes later, they had their chance when a young doctor who introduced herself as Dr. Webb asked if there were any other symptoms.

"Yes, actually," Violet said. "I've been experiencing some woozy moments."

Marigold leaped in, communicating all the things she knew her mother would have said. "She's full-on fainting. Losing consciousness." Dr. Webb's eyebrows shot up, and she noted something on her iPad. Marigold continued, "Multiple times this month. Something very wrong is going on. She fell and injured herself today because she was feeling weak."

"Is that true?"

Violet nodded in defeat. "Unfortunately, yes."

"Hmm. Okay. Got it."

Marigold prayed that was a sign that the doctor had heard them and would act. "We've been waiting on insurance to clear the way for more tests, but it's taking too long." She and Violet exchanged a concerned look.

"Not what we want to hear. Luckily, I have the ability to hurry things along. Let's get that foot wrapped and get a quick blood workup going."

Marigold exhaled. It was a start.

"We can just worry about the foot," Violet said. "My doctor back home is—"

"Slow and old," Marigold interjected. "We'll take the blood work."

Dr. Webb looked from Marigold to Violet. "Sure. Let's do it."

The morning shifted into afternoon, and the tests Dr. Webb ran seemed to offer more questions than they did answers, leading to more tests. But they were closer. It especially helped when Violet got woozy in the presence of a nurse, who immediately got her into bed and took her vitals.

"Yeah, your blood pressure has bottomed out. It was normal when you came in. That's why you're feeling unsteady."

Violet blinked and exchanged another look with Marigold. They were impressive at silent communication. This was something. New information captured in real time.

"I'll let Dr. Webb know and see where she wants to go from here."

They didn't have to wait long to find out. Dr. Webb, who couldn't have been more than thirty, didn't hesitate. "I want to admit you."

Violet's eyes went wide and panicked. "I can't. I have a little boy. I'm a single mom."

"And we have a fantastic support system to make sure Ethan has all the attention that he needs," Marigold said. It wasn't like Violet had a choice, and they both knew it. Her health had waited patiently in line long enough. Within an hour, they had a room, and Marigold finally collapsed down in a chair that had armrests. She hadn't eaten, other than a slice of apple that Violet had forced her to take from her dinner tray that had arrived just after six.

"Hey there. Is it all right if I step inside?"

They both turned at the sound of a female voice, and Marigold blinked to clear her field of vision. Alexis stood in the doorway, holding a cardboard tray containing three coffees in one hand, and a greasy brown bag that smelled like heaven had arrived in the other.

"I'm told these are the best lattes and cheeseburgers in all of Wichita. I have friends who know. Anyone?"

Marigold nearly sobbed at the thought of a burger. She'd had no idea how hungry and tired she actually was until this very moment. Worrying took a lot out of a person. But she had to admit that seeing Alexis in Violet's hospital room rattled her. That was strange.

"I'll definitely take a coffee," Violet said. "This one is gonna need that burger. She missed dinner."

"Yes, please," Marigold said, still climbing out of her haze. "What are you doing here?" It probably wasn't the most welcoming sentence. She'd blurted and didn't know how to backtrack.

"Well, you texted that you would likely be here awhile, and since it had already been hours, I figured you could use some sustenance." She held up a key. "I also have an exceptionally nice hotel room across the street if you need a break. I'm not staying there, but it's available to you." She placed the key on the small counter nearby. "Room number is on the inside of the card, and your name has been added to the reservation."

Was this real? The gesture was incredibly thoughtful. "I don't even know what to say." Marigold took a sip of the comforting warm liquid that squeezed her like a much-needed hug on the way down.

"Well, damn," Violet said. "You're charming. I'm calling it now. Might be snarky on the internet, but you're really starting to make up for that in other ways." Violet shook her finger in Alexis's direction. "Don't sleep on this one."

Marigold felt her face go hot. She turned away and pretended to be interested in something out the window. No one bought it. "No. Of course not." She needed to loosen up and was trying her best to behave like a normal person.

"Why don't you two go for a walk," Violet said. "Find an out-of-the-way table and get your cheeseburger on."

Alexis arched a perfect brow. "You game?"

She turned to Violet, who'd started to look a little tired. "Are you sure you're going to be okay?"

Violet scoffed. "I'm a woman in a comfy bed with a television and a sinfully good vanilla latte. Give me my peace."

"Okay," Marigold said, her heart nervous and her head worried.

She led the way out of the small hospital room to a vending area she'd spotted earlier, complete with a few metal tables and chairs. Except for the two of them, the space was empty.

"I still can't believe you're here." She unwrapped the foil-covered cheeseburger that was still hot as Alexis slid a cup overflowing with fries her way.

"No burger can exist without fries."

She swallowed. "Thank you." The true weight of the gesture was beginning to settle over her. It was unexpectedly kind and thoughtful of Alexis to come up with a list of possible needs and fulfill them. This anomaly of a woman continued to surprise her. Why couldn't she say all of that out loud? She was emotionally frozen in place to a frustrating degree.

Alexis sat back while Marigold ate. She hadn't been wrong about the quality of the food. It was better than any meal had a right to be.

Slowly, as the calories infiltrated her bloodstream, she felt herself coming back to life. Her ability to think returned, and she offered Alexis a genuine smile. "Hi."

"Hey. You hanging in there? I know this whole thing has been scary."

She nodded. "But they're taking care of her. For the first time, I feel like we have a good team on the case. Maybe this sprain was fortuitous in the end."

"I'd like to believe it was. What can I do?"

"Absolutely nothing. You're sweet just being here." It sounded extra polite. They were off with each other. Her fault. Her brain was back on the job, and now she couldn't seem to keep it from overthinking. Marigold wanted to explain herself. To reach out and thread their fingers together, allow herself to shelter in the comfort Alexis offered. But she just couldn't seem to make the leap to allow Alexis in.

"I hope I'm not overstepping."

"Nope. Uh-uh." She tossed in a no-big-deal laugh, but it sounded hollow. "It's just…she's probably going to need me back in her room soon." She winced.

"Got it. And that's okay."

"I'd hate for her to be alone, you know? I don't think she's ever been in the hospital outside of having Ethan."

Alexis stood. "You don't have to explain." She paused. "Just know that I'm available, okay? Free for whatever you need."

Marigold nodded and began to stand.

With a hand out, Alexis stopped her. "No, no, no. I can find my way. You stay here and finish your meal. You'll need it." She lingered a moment in thought. "Maybe I'll hear from you when you come up for air." The smile she offered was tight and didn't reach her eyes. Alexis was smart. She knew she'd been kept at arm's length. The slash of hurt Marigold saw cross her features had been her doing.

She scrambled. "You're amazing for doing this."

"Not at all. But please make use of that hotel room. Can I bring you an overnight bag from home?"

"I'm sure Aster and Brynn can help."

Alexis's gaze fell straight to the ground, and Marigold realized she'd just rejected her again. Why was this serious real-life moment so much harder than making out?

Experiencing Alexis Wakefield outside of their dating bubble, their lust-driven interactions, rattled her. Maybe because it came with a formal stamp she hadn't been prepared for, no matter how much she wanted it? This was her life, her family, her real world. Sacred. When it came to romantic relationships, she was realizing in real time that she wasn't sure how to navigate anything that didn't belong in a bridge-sitting daydream or a spicy romance novel. What was she supposed to say or do right now? This wasn't the time for clever flirtation or physical objectification. This was her world and her heart. She'd not prepared for this kind of moment, which made her feel silly and ill-equipped.

"You take care of yourself," Alexis said, hands at her sides. She leaned in, hesitating briefly before placing a kiss on Marigold's cheek.

"Thank you again. I will."

Once she was on her own, she balled up the foil, tossed the rest of the fries, and headed back to Violet's room, where she found a new face in a lab coat holding his own iPad. Violet looked up as she entered the room. Her tear-streaked face sent Marigold cold and still. This wasn't good.

"What's going on?" Marigold asked. A distinguished man with salt-and-pepper hair and kind eyes looked back at her. She held up a hand. "Hi, I'm the sister."

Violet wiped the errant tears as if embarrassed. "This is Dr. Welsley from oncology. They've found something that could answer a lot of questions, and even though we still need the lab to confirm, they want to get my ducks in a row."

"Oh." The only word she could manage because the air had been drained from the room. *Oncology.*

"Is it okay if we include…?" He gestured to Marigold.

"Yes," Violet said. "You can speak freely."

"Unfortunately, I'm seeing the telltale signs of Hodgkin's lymphoma." He went on about lymph nodes, blood counts, and an enlarged spleen. Marigold tried to take in the details, but her ears buzzed uncomfortably and nausea gripped her midsection.

Violet nodded along like a trouper. Bless her. "And you think it's responsible for my dizzy spells? The passing out?"

"It manifests differently in everyone. But it can most certainly steal your energy out of nowhere, leaving you wondering what happened.

Drops in your blood pressure could also be the culprit. Everything's connected. The body is a complicated place."

"How treatable?" Marigold asked. She wished she'd had a more delicate phrasing. Her vocabulary had arrested. The world was crumbling around her, and despite her efforts to maintain control, every inch of her vibrated with abject fear.

"If it is Hodgkin's, it's highly treatable, and there have been great advances in therapies in the last five years," he said with a nod. "But I'll need to run a few more tests before I offer up specifics. We'll know more this week." He focused on Violet. "If you'd like me to take you on as a patient, I would be happy to do that. The hospital also has a list of oncologists they can match up with your insurance as we continue to explore. Either way, we'll make sure you're taken care of."

He continued, now referencing images on the iPad. However, Marigold's brain had gone soft and foggy. Her emotions swamped everything. She caught snatches. Surgery was likely due to her spleen issue. It was all a movie playing on fast speed. This wasn't real. Their family had already paid enough.

The crux was that Violet had a journey in front of her, and Marigold would be here through it all. It seemed like they were ahead of this thing, and could take it out once and for all.

Once they were alone, Marigold took a seat on the bed next to Violet and pulled in both of her hands. "This is good. Don't you think?" A lie. "It sounds like the doctors are on top of the problem. We caught it in good time."

"The *cancer*," Violet amended, shock etched tightly on her face. She was pale and nodding. "That's what it is, so we should probably use the word. Confront the reality." She dropped her head onto the pillow and arrowed her concern to the ceiling. "All I can think about is Ethan. He needs me, Mare. Tad is not the kind of parent that—"

"I know." Ethan's father, Tad, was an arrogant, selfish, abusive asshole, who Violet had divorced when Ethan was still a baby. He wasn't an active parent, preferring to spend his time looking falsely important, flashing his inherited wealth, and moving from woman to woman. Even his snooty parents had distanced themselves from him. Tad dropped in for birthday parties and Christmas photos before disappearing from Ethan's life again. Should anything happen to Violet, and it wouldn't, there was no way Marigold would let that slimeball in a sport coat raise

Ethan. "I don't want you to worry about that at all. Doctor...who was that?"

Violet consulted the card he'd left. "Dr. Welsley."

"Right. Dr. Welsley said during his spiel that this wasn't a grim diagnosis."

"He said *at this point*."

"And that's the point we're at. So we're okay."

Without a word, Violet reached for Marigold, who was right there for her, enveloping her in a hug that they very much needed. Fresh tears hit, born of fear and love. Violet was more than just her sister. She was her best friend, her partner in crime, her hero, and she tried to communicate all of it in this embrace. She pulled tighter and clung.

"I love you, Vi. You're gonna be just fine. I need you to believe that."

"I'm trying. I promise. And I love you, too."

CHAPTER SIXTEEN

As someone who very much valued the feeling of being in control, Alexis wasn't sure what to make of her reception at the hospital. In fact, the awkward scenario had been on her mind for days now. She'd tried to do a nice thing, step in and help out so things went a little easier for Marigold and her family, but she'd left feeling like she'd been in the way, when it was her goal to be anything but.

She wanted to throw herself into work, yet she didn't have the fortitude to write from her heart, explain herself to her followers quite yet. She went for runs and stopped in at Hole in One, all the while waiting for the woman she missed to resurface.

Marigold had a lot on her plate, though. She'd be good to remember that and not make anything she experienced that day about herself, even if it did feel like Marigold shoved her right out the door. Whether she wanted to or not, Alexis felt a little too vulnerable for her own comfort level. They had recently taken a pretty big step forward on that phone call, admitting to each other that there was something real and important happening between them. And with just one swift rebuff, Alexis felt herself backing the hell up again, grasping for safety, and trying to convince herself she didn't care.

She very much did.

So three days later, when she swung her front door open after a quiet knock, she was relieved to see Marigold standing there. Her fingertips went numb, and to hide it, she feathered them through her hair.

"Hi." Her heart thudded as a bolt of unfamiliar nerves sprouted.

"You're back home. Hey." She'd already said a greeting. Why did she offer a second one? She closed her eyes briefly, an attempted regrouping.

Marigold nodded, but her hands were clasped in front of her tightly. The white knuckles meant she wasn't feeling so carefree. "Can I come in?"

"Of course. Please." She forced herself to brighten, remembering her hospitable side. "Coffee, some water, a glass of wine? We're into the afternoon now."

"Um, no thanks." Marigold shifted her weight, another sign of her discomfort. She hated the distance that hung between them. The conservative exchange didn't quite fit right, like a shirt that was too snug. She didn't know how to fix it.

"I wanted to say thank you for all the trouble you went to when Violet and I were in Wichita."

"How is she?"

A small pause. "Back at home and happy to be there. And understandably shaken by the diagnosis."

"Oh, so they know what…"

"It's a form of cancer that's been having a negative effect on her blood pressure and immune system, but they're hopeful."

"Oh." Alexis's stomach flexed with discomfort. It wasn't good news. Cancer never was.

"I'm trying not to get ahead of myself."

Alexis nodded, taking it all in.

"We talked to her doctor again this morning. He's getting Violet set up quickly for treatment and says we have reason to be optimistic. I like him."

She slid her hands into her back pockets. "That part is really good to hear. I don't know Violet as well as you do, but I can certainly tell you that she is a strong, determined woman."

"Yeah. She is that."

Now what? She was out of her depth. She searched for the magical words that would make this all feel better for Marigold, who had to be in such turmoil. Violet was clearly her best friend, their bond ridiculously tight. Plus, they'd lost their mother to cancer not long ago.

"Anyway, I wanted to tell you how much I appreciate you

arranging the hotel room, which I did use. And for the food. It was nice of you to drive up."

"It wasn't that long of a drive. Plus, I wanted to." Alexis lifted her shoulders. "No problem."

"Except there was."

"Oh." That didn't bode well.

"The problem was that I panicked when I saw you. I'm not used to having a plus-one to traumatic events in my life, and I botched the whole thing."

"I did insert myself and realize now that—"

Marigold took a purposeful, desperate step forward. "But I want one. I want you." That snatched the air from Alexis's lungs.

"Oh." She nodded, struggling to keep up with the twists and turns this conversation was taking.

"I just might need a little practice inside the maze"—she held up a finger—"a metaphor that you likely don't understand, but bear with me. I've never had someone who mattered in the way that you're starting to matter. That meant the moment you walked into that hospital room, my brain couldn't handle all the things happening at once."

"I short-circuited you?"

"Yes. But I'll be ready next time. I'll be better at it."

Alexis felt the brewing of a soft smile. "So, you're saying I should stand my ground."

"Hell, yes. Stand, stand. Stand," Marigold said with such intensity that it almost knocked Alexis over. Her pale blue eyes were wide and imploring. "Because maybe I'm not as put together as I thought I was. I sit on my damn bridge and dream up all sorts of fantastical, romantic, wonderful scenarios, ready for my own love life to find me." She swallowed. "But maybe I forgot to plan for *real* life, too."

Alexis tilted her head, drinking this woman in. The soft turn of her curls, the way her eyes searched Alexis's as she spoke, as if seeking answers within their depth. "Come here," Alexis said, holding out a hand. Marigold placed her trembling hand in Alexis's, and with a soft squeeze it relaxed. She pulled Marigold closer, her gaze never wavering, not for a second. "I've got you, okay?"

"You've got me. I feel it."

"You can trust me," Alexis said, cradling her cheek. She turned and quietly walked them hand in hand to the couch. She took a seat and pulled Marigold onto her lap, her knees on either side of Alexis. Reaching up, she took Marigold's face in her hands and smiled. The quiet moment was all they needed to reconnect and click right back into place. The tether between them was as real and as palpable as the couch they sat on. She couldn't deny it, escape it, or argue. Not that she wanted to.

Marigold touched a strand of her hair, and her gaze scanned Alexis's features. "I've never seen a more beautiful woman in my entire life."

Alexis raised an eyebrow. "Have you seen my sister? That line is generally reserved for her."

"Aspen Wakefield, queen of the screen and the face on magazine covers? Of course I have. Trust me when I say that she doesn't compare." Her voice was achingly sincere. Her eyes dipped to Alexis's mouth. She leaned down and brushed her lips across Alexis's. It caused a shiver, a full-body ripple of wonderful anticipation. She encouraged Marigold, pulling her face down more fully, sinking into the kiss, submerging herself in the haze of lust and possibly something even bigger. An acute tenderness encircled her heart, and she wasn't sure she ever wanted to be without it again. Which meant without *her*. Marigold Lavender.

With a soft urging of her tongue, Marigold requested entrance, and they were off. As the seconds ticked by, her body reached for a more intimate form of attention. Her breasts were grazed by Marigold's with each subtle movement, creating a firestorm that quickly spread. The friction of this beautiful woman moving in her lap left an ache between her legs that grew more and more difficult to ignore. Warm lips were on her neck, caressing, tickling, and working her into a desperate state. She closed her eyes as Marigold began to rock her hips, which pressed the seam of Alexis's jeans up against her center. Sweet Lord, what was happening? The button on her forest-green pants was undone expertly. Her eyes opened to the sight of Marigold's top going over her head and a helping of wonderful cleavage left to greet her. Her mouth went dry, and she swore the Earth shook. Marigold slid off her lap, and what a fucking loss that was. She nearly protested until her pants were eased down her legs and Marigold's mouth found the skin of her inner thigh. "Oh," she murmured in surprise.

"Can I?" Marigold asked quietly, a humble request.

"God, yes," Alexis said and felt her body eased to the edge of the couch. She was wet, and her underwear had to be, too, only now it was gone. Removed by Marigold, whose tongue touched her ever so lightly. The noise was hers, a cry or a whimper pulled automatically from the back of her throat. She lost herself after that, taken on a journey in which she was brought to the edge and then back again. Marigold knew exactly what she was doing, prolonging the dance. Alexis rolled her hips, searching for release, desperate, just in time to have it pulled away. "What are you trying to do to me?" she asked, eyes closed. But she knew and loved every second of it.

"I'm learning you, that's what." The sentence was about the sexiest she'd ever heard. What was even hotter was the way Marigold went straight back to the task at hand. It was the lazy circles of her tongue that had Alexis ready to levitate off the couch. She squirmed beneath the sweet torture until Marigold changed the trajectory of everything, pushing her fingers inside. The climb began. They moved together, Marigold inside her, Alexis on the brink. That's when Marigold began to shower attention on the one spot that was now the center of Alexis's entire universe.

"Fuck," she breathed as she was carried higher and higher with each thrust. She dug her nails into Marigold's shoulders, at the top of the roller coaster. She'd lost all logical thought but was unable to care. The payoff raced toward her, taking over her everything. A cry shook from her throat when it hit, enveloping her like a wave crashing on the shore. She came hard and fast, clutching Marigold, then the couch, searching for anything to steady her out of control, wonderful, head-spinning experience. Marigold continued to rock her through it until the last ripples of pleasure receded. She struggled to catch her breath as she slowly returned to planet Earth. "I think that's what's called losing myself."

"Then let's make you lose yourself more often." Marigold, looking sexy as hell, curls flipped onto the top of her head, joined Alexis on the couch with the most satisfied look on her face. "Because it looked really good on you. Everyone should take a page from that book."

She leaned in and kissed Marigold softly. The sight of her in that bra was beautiful, but the clothing seemed superfluous. They should do something about it. "Did I mention that the owner of this place completely remodeled the primary bath? Biggest shower you've ever seen."

"Wow. That sounds luxurious."

Alexis stood and offered her hand. "I want to see you naked and wet. Join me?"

"I can't believe you just said that." Marigold opened her mouth and closed it again, but her eyes had gone dark. Alexis remembered that look.

"I have a lot more to say. Trust me."

Marigold stood and reached around to unclasp her bra, but Alexis shook her head.

"I'll be handling the undressing. Follow me."

Marigold closed her eyes briefly. "Your wish is my command."

"Dangerous words. But I love them."

❖

The first true cold front of autumn rippled through southern Kansas that next week. Fall was fully in session now. Along with coats and jackets nearly all the time, an excitement danced its way through the streets of Homer's Bluff as the citizens geared up for the holidays ahead. The Lavender House was busier than usual. Something about the colder weather made people want to get serious about their holiday shopping. Marigold was on her own at work, juggling customer interaction with her checkout line. The store pulled quite a few visitors from other towns. The farm and retail space had a strong word-of-mouth business. Women, most specifically, were their most dedicated customers. Groups of them made the trip to Homer's Bluff to stock up on their cute little wares. As the holidays approached, those kind of customers' visits tripled, to the delight of the Lavender family.

"Is there anything I can help you find?" Marigold asked a woman loaded up with purchases. "Those gloves are my favorite. Have you seen the paraffin treatments down the aisle?"

"Oh, I love those. Be right back." She dashed away.

Moments later, Marigold was behind the point-of-sale station, checking out a likely group of grandmas who spoke animatedly about their reservations at Marilyn's.

"I hear it's the nicest little place," one woman said.

"My friend Tina said we should go. That's why I booked it," another woman said as she fished for her credit card. "I might treat myself to a cocktail."

"You should. Try the lemon drop martini." Marigold flashed a smile as she bagged their items. "That's my sister's restaurant. Do yourself a favor and order the pork medallions in Jack Daniel's sauce, and finish your night with the warm butter cake."

Their eyes lit up, and they left happy and hungry.

Though it was closing time, Marigold's night wasn't finished. She missed Alexis and hoped they'd have a chance to spend time together at some point soon. In fact, she'd been living off mini-Alexis daydreams all afternoon. But first she had a meal to cook for her father before she checked in on Violet. In fact, maybe she'd invite her over to eat with them. Ethan could help her stir the potato soup.

"Excuse me. Did you wear your gloves and scarf today?" Marigold asked her dad an hour later as she finished peeling the last of the potatoes.

"I should have. The air had a bite to it."

Marigold went still and stared at him hard. Their mother never would have allowed him to walk out of the house without the proper weather gear. "You take those things with you tomorrow or I'm going to stop my day and bring them to you in front of all your guys like a child on the playground. Is that what you want?"

He eyed her. "You're tough."

"Damn right I am." She touched the tip of her finger to the counter. It was her way of threatening. "You don't take care of yourself, so I have to stay on top of you. You're honestly a little frustrating."

"Fair enough," he grumbled. "I'll set 'em out tonight before bed."

Her bad cop routine worked. "Good."

"Is there food? You said there'd be soup, and I'm here for it." She smiled at Violet, who entered through the back door on crutches. She had less than a week left on them and was counting down.

Ethan dutifully carried her purse like a happy little soldier. "Mom said that you said I could stir."

She nodded, hands on her hips as she surveyed her nephew. "The game of telephone was correct. Grab your stool and get over here." Ethan scurried to the stove, and she put him to work with the biggest spoon she could find, knowing the power it would gift a four-year-old. He wore the matching ball cap Uncle Sage had given him for his birthday, looking like a miniature version of the guy. The brunette model. Genetics was an amazing thing.

Violet took a seat, and Marigold was right there to retrieve the crutches. Her father leaned in. "You taking it easy? Following doctor's orders?"

"I am," she said with a conservative smile. Her light had dimmed since her diagnosis, but it was apparent she was trying to hold it together for the rest of them. Marigold wished she didn't feel the need for the brave front.

He nodded and his brow furrowed. "Now here's the real question."

"Okay." She waited, watching.

He paused. The room felt heavy. "Did you wear your scarf and gloves today?" he asked quietly. "Because if not, MG over here is gonna show up at your job and yell at you."

Violet's eyebrows shot up before the sides of her mouth stretched their way into a laugh. "I'll have to remember that. She can be scary. Thanks for the tip."

Score one for their dad. Violet needed those moments of joy. In her peripheral, something slid by on the stove. "Hey, E, let's try to keep all the potatoes in the pot."

"They just keep hopping out like frogs," he said with a shake of his head. "Tricky."

Violet sat tall, trying to see. "That might be because you're whipping them around like a tornado. Slow stirring. Okay? Slow."

"Slow stirring," he repeated quietly to himself. He was a good kid. Her heart tugged, hoping only positive things for him and his future.

Marigold gave him a squeeze from behind as he worked. "I think you're killing it."

He looked up at her, wide-eyed and worried.

"No. No. That's a good thing."

Ethan relaxed. "Oh."

"I do have news," Violet said, tenting her hands as Marigold chopped the freshly cooked bacon. She paused entirely to listen.

"I have a date for surgery. Two weeks from Thursday."

Marigold came around the counter to stand in front of the kitchen table. "Okay. This is good. Let's get the ball rolling. That's a November date. My lucky month." She danced around and threw a few punches.

"It is?"

"Well, it's my *favorite* month, so now it will be my lucky one, too."

Violet laughed. "I like it. My doctor said it's possible they'll want to follow up with chemotherapy after surgery, but it's a wait and see."

Her father stroked his chin. He was nervous around the topic, and rightfully so. "I've been reading about Hodgkin's. It sounds like it's different in everyone, and symptoms can come on fast."

"Exactly, but so did we," Marigold said, offering more fancy footwork, refusing to focus on anything but the encouraging portions of their plight. Unless, of course, she was alone and then imagined every awful scenario possible. Apparently, it was her new normal. In the quiet hours of the night, instead of her own steamy romantic fantasies, she daydreamed about all the ways her heart might be broken by the universe. It presently felt like she had a lot to lose.

"I'll be happy to stay with the little guy," their dad said.

"That'll be great. It frees me up to be with Violet and Cruz at the hospital," Marigold said, moving back to the stove to add in her cream. Ethan had abandoned his project for his car collection on Grandpa's bottom shelf and was driving the cars off the cliff-slash-coffee table. Something she remembered Aster and Sage doing in that exact same spot. "Soup in twenty. Can I pour anyone a glass of wine? Let's be fancy for once."

"Me," her dad and Violet said in unison, which prompted a laugh.

"Three glasses of the good stuff coming up."

"I have news, too," their dad mumbled. She and Violet exchanged a look.

"All right. Out with it," Marigold said and poured three glasses.

"Do you remember when I high-fived that woman at the grocery store?"

"I still can't believe you did that," Violet said. "You're a unique guy."

"Not so fast." He sat forward with a sly grin Marigold wasn't at all used to on him. "She spoke to me yesterday." He sat back and waited as if he'd just dropped the most exciting grenade and planned to watch it tear through the room. It did.

Marigold did an about-face like a dutiful, celebratory soldier of love and took a seat at the table. "Tell the whole story."

Violet rested her chin in her hand. "Don't skimp on details either."

"Well, first I paused in the ears of corn section and picked up a pack. And then she wheeled her cart around me and grabbed a head of lettuce and said, *Good to see you.*" He paused.

They waited.

"What did you say back?" Marigold asked, drumming her palms on the table, too excited not to.

He shrugged. "Oh, nothing. I just nodded. I thought that was good."

Violet dropped her forehead to the table. "No. Dad. You didn't tell her it was nice to see her, too? She likely thinks you're not interested."

He shrugged, undeterred. "I don't know that I am. Just making a little conversation at the grocery store with a woman."

Marigold nodded. "Okay. Well, next time, maybe you'll strike up a conversation. With words "

"Good idea. You can take turns," Violet offered.

He blinked, unfazed. "Sure. We both seem to do our shopping on Thursday evenings close to dinnertime."

Marigold clapped. "Bam. Now that's the kind of intel you can put to use."

He nodded and sipped his red. "This is nice, but I'm gonna grab a beer. I'm not as fancy as I thought."

Violet stole his glass and poured the contents into hers. "But I am. I've earned this."

Marigold kissed her cheek with a smack. "And more. Gonna check the soup."

"Mare?"

She looked back. Violet's eyes were wide and brimming with tears. "Everything's going to be okay, right?"

Marigold's own eyes filled, and she fought the painful lump that had risen in her throat. "Yeah. It is."

"Okay," Violet said, and nodded.

CHAPTER SEVENTEEN

Hey little sister. It's me, your much more famous and fabulous big sis calling to wish you a fun-filled birthday. I'm actually on a yacht this week in the Med." Some sort of loud horn blasted near the phone. Alexis's sister laughed loudly before coming back on. "I think if you keep having birthdays you might just pass me by." Another laugh, a giggle, really. "I'm just playing. You look good for thirty-four. Almost as good as me. Goals are good for you. Let's catch up real soon. Smooches." Click.

The voice mail ended, and Alexis, who stood in the white and pink striped boxers and tank she'd slept in, nodded because the message was everything she'd expect from her sister. She was fairly certain her mother had forced the call, and that was fine. She'd accept the well-wishing. No one in town would know it was her birthday, so she'd celebrate quietly, maybe treat herself to a cocktail later that evening. The best gift she could imagine was some alone time with Marigold. With all that was going on with her family, her schedule had been more than full. Maybe Alexis would call her after work, see if she could help her relax. Maybe a massage might be in order, she thought to herself, as she sipped her newly made cappuccino. That espresso machine that came with the rental was everything.

Her front door opened.

Wait. What? Alarm bells sounded in her brain because she had the place booked for at least the next two weeks. Had Barney gotten his wires crossed and doubled up, or was she being burgled by the local crook? She imagined there was only one in a town this size.

Deciding to proceed cautiously, she straightened and peered

around the corner, attempting to see who was breaking into the house and how big they were. For combat purposes, she needed their stats. Strategy was key.

Was that humming? No. It was an actual song. Another frown. Why was the intruder singing? It was "The Happy Birthday Song." The criminal, who was female, also knew her name. Once her brain fully caught up, she understood that she wasn't facing a home invasion, but somehow Marigold was there singing to her on her birthday. How did she know? Her jaw practically hit the floor, and her palm flew to her forehead as Marigold appeared around the corner, holding a plate of Hole in One doughnuts arranged in a pretty impressive triangle. A lit candle flickered on top as if waving hello. One thought toppled the rest: Best. Birthday. Cake. Ever. She watched as Marigold lowered the plate onto her countertop.

"Haaaappy Birthday, to youuuu!" Marigold laughed and clapped, looking both adorable and pleased with herself.

"How in the world?"

"Did I score doughnuts?" She shrugged. "I know a place." She went still. "Oh."

"What?"

"Look at you. Your outfit. Your hair. Do you have any idea how sexy you look in boxers and a tank top? You have to be cautious when you wear boxers around me. I'm swooning over here."

Alexis straightened to her full height, which was still a couple of inches shy of Marigold's. "Really? Boxers? Ha. I had no idea. I'm still learning all the things that get your attention."

Marigold sighed. "I'm here to report to you that everything you do gets my attention. From the moment you walked into Marilyn's, you had it. I forgot how to speak."

"You were into me before the whole...You're lying."

"No. Violet got worried because I went completely silent. I'd never seen anything like you."

Alexis took her hand. While she was pulled in by the torturous aroma of those fresh doughnuts, she needed this moment with Marigold more. She kissed the back of her hand. "Thank you for my birthday doughnuts." She grabbed one and took a bite. "So sinful."

"Old-school courting," Marigold said, looking down at the back of her hand, her light blue eyes lighting up.

"I heard you like romance." Another bite of doughnut. What a great morning.

Marigold melted. "In every sense of the word. I've actually figured us out."

"I wasn't sure that was possible." She tilted her head. "What have you discovered?"

"We're the sworn enemies who secretly want to rip each other's clothes off. That's our legacy." Alexis raised an interested eyebrow. Marigold held up a hand. She wasn't done. "Until, of course, the villain—"

Alexis pointed at herself in question.

Marigold nodded wholeheartedly. "Until the villain reveals her softer side and they begin to fall deeper and deeper into the wonderful trenches of love." She shrugged. "I mean, after all, you continue to talk about how in love with me you are."

"I had no idea I was in a trench, though. I should scribble that down somewhere as a reminder."

"Perfect idea. It's important." She gestured up and down Alexis's body. "But you need to change clothes. We have plans."

"How is that possible? Aren't you the only one on at the store today?"

"Normally, yes, but I'm making my brother take a shift, and I even gave him permission to open late and close early so he can still check in on the farm." She folded her arms in victory. "Now go throw on some jeans. We're taking a road trip."

"Hmm. About that. I'm more of a first-class kind of girl," Alexis said in her most aloof, ice-cold villain voice.

"Oh, I will kiss that rich girl entitlement right off your face."

"I dare you," she said in her most sultry voice, hand on her boxer-clad hip.

Thank God Marigold didn't hesitate, pressing her lips to Alexis's and taking wondrous liberties with her hands on Alexis's ass. The kiss was searching and slow. "I can't tell if it's your birthday or mine," Marigold murmured, her hands slipping beneath the hem of her top. She placed her palms on the small of Alexis's back, and their connection snapped into place like a long-lost puzzle piece.

"I love it when you get handsy." Alexis's skin went tingly, and she automatically went up on tiptoe to better align their mouths. She wrapped her arms around Marigold's neck, taking the spot that was honestly becoming her favorite on Earth. The curls tickled her forearms. The curves pressed to hers enticed her in more ways than she could count.

Marigold pulled her mouth away and rested her forehead against Alexis. "While I'd very much like to continue this, we have a date a couple of hours from here and need to get a move on."

"Where are you taking me?" Her excitement level began to climb.

"I'll never tell. Until of course we're close, and then I'll blab like the gossip girl of the seventh grade."

"You are so very specific."

"I'm honored. Striving for just that." She gestured to the hallway with her chin. "While it's a shame to lose the outfit I very much want to fuck you in, you should probably get changed."

"I can't believe you just said that. It was awesome."

Marigold pressed on, refusing distraction. "Dress warm and comfortable."

"Demanding," Alexis said over her shoulder.

"Wait." Marigold chased her down and pulled her into one last, searing kiss. "To tide me over because I'm selfish, as well."

As Alexis walked down the hall, she added an extra sway to her hips, well aware she was being watched, objectified, and admired. A shiver danced across her skin. She loved every second of it.

Ninety minutes later, they were flying down the highway with a playlist Marigold had apparently named *What's Up, Suckers*, underscoring their conversation.

"But if you found yourself locked in your own house for two days, how do you spend your time?"

"I'd just call someone to let me out. My editor. My publicist. Even my mom."

Marigold shook her head. "No. You can't call anyone. You're locked in. What do you do?"

"Spend the time figuring out who did this to me and plot my revenge."

Marigold pinched the bridge of her nose. "I don't think you get the exercise."

"Fine." She tapped her lips. "I think I would probably spend most of it in the kitchen. I love to cook but rarely devote enough time to it."

"I applaud that answer and like it a lot."

"Now you."

"Journaling. Daydreaming. Maybe I'd try to invent something like that guy who made Wordle."

"I appreciate the time you devote to thought." Alexis rested her cheek on the seat and watched Marigold as she drove. "Most people don't slow down enough for that. With smartphones and instant gratification, everything is so immediate. Without other people hitting *like* or *comment*, I used to think what's the point?"

"You don't anymore?"

Alexis shook her head. "No. That's a new and probably valuable revelation. Not everything requires the applause of other people to make it worthwhile."

Marigold nodded. "I couldn't agree more. What else?"

"Is there significance to the one magnet on your refrigerator? I've been curious about the choice." It was a peapod opened in the middle and displaying the peas inside.

"That's for Tillman and me. He's been my best friend, not counting Violet, since we were in the sixth grade. We're peas in a pod. He got that for me a few Christmases ago. He has one on his fridge, too. My turn. Have you ever been close with your sister?"

Alexis thought on this. It was important for her to give Marigold an accurate picture of her relationship with Aspen because the truth wasn't all bad. They'd created enough good memories together over the years, but it would never be the kind of close-knit relationship Marigold knew with her own sisters.

"Complicated question. We're very different people. I love Aspen, and I believe that she loves me back." She sighed. "But there's always been an undercurrent of competition from her. She needs, for some reason, to keep me in my place. When I let her do that, we're generally okay."

Marigold sent her an apologetic look. "But when you stand up for yourself…"

"We clash, and she scrambles to win. At any cost."

"I'm so sorry."

Alexis held up a hand. "No. It's okay. It's all I've ever known. Seeing your family and the way you look out for each other"—she exhaled slowly because this was a confession not just for Marigold but for herself—"makes me want things I never have before. It's strange and kind of great." She smiled softly as her gaze settled on her lap. "I think about how nice it would be to have a family of my own someday. Like yours."

Marigold didn't hesitate. She took Alexis's hand, pulled it to her, and threaded their fingers. She drove the rest of the way just like that, one-handed. Alexis continued to steal glances at their linked hands, marveling how the image could make her feel so many intense and wonderful things. Marigold's passion for romance was perhaps not fanciful at all. The two of them in this car made her feel like she could run eighteen miles and carry the weight of the world on her shoulders if she could only just wake up to Marigold every day. If that wasn't romance in all of its glory, she didn't know what was.

"I really like you," she said, earnestly aware that the words fell short of what she knew was already hovering.

"I like you, too." Marigold kissed the back of her hand. She nodded to the road ahead. "We're about thirty seconds away, birthday girl. Prepare yourself and your taste buds."

That had Alexis sitting up and peering off into the horizon. "What? You know how I feel about food."

"I've heard a thing or two."

A man with two hand-held orange flags directed them into a large parking lot. Marigold turned to her. "Welcome to the sweetest event the state of Kansas offers all year."

"Tell me," Alexis said, releasing Marigold's hand. She placed it on her forehead.

"I've literally never seen you almost lose your cool like this. I didn't realize it was possible. Well, except when you're right about to—"

"What is this place?" Alexis asked, hopping in her seat. She wasn't able to take the suspense any longer. It was her birthday, and if she wanted to be a kid, she planned to let herself. Why hold it in? There was probably nobody else she'd let go in front of. Marigold was her safe spot. Deep within her, she knew it. Alexis didn't have to work to impress Marigold or convince her that she was important. She could just *be*.

"Welcome to the Kansas City Pie Festival."

"Stop." She scanned the horizon. She could make out tents, balloons, food trucks, and…was that a giant slide? This was too good.

"I cannot. There's one thing we do well in the Midwest, and it's pie. Don't believe me?" She unclicked her seat belt. "You're about to find out."

"I could make out with you for hours right now."

"Do you want to skip Pie Fest? I'd be happy to accommodate that request."

"I really don't think we can skip Pie Fest."

Marigold nodded. "I think there's room for both. Let's go. I got us VIP passes, which means we get a one-hour early entry window before everyone else."

Alexis gasped. "You got me first-class pie for my birthday?"

"Nothing but the best for Ms. Wakefield."

She experienced a delicious shiver that shimmied its way from her toes to her hairline. "I think I might like it when you call me that."

"Well, then get ready for more. We might have just found your nickname. Are you ready for pie?" Marigold asked, paired with the most beautiful smile on record.

"Yes, please." She opened the door. "Let's go!"

❖

There's something magical about watching someone in their element. Alexis was surrounded by something she loved and it showed. She sparkled as she walked the rows of booths, surveying her options, chatting with the vendors. This was her happy place. And though Marigold was having a fantastic time, her real joy came in watching Alexis. As they moved from one line to the next, tasting key lime, Texas pecan, buttermilk, strawberry-peach, lemon chess, and every other kind of pie mankind had dreamed up, Alexis never seemed to get bored.

"Wait. We can't skip this row," she said, grabbing Marigold and practically dragging her in the opposite direction. "That big line over there means it's good. C'mon."

The ticket was all inclusive and allowed them to sample absolutely everything on-site, which included a variety of cocktails. Marigold snagged a glass of bubbly from an impressive champagne wall and sipped while Alexis interrogated a man in a fedora about his savory cheeseburger hand pie recipe.

"If I told you, I'd have to kill you or go out of business."

"Come on. Arnold, is it?" Alexis asked, surveying his business card. "You can trust me. I'm not even from Kansas."

"Are you one of the judges?" he asked, squinting.

"No, sir. Just a curious attendee. I'm gonna guess you have pickle in there? Do you have pickle, Arnold?"

He zipped his lip, and sensing a stalemate, Marigold gave Alexis's hand a tug and she surrendered. Somehow that left them holding hands as they went in search of the coconut creme everyone had been gushing about. "I'll be back later, Arnold," Alexis called. She squeezed Marigold's hand. "Hey, let's grab the pie and find a place on the lawn. The band is actually really good."

"The Space Cadets. They're pretty well known around here. They cover everything from The Beatles to Ariana Grande."

Marigold pulled a plaid checkered picnic blanket from her tote.

Alexis marveled. "You're impressively prepared."

"Well, I'm the doughnut shop," Marigold said with a wink.

Alexis went still. "Tori says that to you, too?"

"She says it to everyone. So thereby, we say it to each other. Small towns have a sense of humor, too, Alexis."

She eased a strand of honey hair behind Marigold's ear. "I'm learning so much."

"The loving gaze says a lot. Look at you. You might be obsessed with me." She laughed, hoping it signaled the playfulness of the exchange. She didn't want Alexis to think she was moving too fast. Even if she very much was.

The smile on Alexis's lips waned. "I really might be."

For several beats, they held eye contact as The Space Cadets bellowed "Since U Been Gone" from the bandstand.

Alexis tilted her head and gave her head a slow shake. "I don't want this to end."

"There's lots more pie."

"Us."

"Oh."

"But I have to go home."

Marigold nodded. "It was only a matter of time, right?"

"I love everything about today. Being here has been so wonderful."

"I feel like there's another shoe about to drop." Marigold closed one eye, bracing.

"But it also makes me miss my column, my place in the food scene. So maybe it's time I crawl my way back. Go back to work."

"You can do it." She raised her shoulders. "For what it's worth, I'm sorry that I'm the one that ruined it all for you."

"I'm not. At all."

"No?"

"I think I needed the distance and time to reflect on who I want to be and where I want my career to go." A pause. "Also? It brought me you. I wouldn't trade this time for anything."

It felt as if Marigold had been wrapped in the most wonderful blanket. Those words encircled her with warmth. "Me, too. I mean it."

Alexis sighed. "But if I stay away too long, I worry that I might lose whatever tiny bit of momentum I have left."

"And I'm sure you miss your life."

"Some of it. But it's mine."

Marigold swallowed, understanding that the fairy tale might just be coming to an end. They'd discussed San Francisco and the idea of her joining one day, but did she really have the courage to follow through? If she didn't, the feelings that made her days sparkle would be a thing of the past. She wouldn't crawl into bed with a healthy helping of gratitude for Alexis. Would this whole experience soon be a memory she would take out whenever she needed to remember a time she was truly happy?

That was okay. She understood how lucky she was to have been gifted these many weeks with Alexis. She'd gone her whole life without feeling this way. She could again. Only now she'd know what she was missing, and that knowledge forced an ache in her chest.

"Come with me."

Record scratch. She blinked, processing, reaching, hoping. "To San Francisco?"

"Yes. You said it was something you'd consider. Let's take it one step farther." Alexis turned to her fully. "This isn't just talk. I'm officially asking. Come with me to San Francisco."

Her mind raced, but her heart soared. The ache had been replaced with a sense of euphoria rooted in being wanted by someone she wanted right back. Terror also flared. She'd always dreamed of living somewhere big, bustling, or different than the only town she'd ever really known. This was her chance for love, for adventure! But there were so many factors to consider.

"I don't know. I'd have a lot to work out. I have my home, my job, my family. They need me."

"That's true. But for a minute, put all those things on hold. Just focus on you." Marigold tried to do just that. "Now, what is it that *you* want? No one else."

"I want us. You. San Francisco. All of it." She smiled nervously, realizing the words were out there now.

Alexis leaned in and captured her lips, carrying them to somewhere heavenly as she cradled Marigold's face. "We'll sort it all out. We can work up to it, even. I just want to know that it's what you want, too."

Was this really possible? Marigold pressed her forehead to Alexis's and watched as their entire relationship rewound before her eyes to moment one. The way her heart had stuttered and her words had failed her. There had been missteps. More than a few. Alexis's icy persona that very slowly melted away once she truly got to know her. Her own confusion at how to be a person attached to someone else. In the midst of it all, their connection continued to blossom into a full-on relationship that she wanted more than anything. She was falling. Helplessly. Hopelessly.

"The damn dart throwing." She smiled at the memory of Alexis in casual clothes and schooling the men who'd gathered.

"What are you talking about right now?" She took a big, adorable bite of the coconut creme pie and melted, appropriately distracted. "These Kansas pie people don't pull punches."

"I'm skipping down the path of memory lane. You. That first night you were in town. The jeans. The darts."

Alexis set her plate next to them as if this new revelation demanded full focus. "I love that you were hot on me even when you were so livid."

Marigold touched her forehead. "Oh, sweetie. It was probably part of it."

Alexis looked to the side in thought. "We're into each other when we get along and when we don't. That has to say something."

"You know what made me want to get to know you better? Carrot."

Alexis dipped her brows. "Explain."

"It was the way you were with him. So gentle and loving. I knew nobody who treated their dog with such care could be as bad as I was making them out to be in my brain. I decided then and there to quit making rash judgments about you and give you a chance." She smiled. "I'm glad I did."

"I didn't think it was possible, but I love him even more now. Steak for dinner!" She held out her arm. "Come here. I need you close." Marigold slid until they were pressed together, and with Alexis's arm around her, they listened to the music and enjoyed the gentle chill of the afternoon. There was a new promise twinkling in the air between them. It wasn't just a flippant idea anymore. They were going to make a go of it. Marigold could hardly wrap her mind around it. A thought sprang. "Wait. Does that mean I'm your girlfriend now?"

"Yes. Yes, it does," Alexis said, without delay. "I don't know who you need to notify or what sign you need to hang that says *taken*, but you are in fact that."

A sense of calm and belonging came over her. Alexis wasn't her family, but she was feeling more and more like her home. This was what she'd longed for and wondered if she'd ever have. This was what *joy* felt like.

"Are we going to get naked later?" she asked around a sip of champagne.

"Without a doubt," Alexis said.

"I could get used to this." She sighed dreamily.

Alexis kissed the side of her head. "Please do."

The drive home was quieter. Alexis would occasionally kiss the back of Marigold's hand and smile before drifting away into her own thoughts again. Marigold focused on the happiness factor, rather than the knowledge that she'd be leaving her family behind in Homer's Bluff. She couldn't look at that portion head-on. At least, not yet.

"Let me guess," she said to Alexis. "You're piecing together the ingredients of that cheeseburger pie. Or wait, maybe it's the coconut."

Alexis laughed. "It's like you know me or something." She raised a finger. "Except this time, you'd be wrong."

"Okay. Then tell me. What are you thinking about over there?"

"In this moment, I was thinking how captivating Marigold Lavender is and how unexpectedly lucky I am to have found my way to you. This was my absolute best birthday." She shook her head, her features pulled with emotion. "I don't deserve any of this." Alexis's eyes filled with tears until her cheeks streaked. Whoa. What was happening? The sight was so totally unexpected that Marigold wasn't sure what to say or do. Her heart tugged. She reached over and brushed one of Alexis's cheeks with her thumb.

"I don't know if you believe that certain things are ordained, but I always have. And us? We were. Okay? I know it with every fiber of my being."

Alexis listened, taking a moment before being able to speak again. "Me, too," she whispered. "And I just want to be better for you. I want to give you everything." She swallowed, paused. "I want you to be proud of me."

That night when they came together, it was different. There was a reverence that covered each touch, each look, each passion-filled moment. They weren't hooking up. This was an expression of something so much deeper. "Happy birthday, baby," she whispered shortly before falling asleep in Alexis's arms, happy, warm, and taken care of. Carrot was curled into a swirl in his bed next to theirs, snoring quietly. No other place on Earth could have felt this perfect. They'd earned this. They belonged right where they were.

Yet, when she woke in the wee hours, she was alone. Where had Alexis gone off to? She missed the warmth against her side, the hair that tickled her arm.

The house smelled like popcorn, and the sun had not yet come up. What in hell? She blinked to clear her vision and headed out on what could turn into a search and rescue mission.

CHAPTER EIGHTEEN

Alexis scored maybe an hour of sleep after her memorable night with Marigold. They'd taken their time to explore, savor, connect, and eventually combust. The level of heat had been off the charts. She'd lain there, running her fingers through Marigold's hair until she'd fallen asleep, leaving Alexis with her thoughts. She felt light, motivated, happy, and ready for all that was ahead. Then she was met with an overwhelming sensation to get started on their new life then and there. The words slowly presented themselves to her, and she'd scurried out of bed to capture them, no matter what the hour. She popped a bowl of popcorn on the stove using her special Parmesan recipe, quietly poured some food into Carrot's bowl, knowing he'd join her shortly, and flipped open her laptop. Her fingers itched to get to the keys. She let the thoughts come in bursts as she typed, uncensored, apologetic, and raw.

I learned this year that I've been an asshole for a good portion of my life. Deep breath. *That changes today.*

The letter to her readership flew freely from her heart to the screen, unencumbered by second-guessing or the fear of the judgment that could follow. There were moments in life that were necessary, no matter how hard they seemed. Alexis knew that her words and their assembly in this post fell into that category. An hour later, she surveyed her work with a quick read-through and impulsively posted it for the world to see. In her writing, she vowed to be better. She swore she'd find the good in most any bad situation, and though her objectivity would never be compromised and her reviews would be honest, she would never again let her need to be relevant allow her to belittle other people. Maybe it made her newly boring. Maybe she'd lose a portion of followers. But at the end of the day, she'd be proud of the energy she put into the world.

As far as her career went, she didn't expect to be welcomed back immediately. She'd start from the bottom all over again if that's what it took to reinvent herself for the better.

Satisfied, she stole her bowl of popcorn, found an old sitcom rerun, and settled in on the couch with her dog, keeping the volume low to not wake Marigold.

"You two started a middle of the night party and didn't invite me?"

Alexis and Carrot turned in tandem. The little dog rushed to lick Marigold's feet and scampered back to the couch, which surely was a clear invitation to join them. "We didn't mean to wake you."

Marigold seemed to take in the room for clues. "You just wanted a snack and a show."

Alexis switched off the TV. "Not exactly." She took a moment to gather her explanation. "Something about it being my birthday had me taking stock of everything. And like I said, I want to turn over a new leaf, and that extends to my job. So I had some things to get off my chest, and it couldn't wait."

Marigold took a seat, her expression dialed to concern. "What kinds of things?"

Alexis took out her phone and turned it around so Marigold could read the post. The room went quiet. "Wow. Okay. You say some really humbling things in this letter."

Alexis shrugged. "They're all true. And if I'm planning to go back into the foodie trenches, I need to make it clear that I'll be approaching things much differently. I don't want anyone disappointed or thinking I'm just trying to please the naysayers. I personally believe in the cause. Well, *now*." She shrugged. "I won't claim to have always understood."

Marigold raised her gaze. "You've never been sexier in your life."

Alexis looked down at the white T-shirt she'd slipped into before sneaking out of her room. "This thing?"

"It's your whole vibe." Marigold took a deep breath and exhaled. "And let's not lie, the T-shirt is ridiculously hot, too."

Marigold crawled over the arm of the couch and into Alexis's space. She took the cue and leaned back. "There you go, topping me again."

"You're just too tempting."

"Now, this I did not expect to happen at four a.m.," Alexis murmured, easing her thighs apart for Marigold to settle between. Perfection.

Marigold's eyes danced and then closed as she pressed her hips to Alexis and rocked. "And yet it is."

They managed another two and a half hours of sleep after a little sexy fun on the couch. When Alexis woke to frigid sunshine the next morning, she felt surprisingly renewed. She contemplated a run. Maybe after, she'd drop some coffee at the store for Marigold and Violet, who was set to return in short spurts. Out of habit, she checked her phone. Waiting for her were twenty-eight voice mails and forty-two missed calls. Her notifications on her socials were off the charts.

Carrot licked her nose and sat back as if to say *Surprise!*

She nodded once. "I think somebody heard what we had to say."

❖

November in Homer's Bluff truly did deliver the magic. Its arrival marked the official kickoff to the holiday season, and the businesses worked together to make the place feel festive. For her part, Marigold made sure The Lavender House was outfitted with an autumn wreath, a scarecrow along the front walk, and a cornucopia-turkey-pumpkin grouping overflowing on their front porch. As a special touch for their customers, they served mulled cider from a Crock-Pot in the corner, so guests could shop and sip the flavors of the season.

"Is this your mother's recipe?" Mrs. Flagg asked with an armful of lavender jelly. She held up her cider to clarify her question.

"Originally, yes. With a few recent tweaks from Aster."

"Aha!" Her eyes went bright. "That's why I'm in love. Aster knows her spices."

"She would love to know you said so. I'll pass it on."

Mrs. Flagg looked around the shop. "Where's Violet? I planned to see if she wanted a few jackets that my grandson has outgrown, for Ethan."

"Very sweet of you. I'll ask. But Violet's having surgery this week and taking it easy."

"Oh, that's right. I was so sorry to hear."

Marigold wilted. She didn't want people feeling sorry for Violet.

That meant there was something serious to worry about, and that wasn't going to be the case. She held those feelings of terror at bay, refusing to give them too much attention. "If everything goes according to plan, she should be just fine."

"It's the *everything going according to plan* part that always gets me, though. My Henry had quite the ordeal. We didn't expect it. I wish I'd been ready."

Marigold froze. She realized she was taking shallow breaths. Her heart raced. "Here's your receipt," she managed. Once the traffic slowed, she stole a moment in the storage closet and worked on slowing her breathing. When she returned to the empty store, she made a point to focus on happier thoughts. What they'd all be doing next year with all of this in the rearview mirror. That's when her phone did the vibrating rumba on top of the counter. She snatched it up and smiled. Thank God.

"You have impeccable timing," she told Alexis. "I needed to hear your voice. How's your workday?" Ever since Alexis had posted her apology letter, she'd been slammed with requests for interviews and inundated with direct messages from fans who were willing to offer her a second shot. She responded to as many of the messages as possible, working from the ground up to rebrand. She'd posted her first official review back from the land of the canceled. Appropriately, for Hole in One, which received a rave. Aster couldn't seem to wipe the smile off her face. Her baby was all grown up and famous. Tori danced through the doughnut kitchen for days.

"I've been at my laptop, which means I need a good stretch. Missing you, though. How are you?"

"A little all over the place."

"That's to be expected. Big week." Alexis took an audible breath. "In reference to that, I wanted to talk to you about something, and you can definitely say no."

"I'm listening." Mysterious indeed.

"My agent called. The one who quit returning my messages?"

"Convenient."

"Right? Welcome back, Bob. I guess now I know how loyal you are. But I'm trying to build bridges, not burn them, so of course I was friendly. Anyway, he says that *Morning USA* wants to book me on the show next week. They want to cover the whole journey, the concept of change, forgiveness, and redemption."

"Get out. *Morning USA*? I love that show. Why would I say no to you going on? I'll make a whole brunch buffet that morning, and when everyone goes home, I'll watch it again eight times."

"Well, you can't."

"But I love brunch."

Alexis laughed. "They want you, too. In fact, they only want to do the segment if we can both be there. You're a big part of the angle they're going for. Apparently, that little photo of us has renewed interest since my apology tour."

"They want me? On television?"

"Yes, ma'am. But I realize that's only a week and a half after Violet's surgery," Alexis said, offering an out, "so you have every right to say no."

Violet was scheduled to stay one to two nights in the hospital for the splenectomy, but Marigold would feel more comfortable speaking to her about it first. "Can I get back to you?"

"Of course."

"Not that the offer isn't exciting. I've never been to New York City."

"There's nothing like it."

"It's just that if my family needs me here, this is where I have to be."

"I get it. If it works out, it works out. If not, we'll grab a beer at Larry's and bring takeout to Violet."

Marigold sighed in relief. As exciting as this whole thing was, the idea of being away honestly had her on edge. She was the one who picked up the slack when the other Lavenders were tending to their families, their lives. That sense of responsibility was deeply rooted in her, more so than she'd ever realized. Violet's illness had certainly shined a spotlight. Her sense of obligation was something she was going to have to face at some point. She hadn't confessed to Alexis that she also worried a lot about her big move to San Francisco, which they'd tentatively considered for the spring. How in the world would she bring that up? What would Alexis think?

"Also, there's one other thing. I'll probably need to let go of my Airbnb soon. If we make it to New York, I'll likely head straight back to California after. Things are really starting to pick up again. I don't want to miss my window."

A gut punch. She knew it would be coming soon. How could it not be? "That part's going to be hard." She tried to imagine living in Homer's Bluff without Alexis and couldn't. She didn't want to go back to her old life. That's how important Alexis had become in just a matter of months. Like sunlight on her face after living in a shadow for years.

"Hard for me, too. You have no idea." A pause. "I don't want to wake up with you not next to me."

They'd not slept apart in weeks. In fact, they spent every free moment they had together, talking, kissing, laughing at Larry's. Alexis had become really good at making fun of Sage, and the two had a great give-and-take relationship. "I know you have to go, but I hate the thought of that distance between us. I don't want to lose an inch of what we've built so far."

"Well, you know what? That's not going to happen." Alexis didn't hesitate. "And there's room for you at my place the second you're ready to make the leap. We don't have to wait until spring."

"Maybe." Fear had entered the chat. She closed her eyes and tried to brace against it.

"Once you're there, it will be *our* place, right? Plus, visits galore until then. We have our entire lives just waiting for us." Alexis paused. "Those are the things I tell myself to make it feel manageable in the short term."

Marigold closed her eyes. "It sounds really nice. I just need to make sure the timing is there for the move. That my dad is feeling set up. My siblings are all good."

"I'm incredibly patient, you know. Especially when the woman I'm waiting for is more than worth it. And I was thinking about it, and you should keep your house. We'll need a spot to land with all the visits back to town."

Lots of visits. That was something to hold on to. Marigold smiled, loving how much Alexis just got her attachment to her family. Her need to be there for them, especially now that her mother couldn't be. That was a big piece of this thing. There was no chance she could stay away for long. It really would be the best of both worlds if she could make the leap. Correction. When. When she made it. Focus on the good. She scrunched her shoulders to her ears. All her dreams were coming true. She was about to have a life and maybe a family of her own. She just had to sort out a few fears first. She imagined Violet visiting them in San Francisco. They'd go wine tasting and shopping and sit in the gorgeous parks. One day soon.

With a shaky hand, she had a call to place.

"Well, you're one hundred percent going to New York," Violet said. "I'll have been home from the hospital for a week by that point, bored out of my mind and wanting something to watch on TV. And it better be you who shows up or we're not speaking."

"Are you sure?"

"Of course I'm sure. Cruz took three weeks off and will be here the whole time to help with Ethan."

She exhaled. "That part makes me feel better."

"Plus, I have Dad, Sage, Tyler, Aster, and Brynn—and everyone in town—to try to make up for one Marigold. It will be a tall order, admittedly. But I think we've got it."

She smiled. "Thank you for getting that. I'm the glue!"

"You're the glue who needs to go to New York. I'm serious. I can't believe you're going to be standing in that studio. We grew up watching that show with Mom! You know she's loving every second of this."

"Oh, wow." Tears filled her eyes. "I hadn't considered that part. She would have called all her friends."

"And showed the clip to everyone she met. This is honestly beyond cool. I'm really happy for you." A long pause. "About everything. That means Alexis. San Francisco. All of it. You know that, right?"

"Yeah," Marigold whispered, nodding.

"You've sacrificed a lot for the rest of us, and now I want you to take every little opportunity for yourself. Do you hear me?" There was a feistiness in her voice that Marigold wasn't used to, but it had her attention.

She sobered. "I hear you. I'm gonna try. It's hard to imagine leaving, but I'm working on it." Her heart thudded extra fast.

"I need more than that."

Marigold understood the gravity of the conversation and swallowed. "I promise you, Violet. I will chase every chance at happiness." It was a promise she very much intended to keep. She exhaled. A small smile blossomed. "New York City, get ready."

CHAPTER NINETEEN

The morning of Violet's surgery came in a flurry for the Lavender family. Alexis, who wanted to give Marigold space if she needed it, decided she would be present and available, but would take her cues as they came. If Marigold needed anything, Alexis would be there.

"Stop it. Things are different, and I very much want you there," she'd told Alexis the night before. "There's no one else I would rather hold my hand. Okay? I need you."

"Then you've got me."

The main waiting area was packed with Lavenders the next day. While Alexis had spent time with each and every one of them individually, this was her first opportunity to see them in a group. She looked on as they fluttered around, updating each other in a unique shorthand, teasing each other in the next breath. She'd never experienced a room containing so much overflowing affection before. The good energy was unmatched. She couldn't imagine belonging to a family like this one.

"Thank you for the coffee and pastries," Brynn said, taking a seat next to Alexis on one of the outside rows of chairs. Marigold was in with Cruz and Violet, who would be taken back for her surgery shortly.

"The least I could do. Sometimes it helps to find a way to feel useful."

"I know exactly what you mean. This family is incredibly close, but I think you'll find that they welcome newcomers quite warmly."

"Everyone's been exceptionally warm. Even you the first time we met."

Brynn smiled. "I'm glad for that now. Could have been awkward when you two got together."

"You two doing okay, over there?" Mr. Lavender asked.

"We're great. Is there anything you need, Pop?" Brynn asked, exchanging a look with Alexis that said *See?*

"Me? No, no." His cheeks went red at the focused attention. "Just want this part to be over. Jittery. Just gimme a fast-forward button already."

"Mr. Lavender, I don't know if it helps, but there's a game I like to play on my phone when I'm anxious," Alexis offered. "Baseball."

His eyes lit up. Her instincts hadn't been wrong. "Oh yeah? That sounds fun. And it's Tom." He took out his phone and held it out to her. He was asking for her help, which was honestly heartwarming.

"You got it. I like the batting practice feature, too. I'll show you." She stood, took the phone, and quickly downloaded her favorite game. While she showed him how to play, Marigold sneaked back in the room, and not long after, she felt Marigold's eyes on them. Alexis passed her a smile that was quickly returned.

"Everything okay?" Alexis asked, joining her across the room.

"I think so. They took her back about fifteen minutes ago." Marigold gave herself a little hug. The raw emotion seemed to have a firm grip on her.

"She's going to be just fine," Alexis said. "The doctors said this was a low-risk operation."

"I know. I'm just worried about what they might find. What kind of turn this whole thing might take. I don't want to be blindsided. I don't want Violet sucker-punched." She was talking fast.

Alexis nodded. "I have a good feeling about this."

"Good." Marigold exhaled slowly and flexed her fingers. "I like hearing that. Keep saying those things and squeezing my hand."

"Done."

She looked over at her father. "Thank you for the game. He needed something to ground him. It's been a hard morning on him." She lowered her voice. "I think this environment takes him back to my mom and all they went through."

"I'm happy to help." Alexis nodded and threaded their fingers. "He's really sweet."

The morning stretched into afternoon, and the group slowly traded spots in the room. Coffee cups came and went, and the new, fun baseball game was checked out by many. Finally, Violet's surgeon emerged from the large double doors, mask around his neck. Cruz was the first to approach, but Marigold was right there with him, practically holding her breath. Mr. Lavender gripped the sides of his chair, his knuckles white.

"She did great," the doctor said. Marigold nodded along, encouraging his words, willing them to come out faster. "We were able to leave a portion of the spleen without incident, and she's in the back recovering. I anticipate she'll return to her room in ninety minutes or so."

"Thank God," Cruz said and accepted a hug from Marigold. Alexis felt the relief infiltrate her body as one grouping of muscles after the next began to release. She could only imagine it was tantamount for the Lavenders.

"Did you hear what he said?" Marigold asked, heading straight into Alexis's arms. She buried her face in Alexis's neck and held on.

"It's the best news."

Alexis heard a quiet sound a few feet away. They turned to see Tom Lavender sobbing in his chair, shaking as tears streamed down his cheeks.

"Oh no. Dad?" Marigold said quietly. She let go of Alexis and raced to him. Her arms were around his neck in no time. Aster and Sage moved in, too, seemingly alarmed by what they saw. Sage laid a hand on Tom's shoulder, and Aster knelt down at his feet to catch his gaze.

"It was good news, Pop," Aster said quietly. "She's out of surgery and doing well."

"I'm happy. Really happy. That's all." He nodded, frantically wiping his tears. "I was just so scared."

Aster leaned her head on his chest, and the family spent the next few moments together in support of one another. The scene, the way the kids held on to their father, forced an uncomfortable lump in her throat. Alexis sent a silent thank-you above for watching over Violet and this very sweet family.

❖

"Just checking in to see how you're feeling," Marigold said, as she pressed her phone to her ear with her shoulder as she wheeled her luggage around the corner. They'd been in New York all of twelve minutes, and Alexis had headed off in search of the town car that the network had sent for them. This whole trip had been first-class service. She was feeling rather fancy.

"I'm doing just as good as I was when you called before takeoff," Violet said. "Gonna watch a movie and then take a walk this afternoon when Ethan gets home."

"And your pain?" She waved at Alexis so they didn't lose each other in the chaos of baggage claim.

"I'm a tad sore, but I don't even need the pain meds anymore."

"That's what we want to hear. Okay, I'll check in on you later. I'll also give Dad a call just to make sure he's eating."

"Mare? We've got Dad. Sage is all over it. I'll call him tomorrow. We have everything under control here. Focus on your trip. Make out with your girlfriend in the city and stop thinking about tending to other people, okay? You're off the clock."

"Right. I keep forgetting." She smiled into the phone. "Glad you're okay."

"See you on TV. I can hardly wait. Bye, now."

The prettiest girl in the world approached as she lowered the phone. "Right this way, madame. Your chariot is spacious and has the heat dialed nicely to warm."

"I love this city already."

Alexis took her hand and led the way. Marigold gave her a once-over. She'd upped her fashion game for the city, wearing heeled black boots, killer olive pants, and a sleek white blouse. "I will never get used to the way you look and carry yourself."

Alexis laughed and popped on her shades as they emerged from the building. "Well, now you're just encouraging me." She paused for them to slide into the car and exhaled. "I'm so happy to be here with you right now." She placed a kiss on Marigold's lips that made her knees wobble. This woman was her girlfriend. Life was surreal.

"Snacks for you," Alexis said, handing Marigold a hand-packed bag of her favorites.

"I feel so out of sorts right now. Nobody needs me."

Alexis rested against the seat and faced her, offering the softest grin. "I need you."

Marigold cradled her cheek. "I'm really glad to hear that because I need you right back."

When the New York City skyline appeared on the horizon, Marigold nearly had to pinch herself. She blinked to clear her vision, wondering if this moment was real. "It's gorgeous," she said as they approached the city. "A postcard. I can't believe this is my real life. I should have scheduled a trip before this."

"No, because then I wouldn't have gotten to experience this moment with you."

Marigold snuggled closer and held on as their driver drove liberally through the city streets. She watched as office buildings, restaurants, delis, and theaters zoomed past. This was the kind of excitement she'd been waiting for. "This is amazing."

"There's no place like it. San Francisco also has its own separate vibe. I can't wait to take you to all my favorite food spots, and maybe you'll introduce me to a few new ones you discover. You'll probably make friends with everyone there."

"Well, I am pretty likable. You couldn't stay away. Came all the way back to Kansas."

Alexis laughed loudly. "Isn't that the damn truth? Best decision ever."

Marigold laughed, too, because there was no better way to express her transcendent happiness. Today felt like the start of a new, important chapter in her life. She felt brave, free, and happy alongside the person who was becoming her everything. She wanted to drink in every moment. She was in a private car in one of the coolest cities in the world about to tell her own little love story on national television. How was this her life?

When they arrived at the hotel, they were excited to find that the show had reserved one of their private residences in the resort's tower. Marigold did a little twirl after their self-guided tour. "I'm officially in heaven. I think we're VIPs."

"I know we are," Alexis said.

They had their own fancy little living room, a view of the Empire State Building, and a rather impressive gift basket. All of it was wonderful, but the best part of all was the time they were spending together in their own quiet oasis in the city.

"How would you feel about me answering a few emails before dinner?" Alexis winced. "It shouldn't take too long. Then we can enjoy our night."

"I feel great about it because I'm going to relax, unwind, and pretend I'm swanky."

Alexis stole a kiss. "You are."

After relaxing for a time, Marigold changed for dinner, snuggled up with their itinerary for the next morning, and watched the sun set through the large windows of their suite. With Alexis working quietly nearby, Marigold couldn't help but watch the way she rolled her lips in when she concentrated, smiled to herself when something amusing came across her screen, and typed with intention when strong feelings surfaced. "Are you watching me right now?" Alexis asked from her spot at the table, her eyes remaining on the screen.

"Mm-hmm," Marigold said, setting the itinerary aside and blatantly enjoying the much more interesting view. "You're super businessy over there. Very important. I might be developing a crush on this side of you. I love watching you eat food, but this super serious administrative side now has its place in my fantasies, too."

Alexis eyed Marigold and turned in her chair. Her white blouse came with overly pronounced cuffs, which added to the whole effect. It was a good look for her, sophisticated with a dash of cool. When Alexis slowly undid the buttons on that shirt one at a time, Marigold lost the smile. Levity left the room.

"Okay," she said as her world shifted. "I see where you're going."

Alexis let the shirt fall from her arms as she moved to Marigold. The very pale yellow bra beneath allowed generous views of the tops of her breasts and always impressive cleavage. She took a seat in Marigold's lap. "Work's done for the day. Now what are you going to do with me?"

"I have thoughts," Marigold said, pulse quickening.

Alexis nodded, her eyes wide and innocent. Marigold pulled down first one bra cup and then the other.

"Oh, hello." She dipped her head, caught a nipple, and listened as Alexis hissed in a breath. Marigold bit down ever so softly and was greeted with a murmur of pleasure.

"This might be fast," Alexis said. Marigold took that as a compliment, lifting and massaging.

"Sometimes fast is fun." She cupped Alexis's cheek and whispered in her ear. "Let's go."

Moments later, they were well on their way. Alexis's olive pants went MIA, and Marigold's hand was inside her underwear. Alexis took it from there. With both of her hands on Marigold's shoulders, she set the pace entirely, riding Marigold's hand slowly at first with a sexy roll of her hips back and then forward. The warmth and wonder that enveloped Marigold's hand as she explored amazed her. The dance left her lust-drunk, enhanced by the darkening city sky as their backdrop. She watched as Alexis's hair brushed the tops of her breasts when she picked up speed, bouncing in time.

"So close," she breathed. Marigold could tell. Taking the cue, she pushed deeper, and Alexis broke. As she came, she tossed her head back in silent bliss before the short cry arrived. She rode out the rest of the orgasm like a dream in Marigold's lap, forever mesmerizing her.

"You never disappoint," Alexis said, finally. "I just look at you, and I'm halfway there."

"That goes both ways," Marigold said, still captivated by the near-naked body on display to her. She circled a nipple with the tip of her forefinger. Alexis shivered and kissed Marigold soundly.

"We have reservations in twenty minutes, but I want you first."

"That's okay," Marigold said. "Did you get a look at that bed? There'll be time for more fun later."

"Fuck later." Alexis slid onto her knees and pulled Marigold toward her to the end of the couch.

"Yes, that's what I was saying," Marigold pointed out with a laugh, but she was already being relieved of her heels and pants. The anticipation silenced any argument from her brain. When Alexis touched her gently with her tongue, Marigold about levitated off the couch. Their earlier encounter had left her hot and bothered and halfway there. "Or we could do it now. No time like the present, right. Oh!" Alexis's tongue was lazy and gifted. That circular move stole her next thought. "What are you doing to me?" It was becoming Alexis's signature in her mind.

Alexis lifted her head. "Enjoying myself." She went back to work, and her hair tickled Marigold's thighs—a bonus she didn't realize she needed. They found a rhythm, and it wasn't long before she saw light and stars as she struggled to maintain her sanity. Her hips bucked, and pleasure shot through her, white hot like a speeding train. She surrendered to its power as Alexis held her steady until her body went limp, satisfied in the best sense. *Damn, that was good.*

Alexis raised her gaze, flipped her hair, and settled back on her heels. "What do you say? A fancy dinner?"

Marigold blinked and tried to think and breathe. "Yes, please."

CHAPTER TWENTY

The next morning, Marigold woke up to the distant sounds of the city below, wrapped in the most expensive sheets to ever touch her skin, with a very warm and sleepy woman pressed to her side. Her phone alarm was singing, and that meant TV show day was here. She placed a kiss on Alexis's shoulder, sat up, and silenced her happy little phone.

"We have plenty of time, you know," Alexis said, rolling onto her back. "We're in their third hour, and the studio is literally two blocks from here."

"Yes, but there's excitement brewing in my soul, and I have to honor that with preparedness."

"Well, if it's brewing, sure." A soft chuckle.

Marigold gasped and turned back, the sheet she held against her breasts falling as she pressed herself to Alexis. "You cannot make fun of me. This is my first time on camera. Don't forget."

Alexis wrapped her arms around Marigold. "A television virgin brewing with excitement. Got it memorized now."

"Better." She stole a kiss, leaped from the bed, and made sure her outfit was ready to go. The same town car from the day before was waiting at the curb to drive them the short distance to the studio. A waiting assistant ushered them into a side entrance and issued them badges. Alexis was beaming the whole time, seemingly enjoying the experience through Marigold's eager eyes. They hopped on the elevator and followed the assistant, Joseph, to hair and makeup for a quick touch-up. How was it all happening so fast? It was almost go time.

"Ms. Wakefield, Ms. Lavender, follow me to set." Here went nothing. The in-charge producer directed them to the studio floor, and Marigold couldn't believe how many lights were needed for a simple show like *Morning USA*. She needed sunglasses!

"You'll get used to the lights in a moment," Mikayla Sherman told her quietly while they waited out the commercial break before their segment. *The actual Mikayla Sherman.* While Marigold's stomach felt queasy with nerves, next to her on the couch, Alexis seemed very much in her element. She was used to the spotlight and quietly walked Marigold through what she could expect.

"When we come back to air, they'll toss it to Mikayla," she said in a hushed tone. "She'll introduce the segment, and the camera will cut to us. You'll see the red light jump from one camera to the next. After that, we'll have about four to five minutes of questions and be done. Off to brunch."

Marigold squeezed Alexis's hand. "We got this." She flashed a tight smile, still grappling with the fact that she was now on the show she'd grown up watching, and Mikayla Sherman was every bit as warm as she hoped she'd be. Taller, too. Oh, the stage manager was counting them back. *Gah!*

"Welcome back. Have you ever hated someone so much you loved them?" She turned to her cohost, Heather Jones. "Sounds like a romance novel to me."

"Right? I thought the same thing going through my show notes this morning."

"That brings me to our guests—Alexis Wakefield, a well-known food critic, found herself in a world of trouble after Marigold Lavender, sister of a restauranteur, posted a video rebuttal to one of her reviews." A short clip of Marigold's video played behind them. This was truly wild. With the posting of that video, her entire life had changed. "Fans agreed that Wakefield was too harsh in her criticisms and sent her virtually packing." She turned to Alexis. "This was no small hit. You also lost your column with the *San Francisco Journal.*" Mikayla's eyes went wide.

"That's true," Alexis said. "It was a red letter day."

Marigold winced.

Mikayla continued, "Fans and naysayers on social media were rallying together to make sure you were canceled for good."

"Also true. Some still are."

"Tell us what you did in the midst."

Alexis offered her most winsome smile. "I decided to crash Marigold's hometown as my own personal getaway for, well..." She exchanged a look with Marigold. "It turned into months."

"You can imagine my surprise," Marigold said wryly followed by a grin. That earned a laugh from the cohosts.

"I needed to escape the attention, and Kansas seemed like a good full-circle option," Alexis added.

"Oh, I think of Kansas for all my relaxing vacays," Heather chirped good-naturedly.

"But here's where the story gets interesting," Mikayla said. "You had a few run-ins. You exchanged some terse words."

"More than a few," Marigold said. "Everywhere I went, there she was. Beautiful, yet my sworn enemy."

"But the feelings were flying?" Mikayla asked and gave her shoulders a shimmy.

Marigold nodded. "I didn't know whether to body slam Alexis or kiss her. It was a very confusing time."

Alexis nodded. "I'm so glad she chose the latter."

Heather nodded along. "And now what? Where do you stand?"

Alexis kissed the back of Marigold's hand. "Together. Always."

Marigold felt herself light up. "I know it's not something either of us would have ever predicted, and we can admit that our story is unique, but I think that's what makes it ours."

"Will you invite us to the wedding?" Heather asked.

"I'm in!" Mikayla said enthusiastically. She turned back to the camera. "Just goes to show you, that person getting under your skin today just might be your forever and always. These are the feel-good stories we live for. Marigold, Alexis, thank you for sharing your journey with us."

Moments later, Heather tossed it to the weatherman, who'd be hosting the cooking segment next door.

"And we're out!" the stage manager said.

Marigold exhaled. "That was so much fun and incredibly

terrifying." She was shaking with adrenaline and hoped it hadn't shown on television.

"I just love your story," Mikayla said, offering first Marigold and then Alexis a hug. "And it's good to see you again, Alexis. I applaud the new approach."

"Definitely an improvement," Alexis said, kissing her cheek. "Take care."

Marigold held it together until Joseph dropped them at the side door, and they spilled out onto the sidewalk. Then she had to run in place, her own little victory dance.

Alexis laughed. "I love when you dance out your energy. More! More!"

"That was the most surreal thing I've ever done." Her voice was loud, and she felt like she could run a marathon. She fished for her phone in her bag. "I'm sure Violet is going nuts."

Strangely, the call rolled to voice mail. Her text messages were eerily silent, too. Nothing from Tillman after her appearance, really? She fired off a couple of her own and turned back to Alexis.

"Want to walk to brunch?" Alexis asked. "You seem to have all this energy."

"And see the sights? Hey, we could be tourists after and ride around on one of those double-decker buses."

Alexis laughed. "Or I could arrange a private tour."

"No, no. We have to be where the people are."

"Okay, Ariel, we will be."

Her phone buzzed in her hand. Finally. Tillman. She slid on to the call. "There you are. Did you watch? Was that not just wild?" Her enthusiasm earned her a few curious glances from folks rushing past on their way here or there. Everyone was in a hurry in New York, another unique quality.

"Yes, ma'am. Great job, too! I caught the tail end. I was pulled next door to stay with Ethan. He's here with me now. Say hi to Marigold."

"Hi, Aunt MG," his little voice called out.

She felt her smile dim. "Why were you pulled next door?" He hesitated, which was unacceptable. Not when her heart plummeted and her skin went to ice. "Tillman, answer me right now. Is she okay?"

"Violet went to the hospital. But it's not what you think. I wasn't even sure if I should call. They didn't leave me any kind of instruction for this kind of thing, but at the end of the day, we're peas and I made a game time decision."

"Tillman. Just tell me what's going on."

Alexis watched silently, her features pulled in confusion and concern. She held Marigold's hand, waiting for more.

"Cara's real sick. She spiked a high fever, which can be dangerous in a baby so young. She's been admitted and the doctors are working to figure out what's gone wrong."

Marigold's hand flew to her head. "What? No, no." How could this be happening. She turned to Alexis. "Cara's very sick. She's in the hospital. I have to go." Guilt flared. This was the universe teaching her a lesson, wasn't it? She left, and the world fell apart back home. Why had she given in? This had been a selfish move.

"It's okay. I've got you. Do you want to fly back?"

"I have to."

Alexis nodded and tugged Marigold back down the street, which was good. It was what she needed because her own brain had quit working. She followed, half numb, and watched as Alexis packed their bags, arranged for the car, and got them straight to the airport.

"I shouldn't have come to New York," she whispered as the city streets whipped by in a blur. They seemed garish and unfriendly now. Her thoughts were spinning out of control. Irrational and disjointed. She knew that, but she couldn't stop their trajectory.

"What do you mean?" Alexis asked.

"This feels like a sign. I believe in that kind of thing. I leave town and Cara goes to the hospital."

Alexis dipped her head, forcing Marigold to make eye contact with her. "It's not a sign. It's awful, but it has nothing to do with you."

"Either way. I'm not where I should be, Alexis." She was shaking. "I can't just up and leave, no matter how much I want this." Guilt overwhelmed everything, stomping out any enjoyment from the morning. Her mother would have been there for her family. Marigold hadn't been. "I can't go to San Francisco." It was the first time she'd said the dreaded words out loud. But it was like she couldn't hold them back.

Alexis took Marigold's hands in hers, helping them go still. "That's not something you have to sort out right now, okay? Let's just get you home, and get Cara well. One step at a time."

They were quiet the rest of the ride. She hadn't argued, but she knew Alexis was wrong. There was nothing for her to sort out. She couldn't do it. There was no chance that she could pick up and move from Homer's Bluff. She'd been so naive to think that she could. This was a wake-up call, and she saw the truth so clearly now.

God, it had been a wonderful fairy tale, but harsh reality had arrived and it placed everything in crystal clear focus. Time to wake up and think about the bigger picture. Time to stop the daydreams for good. Look where they'd gotten her.

❖

A day that had started so wonderful had snowballed into a nightmare. Alexis could hardly believe what was happening but pushed her own feelings aside for the greater good. If Marigold needed to get home, she'd move hell or high water to get her there.

The airport was crawling with people, even more so than usual. Her travel apps weren't offering her a whole lot that day, and now she was questioning the move to fly out of LaGuardia. Kennedy or Newark might have been the better bet.

So here they stood, in a massive line, waiting on help. She could feel Marigold's desperation from feet away, which made the discomfort so much worse. Her mind tried to stay three steps ahead. After she secured them seats, she'd need to cancel the agenda for her week ahead. A couple of in-studio podcasts, a meeting with Tatum in San Fran, and a few small sponsorship lunches to discuss the future. She didn't mind postponing. She much preferred to be with Marigold until Cara was better. This was the baby born on the night her life had been changed forever. She felt connected to Cara and hated the thought of her in a hospital bed.

They were next in line at the ticket counter when she turned to Marigold. "I wonder if it's better to fly into Kansas City rather than Wichita. What do you think?"

Marigold placed a hand on her arm. "I think you should keep your flight to San Francisco. Let me go to Homer's Bluff on my own."

Alexis frowned, not following the thread. That suggestion was not in the realm. "No. I'm going with you. I can move my schedule around. That's an easy decision."

Marigold stared at her, wordless. This was not a look Alexis was familiar with, melancholy in nature and mixed with apology, regret.

"What's wrong?" she asked. Her own voice sounded flat. That was because she was afraid.

"Next." The woman at the counter looked at them expectantly.

"You go ahead," Alexis told the man in line behind them.

Marigold looked to the wall. She'd still yet to speak.

"What's going on?" Alexis asked quietly.

"I truly thought I could do this. I've been afraid, but I thought I'd figure a way past it. But after today, I feel like a failure on all counts." She closed her eyes. "I don't want to lose you, but I'm also not sure I can keep you. How do I do both? Help me."

Her mind began to race and her brain downshifted. People all around them were living their lives. Searching for gates, scrolling their phones, sipping their coffee, and her own life was crumbling around her. "I think you're just upset. Don't beat yourself up about this. Your family loves and supports you. They wanted you to—"

Marigold hit the center of her chest with her open palm several times. "But I have to support them right back. My mom is gone and I've tried to…" Her voice was hoarse, the emotion strangled in her throat.

"You're not your mom. You don't have to fill her shoes."

"I can't even get close if I'm running around the country or living in some new city."

"Are you scrapping the plans? Marigold, you couldn't have stopped Cara from getting sick. That was going to happen whether you'd come to New York or not."

"Maybe. Maybe not. But I could have helped in some way, been there for my sister. I don't know what else. But something." She shook her head, seeming at a total loss. "I don't have these answers, but I do know that Violet's still not through her ordeal."

"And when she is, maybe we take another look at things. I can wait." Silence. Alexis understood that Marigold was floundering and looking for a way to fix everything when no human could. Her love was larger than her ability to make everything okay, and it was eating away at her. Unfortunately, her solution seemed to be self-sacrifice.

It felt unnecessary to blow everything the hell up at this point. In the middle of an airport, no less. There was nothing she could do but get out of the way.

"Next," the woman at the counter called.

"I hate this," Marigold said quietly. "I'm so sorry." She walked up to the counter. "I need to get home as soon as possible. As close to Wichita as you can get me."

"How many in your party?"

"Just one. I'm headed home."

Alexis looked on in sadness. *Home.* Marigold was hers. Two hours ago, she'd had everything she ever wanted and a bright future mapped out ahead. Never in a million years did she imagine that the woman who'd woken up in her arms would get on a plane and fly straight out of her life to maybe never return. She prayed it was just cold feet, but the gut feeling that gnawed at her said otherwise.

"So, what do we do?" Alexis asked, grappling, when Marigold returned with her ticket.

"I don't know that there's much we can do. I'm a mess, and maybe I'm broken. I don't know."

"I don't believe that. Maybe I take another look at Homer's Bluff."

Marigold closed her eyes. "You would resent the hell out of me." Alexis stared at the ceiling. She was willing to make that big move for Marigold, but she had to be met halfway. She had to know that she was wanted.

Marigold folded her arms, her posture rigid. There was no effort to take Alexis's hand. In fact, touching felt off the table. "I'm not saying this is the end."

"You're also not saying that it's not."

Marigold's eyes welled up. "I can't imagine my life without you in it. I need courage. I'm fighting for it every which way, but I'm coming up short."

"Don't give up on us."

"Alexis." She closed her eyes.

She understood that Marigold was caught in a tough spot. Alexis wasn't sure how to help, but her heart broke. Not just for herself but for Marigold, too. She wasn't going to be able to convince Marigold that they belonged together no matter the circumstances. She certainly wasn't going to be able to persuade her to follow her dreams and move to San Francisco. The only chance they had was if Marigold came to that conclusion on her own.

And maybe she never would. Alexis had to face that very real possibility. Not everything worked out. This could turn into the biggest loss of her life. But she wasn't ready to believe it.

They stood in front of the security line that would whisk Marigold away from her. The ticking clock was her enemy. There were tears in both their eyes as they moved into this very difficult moment, their good-bye. "When you get to San Francisco, I want you to go slow, okay?" Marigold was talking fast. "Give yourself time to adjust before you jump back into the deep end. Build in time for rest." She gestured to the soft pet carrier. "Carrot's going to want his quality time. He's used to having you home most of the time."

She nodded, attempting a smile, but then giving up. "That's good advice."

Marigold looked skyward. "I hate this. But I'm trying to be strong."

"Come here," Alexis said and gave her hand a soft tug. Marigold moved immediately into her arms and stayed there. If there was ever a moment made up of two people doing everything in their power to memorize each other, to emblazon every inch of the other person onto their heart and soul, this was it.

Marigold dropped to her knees and let Carrot kiss her through the mesh of his carrier. But it wasn't enough, and she unzipped the side. His little blond head automatically popped out, and he looked around sleepily. "You be a good boy. Only zoom with the best dogs. Please keep smiling, too. I never met a more smiley guy than you." He offered a wiggle and swiped her nose with his tongue.

Marigold stood and faced Alexis. "Kiss me one more time, please?"

Alexis didn't hesitate. She didn't care who was watching either. She cradled Marigold's face, brushed the tears away with her thumbs, leaned in and kissed her with every ounce of emotion she had. She refused to concede that this would be the last time. They were meant to be.

"I love you," she said for the first time, meeting those sky blue eyes as Marigold backed away from her to go.

"No. Don't."

She shrugged, helpless and hating it. "I can't not. It's true. I need you to know that if nothing else."

Marigold held eye contact, nodded, and silently turned to join the line. Alexis waited off to the side, watching as Marigold moved farther and farther away. At the last moment, she turned, blew Alexis a kiss, and disappeared around the corner.

Pain slashed. This was awful. Alexis stood there, luggage in hand, her dog by her side, wondering what in the world she would do now.

CHAPTER TWENTY-ONE

The clouds seemed to know Marigold was sad. Instead of the big, fluffy, white cartoon clouds she'd become acquainted with on the flight in, these new clouds were thin, gray, and depressing. She spent the three flights it took to get home staring at them, lost in her own thoughts.

She worried for Cara and Aster and Brynn. She agonized over Violet and her own personal battle. She wondered what Alexis was doing, how she was feeling. And with the little bit of time that was leftover, Marigold indulged her own feelings of loss. She'd never felt more defeated in her life. This was a low she couldn't fathom. She'd come this close to the life she'd always longed for with the woman of her dreams. How had it come to this? The truth was that it was all her fault. She'd shoved away the same fears that now came back to haunt her.

Weary, out of tears, and starving, Marigold retrieved her luggage from the sad little carousel and headed straight to the hospital. Her muscles ached and her head pounded. It didn't matter. She was here now and could help with whatever Aster needed.

All was quiet when she arrived at the three-story hospital building. The waiting room was empty, which made her think that Aster was with Brynn in Cara's room. She'd known in advance that she wouldn't be allowed back to see her niece, but she somehow just needed to be there in the vicinity, putting her good energy into the world. She wouldn't stay long, but she needed to lay eyes on her sister, see that everything was under control. The updates all signaled that Cara was moving in a positive direction, and that was beyond good news.

She took a seat in a green plastic chair and was surprised to see her brother walk in with two cups of coffee. She looked up at him, so grateful to see his face that she nearly launched herself into his arms.

He laughed. "Well, don't spill the coffee now. One of these is for you."

"Hi. I didn't know you'd be here."

"You said you were on your way, so I thought I'd swing by. See how you were." Had he sensed that not all was right with her world?

"You have no idea how much I needed this." Simply a friendly face was enough to bring her to her metaphorical knees after the cosmically brutal day she'd just had. She felt wrung dry, wrecked, and sad. A shell.

"Here." He handed her the coffee, which seemed to be from an actual roaster nearby, rather than the hospital drip version. She owed him for this. "It's decaf. But the heat from the cup always comforts me in a way I can't explain. Lesson I learned a couple of years back."

Wise words from her little brother.

The hospital was smaller than the sprawling complex Violet had been treated in and a lot closer to home. There was only one other family in the waiting room, leaving the place quiet and still. The lights had been dimmed for comfort in the evening hours. In the corner, a television was turned to the nightly news. Sage lifted his chin toward it in reference.

"I watched your interview. You two were awesome. I'm so happy for you, MG."

"Thanks." This morning, the interview, seemed so long ago. Nearly a lifetime, in fact.

"Did Alexis not come back with you?"

"Um, she was going to." Marigold sagged. She met his gaze full-on. "I told her not to. I can't do this thing with her, Sage. I thought I could, but I can't move to San Francisco, leave all of you. I have responsibilities. People I love." Her heart raced, and she dug her nails into her palms. Life felt like a cyclone at the moment, and debris was flying.

Sage held up a finger. "Aster went to Boston for three full years. We missed her, but we survived. Cars and planes exist for a reason." He frowned at her. "What are you doing? Don't sabotage this. You've been so ridiculously happy with Alexis."

"Don't you worry about me. I'm always going to land on my feet. Any updates?"

He sighed and reluctantly moved on. "The doctor was supposed to be by anytime now. Aster said the baby's holding her own, even smiling here and there. They've cleared her to nurse again, which Aster thinks must be a good sign."

As if summoned, Aster appeared in the doorway and moved to them. "What are you doing here? You're back?" She regarded Marigold with surprise. Her brows pulled in as she took a seat. "You didn't have to cancel your trip, Mare."

"Yes, I did." Aster and Sage exchanged a look. She ignored them. "How's my niece?"

"Cuddling in the armchair with her other mom right now. The IV fluids they've given her since this morning seem to have helped rehydrate her. She's perked up quite a bit, which helps my heart." She looked over her shoulder at the door. "The doctor was just by with the lab results, and we now know what she's been fighting."

"And?" Marigold asked, sitting forward.

"Salmonella. Can you believe that? Apparently, you can find trace amounts of it in a lot of common places. Adults fight it off easy. Babies, not so much. The doctor says we'll likely never know where she came in contact with it."

"Get out." Sage's jaw fell open. "So, what's the plan?"

"They'll want to keep her for a couple more days. But it's mainly just supportive care until she feels better." Marigold put her arm around Aster. "It's so scary when they can't tell you what's wrong."

"She's in good hands now," Marigold said and kissed Aster's temple. "This is all the best news if you think about it. They have a diagnosis and a course of action. When this is over, she'll be good as new."

"I'm just sorry you rushed back."

"It was important to me." She tried to make her brain work, to assess what might help. "What can I do to make your life easier? Do you need any supplies or food?"

"Already handled," Sage said. "I went shopping this afternoon. Tyler swung by the house and got all of their necessities."

Aster smiled calmly. "Violet had dinner delivered to the hospital. We're in good hands."

"Yeah." Marigold nodded. "Yeah. I'm so glad." This was all good news. Everything was as it should be. She went home that night relieved for her family and numb to everything else. But in the darkness of her bedroom, she let it all out, crying into her pillow for the strength she didn't have. She missed Alexis more than she could fathom. Marigold had let her down, and she wasn't sure how she'd ever forgive herself for that. She'd deal with the loss she'd brought on herself, but hurting someone she cared about was tantamount.

But there was one more thing.

A tiny little corner of her mind brought forth a question she could scarcely acknowledge. It drifted in and occupied the air all around her anyway. Had she truly made the right decision?

❖

When the Thanksgiving decorations gave way to reindeer and tinsel in the town square, Marigold expected to feel better. Not only did she love the Christmas season, but she thrived on all the events that popped up, usually keeping her busy and in the holiday spirit. There were carol nights at Larry's where they all sang so badly after a few beers that Santa Claus himself would likely beg them to stop. The huge holiday bake sale held as a fundraiser for the elementary school featuring everyone's favorite table, the upright gingerbread Christmas trees. Marigold always spent at least two days baking her contributions. Then there was the wine-pairing dinner, and the holiday carnival, market days, and the big Christmas tree lighting on the grounds of the Lavender farm. Yet she couldn't seem to get excited about any of it.

In the past few weeks, she'd requested space for herself, which Alexis granted. In that time, Marigold had watched her slowly revive her presence on social media. She'd posted three full restaurant reviews that had been well received and captured her new approach to criticism perfectly. Her heart burst with pride for the bit of success she was seeing. She wanted more than anything to pick up the phone and tell her so. She also wanted to update her on Violet's prognosis, which was turning out to be quite positive. Violet had recovered from surgery and was tolerating the followup chemo well. Everyone was thrilled with her progress, including her doctor.

"What are you doing?" Violet asked, eyeing her from behind the register.

"Arranging the lotions by color."

"Why?"

"Because it keeps my mind busy."

"Mm-hmm," Violet said, coming around the counter. "Why don't you just call her?"

"And say what?" Marigold scrunched her shoulders. "I'm sorry we're desperately in love but have lives that don't fit together? That's a pretty short and bleak conversation."

Violet lowered her hands from her hips to her side when she heard Marigold's words. "That's the first time I've heard you admit to actually being in love."

Marigold's instinct was to rear up in defense, deny everything. But she *was* in love with Alexis. "It doesn't change anything. When did we get these Rudolphs in? Adorable."

"Can I ask what's holding you back and receive a truthful answer this time? I'm not discussing Rudolph until I get one, by the way."

"I have responsibilities here."

Violet frowned. "No. You don't. You're an unattached grown-ass woman who can do whatever she wants."

"It's not as simple as that. Who would make the peanut butter chocolate surprise cookies for the bake sale? Who's going to dog-sit when Brynn and Aster take the baby on her first vacation?"

"Other people," Violet said simply. "Don't you think you've waited for your turn long enough?"

Marigold nodded. "I used to. But I gave it a shot and couldn't quite make the leap, okay, so…can we please just not talk about this?"

"Is this about Mom?" Her sister wasn't through.

"What? No." She scoffed and then exhaled. "Maybe."

"Because she would hate this whole thing. She wanted her kids to have everything life had to offer. I've watched the shell of Marigold walk around this town for close to a month now. I've allowed it to happen, and I'm not doing it anymore."

"Why are you so fired up?"

"Because I love you, but I'm furious at you. Do you hear me? Seething with anger. We all are."

A long pause. "Okay. You're all discussing me privately?"

"Kind of." Violet folded her arms. "And we've collectively decided that we miss the version of Marigold that we got when Alexis was around. We like her a lot more than this one."

"Ouch."

"It's true. You smiled. You got up in arms. There was this spark that, let me tell you, was contagious in the best way possible. We all felt it. We were happier, your family, because *you* were."

She paused. She hadn't thought of it in those terms. "Okay. That's fair."

"Will you give it some thought? Calling up Alexis and seeing if there's a chance for a redo?" Violet's smile dimmed. "Because if I've learned anything this year, it's that nothing is guaranteed. Our time here is fleeting, and we have to use it."

Marigold nodded and hugged her sister. "It is. I hear you."

"Good. Now the Rudolph infusers came from that vendor in Seattle I was telling you about." She grinned like the Cheshire cat, proud of the work she'd just done. "If they buy two, we throw the lavender insert in for free."

"The Devil works hard, but you work harder," Marigold said with a shake of her head. "On so many fronts."

"Aww, sweetie, you noticed." Violet raised one shoulder. "I think you're a little bit in love with me, too."

❖

Three days later, Marigold let herself into her dad's place with the intention of making him his weekly dinner and decorating the hell out of his living room. He had the tree up, decked out with the traditional family ornaments, but that was about it. Marigold was armed with the goods. Twinkly lights, snowman statues, a doormat, a wreath, and yes, even a Rudolph infuser.

"Mr. Dad, today is your lucky day!" she called, hanging her jacket on the hall tree. "Prepare to be holiday bombed."

She didn't see any sign of him, which wasn't that unusual. He was likely finishing up his after-work shower and would pop out sooner or later. But as she strung her first set of lights along the top of the wall, she heard distant laughter. Squinting, she followed the melodic sound out onto the back patio, where she found her dad gesturing toward the farmland behind him to a woman, who smiled at him with true delight.

She slid open the door. "Hi."

The duo turned. The woman was about his age with auburn hair and a very friendly smile.

"Hey there, MG." Her dad gestured to the woman. "This is Alice. She's from the grocery store."

"The grocery store?" Marigold shouted and then quickly realized she'd done so. "That's so nice," she offered, much quieter. That's when she realized that they were each holding a glass of wine, and her dad wore an actual sweater, which was about as dressed up as he ever got.

"Alice, this is my middle daughter, Marigold. She's my dinner buddy."

"Not tonight," Marigold said enthusiastically. She gestured behind her. "I was actually just popping out here to let you know that I had supplies to drop off. Holiday decor, that kind of thing. For decorating. At a later date. Not today."

He eyed her curiously. "Okay. Should I do anything special with these supplies? Or…"

"Not a thing." She held out a hand and backed away slowly. She managed a joyful, "Enjoy your evening," before sliding the door closed again and getting the hell out of there before she disturbed the biggest move her dad had made for himself in years. This was something to celebrate! She was dying to tell her siblings and did so on the group text to appropriate shock and awe all around.

This is amazing, Violet typed.

Points for Dad. Proud of the guy, Sage said.

Whoa, Aster chimed in. *Cara and I are cheering for Pop from her postmilk snooze on my shoulder!*

The whole experience put a temporary smile on Marigold's face. That was, until she got home and realized that he'd stayed true to their pact. He put himself out there in a manner that was probably hard for him. She heard Violet's words in her ear from earlier. *There was this spark.*

She hadn't been wrong. And Marigold missed it. Acting on impulse, she picked up the phone and placed a call to Alexis, holding her breath, trying to assemble the perfect arrangement of words. The call rolled to voice mail, and Marigold closed her eyes, resisting the urge to run.

"I don't know how you're feeling, but I'd love it if we could have a conversation. See where we're at." A pause. "I miss you." Another long pause. Was there a time limit on these messages? Sensing hers was about to come to an end, she took the leap and spoke directly from her heart. "And I love you." She slid off the call.

❖

Alexis had never been so shocked by a voice mail message in her life. She listened again to be sure she'd heard correctly. After Marigold had returned to Homer's Bluff, she'd disappeared gradually into the ether. Their contact had been minimal and stilted, quick check-ins that eventually faded into silence. She'd thrown herself into her work as a survival tactic, rebuilding her brand, seeking out partnerships, and trying to avoid thoughts of the one person she'd give anything to speak with, touch, kiss. She was a sad little cliché, spending weak moments scrolling through photos of her time in Homer's Bluff. She lost herself specifically in the shots of her and Marigold on the picnic blanket together at the Pie Fest, or snuggled up on the couch with Carrot at Alexis's Airbnb. Her experiences those months had changed her for the good, and she carried those memories with her every second.

But defeated by the silence, Alexis had recessed into herself, caught off guard now by not only a call from Marigold, but the declaration she'd longed for. Did she buy a plane ticket to Homer's Bluff that day? Absolutely not. She waited until the next morning, along with a few arrangements for when she arrived. She didn't want to waste this opportunity. If there was still a chance for her and Marigold, she was going to give it everything in her power.

"So, you think that's a good idea then?" she asked, phone to her ear as she was driven to the airport.

"One hundred percent," Violet said back. "I approve of the plan. Do you mind if I let my dad know?"

"Um, no. Not at all. I'd appreciate it, in fact."

"Perfect. Safe travels, Alexis."

She clicked off the call just in time for another to come in. She sighed. This was the kind of call she typically dodged. Today, though, she was feeling feisty, determined to fight for what was right.

She answered and forced a smile. "Aspen. To what do I owe the pleasure?"

"Mom said you were traveling back to Kansas today. Why? Is this about that woman you've been flaunting around the news?"

"Actually, yes."

"Level with me. Just us here. None of that is real, right? Just part of your rebound tour. Another way for you to get attention in the press? We've all done it."

Alexis blinked, anger simmering. "No, actually. Marigold matters to me a lot." She paused, because since when did Aspen care about her personal life? This was likely a call placed to garner information she could use to further her own exposure. The last thing she needed was Aspen starting a smear campaign and calling her relationship with Marigold fake and opportunistic. Her heart thudded as adrenaline took over. Time to take no prisoners. Enough was enough.

She leaned forward in her seat. "Listen carefully to me, Aspen. If you take that asinine theory to a single gossip columnist or news outlet, I will tell every reporter who owns a microphone that you slept with Lori St. Michaels and threatened to tell her wife unless she cast you in your first feature film. Your whole career is built on extortion. What's even better? I'm pretty sure Lori would offer up a nice little quote of her own. She's not a fan."

Silence struck, which was honestly blissful. The sound of Aspen squirming.

"I don't appreciate your threat," Aspen said. "Please note that. However, I have zero intention of speaking your name to anyone. How boring. Bye, now."

She grinned, victorious. She'd won the battle, and Alexis didn't plan to let up in the future. Her sister would learn to play nice in the sandbox or face the consequences. She'd been left unchecked long enough. No more.

"We're here, ma'am," her driver said, pulling up to the curbside check-in. She grinned and accepted his hand as he helped her out of the town car.

"I appreciate you, sir."

She adjusted her sunglasses and wheeled her bag to the desk. Time to reclaim her life and win back the woman she loved.

CHAPTER TWENTY-TWO

"Tis the season to be jolly," Marigold sang to herself from on top of a ladder in her father's living room. "I love a good fa-la-la. It's like my tongue's throwing a party." There was a pot of mulled wine with orange slices warming on the stove, and carols playing from the stereo system. Her father ladled them two mugs of the good stuff, came around the couch, and took a seat.

"Okay, now finish the story," she called over her shoulder.

"Not much left to tell. No kissing, but we did hold hands."

"That's big. That's way beyond high fives and friendly wine on the porch. It means this is a burgeoning romance."

He broke into a smile, and his cheeks went pink like Santa Claus. "I don't know. Maybe."

Cute and new. "Best answer ever. We accept maybes around here. In fact"—she hesitated—"I'm tossing around a few maybes myself." In the land of honesty and putting yourself out there, Marigold was becoming more and more comfortable. Ever since she'd told the truth on her call to Alexis, she found herself able to breathe easier. Saying those three little words released her from an invisible binding, freeing her heart. There was something about surrendering to a power larger than herself that put Marigold at ease. Why was she fighting a battle she clearly didn't want to win? She loved Alexis. She craved her. Desperately. She couldn't put the rabbit back in the hat. Had she checked her phone every ten minutes since she'd placed the call? Yes. But she'd not given up hope yet. She'd taken the first step, and that was huge.

"Oh, that reminds me. I have a gift."

"For who?" Marigold said, coming down the ladder.

"You. Sit right there and I'll get it," he said, pointing at the couch. An order.

Curious, she took a seat and waited. He reappeared a moment later with a small green box with a shiny red bow. "I was gonna give you this on Christmas morning, but I decided not to wait." He gestured with his head. "Open the lid."

She did as he asked and found herself looking down at a new ornament for her tree. How awesome. She picked it up and let it dangle in the light. A purple cabin with the words *Lavender House II* written in script on the front.

"Thank you, Dad. What does the two mean?"

"Well, here's the thing. I've been looking for a new investment, somewhere to put my money as I age. And The Lavender House has done really well for all of us."

"I'm so glad to hear that." She was listening but felt like she lagged one step behind.

"But I think we should capitalize on the business model we know works so well and open a second shop. That's when it occurred to me."

"What?"

"I know the perfect person to take our store and run with it. I was thinking"—he held up a finger—"maybe San Francisco."

"Dad." She closed her eyes, touched and overwhelmed.

"Of course, Violet will make a few trips to help get the place off the ground. I'll need to visit here and there to make sure it's in line with the Lavender legacy." He winked at that part. "And we'll need a couple of employees who will run the place when you're back in Homer's Bluff, hanging out with all of us."

She blinked, overcome. "I don't even know what to say. Is this real?"

His smile faded. "I'm dead serious. I believe in you, Mare. You're gonna go out there and do great things for this family, and I'm gonna love watching it happen."

She exhaled and nodded. With the beautiful little ornament still in her hand, she moved into her father's arms. His belief in her meant everything. It felt surreal, but she was starting to see all the areas of her life converge like perfectly fitting puzzle pieces. She exhaled, standing stronger and more determined by the second.

"Hey, MG! You here?"

She craned her neck to see Violet's head poking in from the doorway.

"We're in the living room!"

"Better go see what she wants." He popped her on the arm. "I'll catch ya later. We can talk business."

She eyed him and then Violet. Were they in cahoots? It was difficult to keep up with these people. "What is it you want with me?" Marigold called to her sister.

"I'm a little worried for your bridge."

Marigold stalked to the door. "What's happened to the bridge?"

"I'll show you. But it's not good."

"Why aren't you saying more?" She followed Violet to her car. "It's still standing, though, right?"

"Yeah, but there's a bigger problem. I'd rather the visual speak for itself."

"Okay, weirdo." This was the strangest day. "Did you know about the ornament?"

"Lavender II?" Violet grinned. "We're gonna be twins. Probably on the phone daily, swapping strategies and branding ideas."

"I don't think I've absorbed the proposal yet."

"You will. It's a fantastic idea."

"And you're feeling okay?"

Violet sat back as they turned off the main road. "Never better." She dipped her head and stared off at the bridge in the distance. "Ah, Little Bridgerton. C'mon. Let's go."

Marigold followed her sister, hoping to get to the bottom of this big bridge concern, praying the old structure wasn't in any danger. "Is there any reason that you won't just tell—" But she realized in that moment that Violet was no longer walking beside her. She'd fallen back, leaving Marigold to approach the bridge her…

The thought died.

Everything went still except the sound of the water lapping below.

Standing on her bridge, looking off into the distance, was the most beautiful woman on the planet. "Alexis," she said quietly, her chest squeezing. As her feelings swirled and enveloped, Marigold placed her hand over her heart in the exact moment Alexis turned and looked at her. She wore a white sweater and had her dark hair swept partially back. Was she real? This was really happening?

"Go," she heard a voice behind her say. She smiled. Violet was ushering her along.

Marigold took a deep breath and made her way onto the bridge, arriving next to Alexis, who offered her a soft smile. "I heard this bridge was the place to be."

"A smart person must have said that."

Alexis nodded. "That's true."

She offered her hand and Marigold took it. But instead of allowing herself to be pulled in, she reversed their roles and pulled Alexis to her. It was up to Marigold to put them back together, and she would. She would put in the time and conquer her own insecurities. She would make that promise to both of them because she loved Alexis with all she had in her. Marigold closed her eyes at the sensation of Alexis wrapped in her arms. "I'm so sorry I lost my way. I love you," she whispered, her hand at the back of Alexis's head.

Alexis pulled back, found her gaze, and their connection locked in place. She kissed Marigold softly. "I love you, too. Wherever you live, I live. Iceland? Sure. New York? Let's go. Right here? I'm in."

"Deal," Marigold said, kissing her again. "I'm exploring the concept of a hybrid model." Another kiss. This one deeper. "I just had the most interesting business proposition," she explained when they came up for air.

Alexis tilted her head. "Oh yeah?"

"I can't wait to tell you all about it."

Another kiss.

"Can you stay awhile?" Marigold asked.

Alexis nodded. "Forever."

EPILOGUE

On such an important day, Marigold was up early, already sipping coffee at the kitchen table when Alexis arrived home from her extra-early run.

"Babe, you're up already? You don't have to be at the store until ten. I thought you'd grab an extra few minutes, pamper yourself. You've earned it." She kissed Marigold's cheek on the way to the fridge for water. Marigold followed her progress, loving postrun Alexis. A little sweaty, a lot accomplished. Incredibly hot.

She gave her head a shake, pulling herself back into the conversation. "You'd think, but when there's a momentous occasion, I'm awful at sleeping. I'm a child."

Alexis took three generous swallows, breathed, and then grinned around her water bottle. "I can attest that there's nothing childlike about you. Last night was really good, by the way." She'd dropped her tone for that last part. "I actually can't stop thinking about it."

Marigold gave her shoulders a proud shimmy. "I was kind of proud of myself, too. I think that was a record. I lost count."

Alexis closed her eyes, almost as if drifting back to those very sexy moments. "Oh, I didn't. And it definitely was." She set the water bottle on the counter and turned to Marigold with a clap, clearly meant to focus her thoughts. "Now. Down to business. What do you need from me?"

Marigold looked skyward. "Just your never-ending love and support. Everything's in place. I have the caterers arriving at the shop in a couple of hours, and Marjory will be on register so I can play hostess—greet the customers and educate them about the origin of our merchandise." Marigold had put a lot of effort into getting the new store just perfect in time for her grand opening. Not only had it turned out beautiful, but in many ways it was reminiscent of the original Lavender House, which made her feel incredibly at home between its walls.

Alexis scooped up Carrot and kissed his head. "I have a lot of Instagram followers reposting your grand opening announcement. Should be a good way to get word of mouth out there."

"And I couldn't be more grateful. The response has been huge. Who knew big city people craved the quaint and rustic?"

"Are you kidding?" Alexis laughed. "They're starved for it."

Honestly, this little business venture was shaping up to feel like not just a good idea, but a great one. Her soft opening had pulled in surprising receipts each day. She'd taken photos of the space and sent them to Violet, who was incredibly jealous of the window seats that offered fantastic natural light.

"I'll hop in the shower unless you want to go first."

"Two birds, one stone?"

Alexis's whole face lit up, and she nodded. "You're so efficient. Hey, did the contractor call about the new countertop install?"

"Yes, he's coming on Thursday, so I moved Carrot's grooming appointment to Friday. I can drop him on the way to work."

"You're a lifesaver. I have that podcast Friday morning."

"I know. That's why I made sure I had coverage at the store."

This was life now in sunny, sometimes rainy San Francisco. In the past eight months, Marigold had come to love the place, and the life they were building together. She had new friends, dinner plans several nights a week with her food critic girlfriend, and a new business to nurture into the neighborhood. She'd been worried about losing her connection to her family members, but with visits to Kansas happening quite literally whenever they got the chance, her concerns had evaporated. Plus, the group text with her siblings kept her up to date on any and all town gossip.

Later that afternoon, wearing her favorite purple sweater dress, Marigold greeted one friendly face after another as they explored her store and ate the best canapés in life. "One of the bonus features about this place is the organic nature of the products," she explained to a friendly couple who'd already selected several cuddly throws for purchase. Apparently, they lived just two blocks away. "You'll notice an extra dollar or two tacked on to the price tag, but that's because most everything is sourced from my family's farm, and most of the goods are handmade from vendors we have contracts with across the country."

"I love the concept," the woman said. "And we will be back. I see great gift potential here."

"Or for simply spoiling yourself," Marigold told her.

"I can vouch for how amazingly comfortable those blankets are," Alexis said from a few feet away. "I'm addicted to mine."

"Sold!"

Once the couple moved on, Marigold blew Alexis a covert kiss. Alexis winked in response. This private exchange gave her the energy to finish the day, knowing exactly what she had to look forward to. She'd been on her feet for several hours now, and her social energy was running low, but the exhaustion was well worth it.

"I'm gonna need whatever item will accentuate a sweet pair of dimples," a male voice said behind her.

What the hell? She knew that voice as well as she knew her own, but it didn't make sense. She whirled around, shocked to see Sage and Tyler grinning at her from the food and beverage portion of the shop. "What in the world? How are you here right now?"

"Like we could let this day go without celebrating your success," Tyler said, pulling her into a hug. Her brother beamed, looking on. This was honestly the best surprise ever. She grabbed him next in a bear hug for the ages.

"I was looking for some spaghetti. I like it on Wednesdays at my place with a brewski."

She pulled back at that voice and stared Sage dead in the face. "No."

He nodded. "Oh yes."

She flipped around to see her father grinning proudly. He practically vibrated, which was the cutest thing ever. "I'm really bad at surprises, but I pulled it off, right? You didn't know I was coming." He was so happy he was laughing. This was an amazing sight.

Okay, this brought tears. Since when had her father hopped a plane? He'd done that for her? "You definitely pulled it off. What is happening right now? Hi." She opened her arms and moved to him.

As she rested her cheek on his shoulder, she immediately recognized the brunette who'd just pushed open the door to the shop. "Violet," she breathed. "You're here."

"Like I'd miss the party." Violet hooked a thumb behind her, and Aster, Brynn, and the baby peered around the doorjamb in comical formation. "I brought stragglers. They're here for the food."

The tears ran down Marigold's cheeks as she laughed, tickled, honored, and thrilled. The customers in the store seemed to have caught on to what was happening and watched with big smiles. This was the most wonderful opening ever.

After showing her family around, she finally had a moment to catch her breath. She pulled Alexis into her arms. "You knew about this. I don't know whether to scold you or make out with you."

"Definitely both, maybe together." She made a *can you even imagine?* face before sobering to sincere. "They gave me a small heads-up. Also, we have a fabulous dinner planned at a Michelin starred restaurant. That okay? Are you up for it?"

"With everyone together? I'd give anything."

Alexis kissed her. "Done. Now let's get a family photo in front of the grand opening sign."

Marigold stood taller. "That's the best idea."

"Line up, Lavenders!" Violet called. "Photo time. Make Sage stand in the back so he doesn't ruin the shot. I wish he was better looking."

"Hey, now you've wounded my pride and alerted everyone to the fact that you need glasses," Sage said. "Dad, Vi needs glasses."

"Pipe down and tell me where to stand," her dad said. "And where do I look? I never know. Hi, Aster. Funny seeing you here."

Aster turned. "Right? What an odd coincidence."

"You all, I can't even right now." Marigold took her spot in the middle of the wonderful chaos and pulled Alexis in next to her.

They smiled for the photographer there to cover the opening, as he checked his lens and addressed the group. "On three, we shout *Lavender* and smile. Ready? One, two, three."

"Lavender!" the group yelled. His shutter clicked, sealing the moment in time forever.

Marigold knew without a doubt that she would cherish that photo and her memories of today for the rest of her life. She'd lived in her daydreams for a lot of years, but life in its current form exceeded every single one of them.

"I love you," she said quietly that night to Alexis as they lay in their darkened bedroom, exhausted and happy. Marigold was more tired than she'd ever been but, at the same time, didn't want the day to end.

Alexis kissed her softly in answer and stroked her hair. "I love you, too. I wish I could express how proud I was of you today. You've accomplished so much."

"Only because I have you. Do you know that? You drive me wild on the daily, give me the courage to chase down my dreams, and are the first person I want to decompress with at the end of it all. You're my everything." Another lingering kiss that made Marigold's toes curl. "I didn't know you were possible."

"That might be my favorite sentence ever. Marigold Lavender, you have my heart now and for the rest of time." Alexis took her hand and placed it on her chest.

"Now what?" Marigold asked.

Alexis laughed. "That's just it. We've got a dog, a store, and each other. The sky's the limit."

About the Author

Melissa Brayden (http://www.melissabrayden.com/) is a multi-award-winning romance author, embracing the full-time writer's life in San Antonio, Texas, and enjoying every minute of it.

Melissa is married and working really hard at remembering to do the dishes. For personal enjoyment, she spends time with her Jack Russell Terriers and checks out the NYC theater scene as often as possible. She considers herself a reluctant patron of spin class, but would much rather be sipping merlot and staring off into space. Bring her coffee, wine, or doughnuts and you'll have a friend for life.

Books Available From Bold Strokes Books

Digging for Heaven by Jenna Jarvis. Litz lives for dragons. Kella lives to kill them. The last thing they expect is to find each other attractive. (978-1-63679-453-2)

Forever's Promise by Missouri Vaun. Wesley Holden migrated west disguised as a man for the hope of a better life and with no designs to take a wife, but Charlotte Rose has other ideas. (978-1-63679-221-7)

Here For You by D. Jackson Leigh. A horse trainer must make a difficult business decision that could save her father's ranch from foreclosure but destroy her chance to win the heart of a feisty barrel racer vying for a spot in the National Rodeo Finals. (978-1-63679-299-6)

I Do, I Don't by Joy Argento. Creator of the romance algorithm, Nicole Hart doesn't expect to be starring in her own reality TV dating show, and falling for the show's executive producer Annie Jackson could ruin everything. (978-1-63679-420-4)

It's All in the Details by Dena Blake. Makeup artist Lane Donnelly and wedding planner Helen Trent can't stand each other, but they must set aside their differences to ensure Darcy gets the wedding of her dreams, and make a few of their own dreams come true. (978-1-63679-430-3)

Marigold by Melissa Brayden. Marigold Lavender vows to take down Alexis Wakefield, the harsh food critic who blasts her younger sister's restaurant. If only she wasn't as sexy as she is mean. (978-1-63679-436-5)

A Second Chance at Life by Genevieve McCluer. Vampires Dinah and Rachel reconnect, but a string of vampire killings begin and evidence seems to be pointing at Dinah. They must prove her innocence while finding out if the two of them are still compatible after all these years. (978-1-63679-459-4)

The Town That Built Us by Jesse J. Thoma. When her father dies, Grace Cook returns to her hometown and tries to avoid Bonnie Whitlock, the woman who pulverized her heart, only to discover her father's estate has been left to them jointly. (978-1-63679-439-6)

A Degree to Die For by Karis Walsh. A murder at the University of Washington's Classics Department brings Professor Antigone Weston and Sergeant Adriana Kent together—first as opposing forces and then as allies as they fight together to protect their campus from a killer. (978-1-63679-365-8)

Finders Keepers by Radclyffe. Roman Ashcroft's past, it seems, is not so easily forgotten when fate brings her and Tally Dewilde together—along with an attraction neither welcomes. (978-1-63679-428-0)

Homeland by Kristin Keppler and Allisa Bahney. Dani and Kate have finally found themselves on the same side of the war, but a new threat from the inside jeopardizes the future of the wasteland. (978-1-63679-405-1)

Just One Dance by Jenny Frame. Will Taylor Sparks and her new business to make dating special—the Regency Romance Club—bring sparkle back to Jaq Bailey's lonely world? (978-1-63679-457-0)

On My Way There by Jaycie Morrison. As Max traverses the open road, her journey of impossible love, loss, and courage mirrors her voyage of self-discovery leading to the ultimate question: If she can't have the woman of her dreams, will the woman of real life be enough? (978-1-63679-392-4)

A Talent Within by Suzanne Lenoir. Evelyne, born into nobility, and Annika, a peasant girl with a deadly secret, struggle to change their destinies in Valmora, a medieval world controlled by religion, magic, and men. (978-1-63679-423-5)

Transitioning Home by Heather K O'Malley. An injured soldier realizes they need to transition to really heal. (978-1-63679-424-2)

Truly Enough by J.J. Hale. Chasing the spark of creativity may ignite a burning romance or send a friendship up in flames. (978-1-63679-442-6)

Vintage and Vogue by Kelly and Tana Fireside. When tech whiz Sena Abrigo marches into small-town Owen Station, she turns librarian Hazel Butler's life upside down in the most wonderful of ways, setting off an explosive series of events, threatening their chance at love…and their very lives. (978-1-63679-448-8